Ken M
Yorksh...   ...wn
building ... he
also worked as a freelance artist, greeting card designer and
after-dinner entertainer. He has appeared on television,
radio and as a comedian on the Leeds City Varieties' *Good
Old Days*.

Writing is now Ken's first love – not counting of course his
wife Valerie, to whom he has been married since 1973. He
has five children and twelve grandchildren.

www.kenmccoy.co.uk

D0680261

Two Rings for Rosie

Ken McCoy

piatkus

PIATKUS

First published in Great Britain in 2002 by Judy Piatkus Ltd
This paperback edition published in 2011 by Piatkus

A CIP catalogue record for this book
is available from the British Library.

ISBN 978-0-7499-5688-2

Typeset by Action Publishing Technology Ltd, Gloucester
Printed and bound by
CPI Group (UK) Ltd, Croydon, CR0 4YY

Piatkus
An imprint of
Little, Brown Book Group
100 Victoria Embankment
London EC4Y 0DY

An Hachette UK Company
www.hachette.co.uk

www.piatkus.co.uk

For Lilian M-I-L

Acknowledgements

With many thanks to Stephen Oldroyd for his help with court procedures.

To Judith Murdoch for hinting that there wasn't much wrong with my first attempt at this book that re-writing 90% of it wouldn't put right – as long as I took out half the characters and changed the title. Fortunately I had the good sense to take her advice.

And to Val, who effortlessly picks out all my faults – grammar, spelling, syntax, cheap jokes, dress sense and juvenile behaviour. But I love her anyway.

Chapter One

Duck Street wasn't built for sunshine. It was built to blend in with grey skies and soot. It was built to melt into the fog or glisten, dully, in the rain. The sun only shone on Duck Street on days of special interest. Such as the day war broke out. Rosie Jones was already at war. She was round the back of the Vinery Place Primitive Methodist Chapel fighting off the primitive advances of Joe Brindle.

Word had reached the chapel that an important speech from Mr Chamberlain was due to be broadcast at quarter-past eleven that morning and within minutes the place had emptied. The worried worshippers were scurrying down the pitted tarmac pathway in twos, glancing nervously at the sky and clutching prayer books and hands as if to draw courage from each other in the face of the anticipated hostilities. Joe Brindle was clutching Rosie in places where she didn't want to be clutched. It was the first Sunday in September and what, for Rosie, had started out as a pleasant walk to a friend's house had turned into something unwelcome. On the way there she'd bumped into Joe. He was a big lad, with a dangerous reputation – which often intrigued young girls. He smiled at Rosie and took her by the arm.

'Come wi' me, Rosie Jones. I want ter show yer summat.'

Curiosity triumphed over wisdom as she allowed him to hustle her up the path and round the back of the chapel, where he imprisoned her against the wall with an arm either side of her. She was wishing she hadn't come.

'What is it, Joe?'

'Have yer ever kissed a lad?'

'How d'you mean?'

He leaned into her and kissed her, roughly, then he rubbed his hands over where her breasts would soon begin to make an appearance. She turned her head away, frightened now.

'Joe, I don't want to do this.'

'Course yer do.'

He ran his hand down and lifted her skirt. 'Yer gaspin' fer it. Yer can't kid me.'

Rosie clamped her legs together, trapping his probing fingers. 'Stop it, Joe. Honest! I don't want you to touch me. Certainly not down there.'

'Come off it, Rosie, what d'yer expect? Yer haven't got much up top.'

Annoyance overcame her fear. 'Joe Brindle! Don't be so flippin' rude.' She cast a self-conscious glance down at her as yet undeveloped bosom, well-concealed beneath a thick, woollen cardigan. 'I'm only fourteen, yer know. I'm not fully developed yet.'

He gave a revolting snigger. 'So long as I'm fully developed, that's all what matters.'

'Fully developed? That's not what I've heard.'

'What?'

'Never mind.'

Roughly, he tried to force his hand up her skirt but she pushed him away, causing him to stagger backwards and trip over a kerbstone. He was still falling as she ran to join the tail-end of the departing chapel-goers, leaving him on the ground clutching a twisted ankle. Rosie entered into a conversation with a woman carrying a prayer book, as Joe limped to the low chapel wall and sat down.

'I'll get yer fer this, Rosie Jones!'

But she didn't give him the satisfaction of a reaction; she

2

just carried on her conversation with increased animation as Brindle cursed his luck and Rosie Jones. Seventeen and he still hadn't gone all the way with a girl.

Rosie said goodbye to the woman and breathed a sigh of relief at her narrow escape. If the day ever came when she let a boy do *that* to her it certainly wouldn't be the likes of Joe Brindle. He was a lout and he was common and he had a big gob; and she wouldn't want such carryings-on broadcast around the streets of Leeds. In the meantime, her dad was having no such inhibitions.

Tommy Jones was a self-employed tea delivery man with a bowler hat and a pony-drawn van. He had inherited the company from his father, who had borrowed the idea from a well-known northern tea delivery company. Tommy had added sugar and biscuits to his stock.

Although Sunday was not a normal working day, he was making a delivery to Norah Nesbitt on Maudesly Place. Mrs Nesbitt, whose husband had joined the army around the time Italy and Germany signed the so-called Pact of Steel, would pay Tommy in kind. This suited all parties, including Tommy's wife, Ethel, who didn't like to be troubled by what she called 'physical unpleasantness'.

Norah's drawn bedroom curtains might have aroused suspicion from the neighbours had they not been gathered around their wireless sets in dismal anticipation. Tommy's black and yellow van, with 'Jones's Tea and Biscuits' painted on the side in fancy lettering, was parked outside her front door. The pony was tethered to a lamp-post, its head munching inside a feeding bag. Waiting patiently at the other end of the animal was an old man with a bucket and shovel who had an allotment to tend. Britain had been preparing for the worst for over a year and the old man's allotment was his contribution to the war effort.

Another old man, kitted out in navy-blue overalls and a steel helmet with the letters ARP painted on it, stopped and enquired, 'Any luck?'

3

'Nah ... the only bloke who's havin' any luck this mornin' is Tommy Jones.'

The two of them looked up at the drawn curtains and each felt a twinge of nostalgia at the passing of their best years.

'Good luck to 'im,' said the man with the bucket and shovel.

The ARP warden agreed. 'Aye, get it when yer able.' Then he added, 'Yon useless bugger in Downin' Street's gonna mek an announcement in a few minutes – have yer not heard?'

'I don't need ter listen ter no announcement ter know what's what,' replied the man with the bucket. He looked at the sky which was blue and white and unthreatening, with no hint of war. 'It'll not stay like this fer long. Bloody Nazzies!'

The ARP man looked at Norah's window again. 'Get it when yer able, that's what I say.'

The sun forced enough light through the curtains for Tommy to see all he wanted of Norah Nesbitt's nakedness. Enough to spark the ardour required for the job in hand. The wedding photo of her and Mr Nesbitt was laid face down on the bedside table (out of sight out of mind), and the wireless tuned into the Home Service. A lady with a posh voice was giving a talk on tinned food recipes and Tommy reckoned she'd be better off taking the plum out of her mouth before she started talking. Then Neville Chamberlain came on the air and solemnly explained how Britain had called for an undertaking from Hitler to withdraw his troops from Poland. The lovers paused in patriotic coitus interruptus as their Prime Minister said, 'I have to tell you that no such undertaking has been received and that consequently this country is now at war with Germany.'

Norah switched off the wireless, pulled Tommy back down on top of her and re-ignited their passion with a desperate, bed-creaking urgency in case this was the last time for both of them.

4

Fifteen years previously, Tommy had lost his virginity under the bandstand in Roundhay Park, inadvertently conceiving Rosie and thus trapping himself into marriage to the scheming Ethel Dobson, who valued security over love.

Tommy owned his own house, having inherited it from his dad. His mother died when he was only eleven and his father, from whom he also inherited the tea round, died a month before Tommy and Ethel got married. Number 2 Duck Street was a substantial, end-of-terrace house which had a shop attached to it when his dad had first bought it. But being stuck in a shop all day long was not for Tommy's dad, so he converted it into a store and a stable for the pony and van. His dad had seen Ethel coming a mile off. When you're on the outside looking in, these things are easy to spot, but not when you're nineteen and know no better. His dad had devoted the last precious fragment of his life to warn Tommy off her.

'Kick the graspin' cow into touch, lad.'

'I think I love 'er, Dad.'

Tommy's father gave a rattling sigh, then turned his death-damp face to his son to deliver his dying words: 'Don't talk so damn soft, lad. She's nobbut a pair o' tits an' a big gob.'

In a moment of clumsy confusion, Tommy repeated these words to Ethel, who assured him that these were nothing but the ramblings of a dying man who wasn't in his right mind and she insisted Tommy did the right thing by her. He succumbed to her moral blackmail because she was the only girl who'd ever batted an eyelash at him, much less dropped her knickers. It would be foolish to ignore such promiscuity, which wasn't rife in the 1920s. Tommy figured it was a sure sign of more to come. Ethel's eyes were focused more on his house and business than on Tommy, whose face would never be his fortune. But he was optimistic and hoped that things might take a turn for the better – which of course they never did. He stuck it out anyway, going along with the old adage drilled into him by his late, but revered mother, 'You've made your bed, now you must lie in it'.

Ethel was an attractive woman in an obvious sort of way. She had woven her web and had made the best use of her feminine wiles. It was quite some time after their wedding night before their marriage was actually consummated. Her bedtime migraines and general aches and pains kept the fire in Tommy's loins burning on a very low light – until Norah Nesbitt came along. He didn't love Norah, or she him, but it didn't matter because they had a mutual need which their weekly liaisons took good care of. Ethel had her suspicions which she kept to herself. Perhaps she thought Tommy's secret lover was doing her a favour. Besides, she had a whole host of ailments to nurture without wasting time on an errant husband.

Tommy was thirty-four years old which, in those days, was middle-aged and Norah Nesbitt made him realise just what he was missing. He didn't wait for his call-up papers but joined up in June 1940, two days after the last man had left Dunkirk. It was during his last visit to Norah's bed that they listened to the broadcast of Churchill's speech together. The new Prime Minister had by now replaced the decent but inept Neville Chamberlain, and seemed to represent the bulldog spirit that would be required to see this thing through. The lovers were lying comfortably in each other's arms, having already finished what they had to do rather than leave it until after the expected announcement, which might dampen their ardour. Albert Sandler was singing 'Roses of Picardy' and Norah was humming along in Tommy's ear as the music faded out. Big Ben began to strike and they both mentally counted the bongs until the ninth one died away. There was a brief moment of silence then an announcer said, 'This is London. The Prime Minister, the Right Honourable Winston Churchill.'

Churchill's voice crackled through Norah's wireless as the lovers clung to each other. 'I speak to you tonight at a moment of great danger for our country . . .'

'I hope my old man got out of France all right,' said Norah.

Tommy made no comment; he was listening intently. Churchill's words were striking a chord within him.

'... We shall fight on the beaches, we shall fight on the landing grounds, we shall fight in the fields and in the streets, we shall fight in the hills; we shall never surrender.'

Norah sat up in bed and turned off the wireless. 'There'll be some fightin' in Maudesly Place if my old man comes home and catches me in bed wi' you.'

She took two cigarettes from a packet of Players on the bedside table, lit them both, then handed one to Tommy as he rummaged under the bedclothes for his underpants. She had mixed feelings about all this news. The odds were that her husband, if he'd been lucky, would be one of the 340,000 troops evacuated from Dunkirk by the Royal Navy and the armada of 'small ships' and, if that was the case, he'd be coming home on leave very shortly. This would make Tommy's visits somewhat difficult, which would be a shame because her husband was no great performer in the bedroom.

'What'll yer do?' she asked.

'I think I'll join up.'

'Nay the heck, Tommy! Then I'll be left wi' nobody. What about your Ethel? She'll not want yer ter go, surely?'

'Our lass dunt care twopence about me,' said Tommy. 'I'll get some owd bloke in ter do the tea round. She'll never know I've gone.'

'I think I'll have a word with her,' Norah grumbled. 'Tell her to think of the needs of others, not just herself.'

'Knowin' you, I wouldn't put it past yer ter do it.'

She kissed him on his lips. 'Just mek sure yer look after yersen. After the war's over, happen we can tek up where we left off.'

'Fair enough. How about one for the road?'

She was one of the few things that made sense in his life; she and Rosie.

*

7

At first, Ethel thought him joining up was inconsiderate, selfish even. 'Yer know they're calling up t' youngest first. They wouldn't get round ter you for mebbe a year. By that time it might all be over.'

'I doubt it,' he said. 'If yer worried about the tea-round we can get someone in ter do it.'

It did the trick. 'Right then. I'd best not stand in yer road. Should be right up your street, gaddin' around France wi' all them French tarts gawpin' at yer.'

'We'll not be goin' ter France for a bit. Our lads have only just got back. Did yer not read the papers?' Then he added, 'I shall miss our Rosie.'

'Aye, I expect yer will,' Ethel said.

Rosie accepted the news with equanimity. It was to be expected. Other men were being called up. The war was getting serious with the easy capitulation of France and Belgium, and the mass evacuation from Dunkirk. For the first time since she was a small child she told her dad she loved him, as she ran after him down the street for one last hug. Ethel stood at the gate with her hands in the pockets of her pinny, aware of the muttering faces staring at her through windows and over yard walls. She nodded a curt farewell to her husband who looked back at her over Rosie's shoulder. If his wife had shown even a morsel of regret at his leaving it might have encouraged him to return. But insincere displays of affection were not her style. Rosie had been the tenuous thread that had held them together, but now she was almost grown up and would soon be making her own way in the world. He'd been given the best excuse in the world to make a clean break. Tommy knew as he hugged his daughter that he wouldn't be back. Rosie didn't see the tears in her dad's eyes as he walked away. She had tears of her own to cope with.

Chapter Two

There was a spare room and Ethel, as part of the war effort, was required to take two women as lodgers. They worked in a local factory which had been turned over to making optical instruments on behalf of the War Department which had made Ethel the offer she wasn't allowed to refuse. A year after her dad left, Rosie caught the flu and sat her School Certificate exams pouring with sweat until she was sent home in case she infected everyone else. She left school without the qualification she'd always assumed she'd get and took a job at Brigshawes, the same factory where the lodgers worked. The Minister of Labour, Ernest Bevin, was conscripting women for war work so Rosie figured she might as well jump before she was pushed. It was cleaner work than some of the older girls were having to take at the munitions factories, filling shells with explosives. She could have taken a job in the aircraft factory at Yeadon or the tank factory at Crossgates; or become a lorry driver or joined the Women's Land Army. Jobs abounded in order that men could be released to go and fight Hitler.

She also joined the Women's Voluntary Service and for two evenings a week she washed and ironed various uniforms, made sandwiches and did a bit of marching. Apart from the odd bomb, the war seemed to be passing Leeds by and there was little in the WVS to interest her;

although towards the end she was taught how to drive an ambulance by a besotted Home Guard sergeant who should have known better at his age. Rosie accepted his tuition but declined a suggestive invitation with a slap across his face. Apart from a sparsity of men and irritants such as gas masks, ration books, the black-out and no fresh fruit, life in Duck Street went on as usual.

Mostin Craddock, from Number 27, found himself sitting on a bench in Paradine Hill Police Station for firing his catapult at a barrage balloon. He was eight years old, thin as a rail and a stranger to soap. Impetigo scabs, daubed with gentian violet, littered his scalp, which had been shorn and treated with DDT to get rid of nits. A morning confined to sitting on the 'long form' was considered a salutary lesson for would-be saboteurs, but Mostin was too engrossed in the *Beano* to worry overmuch. He was laughing at the comic's portrayal of Hitler and Goering as Addie and Hermy, the Nasty Nazis, who fought losing battles against Lord Snooty and his Pals, Pansy Potter and Desperate Dan. Mostin's favourite was Mussolini, who became Musso da Wop – 'he's a big-a-da-flop'.

Mostin had also discovered that by blowing into his gas mask he could make a rude noise, which the police found intensely annoying. It was the reason kids rarely forgot to carry their masks with them. By lunch time, the police had had enough of him and a constable was despatched to fetch Mostin's mother, who immediately laid into the desk sergeant.

'Haven't you lot got nowt better ter do than chasin' round after kids what's only playin'?'

'Your lad were discharging a weapon at a civil defence installation.'

'Don't talk like a pillock! He were playin' with his catapult. He couldn't reach our bloody chimley pot wi' it. God knows, the barmy little beggar's tried often enough.'

'There's a war on, missis. Or didn't yer know?'

'Course I know, it's been in t' papers.'

10

The sergeant ignored her sarcasm. 'Yer never know in a war. I've confiscated the lad's weapon an' his name's gone in the book.'

'Does Churchill know?' she said. 'Mebbe yer due for a VC or summat. Anyroad, why aren't you out there fightin' bloody Nazzies instead of arrestin' little kids for neither nowt nor summat?'

'I did my bit the last time round and yer can take him home if yer like. But the little sod dunt get his catapult back.'

'Yer can keep the damn thing. It should come in right handy fer shootin' Nazzie planes down.' She inclined her head towards her son. 'Yer can keep yon little bugger as well, if yer like.'

'We'd rather not, thank you, Mrs Craddock.'

Mostin grinned triumphantly at the policeman, and his mother gave him a crack around the side of his head that propelled him through the door.

Ethel employed a man to do the tea-round and, despite rationing, drew a steady income from it. There was a rapid turnover of employees because she wasn't the easiest person to work for. Rosie didn't work on Saturdays so she went round with the deliveryman, often taking the reins. There was something satisfying about the solid clip-clop of hooves on metalled roads; and the way people's faces lit up and smiled when they saw the little van passing by, pulled by a piebald pony. For a few hours she could see the world as her father used to see it. Sitting in the rattling seat behind the pony gave her a sense of identity she didn't get from her mother.

The streets on the tea-round were mainly brick terraces, darkened by the ever-present cloud of black sulphurous smoke that clung to the Aire Valley. Countless chimneys sent streams of warm soot trailing into the sky to form a mushroom of grey-blue clag which would cool and return to ground, passing more of the same on its way down. Hitler

11

did his level best to bomb Leeds but the permanent pall rendered the city invisible to Germany's night-time bombers. The Luftwaffe did manage to hit the Marsh Lane Goods Station and the City Museum, where a collection of Egyptian mummies died a second death. Part of the Town Hall was hit and quite a few houses, but strategic targets such as Kirkstall Forge and the Barnbow Ordnance Factory survived. She drove the van past a *Yorkshire Evening Post* placard.

BUS KILLS BIRSTALL WOMAN IN BLACKOUT. THIRD YORKSHIRE BLACKOUT DEATH IN TWO WEEKS.

This didn't surprise her because in Yorkshire the blackout had killed more people than Hitler had. But it was a precaution and in war, precautions are paramount, even if they do get you killed. One day Rosie stopped the van outside Mrs Nesbitt's to tell her that her dad had joined the army and that she couldn't have her weekly quarter pound any more. Mrs Nesbitt stared at Rosie for a second, hoping the girl hadn't picked up on her own unintentional double entendre. Or was it unintentional? Surely the girl didn't know anything.

'They've brought rationing in for tea,' said Rosie. 'And you're only allowed two ounces per person per week.'

'Oh, right.'

'So is that all right then?'

'What? ... yes, it'll have to be.' Mrs Nesbitt couldn't resist adding, 'When yer dad comes home on leave, tell him I miss me weekly quarter pounder.'

'I'll do that, Mrs Nesbitt. Me mam was wondering if Mr Nesbitt had come home from Dunkirk yet?'

'Not yet, love. I expect it's all a big mix-up down south.'

It would be another week before she got the telegram saying her husband was 'Missing'. Three days later he turned up on the doorstep. Norah opened the door and promptly fainted.

Rosie counted out the six weeks it would take for her dad to do his initial training. Everyone's dad came home on leave after square bashing.

'Dad should be home tomorrow,' she announced, ticking off the final day on the calendar.

'He wrote to say he can't manage it,' said Ethel. 'Something's come up.'

'What's come up?'

'We're not allowed to ask.'

An awful thought struck Rose. 'Mam ...?'

'What?'

'You haven't had one of them telegrams, have you?'

'One of what telegrams?'

'Mrs Nesbitt got one about her husband being missing.'

'Her husband turned up. He'd been missing in Southampton. It wouldn't surprise me if *she* goes missing when he finds out what she's been up ter.'

Rosie chose not to query this remark. 'I just wondered, that's all,' she said. 'You would tell me if you got a telegram, wouldn't you?'

'Course I'd tell yer. Anyway, yer don't go missing marching up and down a flamin' parade ground. Mind you, I wouldn't put owt past your dad.'

From then on, Ethel cut her short every time she brought up the subject of her dad. There was something amiss and Rosie wasn't being told.

3 September 1943

British and Canadian forces, under the leadership of Montgomery, crossed the Straits of Messina from Sicily and landed in the toe of Italy. It was there that Gunner Tommy Jones met the Italian girl.

The war had kept him celibate for over three years, so he was easily seduced by the batting eyelashes of a plump but pleasant-looking local girl, several years his junior, despite explicit orders from his sergeant to the contrary:

'Until we've been issued wiv contraceptives, there will be no sexual relationships wiv enemy bints wot might be carryin' social diseases passed on by the Krauts.'

13

The threat of catching second-hand German VD made most of the soldiers steer clear of temptation, leaving the field clear for Tommy, who was soon madly in love with the girl and she with him. Their illicit affair lasted three weeks until Tommy's unit had to move on.

Up until his association with the Italian girl, Tommy was reasonably friendly with a corporal from his unit, their friendship stemmed from them both coming not only from Leeds but from the same district. But when the girl came on the scene, jealousy reared its ugly green head.

'Yer shouldn't be havin' it off wi' an Eyetie. They're us enemy,' grumbled the corporal.

'Get stuffed, corporal,' said Tommy.

They never spoke again. A week later the corporal's leg was shattered by an exploding mine and two months after that he was invalided out and took his jealousy back to Leeds. A beer-fuelled conversation between the corporal and his wife started a poisonous campaign of vilification against both Ethel and Rosie.

'Yer know Tommy Jones?'

'Ethel Jones's husband?'

'Aye.'

'What about him?'

'He's only havin' it off wi' an Eyetie bint.'

'Can't say as I blame him. That Ethel's is a right toffee-nosed cow. Thinks she's doin' the world a favour just by bein' alive.'

'Ah,' said her husband. 'But it's not right, is it? We were told not ter have nowt ter to wi' Eyetie women.'

She eyed him, suspiciously. 'Oh aye, an' why would they need ter tell yer that?'

'It were in general,' he explained quickly. 'Some o' the lads weren't married an' these Eyetie bints were handin' it out on a plate.'

'Of course you wouldn't have been interested.'

He diverted her line of thought. 'It's called fraternisin' wi' the enemy. Careless talk costs lives an' all that.'

'So, yer reckon his lady friend were trying to extract information from him?'

'Well, it stands ter reason. I mean Tommy's not exactly Errol flamin' Flynn an' this lass were right nice-looking.'

'Was she as nice as me?'

'Nay, lass, I'd not climb over you ter get to her,' he lied.

'Yer'll tell me owt.'

The following morning the corporal's wife started a rumour that went around the district like Chinese whispers until Tommy was being accused of sleeping with German women and passing over vital secrets to the enemy. Marlene Gedge, two doors down from Rosie and Ethel, got the juicy version of the story. This delighted her no end and she felt it her bounden duty to inform everyone in the street of the traitorous family in their midst.

Marlene was a sharp-tongued harridan who, for years, had carried a chip on her shoulder regarding the Joneses; what with them having the biggest house in the street, running their own business and Ethel flashing off her new clothes at every opportunity.

Rosie had got used to her dad being away. At first, he sent brief letters from various places in England and when he was posted to the Eighth Army in Egypt his daughter followed his whereabouts via the newspapers. But never once had he been home. His last communication was to say he was in Italy and was alive and well.

'He's certainly getting about,' commented Ethel, handing the buff card across to Rosie. 'I wouldn't mind a fortnight in Italy meself.'

Rosie looked at the card. Everything had been crossed out except the printed line that said 'I am well'. It was a relief, but it didn't solve a problem that had reared its head recently. 'Mam, have you heard what people are saying about him?' she enquired.

Ethel glanced at her daughter. 'I have,' she confirmed, 'and I take no notice. It's just a daft rumour and it'll

15

go away as quick as it came.'

'Mam, they're saying he's a traitor. Susan Clarkson told me they're all talking about it at work. What's the matter with him, Mam? He never comes home on leave and now people are calling him a traitor.'

There was an edge to Ethel's voice now. 'How do I know what's the matter with him? I'll tell yer one thing, lady. I know who's at the bottom of it all – it'll be that Marlene Gedge. I'll mark her card for her. You see if I don't!'

Little Mostin Craddock had found a tin of whitewash and was painting a set of 'V for Victory' signs on the street walls in a belated celebration of the Allied Victory in Africa the previous May. Marlene Gedge had gone out to remonstrate with him but changed her mind and did a deal with the boy.

Rosie was just finishing the Saturday tea round when she saw the boy writing the word 'Traitor' on their yard wall. She'd just about had enough. Unaware of her presence, the boy stood back to admire his work before being smacked on the side of his head with such force as to knock him to the ground and send his spectacles spinning from his head. As he lay there, Rosie angrily kicked him up his bony backside.

'Leave us alone!' protested the boy, scrabbling for his glasses and checking that they were unbroken. 'I'll tell me mam o' yer.'

Rosie was horror-struck at what she'd done. She'd known him all his life. 'Mostin, why did you write that?' she asked.

Before he could answer, she felt a shove in the back that sent her to the ground, narrowly missing Mostin, who scrambled away. She sat up and rubbed a sharp pain away from her elbow. Mrs Gedge stood over her. Beefy arms crossed over her low bosom, bare mottled legs, a cigarette between two nicotine-stained fingers and curlers encased within a hair-net in readiness for a night out at the Fforde

Grene pub. If Hitler had known about the likes of Marlene Gedge he wouldn't have been in such a hurry to invade.

'Kick the lad again an' we'll kick the 'ell outa you!'

'Why?' protested Rosie. 'Why are you doing this?'

'Yer known damn well why,' snarled Mrs Gedge. 'Blood's thicker 'n water. Yer'll be t' bloody same. Like father like daughter.'

A crowd had miraculously gathered from nowhere, drawn by the raised voices. Head-scarfed women with arms akimbo. Cloth-capped men, who, for various reasons, were exempt from fighting in the war, watched the confrontation with hands pushed deep into trouser pockets. Assorted dirty-faced, snotty-nosed children, fresh from the Saturday matinée at the local Bughutch. A girl with spectacles that had one lens blocked with sticking plaster and a boy with plasters pinning his sticky-out ears back to his head. The short-socked girls had knee-length frocks and cardigans and ribboned hair and short-trousered boys had toe-scuffed boots or plimsolls or Wellingtons, and an assortment of jumpers, not one without a hole or a visible mend. But they were all in the same boat and elitism only arose at Whitsuntide, when some kids were turned out in new clothes.

All of them were hoping the argument might escalate into something more violent to brighten up the remains of this dull afternoon. With Mrs Gedge involved, the prospects looked promising.

'What's my dad supposed to have done?' asked Rosie.

'He's a traitor, that's what!'

The shouts were now coming from different parts of the crowd: 'My husband's in a prisoner o' war camp while yer dad's havin' it off wi' bloody Nazzies. He wants hangin'!'

Rosie ran into the house in tears. Ethel was waiting behind drawn curtains.

'What's it all about, Mam? What's Dad supposed to have done?'

'I've no idea, love. It's gettin' beyond a joke is all this.'

17

Her hand shook as she took a Swan Vesta from a box and lit a cigarette. 'I could do without all this, I can tell yer that for nowt.' She took a deep drag and shook her head, despairingly. 'I wouldn't care, yer dad's made it pretty plain he doesn't want ter come back ter me.'

'Has he actually said that?'

'Sort of . . . reading between the lines. I think he's tryin' ter let me know gently. Let's face it, we haven't seen hide nor hair o' the bugger since he joined up and he'll have had a bit o' leave since then, surely.'

Rosie felt doubly sad. This was the first time her mother had actually confirmed her fears about her dad not coming back to them. The trouble outside was momentarily forgotten as she asked, 'Did you ever love Dad?'

Ethel was slightly taken aback at this turn in the conversation. 'Good grief, Rosie, what a thing to ask.'

'Well, did you? I know I was er . . .' she searched for the words, '. . . conceived out of wedlock. I just wondered, that's all.'

Her mother drew hard on the cigarette once more. 'They were hard times when you were born, love. A girl had to take other things into consideration. Love never put food on the table nor clothes on yer back, no matter what they say. And you've never gone without.'

'You married my dad because he had a bit of money, is that what you're saying?'

'I married him for a better life than I'd have had otherwise – where's the crime in that?'

'So, you never loved him?'

'I was never passionately fond of him if that's what yer gettin' at.'

A brick shattered the window, showering Rosie with glass. Ethel evaporated into tears. 'They can't do this. I'll not have them do this to us. Not because of something we haven't done.' She headed for the door and Rosie grabbed her arm.

'Don't go, Mam.'

Ethel shook herself free. 'Leave me alone,' she sobbed. 'Why don't you all leave me alone?' She walked uncertainly outside and stood in front of the mob standing by the gate. All the women stood in a line, with arms aggressively folded across pinafored bosoms of varying sizes. Uncertain men formed a second rank and expectant children hung around the perimeter. Ethel looked a pathetic adversary.

'Yer shouldn't throw things through our window.' Her voice was faltering, her eyes on the ground. 'It's not right. We haven't done nowt.'

The crowd went quiet. There was an embarrassed shuffling of feet. Rosie strode past her mother, carrying the brick. She held it out and asked: 'Whose is this?'

There was no reply. Rosie looked at the crowd; taking in all the men and causing them to lower their eyes. 'I can see why none of you lot were called up,' she said, scornfully. 'The army don't bother with cowards.'

It was an unfair comment and there was a muttering of protest from the men; some of them moved off, not wanting to hear any more. Ethel seemed to draw strength from her daughter's support.

'Come on . . . who threw it?' There was a hint of hysteria in her voice. Rosie took her arm, but once again her mother shook herself free.

Across the street a window slid noisily up and a shout of: 'What's goin' on 'ere?' came from a turbaned woman as she poked her head out.

'It's Ethel,' shouted back an anonymous voice. 'See what somebody's written on their wall?'

The crowd instinctively shuffled to one side so the new spectator could read the graffiti.

'Well, they've spelled it right, so it can't be anyone from round 'ere,' commented the woman in the window.

'It were our Mostin,' shouted up Mostin's mother, proudly. 'He's doin' ever so well at sch . . .'

'Who broke my window?' Ethel's voice chopped her off mid-sentence.

Mostin looked up at an old man, whose gaze dropped to the ground. Ethel and Rosie followed the boy's eyes.

'It was you, wasn't it?' accused Rosie. 'Only you haven't got the guts to own up.'

The old man fiddled in his pocket to find his teeth, which he jammed into his mouth as surreptitiously as he could, then, with his tongue, he cleverly revolved the top set until they fell into place. He looked, studiously, at his boots and muttered, 'At least I'm not a traitor.'

He had only come out to watch and had got carried away by the enthusiasm of the crowd. Enthusiasm he found he didn't share when put to the acid test. Besides, it was a bit chilly and looked like rain and he'd come out without his waistcoat. He was a small man, wearing only a khaki, long-sleeved vest buttoned up to his unshaven neck and voluminous trousers, which were pulled up by braces almost to his armpits and further secured by a broad leather belt. He tried to effect nonchalance by lighting his pipe but Rosie could see his hand was shaking.

'You're a flamin' idiot, that's what you are!'

'Now then, lass, don't start callin' folk names,' he protested. 'There's never no smoke without fire.'

'You're a silly old man who's daft enough to believe a load of gossiping old women who don't know what they're talking about,' said Rosie, scathingly. 'You know my dad. He's not a traitor!'

'That's not what we've heard,' shouted Marlene Gedge. She turned to the crowd, trying to incite them.

Ethel's demeanour suddenly changed. Her timidity turned to rage. 'Oh, I knew you'd be behind all this!' She shook her fist at Mrs Gedge, who held up her arms protectively as Ethel screamed at her, 'And what is it you've heard, eh? Go on, tell us, so we all know.'

There was more foot-shuffling and Marlene Gedge stuck out her chin, to show the crowd she wasn't really scared of Ethel. 'We heard he was havin' it off wi' German women and betrayin' secrets.'

'German women?' laughed Ethel, hysterically. 'He's in Italy, yer brainless cow! There aren't any German women in Italy.'

'We're just sayin' what we've heard.'

Ethel stormed back into her yard as Rosie said, calmly, 'My dad's never been to Germany. He was in Africa with Montgomery for a year and now he's in Italy.' She looked scornfully at the men once again. 'My dad's been doing your fighting for you, and all you can do is listen to brainless idiots like Mrs Gedge who tell lies about him.'

'Who d'yer think you're callin' an idiot?' exploded Marlene Gedge. 'I'll rattle yer bloody ear'ole if yer . . .!'

Her voice was choked off in mid-sentence as Ethel flew out of the yard and thrust a yard broom, bristles first, into Mrs Gedge's face. The woman screeched in pain as the bristles broke her skin, then she cowered as Ethel, weeping in anger, rained a shower of blows on her, stopping only when Rosie managed to grab the weapon from her mother's hands.

The injured woman stumbled away, helped by a neighbour. The crowd dispersed. No one wanted to be this mad woman's next victim. Ethel sank to her knees, shocked at what she'd done; inflicting so much pain on her neighbour. And all because of Tommy, who hadn't been home for three years.

Rosie knelt down and put her arm around her mother, risking another rebuff, but it never came. Ethel sank her head into her daughter's shoulder, her resources completely drained. There was a rumble of distant thunder like some monster truck crashing through its gears.

'Let's get inside, Mam, before it starts to rain.'

Her mother nodded and got to her feet.

'I reckon my dad would have been proud of the way you stuck up for him.'

'I didn't do it for yer dad. I just wanted them to leave us alone.'

*

21

Tommy Jones went from a traitor to a hero in the space of one telegram. It was February 1944 and Tommy had risen to the rank of corporal. Churchill had proposed an amphibious landing behind enemy lines at Anzio on the west coast of Italy. The Allies had established a beach head but the Germans fought back fiercely. Tommy's unit came under heavy artillery fire and was ordered to withdraw from their position. A young major was wounded in the leg and had ordered Tommy to leave him where he was, but Tommy, as was his wont, disobeyed the order and carried the man a quarter of a mile to safety. Two men from his unit, seeing what he was doing, dashed out from their cover and took the wounded man from him. Tommy set off to follow them and stepped on a land mine. Little was left of him; not even the letter he'd written to Rosie telling her how desperately he missed her, and how he was coming home on his next leave to see her. He was awarded a posthumous DSM which, if nothing else, put paid to all the gossip of him being a traitor. Mostin Craddock was sent round by his mother to apologise for writing traitor on the wall and even Mrs Gedge came round to make her peace. On balance, Ethel preferred being the widow of a hero to the wife of an absent husband.

Rosie's grief had been cushioned a little by her dad's long absence but she was still numbed by the news. She went with her mother to Becketts Park Barracks and tearfully accepted the medal on behalf of her dad, but she somehow couldn't help feeling he'd let her down. Dying without coming home to see her. She'd no way of knowing if he ever would have come home.

Rosie had developed a mistrust of men. If her dad could let her down like that, then so could anyone. Boyfriends came and went. Mostly they went off to war. Billy Tomelty, her first serious boyfriend was home on leave after completing his initial army training. Although they weren't formally engaged, marriage had been discussed and agreed, but not until the 'war was out of the way'.

On the night before Billy was due to go off on his posting, Rosie's mother had left them alone while she went to the pictures. Billy was a trainee draughtsman and therefore met with Ethel's approval. The fire was low in the grate to combat the evening chill and to keep them warm in their state of partial undress as they lay on the hearthrug, kissing, exploring and, in Rosie's case, determined not to let things go too far like her mother had done.

Their passion was being held in check with ITMA being on the wireless. It was often said that if Hitler wanted to invade England he should do it between half-past-eight and nine o'clock on a Thursday night when the whole nation was tuned in to Tommy Handley; to listen to the antics of such as Mrs Mopp, Funf the bungling German spy and Colonel Chinstrap. Billy eventually got up and turned it off.

'Hey! – I was enjoying that,' protested Rosie. She knew Billy was up to something. He'd been acting strangely lately and had developed an unusual obsession for haircuts, which she couldn't quite understand, but she said nothing. Maybe it was something to do with him joining the army.

He stood over her and looked down, illuminated by the twilight and the flickering fire; the bulge in his loose underpants betraying his excitement. Rosie had on only her brassiere and knickers; neither of which she intended removing. This was as far as things went. Until their wedding night.

'You look nice,' she said.

'Thank you,' he said, then asked, politely, 'Rosie, can we do it?'

'I don't think we should, Billy.'

He hooked his thumbs into the waist of his underpants. 'Shall I take them off?'

She gave it some thought. 'You can if you want. I still don't want to do it, though.'

Billy pushed them off and knelt astride her. It was the first time she'd seen him completely naked and she would always remember how beautiful he looked.

23

'I think we should do it,' he said.

'Why?'

'Well, I'm off tomorrow, and I might not come back. We might never get the chance again.'

'Don't talk so soft, Billy Tomelty. Course you'll come back.'

He decided to push his luck and play on her sympathy. 'But I might not. And I wouldn't want ter die never havin' ... yer know ... done it with yer.' He leaned over, picked up his trousers and removed a small packet from the pocket. 'I got a ... you know what.'

'Have you now?'

Rosie thought it over for a while. It certainly put a different complexion on things. She came to what she thought was a reasonable compromise. 'Tell you what, I'll make you a promise. I promise I'll save myself till you get back then we'll definitely do it on the very first night.'

'I'd sooner do it now, and know I've done it.' He was struggling to keep the disappointment from his voice.

'No,' decided Rosie, firmly. 'I don't want to do it just for the sake of doing it. It's got to mean something.'

'Oh, right.' This was woman's logic, something he didn't understand and therefore couldn't argue with.

'It's just as hard for me,' she pointed out. 'I've never done it neither you know. It'll be all the better for waiting for. And it'll be a good reason for keeping your head down.'

'Fair enough,' he accepted, gloomily. 'I'd best hang on ter this then.'

'I think I'll buy us a new one,' said Rosie. 'I don't know how long they last.'

'I'll hold yer ter that,' he grinned. 'I had me hair cut three times in two weeks before I dare ask t' barber fer one.'

She laughed as the haircut mystery was solved. He leaned forward, kissed her, and whispered confidentially: 'It's on the cards that we'll be off ter France before long.'

24

'You're not supposed to tell me stuff like that, Billy Tomelty. Walls have ears, you know.'

'I thought yer mam were out,' he grinned. 'Anyroad, I'm lookin' forward to it. I've never been abroad.'

'You just stay away from them French girls.' Rosie took the contraceptive from him. 'In fact, I think I'll look after this. I know what you're like about not wanting things to go to waste.'

Then, persuaded by the moment, she unhooked her bra and slid out of her knickers to join him in his nudity. He gazed down at her.

'By heck, Rosie, lass – I've never in my life seen owt so bleedin' beautiful.'

Holding him in her gaze, she reached up and touched him; amazed that something so hard could feel so soft. Like velvet.

'You're a silver-tongued charmer, Billy Tomelty – but I'll not change my mind,' she said, without conviction.

Within a few minutes she'd satisfied him without them going 'all the way'. At the crucial moment Rosie was making almost as much noise as he was. Had Billy held back a little longer she would have let him make love to her. But he never knew this. A month later, on 6 June, Billy died on Sword Beach in Normandy, before he'd even reached dry land. He was eighteen.

Rosie heard the news of Billy's death second-hand in Wormald's chip shop. Two women in the queue were talking:

'Did yer hear about Mrs Tomelty's lad?'

'Aye, I went round to their house as soon as I heard. She's a wreck is Hilda Tomelty.'

Rosie felt herself go cold. She turned to the women. 'Has something happened to Billy Tomelty?'

The women looked at her, then at each other.

'He's my boyfriend,' explained Rosie, anxiously. 'Is he okay?'

The rest of the queue went quiet. Eventually one of the

two women said, 'Yer might be as well goin' round to see his mam, love.'

'I don't really know his mam.'

'She got a telegram this mornin', love,' said the second woman, as gently as she could. 'I think it said ...' she cleared her throat and the queue shuffled its feet uncomfortably, 'Killed in Action.'

'Oh,' said Rosie. She looked at the fish frier. 'A fish and two penn'orth please ...'

The man hesitated then turned to do her order. Rosie placed her money on the counter and left the shop empty-handed.

The tears arrived as she walked in the door. Ethel was in the cellar, squeezing washing through the mangle, prior to hanging it out on the line. Rosie went through to the front room and stared out of the window, seeing nothing. Then she conjured up an image of her lovely Billy standing over her with the bulge in his underpants and politely asking if they could 'do it' – and she'd turned him down.

Had he thought about her as he lay dying? Had he wished she'd said 'yes'? Would he have died happier if she'd let him? It was the least she could have done. If she could only turn the clock back ...

Chapter Three

Number Two was larger than the rest of the houses in Duck
Street. It also had a bathroom which made Ethel and Rosie
almost middle-class by 1940s standards. All in all, losing a
husband and gaining a house and a war widow's pension had
been a fair swap in Ethel's eyes. She didn't say as much to
Rosie, but her daughter couldn't help but notice the absence
of grief when the news about Tommy came through.
Relations between mother and daughter were strained.

Many working women had to give up their jobs to the
men returning home from the war. Some of them did this
willingly, but Rosie had risen through the ranks during her
time with Brigshawes and was now a floor supervisor and
she saw no good reason why she should step aside for a
man of inferior ability. Ethel continued to take in lodgers to
supplement the family income as she'd sold the tea round
and rented out the store and stable to the new proprietor.
She spent some of the money on a holiday for the two of
them at Butlin's Holiday Camp in Filey.

'It's an opportunity to meet a nice young man.'

'Mam, there'll be plenty of nice young men around now
the war's over, without me having to go to Butlin's.'

'Did yer know Joe Brindle's dad's had ter retire?'

'Yes, I heard,' said Rosie. 'Dodgy heart or something.'

'Apparently their Joe's runnin' t' firm now. He'll be
worth a few bob if his dad pops his clogs.'

'Mam, I'm not interested in Joe Brindle. He's a bully and a thug.'

'I know he's got a soft spot fer you.'

'He's a pest. I told him ages ago to stop bothering me.'

Ethel shrugged. 'A feller's a feller. Yer could do worse.'

'What? You think I should marry for money like you did? Look where it got you.'

'Just you mind yer mouth, madam. Yer not too big ter feel the back of me hand!'

The rift between them would grow wider before it healed. The week in Butlin's didn't help. For the past five years most eligible young men had been away fighting Hitler. In Ethel's mind, now was the time for her daughter to set her stall out and find a husband before all the good ones got snapped up.

Rosie had hated every second of the holiday. She hated having to wake to the sound of some idiot shouting, 'Good Morning, Campers' through the loud speakers; and she hated sitting down to eat in a vast dining room where the campers ate and sang inane songs such as 'Bobbing Up and Down Like This', as they bobbed up and down and ate their kippers, which she also hated.

Ethel selling the tea van had broken Rosie's last tenuous link with her dad. This saddened her and increased the burgeoning resentment she felt towards her mother. As for men, it would be quite some time before she met anyone she remotely took a fancy to. And there would never be anyone who met with her mother's approval. Least of all Sean Quinnan.

Chapter Four

Late summer 1947

As he stepped off the boat from Dublin, Sean Quinnan felt the sea-sickness leave him. He'd spent the whole voyage retching over the rail, having already emptied his stomach into the heaving, slate-grey, Irish Sea. But now he sucked in a deep breath of Liverpool air and took his first look at England. He watched the criss-cross of dockyard cranes lurching across the dull, white skyline, loading and unloading cargoes coming from or going to exotic ports on the other side of the world. Had he been a better sailor he might have been tempted to board one of these ships and continue his adventure; in the event it would have been a wise decision. But Sean had a plan and a vague destination and his sea travel ended here. He sat down on a wooden crate and opened the packet of pork and onion sandwiches his mammy had packed for the sea voyage. Up until now they'd been surplus to requirements, but now his belly was empty and he stuffed them into his hungry mouth and drank from a bottle of lemonade. He ducked as a screeching gull dived at him and tried to steal his food. It landed a few yards away and patrolled up and down without taking its eye off him. He threw the empty lemonade bottle at it.

'Clear off!' he shouted. 'Or ye'll feel the length of me boot up yer little seagull bum.'

Then he looked up at the Liver Birds that his mammy had

29

told him to watch out for and his face broke into a broad, excited smile. This was where new lives began. It was his first time away from home; away from his mammy. His oldest brother had been looking after the family farm since their feckless father had died three years ago. The drink had taken him, as their mammy had prophesied. It had taken him in the form of a farm truck that he'd stepped under on his way home from McPhail's. Now Padraig was married with a child on the way and the farm could barely support one family. So Sean had followed his other brother, Michael, to England.

Michael was in London and had advised Sean to try elsewhere for work. Up north maybe, where the lodgings were cheaper. There was work enough in London but his brother was living in a hostel as it was all he could afford. Sean finished his food and got to his feet, refreshed, replenished and ready to face his new future. Someone bumped into him as he emerged from the docks, almost knocking him to the ground.

'Sorry, pal,' apologised the man, hurrying off.

A couple of minutes later Sean realised his watch was missing. It was a brass half-hunter engraved *J.P. Malone. 25 years Loyal Service*. His dad had won it from Jimmy Malone in a game of brag in McPhail's bar late one night. It was the only thing his dad had left him. Everybody and everything in this town was out to rob him. There was a tear in his eye as he asked directions to the station.

He sat on his suitcase and looked up at the destination boards. No train to Manchester for over an hour but one for Leeds was leaving in fifteen minutes. Leeds, he'd heard of Leeds. It was out in the country somewhere, that'd do for him. The destination board had determined his future.

In some ways, Sean was right about Leeds being out in the country. It bordered on a expanse of open countryside stretching to Scotland in the north and to the sea in the east. But the approach to the city from Lancashire was uninspiring. Apart from the bleak, barren Pennines there was no countryside to speak of. Once over the tops, the West Riding landscape barely changed as one industrial town smudged into another. Slaithwaite, Huddersfield, Mirfield, Dewsbury, Wakefield. Hundreds of smoke-belching chimneys stabbed at a sky which looked incapable of ever being blue. Everything beyond the train window was drab. Drab stone factories and drab brick mills and endless rows of drab houses which could surely only house drab people. When the train slowed down, which was often, he saw men in dark cloth caps and headscarfed women; as if no one wanted to expose their heads to the descending grime. It was all a million miles from the fresh clean air of beautiful green County Mayo where he'd lived all his life. But Sean didn't lose heart, maybe Leeds would be different.

The train slowed down to a crawl and began to clatter over several sets of points and his spirits sank when he saw a large brick building with the sign, *Leeds City South Box* and the people in his compartment began to reach for their cases. He had kept his on his knee after the incident in Liverpool. His mammy had sewn a pocket in his underpants for him to keep his money in and he was grateful for her wisdom, but he wished she was with him now. This was an alien land. He didn't belong here, but he knew he'd have to make the best of it. That's what his mammy had told him.

Dere's a million pounds out there, just waitin' for a man to come and pick it up. But ye might have ter get your hands dirty before it comes your way.

He knew what she meant. Hard work paid its own rewards and this was a land of opportunity. He stepped off the train, full of determination to make the best of things. He'd show his mammy what he was made of and maybe he'd be able to send for her to come and live with him. How great that would be!

It was six in the evening when he stood in Leeds City Square and looked up at the equestrian statue of the Black Prince, spattered with the droppings of countless irreverent pigeons. A spiteful drizzle tested his optimism, hard and invisible, like tiny needles of ice pricking at his skin.

All around him were bronze, naked nymphs, each holding on high an illuminating glass moon that cast its light, diamond bright, on to the wet pavement. A soggy paperboy repeatedly shouted what was supposed to be the name of his paper but sounded like, 'Ee-yapos'. People scurried past with heads down and collars up. He looked up at the Queen's Hotel, tall and grey-streaked white, despite it being just ten years old. On the other side stood the soot-encrusted Victorian Post Office building. City Square was an island marooned in a sea of trundling traffic. Trams ran all around him like Red Indians encircling a beleaguered wagon train, each bound for a place he knew nothing about: Swinegate, he didn't like the sound of that; Headingley; Roundhay; Harehills. Where was a good place to look for lodgings? Everyone seemed in too much of a hurry for him to ask, so he posed his question to a purple-nosed derelict woman, submerged beneath a mountain of rags, sprawled on the stone flags and looking incongruous beneath one of the beautiful nymphs. The question was halfway out of his mouth before he realised what he was talking to.

'I'm looking fer lodgings. Do ye know a good place fer a feller ter stay . . .?'

She took a deep swig from a bottle of dark liquid, most of which ran down her various chins, then released a loud, rasping belch, the stench of which made him back away. The woman had skin like a pear that had been hidden for weeks in the bottom of the fruit bowl and picked out with distaste, before being dropped at finger-tip into the waste-bin. She looked up at him and cackled, 'Yer can come 'ome wi' me if yer like. At least yer could if I 'ad an 'ome.'

He smiled politely, and looked around. An advertisement on a stationary tram said, Guinness Is Good For You. Sean took it as a sign and ran across to it, clambering on board just as the bell went.

'Plenny o' seats on top,' called out the conductor as Sean tried to find one downstairs.

'It's all right, I'll stand down here.'

The top deck of the swaying vehicle seemed far too precarious. He smiled at the conductor who was looking at him, only Sean didn't know what was expected. He'd only ever caught the bus into Castlebar. And that was always fourpence.

'Where to?'

'D'ye know where a feller might find some good lodgings?'

'I'm paid to flog tickets not advice. Where to?'

Some passengers tittered. Sean's accent was quite broad. 'I'll have a fourpenny ticket, please.'

'Fourpence, that'll tek yer to 'arehills terminus.'

'Will I get lodgings there?'

'No idea, mate.'

The conductor clattered up the winding stair shouting, 'Fares, please,' and Sean smiled pleasantly to his fellow passengers. He wanted to create a good impression from the start.

A man got up and pressed the bell to get off. Sean took his place and the young woman on the adjacent seat gave him a polite smile. It was the first sign of friendship he'd seen since he'd stepped off the boat from Dublin.

'Bit late to be looking for lodgings,' she said, before returning her eyes to a newspaper she was reading.

'Oh,' said Sean.

Dusk fell and the gas street lights began to flicker on. The halo of each lamp scattered the passing drizzle into a thousand streamers of falling light, a phenomenon Sean had never noticed before.

'That's pretty.'

'What is?' the young lady asked politely, perhaps hoping he was referring to her.

'How the lamps light up the rain.'

She followed his gaze and saw what he meant. 'Yes,' she agreed. 'It's very pretty.'

'Ye don't happen ter know the time, do ye?' he asked.

33

Then by way of explanation, he added, 'I had me watch stole today. It was one the old feller gave me.'

The young lady stretched out a white hand and looked at her watch. 'Twenty-past-six.'

'Thanks. It was a good fine watch an' all.'

'I'm sorry to hear that. Did you tell the police?'

'Well, I had it stole in Liverpool.'

Sean didn't elaborate, it seemed explanation enough. He looked hopefully through the window, willing a green field to come into view. But he was disappointed. Just row after row of dull, terraced streets, then a large, important-looking building, built in heavily ornate Victorian brick and set back from the road.

'What's that place?' he enquired of the young woman.

She looked up from her paper and followed his pointing finger. 'It's a hospital, St James's.'

Through the opposite window he saw a cemetery. 'An' I suppose that's where they bury all the mistakes,' he grinned.

She laughed and folded her paper, resignedly: 'I suppose it is.'

'Me name's Sean,' he said. 'Sean Quinnan. I'm from Ireland.'

The young woman looked for the first time into his dark eyes. 'I'm Rosie,' she said. 'And I think I might know somewhere you can stay. If only for a couple of nights till you get yourself organised.'

Chapter Five

Ethel wasn't too keen. Especially when she heard Sean's accent, but Rosie had long since succumbed to the charm of the Irish construction workers who drank in the Wellington Arms. Besides she'd already promised him somewhere to stay, if only for a couple of nights.

'We've a spare room, Mother, and he's got nowhere to stay the night.'

'It'll do no harm ter put him up for the night, I s'pose,' said Ethel grudgingly. They'd only had women lodgers before but the last ones had left a couple of weeks ago and she was beginning to feel the difference in her purse.

'What part of Ireland are you from?' asked Rosie.

'Castlebar, County Mayo.'

'There's a lot of Mayo men coming to Leeds.'

Sean smiled awkwardly and felt himself blushing under Rosie's gaze.

'Have you got a job?' enquired Ethel, sharply.

'No, but I'll get one, no problem,' he assured her. 'And I got money to be going on with.'

As the two women looked curiously on, he delved deep inside his voluminous trousers and brought out fifteen pound notes. The sight of the money made Ethel's mind up for her. She took all the notes from him and counted out five.

'This'll pay for two weeks,' she said, giving him back the remaining ten.

Sean beamed from ear to ear. 'Will I be stayin' here, then?' he asked.

'Until I say different,' said Ethel.

'Are you after building work?' enquired Rosie.

'I think that's all there is for us Irish fellers.'

'I know someone who might be able to fix you up. He works for Brindle Construction.'

'D'yer see much o' Joe Brindle?' asked Ethel, innocently and hopefully.

'I know his ganger,' said Rosie curtly. 'Barney Robinson.'

'Oh *him*,' withered Ethel. 'I must say I don't know what his wife ever saw in him.' Ethel looked at Sean as if for support. 'She went to Leeds Girls High School and she goes an' weds a builder's labourer. What a flamin' waste. She could have had her pick, yer know. Her dad's a farmer out at Eccup.'

Sean nodded because it seemed the right thing to do, but he sometimes couldn't understand the strange way these Yorkshire people spoke.

'Barney's a smashing bloke,' said Rosie, annoyed. 'And he's a bit more than a labourer. He practically runs Brindle's firm for him.'

Ethel pulled a face and headed for the stairs. 'I'm not feelin' so good,' she muttered. 'I'm goin' up.'

Rosie offered her mother no sympathy. She turned to Sean. 'Joe Brindle's a bit of a slave driver but he pays good money by all accounts.'

'That'll do fer me.'

'Right. I'll see what I can do.'

Rosie saw in him a beguiling beauty rarely seen in lads of his age. He was sturdily built if not particularly tall, maybe five feet eight; with a flurry of jet black hair and a rosy face like a fresh apple. Open and honest. A new page, unwritten on by life, and illuminated by the darkest, most beautiful eyes she'd ever seen. His ears could have been a little flatter but somehow they suited him.

Sean was the first young man Rosie had had any feelings

36

for since Billy Tomelty. She was now twenty-two, struggling with her weight and beginning to wonder if she'd ever find anyone. Sean was seventeen and, on the face of it, far too young for her but Rosie was completely entranced by him. She knew he liked her, there were very few young men around who didn't. There was an undefinable something about Rosie, something you couldn't put your finger on.

Although many had tried.

Joe Brindle was the only son of Albert Brindle, who had built his construction firm up between the wars into something quite substantial. Like his father, Joe was one of nature's bullies; coming from his background he knew no better. His father's idea of discipline was a full-on beating with fist and boot. Mrs Brindle had died giving birth to Joe's younger brother, Ralph; the only person in the world whom Joe had ever had any time for. Joe did his National Service as a Bevin Boy, one of the ten per cent sent to work in the mines to reverse the sharp drop in coal production. Ralph Brindle joined the navy and was killed in 1944. His death severed the last link between Joe Brindle and common decency and humanity. Brindle Construction paid well but they took their pound of flesh. No one worked for them out of loyalty.

Sean was sitting on a pile of concrete slabs, taking his first bite of a cooking apple the size of a small turnip which Rosie had packed in his snap tin, when Joe Brindle arrived on site. Six feet tall and well over two hundred pounds, he had a heavy, handsome, mean-eyed face; a face with neither a soul nor a conscience. He grunted at Sean, 'Who the hell are you?'

The young Irishman winced at the apple's sour taste and spat out a mouthful of white mush, just missing Brindle's boots. 'Sean Quinnan,' he said, without apologising. 'Yer man said I could start this mornin'.'

'Did he now? What as?'

'Labourin', I s'pose. I'm a good worker.'

'That's all you lot ever say. What I need is someone wi' a head on his shoulders, norra thick Paddy that dunt know how to eat a bloody apple.'

Sean didn't answer, he'd been told to ignore all insults such as this, which were common on building sites. He would have to prove himself before anyone gave him any respect.

'Well, don't stand there lookin' at me,' snapped Brindle. 'Get that mixer started and stick a mix in ready for t' brickies if they decide ter show up.'

'No problem, sir,' said Sean. 'I'll do that.'

Sean looked at the concrete mixer, not having a clue how to start it. He could well be sacked before he'd officially started work. Adopting a confident air, he headed towards the dirty yellow machine, attempting a cheery whistle designed to throw Brindle further off the scent. No sound emerged from his pursed lips and he realised that whistling when you're nervous is as impossible as whistling when someone's trying to make you laugh. He gave up and hoped the man would disappear into the cabin and give him time to work out how to start the thing. If he couldn't he'd just tell the man where he could stick his job. Sean wasn't keen on working for such a miserable pig anyway.

He could feel the miserable pig's eyes boring into his back as he lifted the metal cover that was hinged over the small diesel motor. There was a filler cap on the fuel tank. Sean unscrewed it and looked inside. To his disappointment it was full. He looked back at Brindle, whose eyes had followed him every inch of the way.

'It's empty,' he shouted. 'Will I fill her up?'

'Well, it won't run on fresh air.'

Brindle muttered something about thick Paddies and let himself into the site-hut as Sean picked up an empty fuel can and disappeared around the back of the buildings where he sat on a low stack of bricks to await the arrival of the rest of the men, particularly the brickie's labourer, whose job it was to work the mixer. The sky above showed promise. Sort of a washed-out blue, which you'd expect at that time of year, and it instilled optimism in Sean who was determined to make the best of things. A squadron of migrating geese squawked their way south in a drunken V formation and Sean watched them with envy. One day he'd fly to warmer climes; maybe take his mammy with him on a holiday.

An idea struck him and he picked up the empty can and made his way back to the mixer. Under the metal cover was a box with a starting handle in it. Back home his dad used to have a diesel generator that started like this. He clicked it into place and was turning the handle just as Brindle was emerging from the hut. The mixer didn't start and the builder stopped and glared at the young Irishman. 'I think there might be an airlock,' called out Sean, who had heard his dad complain of airlocks in the fuel pipes. Brindle shook his head and turned away. As he did, an arm reached over Sean's shoulder and flicked a switch on the motor.

'It goes better if you turn the diesel on,' said Barney Robinson. 'Try it now.'

A relieved Sean gave the handle another energetic turn, the motor coughed out a cloud of blue smoke, then rumbled into life. He grinned at the man. 'I always forget about the diesel switch,' he lied.

'So,' said Barney, 'you've worked on mixers before then, have you?'

Sean looked at Barney and wondered whether or not to continue with his pretence. Barney grinned and said, 'I'm Barney Robinson. Rosie Jones told me you were a good grafter.'

'I am,' Sean assured him. 'But I nivver worked one of these yokes before.' He inclined his head towards the mixer.

'Well, you'd best get used to it,' said Barney, handing Sean a shovel. 'That's what you'll be doin'.'

'Right, mister, no problem.'

'We want a one-two-four mix,' said Barney.

'No problem,' said Sean, confidently. 'What's a one-two-four mix?'

Barney pulled back a tarpaulin covering a pile of cement

39

bags, took the shovel from Sean and cut one of them open. 'In this size mixer,' he said, 'it's two shovels o' cement, four o' sand and eight o' gravel, in that order – don't gerrem mixed up.'

'Cement, sand and gravel,' repeated Sean. 'I got that.'

'Mix it dry for a minute,' said Barney, 'then throw some water in. We want a two inch slump.'

'Two inch slump,' repeated Sean, uncertainly.

'Like stodgy porridge.'

'Stodgy porridge – I get yer.'

Sean was already counting his shovelfuls as Barney walked away. He wasn't at all sure about his wisdom in setting on this obviously inexperienced Irishman, and if anyone other than Rosie had asked him, he'd have said no. Definitely.

Sean had his head almost inside the drum of the mixer when a labourer drove up on a dumper. Sean turned and beamed at the man who nodded his acknowledgement.

'Come on, Paddy!' he called out, cheerfully. 'T' day after tomorrow's Wednesday. That's half a week gone and nowt done.'

'D'ye think this looks all right?' asked Sean.

The man got out of the seat and strolled across to the mixer. He sniffed inside the turning drum with the air of a chef checking a pan of sauce.

'Smells a bit fruity.'

Men on the scaffolding were grinning and nudging each other. The dumper driver jabbed his middle finger into the mix, then, in the same movement, thrust his forefinger into his mouth and smacked his lips. Sean's mouth opened in amazement as the man surreptitiously wiped his middle finger on his overalls.

'Too much salt,' he concluded.

Sean knew he'd been tricked but wasn't sure how. 'Too much salt's very bad for ye,' he grinned. 'I'll know next time.'

The man laughed and drove his dumper up to the mixer, then got out, unclipped the drum lock and spun the wheel to tip the grey mixture into the dumper. Barney had forgotten

40

to tell Sean how to do this and had obviously instructed the dumper driver to show him.

'Thanks,' said Sean, winding the drum back into position. The sun came out and warmed his back enough for him to take off his heavy jumper. He looked round the site and silently thanked Rosie for getting him such a great job.

Two hours later he had joined the rest of the gang for the morning tea break when Brindle approached. His eyes bore into Sean from beneath permanently scowling brows.

'I reckon yer staying wi' Rosie Jones,' he rasped.

'I am,' confirmed Sean.

Brindle's face contorted into a lewd grin. 'She likes Paddies – I reckon yer must be giving her one.'

Sean didn't see Barney's face set like stone. The Irishman didn't know what Brindle was talking about, some of the other men laughed coarsely. Sean shrugged.

'Sayin' nowt, eh?' Brindle's eyes clouded over. 'Mess with her, an' yer'll have me to answer to.'

He spun on his heels and was disappearing into the hut when one of the men said: 'What d'yer reckon that were all about?'

'I reckon he fancies Paddy's landlady,' laughed another. He made a lewd gesture. 'Is it true then, Paddy? Are yer givin' her one?'

'Leave it!' snapped Barney.

'You an' all?' grinned a bricklayer. 'I shall have ter tell your wife o' you, Barney lad.'

Barney forced out a grin. 'Hey! She's a friend o' mine that's all – an' it's bad enough Brindle goin' on about her without you pillocks joinin' in.'

'So, Brindle fancies her, then?' pressed the brickie.

'He's always fancied her,' said Barney. 'I reckon he fancies her nearly as much as he fancies himself. But I reckon Rosie Jones'd sooner kiss your hairy arse than kiss Brindle.'

'Me too, ducky,' minced the dumper driver.

The brickie threw a half-eaten sandwich at him and the conversation switched to Leeds United.

41

Chapter Six

It was Thursday of the following week and Sean arrived home, sat down at the table and took his first pay packet out of his pocket. Five pounds two and six after deductions.

Ethel said, 'That's a damn good wage for a seventeen-year-old. When I were seventeen I got fourteen shillings a week.'

'He's doing a man's job, why shouldn't he get a man's wage?' defended Rosie, who had taken something of a shine to their new lodger. And she was fairly certain her feelings were reciprocated. She'd been aware of him staring at her then turning his head away as she looked at him. But he was shy; too shy ever to make the first move. Her mother was quite taken by Sean's good looks and had warned her daughter, 'He's too young for you.'

'He's probably had about as much experience with women as I have with men,' pointed out Rosie. 'Which is very little. If I have to sit and wait for a decent bloke my own age to turn up, I'll be waiting forever.'

When Sean was counting his money she took the bull by the horns. 'We should go out and celebrate your first pay packet.'

'That sounds great,' replied Sean. 'Where would we go?'

'The Wellie – Wellington Arms – it's a good night on a Thursday.'

'That sounds like a public house.'

'It is.'

'But I'm not old enough ter drink. I'd hate ter get in trouble wid the police.'

Rosie looked at Sean with her head tilted to one side and rubbed her chin between fingers and thumb as though appraising the trade-in value of a used car.

'Well, you look old enough,' she said. 'And anyway, I'll look after you.'

'Don't look after him too well,' warned Ethel.

Sean refused to touch a drop of alcohol. 'I promised me mammy I'd wouldn't touch the stuff until I was eighteen.'

'I'll get you a shandy then.'

'Ginger beer shandy,' he said. 'I like that ginger beer.'

'I thought you might.'

The lounge bar was only half full, most drinkers preferring to take advantage of the cheaper beer in the tap room. An erratic gas lamp made Sean's shadow flicker against the shiny oak table, at which he sat with his back to the room to reduce the chances of him being exposed as an illegal drinker.

He had been indoctrinated with two opposing views on drinking. His mammy whom he loved dearly, and for whose wisdom he had the highest regard, told him that drink was the devil's claw; *It'll grab ye and pull ye straight down ter hell once ye get the taste*. His father, Declan Quinnan, whom he had also loved dearly, had often taken him into the pub, where he'd sit young Sean on a high stool to drink a glass of lemonade while old Barney McPhail pulled a slow pint of Guinness. His dad would slide the black pint with its creamy white collar in front of his son.

'Would ye look at dat? Who does it remind ye of?'

'It's the dead spit of Father Conlon, Dad.'

'And how can anything that looks the image of a man of God, be sinful?'

'I don't know, Dad.'

It was a well-rehearsed routine, but his dad and Barney McPhail would laugh and Sean would laugh as well, although he didn't know why. Declan Quinnan was a poor class of a husband but a great man for the crack. After a few pints of the black stuff he'd raise his glass and recite his little poem to whoever was in earshot.

Mother Dear I'm over here and nivver coming back,

I'm stoppin' for the pint o' beer, the woman and the crack.

Sean remembered the time his dad had pointed to the clock on the wall behind the bar and told him that it was the oldest clock in Ireland. It was so old that the shadow from the pendulum had worn a hole in the wall. This time everyone in the pub laughed and Sean joined in, hoping that one day he'd understand this strange man who was his father.

Rosie had gone to the bar, leaving him to his own devices. He studiously examined a Tetley's beer mat adorned with a picture of a monocled huntsman, then at a faded print of Goya's Duke of Wellington, who stared reproachfully at him from the wall opposite. It was pictures such as this, plus the peeling, wine-coloured flock wallpaper and threadbare carpet that differentiated the lounge from the tap room, thereby justifying the extra penny a pint.

Rosie's return from the bar came as a relief to Sean. She set a shandy in front of him. It was seventy-five per cent Tetley's Bitter. Rosie wanted him to drop his guard.

'There,' she said. 'It's proper shandy. Don't drink it all at once or you'll get legless.'

He eyed his drink suspiciously.

'It was a joke,' said Rosie. 'They had no ginger beer, but it's practically non-alcoholic.'

He drank the shandy in a series of quick gulps, then set the glass back down on the table.

'Your round,' said Rosie.

He took a florin from his pocket and pushed it across the table towards her. No way would he be persuaded to go to the bar himself, that would be just too illegal.

'There should be threepence change,' he said. Then added by way of explanation, 'I heard yer man tell yer how much it cost last time.'

'It might have gone up since then. It's been all of thirty seconds since I got you that shandy.'

'Would that be another of yer jokes?'

'Sort of.'

'What else did you promise your mammy?' she enquired, sipping a gin and tonic and absent-mindedly balancing his two shilling piece on its edge. 'Did she say anything about girls?'

'She said I've ter save meself until I get married.'

'I thought she might.'

'Although what she meant by that, I've no idea.'

Rosie brightened. 'We all need to save for when we get married,' she explained. 'It's an expensive time.'

'Is that what she meant?'

'What else could she mean? Have you got a girlfriend?'

Sean gave a shy grin. 'Not really. I went to the church dance wid Maureen Flanagan a couple o' times but I have ter say I wasn't exactly keen on the idea. Her own father was prettier than her and he had a face like Muldoon's pig.'

'What about me? Am I prettier than Maureen Flanagan?'

His dark eyes shone into hers as he examined her face. Her mouth was too big and she had a slightly crooked smile. Her eyes were too oval, her nose hooked slightly and her chin was dimpled. Positioned differently, her features could have let her down badly, but nature had been more than kind to her and the juxtaposition of all these imperfections added up to a startling beauty that no artist could ever invent for himself.

'I tell yer, I nivver seen a more beautiful lady on God's earth.'

She was suddenly reminded of Billy Tomelty and the awkward praise he'd heaped on her when she'd lain naked beneath him that time. When she'd refused to 'do it'. A mistake she'd never make again – if the right man came along.

'So, you like big women, then?'

'You're not big,' he argued. 'Not by Mayo standards anyway. I don't like skinny women. Skinny women can be miserable. And ye've got a pretty face.'

'You're not so bad yourself.'

'I know. Me mammy reckons I'm the most handsome divil in the whole family.' He reached in his pocket and brought out a wallet, from which he took a small, black and white photograph.

'Who's this?' asked Rosie, taking it from him.

'It's me when I was a young buck at school. Would ye look at the ears on me? Me mammy reckoned I might be an angel wid wings growing out of me head.'

'Your mammy loves you, doesn't she?'

'And why wouldn't she? Ye can keep it if ye like.'

Rosie laughed and hugged him to her. He responded and then pulled away, aware of watching eyes. Their faces and lips were just inches apart. Rosie gave him a swift, pecking kiss on his nose. He responded with a peck to her lips. They parted once again and eyed each other up. Rosie felt herself being drawn to him until their lips were almost touching. Sean's sudden embarrassment broke the spell.

'I think I'll go to the bar meself.'

'Yes, right . . . I'll have a brandy.'

As the evening wore on, the flirting continued with increasing daring, fuelled partly by drink, but mostly by mutual attraction. On the walk home they kissed for the first time; fully and deeply. Sean's novice lips were well up to the task and Rosie's suppressed libido pushed her body hard against him. The memory of Billy was now foremost in her mind. Tonight she wouldn't be saying no.

They were now back in Number Two Duck Street. She had sneaked him past the room inhabited by her snoring mother who had gone to bed with one of her migraines. Her remedy of three aspirins washed down with half a tumbler

46

of whisky ensured that she would only wake up if disturbed by a violent earthquake or a medium-sized atomic bomb. It had been a good night so far and Rosie had sneaked the family wireless out of the front room for their further amusement. She noisily made a space on her dressing table, set it down and plugged it in, then began to fiddle, laboriously, with the tuner, shushing Sean into silence as she held her ear to the speaker like an expert safecracker. Her face lit up with triumph as the music of Geraldo and his late night orchestra crackled into the room. She began to sway, seductively, as Sean perched on the edge of the bed, not quite knowing what was expected of him.

Doing a strip-tease wasn't Rosie's immediate intention, but the look on Sean's face when she playfully removed her cardigan and dropped it beside him on the bed, tempted her to take it a stage further. His incessant chatter had long since stopped by the time she sat on a chair and slowly unpeeled her stockings. She posed, unsteadily, in just bra, panties and suspender belt, causing Sean's eyes to bulge. The band struck up with 'You'd Be So Nice To Come Home To' and she held her hands out for him to join her in a dance.

'Did they teach you the waltz at the church dance?'

'I was never one fer all that modern stuff – but I can do the Siege of Ennis.'

'Sounds complicated, does it take a long time to learn?'

'Not the way I do it,' he grinned. 'It's a bit vigorous.'

'I don't think there's room in here for anything vigorous,' giggled Rosie. 'Come on, I'll show you how to waltz.'

'I'm no Fred Astaire.'

'I'm no Ginger Rogers but we'll get by.'

'Yer a bit of a naughty lady if ye ask me.'

'I'm not, actually. Maybe it's you who's making me naughty.'

It sounded like a compliment to Sean so he got to his feet, took her into his arms and moved clumsily into a

47

waltz. His feet crushed hers and made her wince but she said nothing. At first he didn't know which part of her to hold. Her back was naked so he placed his right hand further down, keeping her panties between her skin and his hand. As the band moved on to 'You'll Never Know', she pushed herself closer to him and Sean couldn't help but respond. Lit only by the pale gleam of the street gas lamp through a gap in the curtains, they moved round and round the tiny room in a tight circle, his hand on her naked back now, with his little finger just edging beneath the waistband of her knickers into the cleft of her buttocks, the nearest he'd ever had to sexual contact with a woman. She wriggled her bottom, inviting him to continue his little foray, which he did, but not fast enough for her liking. She kissed him, pushed him on to the bed and took a step back, her mischievous eyes fixed on his.

His heart raced and his Catholic conscience melted beneath the heat in his loins as she removed her bra and, with hands on well-upholstered hips, shamelessly thrust out her generous breasts, the first Sean had ever seen. His eyes darted excitedly from nipple to nipple, pink and hard like miniature sombreros, only he was much too polite to say.

Then, inch by seductive inch, she pushed down her lace-trimmed knickers, bought that very day from Marks and Spencers. Her eyes were fixed on his mesmerised face until she stood before him, stark naked. He dropped his guilty gaze to the floor, then allowed his eyes to be drawn up her shapely legs until the dark, seductive V came into view. Then his conscience forced his gaze further up to her marginally less sinful, but equally naked bosom.

'This is a sin of the flesh,' he croaked, addressing his remark to her left breast.

She took a step towards him, her Soir de Paris perfume assaulting his senses and extinguishing his puny resistance.

'Isn't there something in the Bible about God making man in His own image?'

He gave Rosie's question some thought, then nodded. He

was no expert on the Bible but her words had a ring of truth.

'Well then,' she said. 'You're looking upon God's own image. What can be sinful in that?'

'God must be an awful nice lookin' fella.'

'So are you, but I'd like to see more of you.'

She stepped towards him until her breasts were brushing against his face. Her flesh was pale and satin smooth, without a blemish or an unsightly ripple and was evenly distributed about her body in not quite Rubenesque proportions. Sean could see little wrong with Rosie Jones, but the disturbance she was causing in his trousers told him that this must definitely be a sin. Nothing as pleasurable as this would ever be allowed by the Holy Catholic Church. At times like this he wished he was a Protestant or maybe even a Jew or a Hindu. Why should they have all the fun without having to confess it? Rosie took him by his hands, gently brought him to his feet then began unbuttoning his shirt.

'I'll let you do your own trousers.'

Sean did as he was told. They flopped around his ankles as she pulled the shirt from him, relieved to note that his underpants were not the long-john variety, although they were quite substantial. The word demi-john sprang to her mind, bringing a smile which might have been broader had he worn the ones with the pocket.

'What are ye laughin' at?' Sean sounded offended. Rosie pressed her finger to his lips, cutting off his protest.

'Not you, I promise. Well, not you personally. It's your underpants, they're a bit ...' She didn't have the word. 'Just take them off,' she said.

Sean hesitated. His body was whiter even than hers. Hard muscled but in need of a good wash.

As a child, Rosie had always wanted a shower and her dad had installed one over the bath just before he went away. It was his going away present to her – although she didn't realise it. She wrinkled her nose but said nothing. A shower with Sean would get the night off to a good start.

'With a hard job like yours,' she advised. 'You should shower every day when you come home.'

Sean took the hint. 'Back home we only had the tin bath what we had ter fill with pans of water and there were seven of us so we were all in the habit of not havin' the bath too often.'

Rosie pushed a lock of hair away from his eyes and kissed him lightly on his lips. 'It's a habit you might have to break. We English are a bit over sensitive when it comes to, er, body musk, manly though it may be. I think we should start now.'

Rosie was enjoying this reversal of roles. Up until now it had always been the men making the moves, with her playing the part of the protesting virgin. No doubt the drink was playing its part and maybe she'd regret it all tomorrow. But this was tonight and she was having a good time. She hooked her thumbs into his underpants and pushed them down, her eyes not leaving his. A couple of drunks in the street outside began singing loudly and discordantly and Rosie was worried lest they break the mood.

'In fact, I think we'll start by having that shower.' She took him by the hand and led him into the bathroom.

Sean and Rosie lost their virginities under the luke-warm spray, his shuddering knees almost giving way as the moment came. Rosie supported him as he came to a raucous climax, shouting something about Divine forgiveness for his terrible sin. She found this mildly insulting but said nothing.

They stayed there, in each other's arms, for several minutes, with Rosie absent-mindedly soaping his back. Sean's sin of the flesh might have been complete but hers certainly wasn't. She felt him stirring against her stomach and reached down to help him back to life. He was no longer interested in Divine absolution and began to move exploring hands all over her body. She passed him the soap and for the next few minutes they worked up a lather in both senses of the phrase.

'Perhaps we should finish this in bed,' she suggested.

Two tiptoeing, giggling minutes later they were under the sheets in Rosie's bed. This time it was slower and more satisfying. As dawn poked its dim, grey light through the chink in the curtains, Sean woke up. Rosie was fast asleep and the only sounds were the ticking of the clock and the comfortable snoring coming through the wall.

He dressed quickly and slipped back into his own room, unaware of the triumphant sperm which had just completed an exhausting trip along Rosie's fallopian tube and was at that moment politely introducing itself to one of her eggs.

Chapter Seven

The following morning Barney looked at Sean's pallid face. 'I hope you didn't drink your first week's wages in one night,' he said.

'I was only drinkin' shandy.'

'Oh aye? An' how many pints o' shandy did you have?'

'About six, I think. I reckon Rosie was askin' yer man ter fill 'em up wid mostly beer.'

'Rosie? You were out with Rosie?'

'I was. She took me out ter celebrate me first pay packet.'

'Hey, did she mek yer buy a packet o' three ter take home with yer?' guffawed the brickie. The rest of the men laughed.

All except Barney.

Sean grinned. He obviously hadn't a clue what they were laughing at. The brickie pressed on, 'Did yer use all three?'

'All three what?'

'Johnnies – don't say yer didn't use a rubber johnnie.'

The laughter drew Brindle over. 'Yer gigglin' like a bunch o' bleedin' schoolgirls,' he said. 'What's the joke?'

The bricklayer sniggered and pointed at Sean. 'He were having it off with 'is landlady last night. I reckon he were ridin' bareback.'

'They're just havin' him on,' said Barney.

'Is that right?' grunted Brindle, looking at his watch.

'Well I reckon it's time yer got some work done or I'll have you lot off this bloody site.'

'She took him out an' got him pissed,' called out the bricklayer, as he walked away. 'I reckon him and 'er were havin' it off.'

By dinnertime Sean had sweated out any dregs of alcohol left in his system. The memory of his night with Rosie was vivid in his mind – and in his heart. He knew beyond all doubt that he loved Rosie Jones and he would be telling her just as soon as he got home.

'We don't need any concrete this afternoon, Sean,' said Barney as they left the canteen hut after dinner. The ganger pointed upwards to the steel skeleton of the four storey office block they were building.

'We've a load o' slabs comin'. I want you to help off-load 'em. Then you can give us a hand up top to lay 'em.'

Sean followed Barney's pointing finger and looked up, with some unease, at the rolled steel joists, columns and concrete stairways. No walls or floors yet; they were the next items on the agenda. Concrete slabs would span between the steel beams. At least, they would when Sean had helped off-load them and helped the slinger to fasten them on to the crane-line, which would hoist them up to the gang waiting on the top of the structure. Barney Robinson always liked to get the roof on first; it cut down rained-off time. No one liked being rained off, especially Joe Brindle. Sean gave an involuntary shudder as he looked up to where the slab layers were busying themselves fifty feet above him. Sean had spent his life at ground level; the highest he'd ever been was the attic bedroom back home. Had he gone a little higher he might have become aware of his vertigo.

He watched as one of the men walked nonchalantly across a four-inch-wide beam, stopping in the middle to light a cigarette. Sean jumped as a loud horn announced the arrival of a heavily loaded wagon.

53

'Where d'yer want these?' shouted the driver, who had a lazy eye which made it unclear whom he was talking to. Sean looked around, hopefully, but apart from the crane driver whose face was buried behind a *Daily Mirror*, there was no one else to whom the question could have been addressed.

'Did yer hear me?' shouted the exasperated driver.

Sean pointed at himself. 'Is it me yer talkin' ter? I didn't know ye was lookin' at me.'

The driver was used to this misunderstanding, but he wasn't going to take it from a Paddy. 'Who d'yer bloody think I'm talkin' ter?'

His shout brought Joe Brindle to the cabin door. 'What's the problem?' he called out.

'I just want ter know where yer want these off-loadin'. I've asked this feller but he's thrown me a deaf un.' The driver pointed accusingly at Sean.

'He's a thick Paddy, what d'yer expect?' grunted Brindle, directing the wagon to a position within range of the crane. The thought of Sean 'having it off' with Rosie Jones rankled with him. What had this thick Paddy got that he hadn't got?

The day was warming up and Brindle hung his jacket on a pile of bricks. Then he thumbed his braces from his shoulders, allowing them to dangle against his thighs and rolled his sleeves up above his muscular, tattooed forearms. 'We're liftin' 'em straight up top,' he said. 'I'll be workin' wi' yer.'

The man jumped out of his cab and began to untie the ropes securing his load. Between the two of them they had now made Sean redundant and he was at a loss what to do. The driver looked at him, and shouted to Brindle, 'If it were up ter me I'd ban 'em from the bloody country. After the way they performed in t' war.'

'Performed? How d'yer mean, performed?' snorted Brindle. 'They didn't perform, they stayed bloody neutral, the bastards. Didn't lift a bloody finger when we needed 'em.'

54

'It's a different story now, innit?' said the driver, who had avoided military service, having been classified as unfit for combat due to his feet. 'Now we've beaten them Nazzies yer can't move fer bloody Paddies, comin' over here an' nickin' our jobs.'

'And gettin' their leg over wi' our women,' added Brindle, coarsely, with a certain woman in mind. A woman who had been on his mind for years. 'There weren't so many of 'em over here when t' bombs were droppin'.'

'I had a cousin who was killed in Coventry by a bomb,' said Sean.

'Serves the bastard right,' rasped Brindle. 'Them bleedin' U Boats had a field day 'cos that bastard De Valera wouldn't lerrus use his ports.' He spat viciously on the ground. 'Our kid got killed just off Southern Ireland. He were in a frigate guardin' a merchant convoy. There were two Irish ships in it what had just peeled off ter go into their own port.'

'What our lads weren't allowed ter use,' added the driver. 'Because o' that bastard De Valera.'

'He were as bad as Hitler.'

Two pairs of eyes burnt into Sean who dropped his gaze. He didn't know how to defend his fellow countrymen against such abuse.

'They were torpedoed.' Brindle lowered his voice, his eyes narrowing. 'Our young un were twenty years old.'

Rare tears invaded Brindle's eyes. There was a silence as the two men directed their hatred at Sean. He looked up at them defiantly and said, 'I had an uncle killed in the war. He was in the Royal Irish Fusiliers. He got killed in France.'

'Yer a liar!' roared Brindle.

'I am not,' argued Sean, stoutly. 'Plenty of Irish fellers fought in the war.'

'Gerrouta me bloody sight,' snarled Brindle. 'Gerrup top an' make yersen useful.' He shielded his eyes against the morning sun and shouted upwards, 'Barney, I'm doin' the slingin' meself. I'm sending this Paddy o' yours up top. He's neither use nor bleedin' orniment down here.'

Sean needed no second bidding. He trotted up five flights of stairs to where a ladder stood on a pre-cast concrete landing, leading up to the roof where the rest of the gang were wrestling with a half ton concrete slab which the crane was delicately lowering into position, spanning between two steel beams. Once they'd laid two or three of these fourteen-inch-wide slabs their job would become less dangerous as they'd have something safer to stand on. Barney looked at Sean who had arrived at the top of the ladder, then down at Brindle who was standing on the concrete slabs on the back of the wagon talking to the driver. The ganger didn't like his boss, there was something unbalanced about him. Not a man you'd want to go for a drink with after work. He regarded Brindle as a man without humour, compassion, generosity of spirit or any of the other things that help to mould a man into a half decent bloke. No one expected contractors to be stand-up comics, or psychiatrists or parish priests, but a sprinkling of decency never went amiss.

And now Brindle had sent a man, new to the job, up top without a safety harness. If the factory inspector spotted any of them without a harness, Brindle Construction Limited would get an official bollocking, perhaps even a small fine, which Brindle would consider to be well worth the risk. Most of the men preferred to work without one anyway. But to expect a new man to work without one was typical of Brindle.

'You'd best nip back down an' get yourself a safety harness, lad,' said Barney. 'These lads have been doin' this for years. I don't expect you to get as daft as them on your first day. The gaffer'll show you where they are.'

Sean hesitated. He didn't know why his stomach was churning but he definitely didn't fancy venturing out onto those narrow beams with nothing between him and the ground. He descended the ladder and ran back down the stairs. As he stepped off the bottom step the churning stopped. He stood there for a second wondering what had been wrong with him. Brindle saw him. 'Is that it, then? Finished fer the day, have yer?'

The wagon driver grinned and Sean said, 'Barney told me ter get a safety harness.'

Brindle was standing on the back of the wagon, wrapping chains around one of the concrete slabs, assisted by the wagon driver. He turned his back to Sean and stuck a finger in the air above his head, twirling it around as he looked across at the crane driver. The crane driver acknowledged the signal telling him to take it up and pulled the lever that lifted the slab in the air. Brindle held it steady until it was clear of the wagon then glowered down at the waiting Irishman. 'Are you still here?' he snapped.

The wagon driver was laughing out loud. Sean could happily have dragged him off the wagon and thumped him. The young Irishman stood his ground, he was in the right. 'If yer don't stand fer something, ye'll fall fer anything,' his mammy had told him.

'Barney told me ter get a safety harness,' he repeated.

Brindle exploded, 'D'yer think I've got nowt better ter do than bottle-feed the likes o' you. Either gerrup top or gerroff this site!'

Sean hesitated, then slowly turned to retrace his steps. He could hear the wagon driver sniggering behind him. Thumping the man and walking off the job didn't seem like a bad idea, surely not every employer was as bad as Brindle. No, he decided. I'll stick it out and show them what I can do. Barney had already witnessed the scene below and made no further mention of the safety harness.

'Just work with Jim,' he said, when Sean arrived, breath-lessly, at the top of the ladder. 'Do as he tells you an' try not to fall off.'

'I'll do me best.'

Jim was standing at the far end of an eighteen-feet-long, six-inch-wide steel beam. Sean's stomach was churning again, worse than before. He had two choices. Either he could take the risk everyone else up there was taking, or he could chicken out and lose his job. Generally speaking, seventeen-year-old youths are not very good at making wise decisions. Sean Quinnan was no exception.

'Tuck yer trousers into yer socks, Sean,' Jim called out. 'Yer might gerrem caught otherwise.'

Sean tucked his wide, flapping, trouser legs into his socks, took a deep breath, spread his arms out like a tight-rope walker and began his nervous journey. The eyes of every gang member were on him, Barney was contemplating calling him back. It was stupid expecting a man new to the job to take such a risk. He felt like going down and telling Brindle what he thought of him. It had never been the same since the old man had retired. Albert Brindle was a hard, sometimes brutal man, but at least he knew the value of a good worker. Many a time Barney had been on the brink of telling Joe Brindle where he could stuff his job. His heart was now beating as fast as Sean's, who had stopped in the middle, his body swaying, trying to get his balance. Sean was quietly cursing his own stupidity in getting himself into this awful predicament. He'd made many mistakes in his life but this was a beauty. '*Everyone makes mistakes*,' his mammy once told him. '*But it's a wise man what learns by them.*'

Learn by them? This was a poor time to start learning. His gaze, which had been deliberately focused on the steel beam, suddenly adjusted itself to take in the wider picture, making him aware of the ground fifty feet below.

'Oh Jesus . . .!'

He became swiftly disoriented. The world began to whirl around him. His legs wouldn't move and he knew he wasn't going to make it to the other end. And no way could he turn and go back.

'Oh, Mammy, Mammy!' Tears of fear and distress tumbled down Sean's face, mingling with the sweat coming out of every pore.

'Stay where you are,' called out Barney. 'Sean, sit down on the beam.' But Sean couldn't hear anything above his own hammering heart.

The men joined in with their own advice. Hard men, who'd grown to like Sean and were upset to see his tears, feeling somehow responsible for his predicament, especially Barney. Jim put a foot on the beam to go and help him, but was waved away by the ganger who knew that if Sean made a panicky grab at him they could both fall. Barney waved at the men, shushing them into silence until the only sounds were the wind, the dull drone of the crane and Sean's sobbing.

'Sean, lad,' called out Barney, softly. 'Can you hear me?'

Sean swayed left to right then miraculously centralised himself, to sighs of relief from the watching men. The noise from the crane increased as it revved up to give it the power needed to lift another load.

'Can you hear me, Sean?' shouted Barney.

The terrified Irishman nodded.

'Now, you're panickin' over nowt.' Barney was trying to reassure him. 'So just calm down and you'll be right.'

Sean recited his dad's poem to take his mind off the danger he was in.

'Mother dear, I'm over here and nivver comin' back,

I'm stoppin' for the pint o' beer the woman and the crack.'

The men could hear him and exchanged grins. They'd be taking the mickey out of the young lad once all this was over. Barney called out to him in a low voice, 'I want you to squat down till you can sit astride the beam, then we'll come an' get you off.'

Sean nodded again, his breath was coming in short sobs as, with painful slowness, he began to lower himself down to the beam, his shaking hands reached down to grasp it. A sixteen-feet-long concrete slab rose slowly over the edge of the building. It formed the base of a triangle, the other two sides being the chains suspending it from the crane, which began to swing it inwards. The crane driver couldn't see Sean. He was relying on directions from Brindle, who was signalling him to swing his load towards where the young Irishman was standing. Barney saw the danger and almost ran across a beam until he was within sight of the crane driver. He held up a hand for the man to stop, but the crane driver's eyes were on Brindle who was signalling the opposite. The men began shouting desperately for the crane to stop but Brindle continued with his signal. He winked at the grinning wagon driver and sniggered. 'Get yer leg over that, yer thick Paddy.'

Brindle had had the same trick played on him once, the only thing to do was to grab the swinging slab and hold on to it. Suddenly all the shouting stopped as the watching men were mesmerised by the inevitability of the situation. Everyone up there knew for certain that Sean was going to die. Their hearts pounded like steam hammers; they were shocked at their uselessness in such a desperate situation.

Sean hadn't seen the slab. He was squatting on the steel beam, holding on with his hands and about to lower his legs over the side. His breathing became more relaxed, it was going to be all right. *Holy Jesus ... I'll never do this again.* Jim broke the silence.

'Watch out, Sean!'

Sean looked around and saw the slab swinging towards him, less than a yard away. He half got to his feet, his arms outstretched for balance when they should have been grabbing at the slab. It barely touched him but it was enough to knock him off the beam.

He lived just long enough to know for certain that he was going to die. Six seconds in all. For four of those seconds he was teetering with one foot on the beam, screaming in terror and windmilling his arms in a hopeless attempt to propel himself back to safety. As he fell he shouted for his mammy and two seconds later struck his head on a beam two floors below, which broke his fall and knocked the life clean out of him.

'Aw, shit!' cursed Brindle as he saw Sean fall. Men were clambering back down the stairs, saying nothing but fearing the worst. Barney was the first to get to Sean and he didn't need to check his pulse or his breathing to know the lad was dead. He'd landed on his back. His dark eyes were still open, but opaque and lifeless, his pale skin contrasting with the dark blood staining the ground beneath him.

The ganger got to his feet and, quivering with shock and rage, pushed his way through the gathering of men and approached Brindle who was still on the back of the wagon, now lighting up a cigarette. 'How is he?' enquired the contractor, flicking a spent match away.

Barney's voice shook with emotion. 'He's dead, you lousy bastard! This was all your fault.' He was shouting now. 'When the cops come I'll tell 'em what you did.'

'Me?' protested Brindle. 'What did I do? It were that thick Paddy's fault for not watchin' what were happenin'.'

Barney stormed off to the site cabin to ring the police. Brindle, realising the trouble he was in, rushed after him. While Barney was on the phone, Brindle took a half bottle of whisky from a drawer and stuck it in his pocket, then hurried back to where Sean's body lay, surrounded by muttering men.

'All right, lads,' he said. 'The show's over. Yer can all go home. It's okay, yer'll get paid for the full day. The police won't want to be crowded when they arrive.'

Some of them seemed reluctant to move, so Brindle raised the stakes. 'If yer wanna a job ter come back to, yer'll all clear off now!'

The men shuffled away uneasily. They hadn't known Sean long, otherwise their attitude might have been different. When they were safely out of sight, Brindle took the whisky bottle from his pocket and, forcing Sean's mouth open, poured a liberal amount down his throat, then sprinkled some on his clothes. He stepped back and was standing there, reverently, when Barney arrived.

'Honestly, Barney, I thought he were goin' ter catch hold

61

of it. From where I were standin' he looked ter know what he were doin'.'

'Well, he didn't.'

'And whose fault's that then? What were yer doin' settin' inexperienced men on?'

'He'd have been all right with a safety harness,' argued Barney. 'I sent him down for one.'

'I know yer did. I told him ter get one before he went back up.'

'Why didn't he, then?'

'Don't ask me! You're the bloody ganger! What the hell were yer doin' lerrin' him walk out on to a beam without a bloody harness?'

Brindle was in the cabin peering through the dusty window when a policeman approached and knocked on the door. 'Come in, mate,' he called out.

The policeman entered and removed his helmet, more out of habit than politeness. 'Bad do, this, sir. Your foreman over there reckons it might o' been your fault.'

Brindle sighed and shook his head. 'I blame myself as well. I should have noticed he wasn't wearing a safety harness. I told him specifically not five minutes before he fell off ter go get a harness.'

'Do they all wear these harnesses, sir?'

'Well, they're supposed to, but the minute me back's turned ... well, yer know yerself what men are like, tryin' ter take short cuts just to make a bit o' bonus. My foreman, or should I say *ex foreman*, shouldn't have let him work without a harness. Especially wi' the lad bein' new ter the job.'

'So you're saying it's your foreman's fault and you're sacking him?'

'Let's just say I don't want to risk it happening again. At the end of the day, officer, everything that happens on this site is my responsibility. I'll have ter carry the can for this. It goes wi' the job.'

'Just one other thing, sir.'

'Yes?'

'The young man who fell. He smells quite strongly of drink. Was he a heavy drinker, sir?'

'Oh heck! No idea, mate. As I said, he only started last week. I hardly knew him. Yer'd be better off asking the man who set him on.'

'Would that be your foreman, sir?'

'Yes.'

In the distance, Barney Robinson was staring at the two figures talking inside the cabin as if he knew what was being said. Brindle caught sight of him through the window. The ganger scowled at his boss, spat on the ground and walked off the site.

A bike leaning against the yard wall betrayed the presence of a visitor to the Jones household. Barney was sitting at the table opposite Ethel, drinking a cup of tea when Rosie walked in.

'Hiya, Barney. Knocked off early?'

'Yeah . . . I, er . . .'

'There's been an accident, love,' explained Ethel.

'It's Sean,' said Barney. 'He had a nasty fall.'

Her mother added, 'He's dead, Rosie.' She saw no reason to prolong the tension.

'Dead?' said Rosie. It was such a short word to announce the end of a life. She sat down heavily.

Barney explained grimly, 'He fell off the top, hit his head on the way down.'

Rosie looked at him, disbelievingly. 'Hit his head?'

He nodded again.

'And he's dead?'

'Sorry.'

Rosie sank her head into her hands. Immersed in a confusion of sadness and guilt. This lovely boy she'd only just spent the night with. Dead. She was crying when she said, 'This is my fault. I got him that job.'

'It's nobody's fault,' said Ethel. 'These things happen,

63

especially on building sites.' She looked at Barney. 'Don't they, Barney?'

'Aye, they do.' He could have added his reservations, but this wasn't the time. He got to his feet. 'Anyway, I just thought it might be better comin' from me than from someone else.'

'Thanks, Barney,' said Ethel. 'And if yer know of anyone who wants a room . . .'

Barney was shocked by her insensitivity. 'I'll be off then,' he said.

Rosie's face was streaming with tears. 'If he hadn't met me he'd be still alive . . .' she sobbed.

'Don't talk so daft, Rosie.'

Barney closed the door on their conversation and pushed his bike out of the yard. He felt as guilty as anyone.

The newspapers had got hold of the story that Sean had been drinking. The police refused to deny this and Brindle allowed the rumour to flourish by means of his faint-hearted denial. 'Look, the lad's dead. Why upset his family by telling a story like that?'

'But he did smell strongly of drink that morning, didn't he, Mr Brindle?'

'All I can say is if the lad had a drink problem he certainly paid the penalty. Let's not make things worse fer his family.'

It was the excuse he needed in the event of anyone taking legal action against him over Sean's death. The Factory Inspectorate had already issued a written warning for him to ensure safety harnesses were used at all times. Brindle would heed this warning, until he saw fit to ignore it once again.

Barney wasn't at the Coroner's Inquest. The police had reluctantly absolved him of blame and obviously didn't believe his version of the story. 'You were the person on the spot, sir,' they pointed out. 'We could ask you why you didn't stop him, but we won't, because it will do no good.

It was clearly an accidental death and for you to suggest otherwise might get you into more trouble than Mr Brindle.'

The police believed that the evidence of Brindle and the crane driver would be sufficient to determine a verdict. The crane driver accepted no blame, pointing out that he was unsighted and was relying on Brindle's instructions. Brindle said he assumed Sean knew what he was doing and couldn't understand why he fell off. The police threw a little light in that direction by mentioning the smell of drink on Sean's breath.

The Coroner declared that Sean's death was accidental and, four weeks to the day after he had stepped off the boat at Liverpool, Sean Quinnan was being flown back to Ireland in a coffin, to be buried beside his father in the Church of St Mary Magdalen in Castlebar. He had left behind little evidence of his stay in England apart from the burgeoning guilt and despair in the heart of Rosie Jones. And the baby boy in her womb.

Chapter Eight

The Wellington Arms was busy, as it always was on a Friday lunchtime. Rosie's glance rested on the table she'd shared with Sean. It had been the best night of his life. That's what he'd told her, and she'd said it had been the best night of her life as well. Which was true. After he'd left for work that morning she'd made up her mind to tell him just how much she thought about him. How he wasn't just what people called a 'one night stand'. But she hadn't told him and now she'd never be able to. Maybe that was the saddest thing of all. Sadder even than not letting Billy Tomelty make love to her.

She rarely went into pubs on her own, but she figured she'd catch Barney in here. This is where she'd seen him when she asked him to give Sean a job. How she wished she'd minded her own business. She blamed herself entirely. It was two weeks since his death and she'd barely stopped crying. From the look of him, Barney didn't seem too pleased with himself either. 'All right, Barney?' she said.

He watched her sit down beside him. Today he looked a little older than his twenty-eight years, with his sad, brown eyes and unruly hair which wouldn't say 'no' to a comb now and again. His teeth were white and even and someone at some time had taken exception to his nose, which didn't appear to be its original shape. But, all in all, his face was not unpleasant, neither was the man behind the face.

'I can't stop blaming meself, Rosie,' he said.

'It wasn't your fault.'

'I've never seen anyone behave like him. He just . . . he just panicked.'

'It's thought he was suffering from an attack of vertigo,' explained Rosie. 'I spoke to his mother on the phone, she reckons he was always scared of heights. He wouldn't even go upstairs in church. It was something he never admitted.'

'I wish I'd known,' said Barney. 'Jesus, Rosie, I'm sorry. He was a good lad, everybody liked him.'

'He was a lovely lad.' Rosie felt tears welling again; she hadn't trusted herself to say two words about Sean since his death. There were purple rings beneath her hazel eyes, and the spark had gone out of her. 'The papers said he'd been drinking.' She searched Barney's face for the truth.

He shrugged. 'So I heard.'

'He'd been out with me the night before. Do you think it was my fault?'

Barney shook his head. He wanted to know what they'd been up to, how far things had gone between them; but it was none of his business. 'He was a bit queasy first thing, but he was all right by dinnertime. He ate all his sandwiches – and one o' mine.'

'So, what do you think?' enquired Rosie.

Another shrug. 'They reckoned his breath smelled o' drink but I never smelled owt on him – an' I were the last person anywhere near him. If I'd have smelled drink on him I'd have sent him packing.'

'That's what I thought,' said Rosie. 'Sean was sober when he left for work.' There was a long silence before she added, 'We slept together. Neither of us had done it before. You don't suppose it could have . . . I don't know . . . had anything to do with that?'

Barney inwardly cursed himself for feeling jealous of a dead man. 'No, Rosie, I don't suppose anything of the sort. We can drive ourselves mad if we keep thinkin' like this.'

He laid his rough hand on hers and squeezed. She felt oddly comforted.

'I can't understand why he'd smell so strongly of drink,' she puzzled.

'If anyone sues for compo,' said Barney. 'Brindle's gonna say he'd been drinkin'. If Sean had been drinkin' it gets him off the hook.' He went quiet. He'd worked out his own scenario of events but didn't know whether to confide in Rosie. He hadn't realised how close they'd been, her and Sean. Maybe he owed it to her to tell her what he thought had happened. It wasn't as though he'd a job to lose, he hadn't been anywhere near the site since Sean's death. Brindle had sent his wages and P45 the following day and Barney was due to start another job next week. He took a long gulp of beer which seemed to decide him. Wiping his mouth with the side of his hand, he looked at Rosie. 'I could never prove nowt but I reckon Brindle might o' made it look like Sean had been drinking.'

Rosie felt a mixture of anger and relief. Relief that someone else believed he hadn't gone to work drunk.

'None of the lads thought he'd been drinkin' either,' went on Barney.

'What do you reckon happened?'

He scratched his chin. 'Well ... and this is only me guessin', I know Brindle kept a bottle o' whisky in his cabin. I know that because I often had a sly taste meself when he wasn't about.' He paused and Rosie knitted her brows, trying to guess the rest. She couldn't, so he continued, 'When I was on the phone to the police, Brindle told the lads to clear off. He was on his own with Sean for about a minute before I got back to him. He had time to pour some whisky into Sean an' mek him smell like a distillery.'

'The lousy pig!'

'It's only a guess,' warned Barney. 'I could be wrong.'

'You could be, Barney,' agreed Rosie. 'But you're not, are you?'

'No,' said Barney. 'I don't think I am. Brindle killed

Sean as far as I'm concerned ... an' then he did that to him.'

'Killed him? How d'you mean, killed him?'

Barney shook his head. 'I don't suppose he meant to actually kill him. He were playin' one of his stupid games. When that slab knocked Sean off, the crane driver was workin' to Brindle's directions.'

'You mean Brindle deliberately directed the slab into Sean?'

'No doubt about it.'

'He murdered him. Brindle murdered my Sean.'

Barney looked at her, his eyebrows slightly raised. She was in tears.

'Were you, er ...?' he asked. He was asking if she'd loved Sean and secretly hoping she'd say 'no'.

'Did we love each other?' Rosie shrugged. 'I don't know, maybe love's too strong a word. He was the loveliest man I've ever known.'

'Man? He wasn't much more than a boy.'

Rosie nodded. 'He still looked at the world through a child's eyes. He saw beauty in the oddest things.' She remembered their first meeting on the tram. 'Like rain lit up by a gas lamp.'

Barney shook his head, not understanding and Rosie nodded at him: 'I know,' she said. 'And I didn't see it either until I looked.' She paused, then added, 'He thought I was beautiful as well.'

'Nothing odd about that.'

Rosie placed her hand on his and smiled. 'He died quickly, didn't he?' She sought Barney's reassurance on this.

He snapped his fingers. 'Quicker than that.' There was no point mentioning the moments of terror that preceded Sean's death.

Her eyes misted over again. 'Jesus, Barney, he didn't deserve to die like that. A victim of a stupid practical joke.'

They sat in silence as Barney allowed her to get on with her moment of grief. She wiped away the tears with the ends of her fingers, pushing them off the sides of her face as she recovered her composure. 'What can we do about Brindle?' she enquired.

He shrugged. 'In a word, nothing. Sean's buried some-where in Ireland and the Coroner says it was accidental death.'

'Did the police ask you for a statement?'

'Not after that first day. I said it was Brindle's fault, he said it was mine.'

'And you weren't asked to give evidence at the inquest?'

Barney shook his head. 'Mebbe I should've gone anyway. But to be honest, Rosie, I wouldn't have known what to do, and I can't stop blamin' meself. If I'd known the lad had a problem with heights I'd never have . . .'

She placed her hand on his mouth. 'Don't,' she admon-ished him, gently. Barney was a decent man. 'You've nothing to blame yourself for, Barney. The only person to blame is Brindle.'

'And he's got away with it.'

'Not if I can help it.' She got to her feet. 'You'll have to excuse me.'

'Are you okay?'

Rosie held her stomach. 'I think I must have eaten some-thing that . . . phew!'

She turned and dashed to the Ladies. Her baby was beginning to make his presence felt.

It was Susan Clarkson who made Rosie see what she didn't want to see. She'd been at school with Susan, who was her one remaining unmarried friend. They were at the Astoria Ballroom at Brigshawe's Christmas dance, which always took place in November because it was cheaper to book. Rosie had missed two periods but had put it down to the shock of Sean's death. Besides, as far as she knew, they'd made love in her 'safe' period. Fred Dimmock and the Footstompers had struck up with a quickstep and the two of them were sipping gin and tonics, smoking Sobranis and half-expecting to get split up by a pair of lads from Accounts. Susan looked at Rosie's dress, which was bulging at the seams.

'By heck, Rosie,' she commented. 'You've put a bit o' weight on since you got that frock.'

'That's what I like about you, Susan. You're so tactful.'

The two hopeful suitors smiled at them from the edge of the floor. One of them had taken a shine to Susan, and she to him. Rosie did a double take of the other one and decided she didn't fancy him. She turned her back to them and said forcefully, 'You're not lumbering me with Peter Ellis. He's all Brylcreem and acne and half his teeth are missing. If they split us up and I'm lumbered with him, I'm sitting down.'

Since Sean, no man had a hope of measuring up in her eyes.

'Give over, he's a right laugh is Pete,' argued Susan.

'Have you seen his teeth? They're like a set of piano keys.'

'He's had a bit of dental trouble,' said Susan, 'but it doesn't make him a bad lad.'

'Tell you what,' Rosie suggested. 'You dance with Pete and have a laugh, I'll have the other one. You can catch acne off a lad, you know.' Much of Rosie's medical education had come from her hypochondriac mother.

'Gerraway, you daft ha'porth,' laughed Susan. 'They're only pimples. It's not bubonic plague.'

But Rosie was adamant. 'I don't care, I'm not dancing with him.' She gave the two young men an insincere smile, then said to Susan, 'And have you seen the size of his shoes? They're like flippin' violin cases. I'm not having them great big clodhopping things treading all over my new shoes. I paid eighteen and six for these from Saxone.' She clutched her stomach as the men approached. 'It's no good, I'll have to sit down,' she said, going back to her seat. Her friend looked daggers at her for being so theatrical.

The hapless young men were left stranded on the dance

floor as Susan followed her. 'What were all that about? I thought ... Good grief, Rosie, are you okay?'

Rosie was already dashing up the stairs to the toilets, closely followed by her friend, who waited outside the cubicle door as Rosie knelt in front of the toilet bowl to avoid splashing vomit on her dress. As she emerged, Susan was leaning against the wash basin, lighting a cigarette, with a knowing look on her face.

'I'll have one of them,' said Rosie.

'Not in your condition you won't.'

'What? ... I'm all right now.'

'You'll not be all right for a few months yet,' observed Susan. 'Rosie, I think you should see a doctor.'

Rosie went back into the cubicle and sat on the seat, speaking to Susan through the open door. 'You think I'm pregnant, don't you?'

Susan shrugged. 'You tell me.'

'I can't be.'

'If you definitely can't be, I must be wrong.'

'Well, it is theoretically possible,' conceded Rosie. 'I have missed a couple of periods ... and there was someone.'

'So,' summarised Susan, who might have shown more compassion had she been sober. 'You've had it off wi' some feller, you've missed two periods, you've put on weight, you're throwing up all over the place and with only that to go on you think it's theoretically possible that you're pregnant. My God, Rosie, I'm impressed. You've got a mind like a steel trap.'

Rosie stared at her. She was carrying Sean's baby. 'I'm pregnant, aren't I?' she said.

Susan nodded. 'I think you might be. Who's the lucky man?'

'Just somebody ... somebody I know.' She didn't want to attach any stigma to Sean's memory.

'And this somebody you know, is he married?'

'What?' Rosie's mind was racing too fast to cope with

Susan's questions. 'No,' she said. 'He's not married.'

'Well, that's something. You need to see a doctor to make sure.' Susan smoked her cigarette down to the tab end and crushed it under her shoe. 'What d'you wanna do?' she asked. 'Go home?'

Rosie tried to grasp the enormity of her problem as it unfolded in her mind. She retched again and tried to turn round to get her head over the bowl but was a fraction too late and what was left inside her splashed down the front of her dress. A long plume of vomit hung from her mouth. She wiped it away with the back of her hand. Tears streamed down her face as she took long, deep breaths to regain control of herself. 'Keep this to yourself,' she warned. 'I don't want it all round work on Monday morning.'

'I'll take you home,' said Susan. 'Give me your ticket and I'll get your coat.'

'I want you to promise.'

'Don't talk so soft! Course I promise. Blimey, Rosie, what d'you take me for?'

Rosie fumbled in her bag for her ticket and found the photo Sean had given her. A small smiling boy with ears like an angel's wings. The father of her unborn child.

Ethel had re-let Sean's room with indecent haste. At least that was Rosie's opinion.

'Life goes on,' said Ethel.

Rosie hated her mother at times.

The new lodger's name was Sidney. He was in his forties, earning good money as a travelling salesman in soft furnishings, and apparently single. Ethel set her cap at him almost before he'd walked through the door.

'He's a very nice man,' she said, as Sidney heaved his suitcase up the narrow stairs.

Rosie wrinkled her nose. 'I don't like him. He smiles too much.'

'Typical o' you is that. Not liking someone because he

smiles. That's what this house needs – a few more smiles.'

'Mam, I do hope you're not going to throw yourself at him just because you think life's left you behind.'

'Throw myself at him? Good grief, Rosie, I've only just met him.'

'I could see the glint in your eye. He's got a car and he isn't short of cash.'

Within a week, Sidney had moved into Ethel's bedroom where she bestowed her favours much more freely than she ever had with her late husband. The ends justified the means. Just as they had all those years ago with Tommy.

Sidney took full advantage of everything on offer but couldn't help but be attracted to Rosie. Her beauty wasn't just skin deep and her secret pregnancy had given her an extra bloom. He tried his hand the first time they were alone together; working on the 'like mother like daughter' theory. Rosie was coming out of the bathroom, when he slid his arm around her.

'Rosie,' he murmured. 'I get the impression that you quite like me. Am I right?'

'I think you're okay,' she lied.

'Okay? I think you can do a bit better than that.' His manner was oily now and Rosie pushed his arm away.

'I'd prefer you didn't do that. What would Mam say?'

'What she doesn't know won't hurt her.'

'It won't hurt her because there won't be anything for her to know.'

He held up his hands. 'Sorry, just being friendly.' He rubbed his thumb against his forefinger, indicating paper money. 'I think you'd find me very grateful.' He winked knowingly, then reeled as she slapped him hard across his face.

'I think you'll find yourself out on the street once Mam finds out what you're up to!'

But Ethel refused to believe her. 'What? ... You're saying Sidney offered you money to *go* with him?'

'Yes.'

'Well, I think we'll see what *he* has to say about it.'

'Mam, he's hardly likely to admit it.'

'Just the same, he's entitled to have his say.'

'But why would I say it, if it wasn't true?'

Sidney not only denied it, but turned the incident on its head. He took Ethel out of her daughter's earshot for a confidential word.

'Go easy on her, love. She's twenty-two and hasn't got a young man of her own. Maybe she feels a bit left out.'

Ethel wasn't convinced. 'That's not a proper reason fer sayin' stuff like that about you.'

He put his arm around her. 'All right, if you must know the truth, Rosie tried it on with me. I turned her down as gently as I could and she burst into tears; end of story. Maybe she can't believe a man can prefer her own mother over her. She's a good-looking girl, she'll get someone of her own.'

'She tried it on with you? – my Rosie?'

'Oh heck! Me and my big mouth. I didn't mean to tell you that.' He put his arm around her. 'Look, Ethel, promise me you won't make a big thing of it. It's best forgotten about. You'll only embarrass the girl. We've all got to live together under the same roof.'

'She'll have ter find a roof of her own if she tries that again.'

Sidney stood behind Ethel as she confronted her daughter. 'I've had a word with Sidney, and we've decided we don't ever want to talk about this again.'

Sidney leered at her over her mother's shoulder. 'What are you smirking at, Sidney?' snapped Rosie. 'Just because you've fooled Mam doesn't mean you'll get away with it forever.'

Ethel exploded. 'Any more talk like that, lady, and you can find somewhere else to live.'

'Oh no,' seethed Rosie. 'I'm not going anywhere. I want to be around when you find out just what a slug he is.'

*

75

Sidney's presence was a double blow to Rosie. It prevented her from confiding in her mother about her condition. Somehow she knew the news wouldn't be received sympathetically, despite Ethel having once been in the same position herself. A week after Susan Clarkson had read the signs, Sidney heard her being sick in the bathroom. He'd noticed the weight gain and the colour in her cheeks.

'Does your mother know you're pregnant?' he asked speculatively.

'What?'

She hadn't denied it, which confirmed it in Sidney's eyes. 'I just wondered if Ethel knew.'

'There's nothing to know.' She turned and walked away from him, but her denial had been too slow and too half-hearted.

He grinned and shouted, 'Hey! It's a good job I turned you down – I might have been accused of being the father.'

Rosie got to her mother first. It wasn't the ideal way to break the news but better than having Sidney tell her.

'Mam,' she said. 'I've got something to tell you.'

Sidney was coming down the stairs.

'And I'd like to tell you in confidence.'

Ethel called out: 'Sidney? ... could yer leave us for a minute, pet. Our Rosie wants a word with me.'

'Oh right,' he called back cheerfully. 'I expect it'll be about her bein' pregnant. I'd best leave you to it.'

Ethel whirled round, shocked. Rosie flopped down in a chair. That awful man was making her life a misery. Ethel folded her arms and glared down at her.

'I'm listening,' she said sharply.

'All right,' admitted Rosie, quietly. 'I'm pregnant. I did want to tell you in my own way and of course your lover boy knew that, but that's the sort of worm he is.'

'Don't you go callin' other people names after what you've just told me.'

'Oh dear, I'm ever so sorry,' Rosie couldn't keep the

76

sarcasm out of her voice. 'It makes me nearly as bad as you, doesn't it?'

'It makes you a slut, that's what it makes you. And to think I doubted Sidney when he said yer'd tried it on with him.'

'At least I *loved* the father of my child,' retaliated Rosie. 'I didn't get pregnant just to get my hands on his house.'

'Oh aye, and who is the father?'

'It was just a man,' she said, 'who's not around any more. It was my first and only time.'

'Not around? You mean he's buggered off and left you in the lurch?'

'You make him sound bad – he wasn't.'

She didn't want to muddy Sean's memory by having him share her disgrace. Ethel took a few paces up and down before banging her fist on the table in exasperation. 'Well, if this doesn't put the tin hat on it! Pregnant and no father to turn to. Good God! As if it's not bad enough everybody knowing me husband ran off wi' a flamin' Eyetie. What sort of a man'd do this ter yer?'

Rosie got to her feet and thrust her face, angrily, into her mother's. 'A man worth a hundred of that slug you share your bed with!'

Ethel recoiled at her daughter's venom, then retaliated, 'My God! – and after all I've done for you, this is how yer repay me!'

Rosie's anger turned to scorn. 'Oh you're a tower of strength, you always have been.'

'Never mind all that, Miss Sarky. What're yer gonna do fer money? Babies don't feed theirsens yer know.'

'I'll manage, don't you worry about me.'

But she didn't know how.

She planned on keeping it a secret until the baby showed. Within a couple of days it was all around the street and Rosie was furious.

'What was all that rubbish about you not being able to

hold your head up round here? If you're so ashamed of me, why didn't you keep quiet about it?'

'I'm sure I don't know what yer talkin' about,' insisted Ethel. 'I haven't breathed a word to anyone.'

'Well, if it wasn't you it must have been Sid the Slug. Did I tell you he offered me money to go with him?'

'How dare yer talk like that? Yer know I'm not a well woman!' Ethel was almost in tears. 'You talk ter me like that an' yer can pack yer bags an' find somewhere else ter live.'

'Oh, you'd like that, wouldn't you?' Rosie was angry now. 'Out of sight out of mind. The only thing you care about is yourself and all your non-existent ailments.'

'Non-existent? I'd just like you to feel as poorly as me. You'd know what it was like then.'

'Give over, Mam. You get a pimple on your face and you're in bed for week in case it's smallpox.'

'Yer get all this from yer dad. He were a heartless bugger as well. Just pack yer bags and get out of my house.'

'*Your house?* This isn't *really* your house, it's Dad's – and Granddad's before that.'

Her mother burst into tears. 'I've got one of me migraines, I'm goin' upstairs. And I want you out of this house when I come down!'

As her mother ran up the stairs, Rosie flung herself into a chair to wait for her anger to subside. How could her mother go round telling everybody? Couldn't she have put her daughter first, just once? Even if it wasn't her, it would have been her fancy man, Sid the Slug, who'd slithered out from under a stone to make her life a misery.

It was only a question of time before the news got round to Brigshawe's. By the time Sidney got back from work that evening, Rosie had packed her bags and was living with Susan Clarkson.

'It's only for a couple of nights until I find somewhere else.'

78

'It'll have to be,' said Susan. 'I'm afraid my mum and dad don't approve.'

At work the following day she was called into the manager's office. His eyes went down to her stomach.

'Miss Jones, as you know, we're having to cut back on staff.' Rosie didn't know this, but she didn't interrupt. 'And . . . erm. Well, not to put too fine a point on it . . .'

'You're sacking me because you've found out I'm pregnant,' she said.

'Not er . . . exactly. You've been an excellent worker but the company has a strict policy on er . . .' He cleared his throat. 'On pregnant women in the workplace. Always a danger of an industrial accident and Brigshawe's can't afford that.'

'When do you want me to leave?'

He opened a drawer in his desk and took out an envelope. 'I've had a word with personnel and er . . . and in lieu of notice we're giving you two weeks pay, which is a week more than your entitlement.'

Rosie leaned over and snatched the envelope from him. 'I'm entitled to be treated fairly, that's what I'm entitled to, you smug little wart!'

Chapter Nine

Two weeks' money after deductions, amounted to seven
pounds two and six. Rosie had no savings, so this was it; all
her worldly wealth. As a stop-gap she rented a cheap, first-
floor room on Royd's Road which was one of the few roads
in Leeds that made Duck Street look posh. The future was a
murky world that she wasn't equipped to handle just yet.
Next week was as far as she allowed herself to think.
Anything beyond that and she'd go potty.

The room was small and damp with a concave bed,
peeling wallpaper and creaking floor boards. It had a cheap
and chipped three-drawer chest, a table, two chairs (one
easy, one dining) a cracked sink with no hot water and a
two bar electric fire with only one bar working. On the wall
was pinned a print of The Boyhood of Raleigh; its colours
were faded but they were still more cheerful than the
brown, wilting curtains.

She shared a tiny kitchen with the other occupant of the
first floor. It contained two gas rings, an ancient gas oven
and a bath, which was covered over, when not in use, by a
pine board which needed a good scrub.

The smell from the landlord's ancient and incontinent cat
might have been pervasive were it not completely obliter-
ated by the stench from the lubricating oil factory just
across the street that made its product from, among other
things, human waste, which arrived in 'honey wagons'

several times a day. But it didn't matter because it was only for a week until she found something better.

On fine days she went to the café in Paradine Park and on cold or rainy days she'd go to the library on Compton Road. Her funds didn't run to a wireless, but the landlord, who occupied a couple of rooms below her, played his own wireless loud enough for her to hear.

One week ran quickly into two and her seven pounds two and six was down to under four pounds and Rosie knew she'd have to get a job.

Someone at the café knew someone who worked at Marsden's Clothiers who needed a sweeper-up for twelve hours a week, evenings only. It only paid one and six an hour but eighteen shillings a week would pay for her rent and leave ten and six to spend on luxuries such as food and the electric meter. She'd have to stop smoking, she'd already decided that. It was in the baby's interests. She'd read somewhere that babies of women who smoked could be born with deformities.

Rosie started at Marsden's three weeks after she'd left home. She was one of three women who went in to sweep up after the clothing workers had gone home. It was arduous work for someone not used to physical labour; and still she blocked out the spectre of her dismal future. It was the only way. Something surely would turn up.

In the room next to Rosie lived an old man called Basil, who spent his days in a haze of cigarette smoke.

'Never smoked afore I came ter live here,' he told her when she knocked on his door to ask how to turn on the gas in the kitchen. 'Kills the smell from over there. They're Germans what run that factory. Did yer know that?'

'No, I didn't.'

'Well, they are. We locked the buggers up durin' the war an' now we've let 'em out what thanks do we get? The buggers are making oil outa 'uman manure.'

'I wondered what it was.'

'Well, that's what it is. Oil outa 'uman manure. What

81

sort of a mind thought up an idea like that, eh? A bloody Nazzie mind, that's what. Yer'd never catch a Yorkshireman makin' oil outa nowt like that.'

It was a smell that wouldn't be troubling Princess Elizabeth who, that November, got married to her distant cousin, Philip Mountbatten of Greece. Rosie, in desperate need of a husband, would have settled for someone not quite so high born. She was existing entirely on her wages now that her meagre capital was gone. She considered packing in her job and going on the dole, which wouldn't have left her much worse off. But Mr Lazarus, the skeletal and therefore aptly named landlord, lived on the ground floor and made his views very clear when he let the room to her.

'So long as yer not a dole merchant. I've had dole merchants afore an' they're nowt but trouble.'

It took Rosie less than a week to cause trouble. She'd gone to bed early to save money on the electric fire. Where they'd been hibernating she'd no idea, but they came out to play that night. An itching on her leg woke her up, then she felt something run over her face. Screaming in horror, she flung the bedclothes off and ran to the light switch. She could see them from across the room. Dozens of bedbugs scuttling across the white sheet. Rosie grimaced and slapped her face. One dropped to the floor, dead. Within seconds she was banging on Lazarus's door until she heard him moving about, grunting and grumbling. He came to the door and blinked his eyes at her, trying to bring her into focus; then he gave a wide, toothless yawn and smacked his lips. His face seemed even more shrunken than usual. He had obviously awoken from a deep sleep. The front of his striped pyjama trousers hung carelessly open and Rosie averted her eyes, not wishing to see whatever revolting sight might be on display.

'Mr Lazarus, my bed's alive with bugs.'

'Yer what?'

She raised her voice. 'My bed's alive with bugs!'

82

'Oh aye, an' what d'yer want me to do about it at this time o' night? Sing 'em a bloody lullaby an' send 'em all ter sleep?' His reedy voice matched his limp face.

'How am I supposed to sleep in a bed full of bugs?'

He eyed her up and down and made her feel uncomfortable. 'Yer can sleep in my flat for the night, if yer like. I'll get yer bed sorted out tomorrow.'

'No thanks.'

When she got back, the bugs had mysteriously disappeared. She threw the mattress out of the window and slept on the chair. The next morning Lazarus banged on her door.

'Is that my mattress in t' back yard?'

'Yes, I threw it through the window.'

'And have yer got no respect for other people's property? I'd never have let yer the room if I'd known yer were going ter treat me furniture like that.'

'Furniture? It's a festering old mattress alive with bugs. It wants burning.'

'It does now,' snapped Lazarus. 'That's all it's fit for after your antics. It's been out in the open all night, thanks to you. Every cat in the street could o' peed on it for all I know.'

'Starting with that stinking creature of yours, no doubt.'

'Yer what?' Lazarus had a talent for selective hearing. Rosie didn't pursue it.

'I said it couldn't smell any worse than it did already. That mattress was a health hazard.'

Lazarus scowled. 'If yer not happy wi' me premises, why don't yer sling yer bleedin' hook? Yer pay for what yer get in this life. If yer want better, yer pay more.'

'I can't afford any more,' said Rosie, hating herself for having to make such an admission.

'Well, if yer want ter stay here, yer'll have ter,' smirked Lazarus, revelling in having the upper hand over this pretty young woman. 'Yer'll have ter pay for a new mattress for a start.' He held out his hand. 'Ten bob please or sling yer hook.'

83

'Ten bob? That mattress wasn't worth twopence.'

'Yer want a decent mattress, yer pay for a decent mattress.'

'I'll give you five shillings, but not for something you've dragged up out of your cellar.'

'Seven and six,' compromised Lazarus. 'And yer'll get what yer given or yer can take yer bleedin' hook.'

It seemed a worthwhile investment to have something half decent to sleep on. 'I want to see the mattress first,' she insisted.

Half an hour later Lazarus poked his head around her door. 'It's downstairs, yer'll have ter fetch it up yerself. My back's givin' me some gip.'

Rosie followed him down the stairs to look at the new mattress. Basil, who had heard the commotion earlier, followed. It looked clean enough. Not brand new but a vast improvement on the one she'd turfed out of the window.

'What's that smell?'

Lazarus grinned and held up a cardboard box which bore the emblem, Fullerton's Bug and Flea Powder. 'I gave it a light dusting,' he said. 'With it not bein' absolutely brand, spankin' new.'

He gave the mattress a smack with the flat of his hand; it threw up a cloud of fine dust which made Rosie's eyes water.

'I don't wonder it kills the bugs,' she said. 'It might be the death of me.'

'The smell won't last,' Lazarus assured her. 'That'll be seven and six.'

Rosie reluctantly handed him three half crowns. 'While I'm at it,' she said. 'Could you turn the volume down on your wireless, please? The people in the next street have been complaining.'

Her irony fell on deaf ears. 'Yer what?' said Lazarus.

With Basil's help, Rosie lugged the mattress up the stairs. She caught a whiff of the smell from the factory over the road as it mingled with the bug and flea powder. 'It's real five star accommodation is this.'

Basil chuckled. 'It could be worse.'

'How?'

The old man scratched his head. 'Well, I can't think off-hand – but there must be summat what's worse than this.'

'I was hoping there wasn't. Please tell me this is as low as I can sink.'

Basil gave this some thought, then his face brightened. 'There's rats as well,' he said. 'I heard one last night. I've got some stuff ter put down, if yer want some.'

'What? Rat poison?'

'Aye, good stuff an' all. Soak it on a bit of old bacon an' tomorrow mornin' yer'll have a dead rat – big as a rabbit. You mark my words.'

Rosie heaved the mattress on to the bed and sat on it. Her head slumped disconsolately between her hands. 'Jesus! What the hell am I doing? What a mess!'

Basil hovered for a second, then left her to it. In a few weeks it would be Christmas. Should she go back home, cap in hand and throw herself on her mother's mercy? Of course there was no guarantee that she'd be welcome. Certainly not with Sid the Slug around. It was he who had spread the word about her pregnancy, she knew that now. Had it not been for his big mouth she'd be still working at Brigshawe's and wouldn't be living in this rathole. No doubt, her mother could have stopped him if she'd really wanted to. She'd seen through her mother around the time her dad left. Seen her for the silly, self-centred woman she was. If Ethel Jones had a capacity for giving, it was well hidden. Taking was what she was good at. Rosie would only go back if it became a matter of life or death.

At first, she'd treated herself to at least one decent meal every day, cooked on the gas rings she shared with Basil, although the old man only seemed to use them for boiling his kettle. What he lived on was a mystery to Rosie. Every time he opened his room door the landing was engulfed in stale cigarette smoke. As far as she could work out, Basil's diet consisted of Brooke Bond Tea and Capstan Full Strength.

She had to budget for her week's groceries: two loaves, two eggs, four pounds of potatoes, quarter pound each of margarine, sugar and tea, one packet Dalton's Cereal Flakes (cheaper than Kellogs), three pints milk, two rashers bacon, two tomatoes, two apples and two ounces of Mint Imperials – everyone needs a treat now and again. On Friday night she'd treat herself to fish and chips from Wormald's, only sneaking into the shop when there was no one in she knew. Purely through pride she'd cut herself off from all of her friends. There was no way she would ever let anyone see what she was reduced to.

Her pregnancy, combined with the smell from across the road, meant that she threw up most of what she ate, which was a waste of much needed nutrition, but what could she do?

Winter was a mixed blessing. Without a fridge the milk kept fresh, and the stench from the oil factory wasn't quite as pungent as in summer. On the down side the electric fire sent the coin meter whirring to the extent of four shillings a week. Lazarus was allowed to set his own tariff on the meter and Basil reckoned he made at least a hundred per cent profit. When Rosie went down with flu she took to her bed and relied on Basil to feed her tins of soup, cups of tea and aspirin. He was despatched to Marsden's to persuade them to keep her job open until she had recovered and they said a week and no longer.

By Friday evening she was no better. With not enough money for the rent and little for food she decided to drag herself back home to her mother. Her eyes were red-rimmed, her nose dripping like a leaky tap and her skin damp with sweat.

'Yer in no fit state ter be goin' nowhere,' said Basil when she told him. 'Just look at yerself. Yer like a wet dishcloth.'

'I know,' she shivered. 'And you shouldn't be coming near me.'

'Nay, lass,' said Basil. 'I'm past carin' about all that.

T' best bit o' my life's long gone. Wi' a bit o' luck a decent dose o' flu might just see me off. I'll not regret that.'

'You shouldn't give up on life like that. There's always something.'

'Yer right, lass,' he conceded. 'There's you fer a start. Yer've made me smile now and again, I'll grant yer that.'

Rosie couldn't remember ever making him smile but she didn't question it. She certainly couldn't remember the last time *she* smiled. Looking through the window at the leaden sky, she asked, 'What's it like outside?'

'Brass monkey weather. Why don't yer get a taxi?'

Rosie gave him seven and sixpence. 'Pay my rent for me, will you? I've got two bob left between me and the workhouse.'

'That's all a taxi'll cost. Surely yer mam'll not kick yer out in your state.'

Rosie blew her nose and said dismally, 'You don't know my mam.' Then she conceded, 'No, you're right. She'll probably be pleased to see me.'

'That's the ticket, lass,' smiled Basil. 'You wait there. I'll nip outside and ring fer a taxi.'

The taxi pulled up outside Number Two Duck Street and the driver said, 'One and six, love and I hope ter God yer haven't passed nowt on ter me. I've got a livin' ter make.'

Partly out of guilt she dropped a two shilling piece in his hand and told him to keep the change. He looked at his tip and muttered a grudging 'thank you'; his gratitude not extending to him getting out and opening the door for her and her suitcase.

The effort of heaving it across the yard left her breathless. She leaned against the wall to recuperate. The door opened. Two small girls looked up at her and said nothing.

'Who is it?' came a voice from inside, swiftly followed by the appearance of a woman in her thirties, who gave Rosie a questioning smile, then looked down at her suitcase and said, 'Not today, thanks.'

87

Rosie looked around to check her location. In her state she might be at the wrong door. No, this was it. Dark green with her initials carved into the door jamb. Her dad had played hell with her for that, but it had been Barney Robinson who put her up to it. He wanted to carve '= BR' underneath but she wouldn't let him. They didn't 'equal' each other, they were just pals. She frowned at the woman and asked, 'Who are you?'

The smile left the woman's face. She became defensive. 'Who am I? Who are you?'

'I live here,' said Rosie. 'At least I did up until a few months ago. Is my mother in?'

'Your mother?'

'Yes, my mother,' said Rosie, irritably. 'Ethel Jones. She owns this house. Do you mind if I come in? I'm freezing to death out here.'

'Well, I do mind. As a matter of fact I mind very much. Me and my husband's renting this house fair and square from Mrs Jones, and she said nothing about any daughter moving back in.'

With that she closed the door in Rosie's face, leaving her shocked and dejected. She knocked again, only to provoke an angry shout from within.

'Go away!'

Determined, she knocked again. This time the woman relented and opened the door a crack.

'Look,' pleaded Rosie. 'I'm not feeling so good and if I can't stay here, I need some bus fare to get back to my digs.'

It was the first time in her life she'd begged for money. There would be worse moments in her life, but up until now there'd been none as bad as this. The woman disappeared for a second, then she came back and gave Rosie sixpence. The door closed again; gently this time.

It rained as she stood at the bus stop. But it was a soft, harmless rain that cooled her fever. Everything good in her life had deserted her. She'd lost her dad, her job, her home,

Billy Tomelty and Sean. Then she thought of Sean and the baby inside her and she cried, her tears mingling with the rain. How on Earth could she possibly bring a child into this rotten world?

Basil was at first saddened by her return, then he nodded in sympathy as she told him the reason. He carried her case up the stairs and ordered her to bed, where she stayed until Monday morning when necessity dictated that she return to work. As she was leaving, Lazarus popped his head round his door.

'Yer know yer missed your rent last week?'

'I'm a little better, Mr Lazarus, how nice of you to ask.'

'What?'

'I've been ill, or didn't Basil tell you?'

'I'm running a boarding house not a hospital. Am I expected to give yer free rent every time yer've got a runny nose? Wait there, I'll get me book.'

She hadn't the strength to argue. Basil had given her back the rent money, but it was all she had and it didn't leave her anything for food, unless she could borrow off one of the other women. Which was unlikely.

That night she came back from Marsden's as exhausted as she'd ever felt in her life. One of the women hadn't turned up and Rosie had had to sweep the vast floor of the trouser room all by herself. Hopefully it would put extra money in her pay packet which would be welcome, but no more than the couple of shillings that one of the women had lent her to tide her over. The ten minute walk home had taken her over half an hour, with her having to stop for a rest every few minutes. When she got back, despite the chill in the air, her skin was running with sweat, every bone in her body ached and she knew she couldn't go back to work if she still felt like this tomorrow. This would mean she wouldn't be able to pay the rent and she wouldn't put it past that pig Lazarus to kick her out just before Christmas.

His door was ajar when she passed. Rosie could hear him in the back room, talking to another tenant. The sound of his whining, tinny voice set her teeth on edge. She had already walked past the door when she realised what she'd seen. On his table was the cash tin where he kept the rent from this and other squalid houses he rented out. And the key was in it. She retraced her steps. He was well engaged in conversation with no sign of any winding-up remarks.

It was desperation rather than daring that sent her creeping into the room. With a shaking hand she turned the key and picked up a wad of notes lying on top of all the loose change. She estimated there was about twenty pounds altogether; in pound and ten shilling notes. Rosie stuffed half the notes into her pocket, replaced the other half and locked the tin. Then she heard his footsteps coming up the hall. Within two seconds he'd be back in the room.

She darted round the back of the settee and crouched down between it and the wall, disturbing the slumber of Lazarus's cat, which hurled itself across the room towards its owner, scuttling between his legs and disappearing up the hall.

Rosie's heart was thumping noisily and sweat was dripping down her face. She heard him pick up the box and 'tut' to himself – probably for leaving it with the key in. The key rattled in the lock. This was it. She heard the lid close almost immediately with neither a curse nor any sound of distress and she thanked God she'd left half the notes there. He'd obviously just given the contents a cursory check. Was that what she'd had in mind when she'd only taken half? Rosie had no idea. It was just an instinct.

A drawer scraped open and shut as the tin was put away. Rosie's breathing was almost as rapid as her heart rate. It was only a question of time before he heard her. He gave a loud, uninhibited belch followed by a disgusting fart, then he sat down on the settee, now only a few inches away from her. A crackling of newspaper and the turning of pages indicated that there was little in the *Evening News* to catch his interest. He gave a smaller belch, more of an aftershock compared to the first one, and Rosie sincerely hoped he wouldn't match it with a second blast from the other end. Then she heard the sound of the paper being folded and cast to one side.

Rosie was holding her breath, and releasing it as slowly and quietly as she could. Then she felt a sneeze coming on and clamped the bridge of her nose between forefinger and thumb; frantically stifling the impulse. God! Surely he knew she was there. Were he a dog he'd be able to smell her fear. She could certainly smell the cat pee. The animal had obviously marked out its territory around the back of the settee. How could Lazarus stand it? This had to be the smelliest room in the smelliest house in Yorkshire.

The wireless came to her temporary rescue. That, coupled with Lazarus's slight deafness. He got to his feet, tuned it into a station crackling out brass band music, turned up the volume and sat back down in the settee. Rosie felt a measure of satisfaction that this man's life seemed even more boring than hers. Her strength was ebbing from her and she lowered herself onto the linoleum floor, wishing the skinflint could have splashed out for wall-to-wall carpet. She lay there for over half an hour, breathing in house dust and cat pee fumes until cramp set in to her left leg, causing searing discomfort. She so desperately wanted to stretch it out and rub away the pain but the pain wasn't as acute as her fear of discovery. The wireless programme had now changed to one transmitting gardening hints and Lazarus began to snore. It was an irregular sound, half snore, half cough; the sort of snore that might suddenly wake up the snorer. Her mother had been like that after a few drinks.

Rosie's condition was now dire and she couldn't stand being in that cramped, cold space a second longer. She crawled out and headed for the door. Her nose dripped on to the floor and she resisted the urge to sniff. Halfway across the room, Lazarus gave a loud snort, which was followed by a worrying silence. Her back was to him and she could feel his eyes on her as she waited for his shout of rage. The snoring had stopped, so he was awake; no doubt

91

curiously waiting to see what she would do next. Enjoying himself at her expense. She daren't turn round to see. Instead she continued on her despairing, shuffling, nose-dripping journey. When she arrived at the door she got to her feet. Rivers of sweat were running down her body. Never in her life had she felt so drained and so hopeless and so sick to death of men controlling her life. She gave her nose a resigned wipe with her sleeve and turned slowly to confront him; to look down, with all the defiance she could muster, at his sneering face.

Lazarus was fast asleep; mouth wide open, false teeth displaced and drooling down his chin. A ghastly, but welcome sight.

Rosie silently left the room, went quickly up the stairs then flung herself on to the bed and dissolved into a fit of sobs. How the hell had she sunk so low? Stealing from people, almost getting caught. Just the skin of her teeth away from being locked up as a thief.

Then a feeling of relief set in, turning into a sense of triumph. It was a small triumph but it made her feel better. She'd beaten one of the bastards, one of those men who made her life a misery! Sidney the Slug, Joe Brindle, the manager at Brigshawe's – even her dad came to mind. But she dismissed this. Her dad had never wanted to make her life a misery. He'd just left her.

Maybe that was worse.

Rosie counted the stolen money. Nine pounds ten shillings. The sweat from her fever was now mingling with adrenalin-induced perspiration. She stripped down to her underwear, climbed between the sheets and tried to go to sleep. But her racing mind denied her this escape. It was turned ten o'clock when she heard Lazarus moving about in his room below and she felt a desperate need to go down there; to return to the scene of the crime like a true criminal. She put on her dressing gown and crept back down the stairs, with the money stuffed inside her knickers for reasons she couldn't even explain to herself. As she stepped off the bottom step, he opened his door and Rosie jumped with fright.

'All right?' he said.

'Er ... yes.'

'Good God! Yer don't look all right. Don't come near me wi' whatever yer've got. I don't want none o' that.' He headed for the lavatory then paused. 'Did yer want me for summat?'

An idea occurred to her. 'Er ... yes. I, er ... I thought I might have dropped some money on the stairs. I seem to have lost five shillings.'

'Five bob? Are yer sure yer dropped it on the stairs?'

It seemed a good idea to plant the idea in his mind that there was a thief about. When he discovered he'd been robbed, Rosie would be the last person he suspected. 'Well, to be perfectly honest,' she lied, 'I thought I'd left it on my table when I came down to the lavatory earlier on.'

'Been ter the bog? I hope yer haven't left any of yer germs in there.'

'But it's not there,' she said. 'So I must be mistaken – unless someone's been in and taken it.'

'I hope yer not insinuatin' that *I* might have taken it!'

'Oh, no,' she said quickly. 'It's just such a puzzle, that's all.'

'Mind outa me way, I'll have a quick look.' Lazarus worked his way slowly up the dimly lit stairs, eyes scanning every step as Rosie pretended to search the hall between the stairs and the toilet. 'Well, there's nowt on these stairs,' he reported.

'Oh dear,' said Rosie. 'I can't really afford to lose five shillings.'

'Well, it'll teach yer to be more careful. Just don't expect me ter be knockin' it off yer rent.'

'I can't understand what happened to it. Do you suppose Basil might have seen it?'

'I very much doubt it. He's not been in all day. Gone ter visit somebody. Went off first thing this morning.'

It was a relief to know that Basil wouldn't be a suspect. She decided to make her story sound authentic. 'I don't suppose I could pay two and six less this week and make it up after Christmas?'

'Yer right, I don't suppose yer could. I'm runnin' a business norra charity. Anyway I'll have ter dash before I pee meself.'

Lazarus opened the lavatory door and looked inside, as though expecting to see the whatever it was that Rosie had left there. He lifted the seat wishing he had his own private bog; but there wasn't much point now, not with this house.

Rosie knocked on his door the following afternoon. That morning she'd been to the doctor who had given her a prescription to reduce her temperature and had recommended bed rest; but there was still the worry of discovery hanging over her. No sense of guilt, just the fear of being caught. She needed to know the situation. As Lazarus opened the door she gave a hopeful smile and asked: 'I was just wondering. Are you sure I can't pay you two and six less on Friday and make it up . . .?'

'No, yer damn well can't. And stand back, I don't want ter catch yer germs!'

There was no hint of suspicion in his voice, nor in his manner. Had Lazarus thought for one second that she might have stolen money from him it would have been written all over his ugly face.

'You see,' she said, innocently, 'I've been to the doctor and he's told me to go back to bed until my temperature goes down – which means I can't go to work.'

'I'm sorry,' he muttered. 'I'm not a charity. Yer'll just have ter get it from somewhere.'

'It's just that I never found my five shillings.'

'And I never found my ten quid.'

'What?'

'I'm ten quid short in me rent box. God knows how. It was all there last night, I counted it.'

'Have you told the police?' she enquired. 'Someone must have stolen it. Probably the same person who stole my five shillings.'

Lazarus scowled. 'I reported it, but they just looked at me daft. They couldn't fathom out why a thief'd only steal half of it.'

'Well, you have to admit, it does sound a bit odd.'

'Don't you start an' all,' he grumbled. 'That's all I bloody need. I know what I know. If the coppers don't believe me, what am I supposed to do?'

'Well, I believe you,' sympathised Rosie. 'Because I think the same person stole my five shillings – did you tell them about my five shillings?'

She was definitely in the clear and enjoying herself now, at his expense.

'Oh aye,' he muttered, bad-temperedly, 'Don't yer think I've enough ter worry about?'

'It'd have done no harm to mention it.'

'Well, I didn't, and there's an end to it.'

'I don't know,' said Rosie, disapprovingly. 'There's some weird things going on in this house. Money going missing like that.'

'I just hope your money's not missing on Friday.'

Rosie took the rest of the week off work, but it didn't affect her employment. When she went back they were still one woman short. It was that sort of a job.

Chapter Ten

When Rosie returned to Duck Street to get her mother's address, the tenant was most apologetic about her treatment of her that day: 'I was just a bit worried about yer moving yerself in, and there bein' nowt I could do about it.'

'That's okay. Did my mam leave an address?'

'Well, we pay us rent to an agency but she did leave an address for letters somewhere. I think she moved down to Birmingham with this feller.'

'That'll be Sidney the Slug,' said Rosie.

'He made my skin crawl,' said the woman. 'Undressed me with his eyes every time he looked at me.'

Rosie sent her mother a Christmas card, deliberately not including Sidney in the greeting. A few days later she received a parcel from her mother containing a book written by a young war widow entitled *All On Your Own*. It was a guide to motherhood when the father was no longer around and there was no one else to look to for help. Rosie took it as a savage hint about how much help she could expect from her mother. In a fit of pique she posted it back to Ethel with a cryptic message written inside.

Your need could be greater than mine.

Ethel, weakened by a bout of diarrhoea, took it as a slur

on her own morality and vowed never to speak to her daughter again.

'What're you doing for your Christmas dinner, Basil?'

The old man looked through the smoke haze at Rosie, peering round his door.

'Nowt special.'

'I thought I might cook something,' she said cheerfully. 'It'd be just as easy to cook for two.'

'Thanks for the offer, but ter be honest, love, I can't afford nowt. I've only got me pension an' that doesn't go far.'

'It might if you didn't smoke so much. You should open a window.'

He gave a rasping, rattling cough and said, 'I've told yer why I smoke so much. Still, it's not so bad at Christmas. There won't be any manure deliveries for a few days.'

'Then it truly is the season of goodwill.'

'What're yer thinkin' o' cookin'?'

'A proper Christmas dinner. Turkey, the lot. And before you say anything, it'll not cost you a penny. Call it a "thank you" for looking after me when I was poorly.'

'I don't need rewarding for doin' a kindness to a friend. God knows I haven't got many left.'

'I'll be offended if you refuse.'

'Well, I wouldn't want to offend yer.'

As Christmases go, it was one she would never forget. On Christmas Eve, Basil announced he was a regular once a year churchgoer and took Rosie to Midnight Mass at Saint Augustine's.

'Never missed a Christmas, man and boy. Once a Catholic, allus a Catholic.'

She hoped she was the only one who saw him take a shilling from the collection plate as it was passed along their row. Surely this was a worse crime than her stealing nine pounds off Lazarus.

'I saw that!' she whispered.

'It's Christmas,' he muttered. 'I'm bloody entitled.'

A lone choir boy began to sing *Adeste Fidelis* with a sweetness and purity of pitch that brought tears to many eyes. Including Basil's.

On the way back, a flurry of snow had him shivering and grumbling, 'Could right do without that.'

'Don't be such a grump,' scolded Rosie. 'It'd be nice if we could have a white Christmas.'

'I saw enough snow last yer. It were like livin' in the bloody North Pole – thick o' snow, right up to the end o' March. Nearly did for me.'

'We used to go sledging in Roundhay Park,' she remembered, determined not to have a damper put on her Christmas. 'My dad made me a sledge when I was a kid. Me and Susan Clarkson spent many a Sunday afternoon sledging down Hill Forty.'

It was only last winter, but it seemed like a lifetime ago. She went quiet as her mind went over the events of the past few months. So much had happened, it was hard to keep up.

'I'm right lookin' forward ter me dinner,' said Basil, who didn't want to talk about snow.

The oven in the kitchen wasn't ideal for cooking a turkey. On top of which, Rosie had never cooked one before, but it was just about edible; as were the sprouts and potatoes.

'Best Christmas dinner I've ever had,' Basil announced. He sat back in her easy chair and scratched his scrawny stomach.

'I do hope not,' she smiled.

He offered Rosie a cigarette, which she refused. 'I didn't say the tastiest, I said the best,' he said. 'There's more ter Christmas dinner than food.'

'If you say so, Basil.' She took a bottle out of one of the drawers. 'Would you like a drop of brandy and a chocolate?'

'I wouldn't say no.'

She poured a generous measure into a cup and handed it to him, then opened a box of milk chocolates.

'Have yer come into money or summat? One minute yer skint, next minute it's all turkey and brandy and chocolates.'

Rosie had to tell someone. 'You could say this comes courtesy of our landlord.'

'Yer what? Owd "Death Warmed Up" paid fer this? Pull the other one, it's got bells on. He wouldn't pee on yer if yer were on fire.'

'Well, he doesn't actually know he's treating us,' explained Rosie. 'And I think it's better it stays that way.'

The old man suddenly roared with laughter. Two nicotine-coloured teeth vibrated above a furry tongue. 'It were you, yer bugger, weren't it? What nicked 'is money.'

She nodded, guiltily. 'I was desperate.'

'And yer told me off fer nickin' a bob off t' collection plate.'

'There is a bit of a difference,' protested Rosie. 'Lazarus steals from us every time we switch the electric on.'

'Hey!' he grinned from ear to ear. 'Don't get me wrong. I'm not judgin' yer, lass, I only wish I'd had the chance meself.' He held out his cup, chuckling to himself. 'By heck! That's the best thing I've heard in a long time. Nickin' yon bugger's brass from under his nose.' He let out another loud roar of delight and slapped his thigh repeatedly. 'By God, lass, yer've got some nerve I'll grant yer that!'

Rosie grew increasingly embarrassed. Basil seemed to be getting the wrong impression of her.

'I'm usually very honest,' she insisted. 'I've never done anything like it before. And I will give it back as soon as I can afford it. Probably anonymously.'

'Hey, don't go spoilin' things, lass. Give the bugger nowt. I'd sooner wipe me backside on it than give it to him.' He held out his mug. 'Fill me up, lass. I don't feel as guilty at takin' yer charity now.'

She poured him some more brandy, then held her own cup out for a toast.

'Merry Christmas, Basil. And I hope you have many more.'

'Nay, lass. It'll be the last one I have here, that's for sure.'

'Oh?'

'Didn't yer know?' he said, sticking a chocolate in his mouth. 'They're pullin' this lot down ter put a new road through. It's being compulsorily purchased.'

'When?'

'New Year sometime. I've seen blokes comin' round measuring already. Firm called BJK Limited according ter what it says on their van.' He tapped beneath his eye. 'I allus keep me eye out fer things like that. Yer never know.'

She resisted the temptation to ask, 'You never know what?'

'Not before time, neither,' he went on. 'It's no place for a pregnant woman.'

There was a silence between them, then she asked: 'Is it that obvious?'

'Not to the layman, no.'

'What are you then, some sort of doctor?'

'No, I'm a father. Father of five as a matter of fact. Lost one lad in the war. Best o' the lot on 'em as well. Youngest an' best. He'd have suited you down to the ground would my Victor. He were a divil at times but he were happy as a lark.'

'He sounds nice.'

'Nice? I'll say he were nice. He could sing an' all. By God he sang like a bloody angel and he thought the world of his dad. You heard that lad singin' in church last night?'

'Yes, he had a lovely voice.'

'Yer what? My Victor could have sung the arse off him.' He took another chocolate and chewed, noisily; chocolate juice escaped from his mouth and dribbled down his chin. 'The others don't give a bugger about their old man. Four

100

lumps o' shit and an angel, that's what I had. And God took the angel.'

'Is that why you took the money off the plate?'

'Why shouldn't I?' he said defensively. 'He took a damn sight more off me.'

She couldn't argue with that, so she didn't try. 'With me it's the other way round. My parents didn't care about me.'

'I wish I were yer dad. I'd swap all four o' mine fer one like you.'

'My dad's dead, so I shouldn't speak ill of him.'

'Sorry about that, lass. I take it the bairn's father's not around, neither?'

'The baby's father's dead as well.'

'By heck, lass! Yer've not had much luck wi' yer menfolk.' There was a silence as his eyes misted over. She didn't ask why. Maybe it was sympathy for her, or the memory of his beloved Victor – or maybe he just had watery eyes.

'Yer 'avin' a rough time of it, what wi' one thing and another,' he commented.

Rosie nodded, glumly. 'The good thing is that it can't get any worse – can it?'

He grinned at the underlying humour in her voice. 'I shouldn't think so, lass. But it can be a wicked world right enough.' He gave her a rheumy-eyed wink and said, 'Summat'll turn up for yer. You mark my words.'

On New Year's Day 1948, Basil had a stroke and died in his bed. Rosie went to his funeral and stood at his grave alongside his four surviving children who couldn't summon up a tear between them. As she glanced along the row of expressionless faces, she was sorely tempted to tell them what Basil thought of them, but she didn't. One asked how she knew their father and she said they'd once had dinner together and wasn't he the most charming man and he didn't deserve to die alone in a squalid room with no one to say goodbye to.

That evening she met George Metcalf.

Chapter Eleven

George Metcalf didn't come from a wealthy family. His father had been an accounts manager with a clothing firm and had died leaving his wife a small house and a smaller pension. George, much to his mother's horror, ran away to join the army at the age of fifteen and within three months had lost his left leg at the Battle of the Somme. Nine years later he lost his beloved wife to tuberculosis. He had a daughter whom he loved dearly, but who eventually became a disappointment to him. A year after his wife's death he went off to university to study civil engineering, leaving his daughter in the care of his mother.

With his honours degree he quickly got a job as a site engineer and when his mother died suddenly, George sold the house he'd inherited and formed his own road building company. Hard work and enthusiasm reaped its own rewards and George enjoyed financial success. His personal life was a different matter altogether.

George and his daughter, Barbara, came as a package. Many women liked him, and were prepared to accept his strange sense of humour and his tin leg. But putting up with Barbara was just too much of a sacrifice. A sacrifice that even George's money couldn't compensate for. By the time he was forty, he had given up looking.

The Royd's Road improvement was one of his biggest contracts to date. He had just finished doing some preliminary survey work when, further down the street, he saw a young woman trip and fall. She wore a headscarf and her clothes were drab and maybe he wouldn't have paid too much attention had he not seen her earlier in the day, all dressed in black. At the time he'd thought how strikingly pretty she looked.

In years to come, Rosie would think back and reflect on how the whole pattern of her future was decided by the daftest thing. Had she not had a loose heel that evening, her life would have followed a completely different path.

But her heel *was* loose as she left the house to walk to Marsden's and work up a sweat for three shillings. It broke as she walked down the footpath, sending her off balance, almost into the road. She was sitting on the kerb, cursing, as George was opening the door to his firm's van, parked up the street. He walked towards her and asked if she was okay.

'Do I look okay?' were the first words she ever spoke to him.

Her annoyance made him grin. 'As a matter of fact, you do. At least you would if you were the right way up.'

Rosie was in that stage of pregnancy when women begin to bloom. When that glow of inner motherhood pervades their bodies. She also looked very ungainly, sitting on the kerb with her dress halfway up her thighs, which George couldn't help but notice were very nice thighs. She smiled and got to her feet, embarrassed at having snapped at this pleasant man.

'Sorry about that.'

'That's okay,' he grinned. 'I expect you were a bit un-balanced.'

'Just a bit.'

'Can I give you a lift anywhere?' What prompted him to make such an offer was beyond him.

'Hey, I've heard about men like you.'

'Really?'

'Men who go round picking up fallen women.' She sat on a low wall and examined her shoe. 'Damn! I'll have to

103

go back and change my shoes.' She looked at her watch, then at George. 'What did you say about a lift?'

'Where do you want to be?'

'Marsden's, I work there on a night. I only put these shoes on because I fancied calling for a drink on the way home.'

He walked over to her and examined her shoe. 'Nothing that a spot of cobbling won't put right.'

She looked up and down the street. 'Do you know? There's never a cobbler around when you need one.' It had been a while since she'd had a silly conversation with anyone. This man had somehow lifted her spirits after that morning's funeral.

'Need a helping hand to get back in the house?' He had an agreeable voice, humour wasn't far below the surface.

'No, it's okay.' She took her other shoe off and walked back to the house in stockinged feet with George walking beside her. He was dressed in work clothes with mud sticking to his boots from a recent site visit.

'I gather you work for . . .' she squinted at the van, 'BJK Limited.'

'Er, yes.'

'What do you do?'

'I'm an engineer. We're putting a road through here.'

'So I gather. Putting me out of house and home as well.'

'Oh, I'm sorry.'

'Don't be. It's the best thing that could happen to this place. I came here for a week because I had nowhere else to live. That was nearly three months ago. I hope you'll be pulling that place down as well.' She pointed towards the oil factory.

'I'm afraid not.'

'Pity. My name's Rosie, by the way. Rosie Jones.'

'Pleased to meet you, Rosie. I'm George Metcalf.'

He dropped her outside Marsden's at five to six. 'If you still fancy that drink,' he said. 'I'll be passing here in a couple of hours.'

Considering she'd told him she only worked for two

104

hours, this seemed more than a coincidence, but he seemed a nice enough bloke; even if he was old enough to be her father.

'No strings,' he added. 'Just a drink and a chat.'

'Might take you up on that,' smiled Rosie. 'I finish at eight.'

His van was parked by the kerb as she came out. She waited until her two workmates had walked in the opposite direction before letting herself into the passenger seat.

'I wasn't sure you'd bother,' she said. 'Me looking like I do.'

'You look fine to me, Rosie Jones. Where's it to be?'

'Anywhere . . . just a drink and a chat.'

He caught the hint of caution in her tone. 'Hey!' he laughed, easily. 'I'm not a cradle snatcher, just a bloke in a van who thinks you're funny. But I expect you to pay your corner. And I don't want you taking advantage of me, I've got a tin leg.' He tapped his leg with his pipe to prove it.

'Really? I'd never have known.'

She wanted to ask how he'd come by it, but decided she didn't know him well enough. Perhaps after a couple of drinks.

He drove out into the country to a pub neither of them had ever been to and gave her a very potted version of his life, missing out the part where he actually owned the company he worked for. Rosie told him what she wanted him to know, missing out the fact that she was pregnant. This was a one off date – if it could be called that – so why should she burden him with all her troubles? He now knew she'd fallen out with her mother and had lost a good job and was currently searching for another, and a decent place to live. He also knew that she was attractive and funny and that he wanted to be with her more than any woman he'd ever met since his wife died. Of course that was completely out of the question because he was far too old for her. After a couple of drinks she considered she now knew him well enough to ask him about his leg.

'When did you lose your leg?'

'Nineteen-sixteen in France. A German shot it off. At least I think it was a German. There was so much stuff flying about, it could have been anybody.'

'You must have been quite young.'

'Fifteen – I lied about my age when I joined up. Daftest thing I've ever done.'

'Did it hurt?'

It was the sort of question a child would ask, which was part of her charm. To his recollection he'd never been asked this before, and wondered why. Maybe no one had been concerned enough.

'Yes, as a matter of fact it did hurt.'

She took his hand across the table and squeezed it. 'I'm sorry,' she said.

'It happened before you were born, Rosie.'

'I'm still sorry. I imagine it was a very nice leg.'

'Not bad, as legs go. The foot was especially nice. You'd have liked the foot.'

'Do you have a photograph of it that you keep next to your heart?'

He shook his head, sadly. 'Not even a piece of toenail in a locket. All I have to remember it by, is my other foot.'

When he dropped her off later that night, she didn't notice the stink or the squalor of her surroundings. She'd had the best night since ... since that night with Sean. On their way home he'd casually said, 'There's a good film on at the Odeon this week. *Easter Parade*.'

'Fred Astaire and Judy Garland,' said Rosie. 'I like him but I'm not so struck on her.'

'You must have liked *Wizard of Oz*, everyone liked that.'

'That was when she was a kid. I saw her in a picture a few months ago. She talks as if she's going to burst into tears any second.'

'You're talking about the woman I love.'

'Careful,' grinned Rosie. 'She's young enough to be your daughter.'

106

'So are you.'

I am, aren't I, she thought. But what does it matter? He's a friend that's all, and very good company. 'Is it on on Friday?' she asked.

'I think it's on all week. I could pick you up after work. We could go to the second house.'

'I'd like that.'

'Right, it's a . . .' He cleared his throat. 'It's a date. You can buy me fish and chips on the way home.'

'You've got a deal,' Rosie said. 'You pay for the pictures. I'll get the fish and chips.'

He gave her a lazy smile. She liked the way he smiled and tried to picture him twenty-five years ago. He'd have been a bit of all right; tall and handsome and definitely a looker. He wasn't so bad even now.

Possibly influenced by George's enthusiasm, Rosie enjoyed the film and on the way home in his van, he turned on the windscreen wipers to clear away the fine drizzle and, using them as squeaky metronomes, they launched into a lusty but tuneless rendition of *We're A Couple of Swells*.

As they sang, he held the wheel with one hand and with the other he tapped his tin leg with his pipe. Rosie broke down into a snorting giggle.

'Excuse me, young lady,' he said. 'I don't know what you've got to snigger about with a voice like yours. You couldn't hold a tune in a bucket.'

'Don't go blaming me. It's your leg tapping that's throwing me off key.'

'Ah, sorry about that. The problem is I sing mainly in B flat and they've given me an F sharp leg. Tell you what, before we go out again I promise to get my leg re-tuned if you do the same with your voice.'

Rosie was still laughing when he pulled up outside her house. She sat back, allowing her amusement to subside. This seemed an opportune moment to tell him her secret. Now was as good a time as any.

'George, I've had a lovely evening.'

'Me as well. The best for a long long time. We should do it again.'

'Maybe you won't want to when you find out what sort of a girl I am,' she thought to herself. 'There's something I probably ought to tell you,' she said, 'And I don't know how to put it.'

The humour went from his voice. 'Ah, you mean you want to get the words in the right order to make it sound right, so as not to upset me?'

'Something like that.'

George's heart sank. He should have seen this coming. What was he thinking of, at his age? He tried to inject a cheerful note into his voice. 'Do these words include: "You're much too old for me and we shouldn't see each other again or things might get too complicated"?'

'Oh no,' Rosie assured him. 'Your age never crossed my mind. Well, it did, but it's got nothing to do with what I need to tell you.'

'What is it then?'

'I'm pregnant.'

He sat back in his seat and lit his pipe. It reminded her of her dad's pipe, but there the similarity ended. Her dad was probably younger than George, but not as youthful. A woman would already be asking intrusive questions, such as: who's the father? and when did it happen? and is he going to do the decent thing and marry you?

As she waited for his reaction, Rosie concentrated her gaze on the damp, gas-lit street beyond the windscreen. A couple, about her age, were walking slowly towards them, obviously drunk. She clung to him with both arms as they leaned against the lamp post and began to kiss passionately, both pairs of hands began to explore places which would be better explored in private. It made both George and Rosie feel even more uncomfortable. The woman did a double take of the watching pair and whispered something to her boyfriend who advanced unsteadily on the van and hammered belligerently on the side window. Rosie wound it half down.

'Hey! What yer think yer lookin' at?' he slurred.

'If you don't want an audience you shouldn't do it under a lamp post,' retorted Rosie.

'We'll do it where we like! Yer bastard perverts!'

'Watch your language in front of a lady!' snapped George.

'Oh aye? An' what yer gonna do about it, grandad?'

Angrily, George opened his door, and despite Rosie's protests, climbed out of the van. Rosie got out quickly and positioned herself between George and the drunken man. The girlfriend suddenly appeared and grabbed her hair. Instinctively, Rosie swung her arm in a powerful arc and slapped her aggressor across the side of her face, causing her to lurch into her boyfriend, Both fell into a tangled heap on the floor.

The fallen man moaned and cursed as he struggled violently to extricate herself from under his girlfriend, who began lashing out at him in senseless, drunken anger. He crouched under a hail of blows, then, in self-defence, wrestled her to the ground, inflaming her temper even more. She fought and kicked like a trapped vixen, her language colouring the night air. Windows opened and shouts of protest came from offended residents. The battling pair were completely oblivious to everything, including the bemused presence of Rosie and George.

'Right,' said Rosie, backing away. 'I er . . . I think we should leave them to it.'

'I agree.'

George's innate good manners had him holding the passenger door open for her. The couple were still fighting on the ground as he drove away.

'I thought it might be wise if I didn't go inside while they were there,' Rosie explained. 'I don't want them to know where I live.'

He laughed. 'I doubt if they remember where *they* live. They'll wake up in the morning wondering where they got all their bruises from. It's probably a normal night out for them.'

George's mind buzzed as he drove; it had been an eventful few minutes. Her last words before the fracas were still foremost in his mind, '*I'm pregnant*'. 'By the way, thanks for stepping in back there,' he said. 'That was quite a whack you gave that girl – didn't realise you had it in you.'

'Neither did I, to be honest,' said Rosie, defensively. 'I don't normally go round hitting people – it was just a reaction to her pulling my hair.'

'Hey, don't apologise. Having only one leg might have been a bit of a drawback had it got nasty.'

'Oh, I'm sure you'd have coped. He was even more legless than you.'

George laughed again and realised how much he wanted this young woman. He stopped at a set of traffic lights. 'About this pregnancy thing, I, er, I suppose it's none of my business.'

'None at all. But you're a friend and I thought you ought to know. Actually, I thought you might have noticed.'

'Well, it did cross my mind, but it's not the sort of thing you actually ask. If you hadn't been, you'd have felt insulted.'

'Possibly. Although I'm not exactly a stick-insect at the best of times.'

'I assume you're on your own in all this?'

'Very much so. The baby's father's dead.'

'Oh dear, I am sorry.' His grief was genuine. He took her hand and she felt oddly safe.

'And my mother's frightened of the shame I'll bring on the family. That's why I left home.'

'Oh dear.'

'I got the sack for the same reason,' she went on. 'That's why I took a cleaning job – to keep body and soul together.'

Concern was etched on his face and she reached out to stroke the worried lines smooth again. Her lips touched his and he felt a magnetism. But did she?

110

'You mustn't worry about me,' she said. 'I'm as fit as a butcher's dog.'

He squeezed her hand. 'I think you've just proved that. If I can help in any way, I will.'

'You don't know how much your friendship means to me, George.'

He wanted to hug her to him but didn't dare, he might be tempted to try something which would destroy their friendship. She looked so young, younger than his own daughter. What the hell was he thinking about? Keep your hands and your thoughts to yourself, George Metcalf. The lights changed and he swung left in order to head back to Rosie's house. The drunken couple had gone by the time they arrived.

'All clear,' he grinned. Then he took a pencil from the glove compartment and wrote two sets of numbers on the back of a petrol receipt.

'My phone numbers,' he explained. 'The work number's a direct line through to me. If a woman answers, it'll be Mrs Drysdale, the office manageress. Just tell her who you are and that you want to speak to George. I'll tell her to expect your call.'

'Won't you get into trouble? I used to get into trouble at Brigshawe's for taking personal calls.'

'Well, I don't make a habit of it,' he said. 'So it should be okay.'

He watched as she got out of the van and took a couple of paces across the pavement. She smiled back at him and returned to peck him on the lips; then she gave him a last wave and went up the path and through the door. It took him a full minute to collect himself sufficiently to start the van. Perhaps the date had been a mistake. His infatuation with her was growing into an obsession, which was unhealthy in a man of his age. The fact that she was pregnant didn't detract one iota from her appeal. With the baby's father being dead it made her quite vulnerable to predatory men. Men such as him.

*

111

Rosie sat on her bed, stared at herself in a mirror hung on a nail in the wall, and saw a fat frump who was growing fatter by the day. She scarcely dared think of the future. Her surroundings were less than basic, certainly not the ideal place to bring up a baby. How the hell did she get into this mess?

If only George were a few years younger she could make a play for him. What was she thinking about? She'd never try and take advantage of such a lovely man. He was lovely though, wasn't he? She smiled as she remembered their nonsensical conversation about his tin leg being out of tune. Pity about his leg. Still, a one-legged George would be highly preferable to the drunken lout she'd seen earlier. She switched her thoughts to more urgent matters and took herself and her unborn baby off to the bathroom, gently cursing it for pressing on her bladder so much.

Rosie had been throwing up all morning. She was having a bilious pregnancy and, with a churning stomach, she walked with an uncertain step to the phone box at the end of the street and rang George.

'I was just passing the phone box,' she lied. 'And I thought I'd give your number a try.'

'Checking to see if the number was genuine, eh?'

'You wouldn't be the first feller to give me a wrong number.'

'Some men are idiots.'

She felt herself blushing at this oblique flattery and couldn't think of a reply.

George sensed her awkwardness and asked, 'How are you?' He sounded pleased to hear from her. It had been a week, and he was despairing of ever seeing her again. She probably had boyfriends galore, all her own age.

'If you must know,' she admitted, 'I've been throwing up all morning. When I've finished talking to you, I'm going to decorate this telephone box with my breakfast then ring in and give work a miss tonight.'

'Ugh! – I think I'd better pop in and see you after I finish. You sound as though you need a bit of looking after.'

'There's no need.' She hoped he wouldn't take her protest too seriously.

'Put the kettle on at quarter-past-six. I'll be there at twenty-past.'

'Give the doorbell two rings,' she said. 'Then I'll know it's for me.'

'Two rings for Rosie, eh?'

One ring would be enough, she thought, as she walked back, providing the right man gave it to her. But she walked with a lighter step, and knew she'd be watching the clock move slowly round to quarter-past-six. George was like the father she'd never known, not bad looking either. If he was younger she could quite fancy him. Oh heck! Maybe she did fancy him, but wouldn't admit it to herself. Behave yourself, Rosie Jones, he's twenty-odd years older than you. Not even you could fancy someone that old.

She opened the door as he was halfway through a second, prolonged ring.

'Thought I'd made sure you'd heard the first ring before I started on the second,' he explained, cheerfully. He had brought flowers. She didn't have a vase to put them in.

'Oh, you shouldn't have, they're lovely. I'll just take them up to the kitchen and put them in a vase.'

He followed her up the stairs to her tiny room and just stopped himself from saying, 'You can't bring a baby up in a pokey hole like this'. Rosie disappeared into the communal kitchen, turned on the sink tap and laid the stems underwater. Then she lit a gas ring and put the kettle on, before joining him in her room.

'It's a bit pokey, I'm afraid,' she commented. 'But it's all I can afford at the moment.'

'It's er ... it's very nice.'

She stared at him with raised eyebrows until he asked, 'Why are you looking at me like that?'

113

'Seeing how long you can keep a straight face.'

'All right, it's not very nice. How on earth do you live with that smell?'

'I have to cut my cloth to suit my purse . . .'

'Right.'

George's mind was racing. He had the solution to all her problems, but would she prefer to stick with the alternative? He could hardly blame her. His reflection looked back at him from the mirror on the wall, the crack splitting his image slightly. He moved slightly to one side to remove the distortion. Did he look old? Not from where he was standing. Who was he trying to kid? There's no fool like an old fool they say. Rosie's smiling face appeared beside his in the mirror.

'We make a handsome couple, don't you think?'

'Twenty-five years ago, maybe.'

'I wasn't born twenty-five years ago.'

There was an awkward pause, then George said, 'I didn't come here to talk about the good old days, I came for a cup of tea.'

She threw him a mock salute. 'Yessir, coming up, sir. The kettle's already boiled.'

'You only salute officers,' he pointed out. 'I never rose to such dizzy heights.'

'I bet you were good at what you did.'

'I was a bugler.'

She turned to look at him, narrowing her eyes and trying to peel back the last thirty years. 'I can just picture you,' she said. 'The brave bugle boy. Bullets whistling all around and you bugling away like a good un.'

He laughed. 'I didn't do much bugling when we went over the top. I was too busy being terrified.'

'I bet you were brave. Did you get a medal?'

'Nothing special, just two campaign medals.'

'They sound special enough to me. It means you were there.'

'At the time I'd rather *not* have been there,' he admitted.

'The whole war was a senseless mess from start to finish.'

'What war isn't?'

He followed her on to the landing and stood behind her in the kitchen as she poured the water into the teapot. It was even more dismal there than it was in her room. He felt guilty when he saw the flowers lying in the sink; she probably didn't have a vase and she must feel embarrassed. A bare, forty-watt bulb hung above her head, illuminating the sparse facilities of the small, brown room with its stained lino and white-washed walls, splashed with years of fat. Hanging from the light was a sheet of fly-paper, covered with tiny victims. Rosie saw him looking at it and grimaced.

'Basil used to change that,' she said, 'but he died. I s'pose I'd better do it.'

'It's okay,' said George, gallantly. 'I'll do it.'

He unhooked the fly-paper and dropped it in a waste bin under the sink. Rosie handed him a fresh sheet. 'Normally you don't get flies this time of year,' she said. 'I think it's that place across the road that attracts them.'

The steam from the kettle, intensified by the cold air, quickly filled the whole room, forcing Rosie to waft it away with one hand. As she poured the steaming water into the teapot, he asked, 'For God's sake, Rosie, what are you going to do?'

She ran his question through her thoughts. 'Honest answer?'

'Honest answer.'

She put the kettle back on the gas ring, replaced the lid on the teapot, then turned to face him.

'I don't know.'

Suddenly her face crumpled and she was in his arms, sobbing on his shoulder. He felt the warmth of her coming through his coat as he hugged her close to him. They stood there for a while as George tried to pluck up courage. His heart raced, terrified of the rejection she had every right to subject him to. Christ, this was worse than the Somme. He took a deep breath.

'I er ...' His courage failed him. 'I wondered if you fancied going to the pictures again.'

'That'd be nice,' she smiled through her tears. 'We get on all right, don't we?'

'Like a house on fire,' he agreed.

They went to the pictures three times during the next two weeks. They saw Deborah Kerr in *The Black Narcissus*, Linda Darnell and Cornel Wilde in *Forever Amber*, then to suit George's taste, Rosie insisted they go see Randolph Scott in *Badman's Territory*. His first formal goodnight peck had graduated into something longer. Something less platonic. Each time George steeled himself to ask the question and each time his courage failed him – or was it simply common sense prevailing? Bumping into Joe Brindle didn't help.

He was at the builder's merchants when Brindle called to him across the yard.

'Hey up, Hopalong – I reckon yer shaggin' that slag Rosie Jones. I should be careful. Yer never know what yer gonna catch from her.'

'It's right what everybody says about you, isn't it?' retorted George, angrily. 'All mouth and no brains.'

'Were it you what put her up the stick?' sneered Brindle. 'I'd have thought yer were past it at your age.'

'Brindle,' seethed George. 'You're a fat useless joke. If you hadn't been able to take over your dad's firm you'd have been sweeping the bloody streets for a living!'

Brindle pushed customers to one side as he stormed across to where George had been discussing drainage pipes with the yard man. Without hesitating he swung a punch that sent George sprawling.

'Now who's a big joke?' he snarled.

George wiped the blood off his nose and decided not to move. He knew he was no match for Brindle so there was no point trying. He was also scared, but he wasn't going to let Brindle know this. He looked up at the bigger man.

'*You're* a big joke, Brindle,' he said, steadily. 'And

that's not just my opinion, that's what everyone thinks. A big, brainless joke.'

Brindle swung a kick at George and caught him in the ribs. Two yard men intervened and stood between Brindle and the prostrate George. The manager came hurrying over.

'I think you'd better leave, Mr Brindle.'

'Brindle didn't move.

'I'll call the police if I have to,' warned the manager, nervously.

Brindle spat contemptuously on the ground and strolled away. The manager looked down, apologetically at George. 'I er . . . I hope this won't affect our business relationship.'

George clutched at his bruised ribs, saw the funny side and started to chuckle; grimacing, as laughing hurt his side. The two yard men joined in as the worried manager held out his hand and pulled George, painfully to his feet. Ever the businessman, George suggested: 'Twenty-five per cent off my last month's account might ease the pain.'

The manager hesitated, then offered. 'Fifteen.'

'Twenty and I won't take my business elsewhere.'

'Agreed,' said the manager. 'I'll knock it off Brindle's trade discount. He can take his business elsewhere if he doesn't like it.'

George's eye was black when he saw Rosie later that evening.

'Don't tell me,' she grinned. 'You walked into a door.'

'Something like that,' he said. 'Only this door was called Joe Brindle.'

'Oh, him.'

'I gather you know him?'

'I do – he's always had a . . . a thing about me.'

'Ah, so you're to blame. He was accusing me of being the father of your baby.'

'Oh, and what did you say to that?'

'Not much. I didn't see the sense in arguing with him. I just called him a few names.' He rubbed his side. 'As it turned out, there wasn't much sense in that, either.'

'Well, it's typical of him to attack a one-legged man twice his age.'

'Hey! – you make me sound like a useless old man,' protested George. He fingered his swollen eye, ruefully. 'I must admit, I don't fancy the return bout.'

'Joe Brindle's a coward,' Rosie assured him. 'One day he'll really get his come-uppance.'

She told him the story of how Brindle had caused the death of Sean, but omitted to mention that Sean was the father of her baby. The pair of them were on the tram, on their way to the Clock Cinema to see Humphrey Bogart and Lauren Bacall in *The Big Sleep*; George's choice of film. He had arrived on foot, saying he couldn't get the van that night. When Rosie gave him her answer he didn't want it influenced by any outside factors; such as his being relatively wealthy. But he couldn't keep his secret much longer. Rosie was the least curious woman he'd ever come across. She hadn't even asked him where he lived or why he had never re-married.

As they alighted from the tram at the Fforde Greene pub, just across the road from the cinema, George suggested, 'Fancy a drink instead? We can always see the picture another time.'

'Suits me,' said Rosie, who didn't like the way Humphrey Bogart talked through his teeth. He wasn't her idea of a matinee idol. She linked arms with George and they darted across Roundhay Road, dodging the evening traffic. Somehow the age gap didn't seem to matter any more. They shared a comfortable compatibility, relaxed and happy in each other's company. But for George it was a lot more than this. He loved Rosie as he had never loved anyone before. And tonight he had to tell her. And then he had to ask her. They found a table in the best room and settled down behind a couple of drinks. Rosie opened the conversation with a question of her own.

'You know when I asked you about your leg and how you lost it, you went all quiet.'

George shrugged. 'The best way to deal with an event like that is to blot it out of your memory. I try not to think about it.'

Rosie looked at him for a while. He returned her gaze but knew he was failing his examination.

'I think there's more to it,' she commented, at length. 'I think maybe there's something that you've kept to yourself all these years.'

He smiled but his smile was a bit too grave.

'I'm right, aren't I?' she pressed.

'Maybe it's something you've got no right to know,' he replied.

'Maybe it is,' she conceded. 'Maybe it's something only someone very close to you should know. Did your wife know?'

He shook his head. 'No, she didn't.'

'So, there is something!' she cried in triumph, loud enough for people on the next table to hear. Heads turned, wondering what that something was. Rosie winced apologetically at George and said, 'Sorry.'

'That's okay,' said George. 'I probably should have told her, but it was too near the event. At the time I was desperately trying to block it out. It was the only way I could cope with it.'

'Can you cope now?'

'You mean can I tell you?' he smiled.

Rosie looked at him, innocently. 'A problem shared is a problem halved.'

He saw a golden opportunity. 'What makes you think we're close enough to share my dark secrets?'

'I just think we are, that's all,' she said. 'I get on with you better than anyone I've ever known, if you must know.'

He reached across the table and took her hand. 'I have similar feelings,' he said, quietly. 'Similar but stronger.'

'Oh?'

'I know you'll think me a silly old sod but I'm actually in love with you. Daft, isn't it? An old fogey like me.'

119

'Oh.'

'Oh indeed.'

She squeezed his hand. 'I think you're a silly sod at times but you're not old.'

'I'm old enough to be your father.'

Rosie tapped the side of her head. 'Not in here. In here we're the same age.'

For her to have told him she loved him would have been too much to ask, but she hadn't been shocked by his own declaration, so it was time to press on, 'You know what would solve a lot of problems, don't you?'

She shook her head, uncertainly. If she knew, she wasn't going to help him out.

He took a nervous breath and said, 'Us getting married ...'

'Oh!'

'... would solve a lot of problems. Rosie, you keep saying, Oh.'

'I know – sorry.' She rested her elbows on the table and laced her fingers together, her face screwed up in thought, thumbs pressed to her lips. 'I'm trying to think. I wasn't expecting this. It's quite a big decision.' Then, as though she'd just understood the situation she said, 'George ... you just asked me to marry you.'

'I know – I remember.'

'But you're old enough to be ...' She bit her tongue but she'd said enough. His heart sank, reality set in.

'Sorry,' he said. 'It was a daft idea. I get these daft ideas. So, just forget it ... and I'll go because I've embarrassed you.' He got up to go, annoyed at the cack-handed way he'd handled things. She stayed his arm.

'Hold it, mister! Where do you think you're going? I can't just forget it. I mean, are you sure?'

George laughed ruefully. 'Sure? I've never been so sure of anything in my life. I happen to have fallen in love with you. It apparently happens to men of my age, particularly foolish old men.'

'You're not old. If you were eighty, that'd be old, but

120

you're only what?' She did a mental calculation. 'Forty-seven? That's barely middle-aged.'

'To you I must appear positively neanderthal.'

'If I knew what you were talking about I might give you an argument.'

Rosie sipped her drink as she collected her thoughts. It was certainly a good offer – and right out of the blue. The last thing she expected.

George was beginning to realise that she hadn't said 'no'. This meant there was hope. He must tread carefully and not blow his chances completely.

'Look,' he said. 'I know you probably don't even fancy me or anything.'

'Ah, that's not true.'

'What?'

Rosie shrugged, confused. 'You're a good-looking man. You've still got all your hair, and your own teeth by the look of it.'

'I'm fifty per cent short in the leg department,' he pointed out.

'Thirty per cent,' said Rosie. She sipped her drink, contemplatively; running through the practicalities of his offer and amazing herself at the thoughts going through her head. How old would he be when she was forty? Sixty-four. Her Grandad Dobson was only sixty-two when he died and he'd looked prehistoric. Would George look ancient when she was forty? What about children? He's hardly likely to want children at his age. Still, she was guaranteed at least one of her own.

'I don't actually love you, you know.'

'I know.'

'You're a nice man; maybe I could grow to love you.'

'Rosie, I'm not asking you to decide this thing straight away. I'm just presenting it to you as an option.'

She took his hand and squeezed it. 'When I said I didn't love you, what I really meant was I don't know how I feel about you. I like you very much. We seem to get on very well.'

'It's a start,' he said.

'It is, isn't it?'

'As a matter of fact, it's a very good start,' he pointed out. 'Most married couples aren't actually friends with each other.'

'I'd have to agree with you there,' laughed Rosie. All of a sudden her prospects seemed brighter. The hopelessness of her situation made this an easy decision to make. She'd been offered a way out of her mess by a nice, kind man with whom she got along very well. What was her alternative? Off-hand she couldn't think of one. There was a possibility that her child might be taken away from her if the powers that be thought she wouldn't be able to support it. She finished her drink and laid the empty glass on the table. A slow smile spread across her face as she saw her opportunity.

'While I'm thinking about it, why don't you tell me your secret? Maybe it's something I need to take into consideration.'

George shook his head at her female subterfuge. 'It probably is,' he admitted.

Rosie did a double take of the couple sitting at the next table. They looked away quickly. 'I know our conversation's fascinating,' she said, sharply. 'But it *is* private.'

Without a word, the disappointed pair got up and left the room. Rosie returned her attention to George. 'Right,' she said. 'You now have my full attention.'

He rubbed his hands across his face as if trying to massage his memory, then he rested his chin on them, elbows on the table, and looked at her. 'Rosie,' he said. 'This is unbelievably confidential.'

'Husband and wife stuff, eh?' she smiled, reassuringly.

'Don't toy with me,' he said, sharply.

Her expression changed to one of contrition. 'George, I'm sorry. I wouldn't upset you for the world.'

'I know. It's just that I've never told anyone this – and maybe I didn't expect to.'

Rosie said nothing. This was his time.

'I'd been in France for three months,' he began. 'Regretted joining up after three days. Still, some days were better than others. The blokes were kind to me – especially Sergeant Woodgate.' Just repeating the man's name seemed an effort. George took a drink of his beer. 'Smashing bloke. Mid-thirties, regular soldier – Old Sweats, we used to call them. He came from Salford.'

He paused to light his pipe. Rosie encouraged him to continue, 'What was it like? The Somme?'

'Noisy,' he said. 'Noisy and muddy and terrifying. We'd been shelling the Hun for days . . .'

'Why did they call them the Hun? . . . Sorry, I'm interrupting.'

'Not sure,' he said. 'Something to do with Attilla I expect.' She regretted distracting him, as he was now taking time to recollect his thoughts.

'When the order came for us to go over the top it was supposed to be a formality,' he went on. 'According to the top brass we'd wiped them all out.' He frowned as he brought back the memory of that day. 'The sun was shining, only you couldn't see it through the smoke. All I could see were smoky shadows all around me. We all had fixed bayonets. At first there was hardly any stuff coming our way; then they opened up. Jesus! it was bad. I was nearly bent double, trying to make myself as small as I could – and I wasn't all that big to start with . . .'

Rosie tried to picture the scene. He rubbed his forehead then ran his hand around the back of his neck.

'Sergeant Woodgate was behind me. "Keep moving, lad", he kept saying. Not harshly – more encouraging. He knew I was terrified. Christ! You'd need to have been an idiot not to have been terrified. Then men started to fall down. You'd hear them cry out and fall and Sergeant Woodgate just kept saying, "Keep moving, lad". He didn't sound frightened, but he must have been, mustn't he?'

Rosie nodded.

'Then I fell. I wasn't shot or anything. I tripped over a

body. Sergeant Woodgate stopped and looked down at me. "All right, lad?" he said. I said, "Yes thanks, Sergeant." "Good lad," he said. "Keep moving".' George took a deep drag on his pipe.

'The guns were deafening. Machine guns, shells, rifles. Christ, it was noisy. Then Sergeant Woodgate fell down. I stopped and asked him if he was okay. Jesus! ... his insides were spilling out and he started screaming in agony. I mean really scary screaming. I shouted for a medic but no one heard me. There was too much noise. I stood up and looked around but I couldn't see anyone. Just smoke and flashes and explosions and bullets cracking past my head.'

George had obviously come to the climax of his story. The bit he'd kept secret all these years. He shook his head at the memory of it.

'Is that when you got shot?' ventured Rosie, gently.

He shook his head again. 'Sergeant Woodgate was in so much agony. God, he was in a mess – we both knew he was going to die. I leaned over him and told him it'd be all right. His eyes were wild and he was trying to lift his pistol. "For God's sake, help me," he was screaming. "I can't bloody stand this."'

George frowned deeply and looked at Rosie. 'He wanted me to help him commit suicide. But I couldn't do it. He kept trying to lift his pistol to his head. Then he said, "Shoot me, lad," but I couldn't. I started crying. Christ! I was only fifteen. "I've given you an order", he was yelling. "If you don't obey an order I'll bloody well shoot you". His gun was pointing at me and his other hand was clutching my uniform so I couldn't get free. I told him I couldn't do it – so he shot me in my leg. I didn't feel much at first, then he was pointing the gun at my head and screaming, "I'll do it". Honest, he was off his head. I took hold of the barrel and twisted it round, so it was pointed at him.'

Tears were coursing down George's cheeks now. Thankfully his back was to the room so no one noticed his distress as he stumbled on with his story: 'He couldn't pull

124

the trigger. He didn't have enough strength left. At that point we both knew I could have taken the gun off him and left him to die. Then he went quiet and gave me this ... this pleading look. I can hear his voice now. "Please, lad. Just do this last thing for me".' George looked at Rosie then lowered his eyes. 'So ... I shot him.'

They sat in silence for a long time. Rosie was waiting for George to speak first.

'A few minutes later two medics turned up. They took a quick look at him then bundled me on to a stretcher. Fortnight later I was back home in Blighty. A one-legged war veteran at fifteen. The papers tried to make me out to be a hero, which made it even worse. Many's the time I was on the verge of telling people what happened. Then the war ended and I was just another cripple. Which is how I preferred it.'

Rosie kissed him affectionately. 'I think you were incredibly brave.'

'I don't want you to tell anyone.' He wiped away his tears with his hands.

'I wouldn't dream of telling anyone.'

'If I'd been a bit older I think I could have handled it a bit better. But at the time I thought I'd murdered him. Thought the same for years. Maybe I still do.'

'The cruellest thing you could have done was to have left him to die in agony. That was your other choice.'

'Not much of a choice, was it?'

'We all have to make choices in life,' said Rosie. 'Like me. You've given me a choice. A choice between a lovely man like you, and not knowing how I'm going to manage.'

'You don't have to give me your answer right now.'

'I've no intention of telling you right now. But I won't keep you waiting. I'll tell you tomorrow.'

'Tomorrow it is – and by the way, if your answer's no, I'll still be around to make sure you come to no harm. You're stuck with me, either as a friend or a husband ... so, what shall we do with the rest of tonight?'

'Tonight I just want us to enjoy ourselves,' said Rosie, leaning over and giving him another kiss. 'Now, I've given up smoking,' she said, handing him her empty glass, 'because I read somewhere that it might harm my baby, but I haven't got to the bit about the evils of drink ... not yet anyway.'

George stood up to go to the bar. 'Do you know,' he said. 'I've read so much about the evils of drink recently, that I've decided to give up reading.'

They were very much worse for wear when they left the pub at closing time. Across the road, in a side street, an unhappy looking ragman's horse, still harnessed to a cart, was tethered to a drain pipe. Its owner was probably in the pub.

'That's very very cruel,' said Rosie. 'No way to treat anaminal.'

'What's anaminal?' asked George.

Rosie giggled and dragged him across the road. 'I can drive one of these y'know.'

Before he could protest she unhitched the animal and climbed into the driver's seat. George, reluctantly, got up beside her. Rosie expertly flicked the reins and the wooden-wheeled cart clattered over the cobbles. The horse, seemingly appreciative of Rosie's driving, picked up its feet and was soon trotting at a fair speed up Harehills Road. George began singing an off-key version of 'The Donkey Serenade' and tapped his leg with his pipe. Rosie joined in, lustily, and flicked the reins to give the horse encouragement. It misunderstood her signal and burst into a trot, then a canter; its iron-clad hoofs clattered and sparked against the stone cobbles. George stopped singing.

'He seems to be getting a bit giddy,' he sounded worried. 'I think you should slow him down a bit.'

'I'm trying to,' Rosie said. 'But he's not taking any notice.' She sawed desperately on the reins, but the horse had taken the bit between its teeth and had decided to have a good time.

'Is there a brake or something?' enquired George.

As he spoke, they turned the bend into Beckett Street. The cart parted company with the racing animal and careered across the road towards the police station, where it came to a halt, jammed against the door. Rosie and George scrambled out as a policeman was trying to squeeze past to have a word with them.

'Hey, you two!' he called out, angrily. 'Come back here, I want a word.'

But they were already round the corner out of sight and moving swiftly.

'Is this the sort of thing I can expect if you say yes?' enquired a breathless George.

'Don't count your chickens, George Metcalf,' giggled Rosie. 'I must say, it's been an interesting evening – what with one thing and another.'

As she lay in bed that night she considered her options, such as they were. She could either throw herself on the dubious mercy of the State or she could marry George; or she could turn him down but still accept his kind offer of help. This third option seemed a useful compromise, but only in the short term. Favours have a habit of drying up on people who rely too much on them.

It seemed there were two obstacles preventing her from saying 'yes'. First, she didn't love him. Or did she? She was definitely attracted to him, maybe that was enough. Under the circumstances beggars can't be choosers. It was the second obstacle which seemed the most insurmountable. Sex. Would George be able to satisfy her? Had his sex drive been blown away along with his leg? Was that why he'd never re-married? Her night with Sean had awakened a need. No, she could never marry a man who couldn't make her happy in bed – and there was only one way to find out. She'd give George her answer tomorrow night.

Chapter Twelve

George parked his car on the main road and walked down Rosie's street with his heart thumping. She was the only woman he'd had any deep feelings for since his wife died. She'd been about Rosie's age when it had happened and it had left him devastated; convinced he'd never feel the same about anyone ever again. And until recently that had been true. Somehow he knew this was his last chance for happiness. If she said 'yes' he'd take her straight out of this dump and find her somewhere decent until they got married. What was he thinking? He'd get her out of this dump whatever she said.

Rosie had thrown caution to the winds and greeted him in her dressing gown. Her hair was still damp from the bath she'd just had and her body was smelling of the lavender salts she'd been soaking herself in. With poor old Basil gone she had the kitchen-cum-bathroom to herself and if she lay back in the deep, iron bath and shut her eyes she could easily block out her grim surroundings and transport herself to somewhere far more salubrious. Imagination was one luxury which couldn't be taken away.

'Sorry,' she said. 'I forgot the time. Must have nodded off in the bath. By the way, how did you feel this morning?'

'Rotten.'

'Good ... so did I ... I was hoping morning sickness

couldn't get as bad as that. I'm off the drink until the baby's born.'

'Very wise,' he said. 'You smell nice.'

'Thank you.' She stepped aside to let him past. 'Age before beauty.'

Then she watched him climb the stairs to her room. It was hard to tell he had a tin leg, so adept had he become at walking on it, only displaying the faintest limp. As he entered the room her voice came from behind him.

'George, I want you to kiss me, please.'

He froze for a second then turned to see her dressing gown hanging loose and untied. He took her in his arms and kissed her gently, pushing his chest past her gown and against her naked breasts.

'I meant it when I said I love you.'

'I know you did, George.'

She removed his jacket, almost ceremonially, as a prelude to what was to come. George felt suddenly awkward and Rosie sensed the tension in his body.

'What?' she asked.

'I feel like I'm on trial.'

'Don't be silly.'

'Rosie, I'm not being silly. I know what's going on, I'm not stupid. You want to know if I'm any good in bed.'

'No, I don't . . .'

'Rosie, credit me with some intelligence. Firstly I'm old enough to be your father, and secondly I have a tin leg. Three strikes and I'm out. That's what this is all about, isn't it?'

She shrugged, he was right but she wasn't going to admit it. Was she being a slut? Or just practical?

'Do you have anything to drink?' he asked.

'Yes, of course.' Rosie fastened her dressing gown, opened the dresser drawer and took out the remaining quarter bottle of brandy.

'You must think I'm a bit of a tart. Throwing myself at you like that. I just needed to know, that's all.'

George took the bottle from her and, in the absence of a glass took a deep swig. 'No, Rosie, you're not a tart. You're a pragmatist.'

'Oh heck! That sounds even worse.'

'To you, the end always justifies the means.'

His words struck a chord with Rosie. He could have been talking about her mother. Was her marrying George the same as her mother marrying her dad? God! she hoped not.

'You make it sound like a marriage of convenience,' she commented, gloomily. 'I wouldn't want that.'

George realised he'd said the wrong thing. 'No, no – it'd be nothing like a marriage of convenience,' he said quickly. 'A marriage of convenience is a loveless marriage. Which wouldn't be the case with us. Not as far as I'm concerned, anyway.'

'Nor me,' she smiled. '*Liking* someone a lot can sometimes be better than loving them.'

'It's important to get on,' George said. 'And we get on, don't we?'

'Yes, George,' agreed Rosie. 'You and me go together like a horse and cart.'

They laughed together at the memory of last night. 'Look well if we'd been arrested for horse stealing,' grinned George. 'They used to hang horse thieves you know. It would have been a double hanging.'

'Poor start to a marriage,' said Rosie.

He looked at her, hopefully, asking the question with his eyes. Her face broke into a broad smile.

'I'd love to marry you, George.'

They embraced. He with love, she with happiness and relief.

'George,' she said. 'To get things off to a good start, do you think you could make love to me?'

'So long as I don't have to take my leg off. I think there's something very forward about taking one's leg off on the first date, don't you?'

'There's nothing else made of tin down there, is there?'

'Oh no – I had that made out of finest English oak.'

'Big oaks out of little acorns grow.'

'Not so much of the acorn, Miss Jones.'

Their lovemaking was careful and gentle and deeply satisfying for them both. George passed the test as he knew he would and Rosie lay beside him as happy as she'd ever felt in her life. He placed his hand on the bulge in her tummy and asked:

'Does anyone, apart from you, know who the father is?'

The thought had never occurred to Rosie. As far as she was concerned it was a secret between her and Sean.

'No one, not even my mam.'

'So there's no reason why the baby couldn't be mine?'

'The father is Sean Quinnan.'

'You mean the Irish lad who Brindle . . .?'

'Yes,' she cut him off. Not wanting to spoil the moment by talking about such a painful subject. Then she realised he deserved an explanation.

'It was the first time for both of us,' she said. 'He was a lot younger than me, but there was something about him that I'd never felt for a man before.'

'I know the feeling.'

She smiled and squeezed his hand and he hoped she'd say she felt the same for him. But she didn't and he accepted it. What they had was enough. They lay there, not talking for a while, not needing to; happy in each other's company.

'It's a good sign, is this,' he said at length.

'What is?'

'Being able to enjoy a comfortable silence. It's a sign of compatibility.'

'Is it? I didn't know.'

There was another long silence, then he asked, 'Do you think Sean Quinnan would mind if I stepped into his shoes?'

'Sean didn't know about the baby.'

'So, no one's to know I'm not the father?'

'I don't suppose so. There's no reason I couldn't have er . . . *known you* around the time I knew him.'

131

He placed an arm around her and hugged her to him. 'There's something else you don't know about me,' he said. 'Which is quite important if we're to get married.'

'Oh dear.'

'You know the firm I work for?'

'BJK Limited?'

'That's right. You see, I don't just work for the firm – I actually own it – well, eighty per cent of it.'

She allowed this revelation to sink in. 'So, you're quite rich, then?'

'I think the word is comfortable. But I have enough for my fiancée not to have to spend another night in this place.'

She frowned and suddenly froze away from him. 'What? You're going to sweep me up on your white horse like a knight in shining armour, is that what you had in mind?'

There was an edge to her voice that he didn't like. He needed to nip this in the bud.

'You're mad at me for having money.' He ran a fingertip down her arm.

'No, I'm not.'

'Yes, you are. You've gone all tense on me.'

She thawed a little. 'I just don't understand why you didn't tell me earlier.'

'I apologise, but two minutes ago you thought I was just another working bloke who gets his hands dirty every day. Which, incidentally, I do. My firm doesn't run itself. I used to be a site engineer. Started my own company when I was twenty-nine. Struggled for a few years, but came out the other side relatively unscathed.'

'Yes, I know, but you're the boss. You must think I'm a right money grabber. If I'd known you were the boss I'd ...'

'You'd have what? Thought twice about going out with me in case I thought you were just a gold-digger? That's precisely why I didn't mention it.'

'So you thought I might be capable of a bit of gold-digging, did you?'

'I wanted to know I had enough going for me without me having money.'

'So, you were testing me?'

'Pot calling kettle black?' he countered.

'It's not the same.'

'Oh, yes it is.' George leaned up on one elbow and stared down at her. 'Are we still on then?'

'Course we're still on. I'm not as shallow as that, you know.'

'Never thought you were for a minute.'

'Mr Metcalf . . .?'

'That's me.'

'Do you have any other surprises for me?'

He lay back and looked up at the cracked ceiling. 'Well, I have a daughter about the same age as you.'

'A daughter? How come you never mentioned her before?'

'Oh, I don't know. Maybe it's because I don't look upon her as a daughter any more. We're sort of estranged.'

She knew that he'd once been married and that his wife had died. But he hadn't mentioned a daughter. He seemed miles away, still staring at the ceiling.

'God, she was so small when she arrived. I never thought I could love anything so much.'

'What about your wife? You must have loved her.'

'Yes I did. I loved her very much. But the love you have for a child is different. They're so helpless and beautiful and totally dependent upon you. There's a magnificence to it that can't be explained, only experienced.' He placed his hand on her tummy. 'You've got all that to come.'

Rosie smiled and knitted her fingers over his hand. These were the first positive words she'd heard about her pregnancy.

'What happened to her?'

'To Barbara?' George gave a quick, dry laugh. 'I went off to university when she was three years old, that's what happened to her. I figured I'd missed out on my education,

133

what with the war and my leg and my wife dying. I needed to do something with my life. I was working in a dead end job and one day I decided I wanted to be a civil engineer.'

'Why a civil engineer?'

George smiled. 'Daftest reason in the world really. Apparently I have a very distant ancestor who had an even worse disability than mine. He became a famous road engineer. Jack Metcalf – or Blind Jack of Knareborough as he was better known.'

Rosie thought for a second, then said, 'Hence the BJK?'

'Precisely.'

Rosie said, 'I haven't got any famous relatives. In fact I haven't got any relatives worth that,' she snapped her fingers. 'They say you should always follow your dreams ... trouble is, I don't know what my dreams are.'

'I think I know what my dreams are,' he said, hugging her to him.

'Tell me about your daughter.'

The contented smile left his face for a second. 'As far as being a father's concerned,' he began, 'going to university, then starting a business was the worst move I ever made. During all this time my mother looked after Barbara – spoiled her rotten.'

'And did she stay spoiled?'

'She was okay until she was about nine or ten, then she went off me. I thought it was just a phase. If it was, she never came out of it.'

'Where is she now?'

'Oh, she got married and went off to live with her husband in Australia. She sends me the occasional Christmas card.'

'And will I be acquiring any instant grandchildren?'

'Not that I know of. I've often wondered if she's too selfish to have children.'

'Good grief! You *have* got a low opinion of her.'

George gave a small laugh and shrugged. 'Rosie, she's the biggest pain in the arse you're ever likely to come across.'

'And how old is my future step-daughter?'

'Twenty-five.'

'But you once loved her more than anything in the world.'

'Oh, I probably still do. But that doesn't stop her being a pain in the arse. She's not a wicked woman, she's just very self-centred but doesn't realise it. I suspect she'd be mortified if she knew what I think about her. I don't really blame her. It's just the way she turned out.'

Rosie kissed him on the lips. 'I want to get married as soon as possible and I'm going to tell everybody it's because you're a dirty old man who got me into trouble and you want to make an honest woman of me.'

'Sounds about right.'

'Oh, and by the way, I'm pleased to inform you that you passed your physical with flying colours.'

'Maybe you'd better check me out again, just to make sure.'

'Yes, but not in this dump,' said Rosie. 'If you absolutely insist on making me a wealthy woman, I may as well make a start right now.'

Chapter Thirteen

To add as much respectability to their relationship as they could muster, Rosie had moved into a small hotel rather than straight into George's house. She had given up her job at Marsden's and was shamelessly enjoying the luxury of being a 'kept woman'. The wedding was due to take place in a month.

A lavish ceremony suited neither of them, they were both agreed on that. The age discrepancy and the obvious third party preceding Rosie down the aisle would be a gossip-monger's dream. They settled for the Register Office in Park Square and a small, but select reception at the Lakeside Hotel. Just people they actually liked, no matter who took offence at not being invited.

'It's our day, not theirs,' said George. 'Will you want a bridesmaid or anything?'

'I'll invite Susan Clarkson to be maid-of-honour.'

'I'll ask my nephew to be best man. Then Susan won't feel out of place.'

'I think Susan would like that – especially if he's anything like you.'

He smiled, then grew serious. 'I'll have to go through the motions and invite Barbara and her husband.'

'Would she come all that way?'

'Doubt if I'll even get a card.'

'In that case I suppose I'd better go through the motions and invite Mam.'

The train journey back from Birmingham gave Ethel time for contemplation. It had been a difficult afternoon. Some might say disastrous. She was looking through her handbag and took out the wedding invitation from one of the pockets where she'd stuck it with barely a glance when it first arrived.

Her time with Sidney in Birmingham had been a daft adventure. It had happened at the time of most women's lives when they're looking forward to nothing; just old age, infirmity and in her case, loneliness. He'd been transferred to the Midlands and had suggested she go with him – and on a whim she'd agreed. Sidney had been the spark that had set her alight once again; after her endurance of the war, her ill health and her daughter. Even the job she'd got in Birmingham had livened up her dull life. It was only as a dress-shop assistant but it made her feel part of the world once again. Had her migraine not felled her that morning she'd have been none the wiser. The boss had insisted she go home.

Sidney was not only in bed with another woman, but going at it with such gusto that neither he nor his moaning floozy were aware of her standing over them until it was all over. Then Sidney came out with the classic line:

'Ethel! er . . . It's not what it looks.'

'Really? Well, it looked for all the world as if you were banging the arse off her.'

The girl was at least twenty years younger than Ethel and annoyingly pretty.

'Sidney and me are old friends,' explained the girl, in a thick Brummie accent.

Ethel said, 'How nice for you both.' Then, suddenly defeated, added, 'I'd better pack my stuff.'

They watched from behind the bedclothes; their eyes following her as she angrily packed her suitcase. Ethel didn't know which was worse, her sadness, her anger or her embarrassment. Sidney's wallet was on the dressing table, stuffed with notes. She stood between it and him, shielding it from his view, then stuck it in the case. It was something. It would be nice to think the girl was expecting payment for her services.

The most annoying part about all this was that she wouldn't be able to move back into Duck Street for a while. Not until she'd given proper notice to her tenants. Maybe Marlene Gedge would put her up; she'd got on better with Marlene since Tommy died. Perhaps it was because it put them on equal footing. Marlene's husband had long since done a bunk.

Rosie had been right about Sidney all along. What was it she'd called him? Sidney the Slug – sounds about right. It'd do no harm to make things up with Rosie, especially now she was getting married.

As the train clanked into Leeds City Station the clock on the Parish Church said six-thirty. Ethel put the wedding invitation back in her handbag. There'd been no accompanying letter as a mother had a right to expect. At best she'd be just a guest.

You are cordially invited to the wedding of George Vincent Metcalf and Rosemary Anne Jones at the Leeds Register Office on the 8th March 1948. And afterwards at the Lakeside Hotel.
R.S.V.P.

Ten thousand miles away, in Australia, Barbara Hawkins was turning the envelope over in her hands, puzzling as to its sender. It was postmarked England but she didn't recognise the writing. Rosie had addressed all the wedding invitations. Barbara gave up guessing and ripped it open. Her lip curled visibly as she read the card. This was the first she'd heard of Rosemary Jones; probably some ancient, dried up crone who had taken pity on her dad in his dotage. Maybe she had money. That would be good, it would add to Barbara's inheritance. She left the accompanying letter unread on the kitchen table and went into the garden to enjoy the Sydney sunshine. Her husband was the first to read it when he came in from work.

'The old dog! I thought you said he was past it.'

'Past what?'

'Past *you know what*. I don't want to sound rotten but she must be marrying him for his money.'

'Paul, what the hell are you talking about?'

'Your dad, marrying this twenty-two-year-old bird.' He looked at his wife, despairingly. 'You haven't read the letter, have you?'

Barbara snatched it from him and sat down. Her eyes angrily scanned the first page, and threw it on the floor as she read page two, where her father had casually mentioned Rosie's age, 'She's only twenty-two but what does age matter? I love her dearly.'

'The gold-digging little whore!'

'Steady on, Babs. You haven't even met her.'

'No, but I soon will, and don't call me Babs!'

'Barbara, I'm not sure we can afford a trip to England right now. Besides I've only just been given my new department and I'm not sure I'd get the time . . .'

'You won't be going! I can handle this myself – and I'm not paying, Dad is.'

She arrived two days before the ceremony and ensconced herself in her old bedroom as if she'd never been away. At first she made no mention of Rosie; her plan had been formulated on *The Empress of India* on the way over. George had volunteered to pay for her passage when he'd heard she was coming alone. A return passage for two would have been stretching his pockets.

Barbara was aware that she looked older than her twenty-five years; but for once she didn't mind. It would help to accentuate the ridiculous age discrepancy between her father and this young flighty piece. For this purpose she wore no make-up for her first meeting. She held out her hand as Rosie walked, nervously into the room.

'Ah, so you must be my future step-mother.'

The amusement in her voice didn't extend to her eyes. Rosie was pretty in an unrefined sort of way but she was larger than Barbara had expected, lumpy almost. They made to kiss cheeks and missed the respective targets by several inches.

'Pleased to meet you.' Rosie's tone was cordial but not over-friendly. She knew George loved this woman and therefore accorded her appropriate respect. 'I've heard a lot about you.'

'I dread to think what that might be.' Barbara spoke through a fixed smile, like a ventriloquist's dummy.

'Now then, Barbara,' said George. 'I wouldn't say anything bad about you. Not to your face anyway.' He said it with a grin, then added, mischievously, 'Anyway, I was rather hoping you might have presented me with a grand-child by now.'

Her reply was curt, 'We haven't started planning a family yet.'

Rosie got the impression that children were the last thing on her agenda. She patted her stomach. 'We have,' she said.

Barbara's jaw fell. 'What?'

George hadn't told her. He thought it would be easier to let it drop out into the conversation. 'You're pregnant?'

'I thought it might be obvious.'

'I thought you were just . . .'

'Fat? Well, I am a bit on the plump side, but not this fat. My . . .' she looked at George. '*Our* baby's due in two months.'

There was a long silence as Barbara built up a head of steam. She turned her back on Rosie and stood almost nose to nose with her father.

'Bloody hell, Dad! I wondered why you were getting married. I mean . . . what the hell are you thinking of? You can't marry her just because she's pregnant. You've got money, just pay her off.'

Rosie stared from father to daughter, her anger barely

140

contained. George's mind was racing for the words that would save the situation, but there were none. Rosie had stormed from the room before he found his voice.

'Good grief, Barbara! That was a rotten thing to say.'

Barbara was defeated. All her careful planning had been knocked away by this unborn sibling. It was a hurdle too big for her to surmount. The baby would be just too much of a rival for her. The argument she'd had with her dad after Rosie had left hadn't been according to plan either. She ended up placating him; apologising even. They'd never been close, but he was the only father she had. She'd never grow to accept Rosie. That would be too much of a compromise.

'You don't have to accept her,' said George. 'You live ten thousand miles away and rarely keep in touch. To be frank, Barbara, you have no right even to voice an opinion about her.'

'If I had a right to an opinion I'd say she was far too young for you.'

'The thought had occurred to me, but it's not a problem to either of us.'

'Not yet.'

George shrugged. 'You can't have everything. We'll both be taking what we can out of this marriage.'

He offered his daughter a cigarette. A token of peace. She accepted his light and blew out a stream of smoke that just missed his head. Rosie had to be a gold-digger, why else would she want to marry a wealthy, one-legged man more than twice her age? There was no advantage in pursuing the point, so she settled for an amnesty. 'Maybe I resent you loving someone other than the mother I never knew.'

Her father smiled at this. 'I've only ever loved four women in my life. My mother, your mother, Rosie . . .' He placed a hand on each of her shoulders, before adding, '. . . and you.'

He waited for her to respond. For her to tell him she

loved him would be a first. Even as a child she'd never said those three words, not to him anyway. Maybe it was too much to expect. She stubbed her half-smoked cigarette out in an ashtray and glanced in a mirror.

'I'm supposed to be giving these damn things up. God! I look a sight. I think I'd better put some war paint on.'

He watched her leave the room and sighed as she clumped up the stairs. Anger in every step.

The wedding passed without incident. Just three frozen smiles amongst an otherwise happy and approving congregation; in ascending order of treachery: Ethel, Barbara and Ernie Scrimshaw.

Barney and his wife had been invited but they didn't turn up. He told Rosie that his wife hadn't been feeling well. But he didn't sound convincing.

Chapter Fourteen

George was already fuming when Ernie walked in to his office in answer to his urgent summons. It was George's first day back at work since his Italian honeymoon. His life had taken a turn for the better. He and Rosie had laughed and loved for every second of the three weeks they'd been away. But when life's good there's always an Ernie to spoil it. Ernie Scrimshaw had been with him for five years; recruited at a time when most of the half-decent able-bodied men were otherwise engaged. It had been a big mistake to allow him to buy into his company. At the time, Ernie's money had come in handy. George had been stuck with a bad debt and the bank had been on his back. Taking Ernie's money seemed a reasonable thing to do. He had a degree in civil engineering and had spent twenty years working for various local authorities, ending up in quite a high position. What Ernie hadn't mentioned was all the promotions he'd been given were to get him off various people's backs. In local government it was possible for a gross incompetent to be promoted way up the ladder.

'Ernie, I want you to tell me I'm wrong.' George held up a thick file and fixed his junior partner with a despairing glare. 'I want you to tell me this isn't the real Parkside Road tender and that you've already submitted another copy and that we haven't missed the submission date of a tender I've been working on for three months.'

'Oh damn!' said Ernie, snapping his fingers in mild self-rebuke. He was a large, inadequate, moon-faced man with thinning hair and floppy chin. Late forties, divorced with no children and poor prospects of remarrying. Men like Ernie rarely got a second chance.

George buried his head in his hands. 'I don't believe it. I don't believe anyone could be that stupid. It was the last thing I told you before I went away.'

'You hadn't finished it,' said Ernie, lamely.

'Of course I'd finished it!' roared George. 'I asked you to check the figures and countersign it. I specifically asked you to take it personally to the council offices and not trust the post.'

'Maybe it's n-not too late,' said Ernie, feebly. 'Maybe they haven't opened the tenders yet.'

'You moron! They'll have opened them five bloody minutes after the submission time expired. The job'll have been let by now!' George rubbed at an ache in his thigh. The English chill contrasted greatly with the weather he'd just left, exposing his damaged limb to aches and pains. This didn't improve his humour. 'I could fire you, Ernie, and just send you your share of the profits once a year. In fact, in the interests of the company I ought to do that. If you were any more stupid I'd have to water you twice a bloody week!'

Ernie reddened. Mrs Drysdale, George's secretary, would be able to hear what was going on and God knows who else.

'I'm putting you in charge of site supply!' George thundered. 'If you make a mess of that you can look for a job outside the firm.'

This was a menial office job, taking orders from site and relaying them to the suppliers.

'Yer can't do that ter me!'

'I just have.'

Ernie tried to think of a good argument but he couldn't. All he could come up with was a petulant, 'I won't do it.'

'Fair enough, I've told you what the alternative is.'

Ernie stamped out of the office, unsure of what to do. He'd always been jealous of George's general superiority; his major share-holding, his business acumen and greater intelligence. Ernie had a superior number of legs, but that was all. Not submitting the tender had been a simple mistake. He'd stuck it in a drawer and had forgotten about it. A mistake which anyone could have made. That was the defining moment. The moment when he actually began to hate George. As he walked across the yard he was struck by an idea which would benefit him more than BJK. Spinning on his heels, he went back into the office.

'I'll take yer poxy job,' he said, then walked out.

Had baby Edward George Metcalf hung about for another few weeks he could have been born courtesy of the new National Health Service designed to take care of him from the cradle to the grave. As it was, he first saw the light of day in the Oakwood Grange Nursing home. George had paced up and down the waiting room in the traditional manner; then on hearing the news he had handed out cigars to all and sundry and no one suspected that he was not the proper father.

All in all, as marriages go, and under the circumstances, Rosie and George were doing okay. Their home was a world away from Duck Street, much less Royd's Road. Oak House was a five-bedroomed, stone-built, Victorian house in half an acre of garden. It was more than Rosie had ever dared dream about. George had bought it just a few years after he'd started his business; hoping it might one day provide a home for the wife who would become a mother to Barbara. But it was never to be.

On warm evenings Rosie would sit on a seat beneath the oak tree, after which the house was named, and read Enid Blyton and Rupert Bear books to little Eddie who was too young to understand much, but enjoyed the sound of his mother's voice. The scent of roses and new mown grass softened the memory of the time she'd sweated out her fever in that foul little room in Royd's Road. There was a pond and a fountain with a stone boy peeing in the air, which always made Eddie laugh. Then he would fall asleep and she'd put the book down and just sit with him in her arms; her contentment unmatched by anything she'd ever known. The calm of the evening would be disturbed only by the singing of birds whose songs she couldn't identify, or felt the need to. Duck Street was only ever visited by starlings, sparrows and pigeons – back street birds – squawkers and twitterers rather than whistlers and warblers. The difference in birdsong seemed to epitomise her change in circumstances. Sometimes she'd sit there for hours and George knew not to disturb her. It was her quiet time.

Once she'd thought about anonymously returning the nine pounds she'd stolen from Lazarus and then she remembered what a miserable pig he was. Instead she went to St Augustine's church, bought every candle in the Lady Chapel and lit them all in the hope they might buy Basil out of Purgatory so that he could join his son who could sing like a bloody angel.

She'd grown to love George; even if she didn't enjoy that deep, searing passion many women search for, but only the lucky few actually find.

If this made her life less than perfect, her actual lifestyle was idyllic by anyone's standards. They holidayed in Italy and France and Scotland; she had her own car and a husband who doted on her. Her own parents had settled for much less.

Edward George had, by mutual agreement, become Eddie. George's fatherhood was never mentioned, not even between the two of them. As far as the world was concerned, George was Eddie's natural dad. Although young Eddie had his real father's eyes, which was enough to keep Sean in Rosie's mind if not in her heart; and the boy was a constant reminder of her hatred for Brindle.

146

No more children had arrived, despite their best efforts. Rosie assumed it was George's age and she made no comment. All they could do was keep trying. Much of her time was spent going round the sites with her husband, learning the business so she could have intelligent discussions with him. George was pleasantly surprised at the interest and aptitude she showed and he spent many evenings teaching her about engineering and surveying and the tricks of the trade, many of which weren't taught in any books. Rosie proved to be a willing and able pupil.

If there was a blot on her horizon it was the continued existence of Joe Brindle, who was in the same business as her husband, so his name kept cropping up. To Rosie he would always be the man who murdered the father of her son, and George was patently aware of this.

When Brindle snatched the Boswell Court Nursing Home from under their noses it was more of an irritation to her than it was to George. BJK Ltd had moved into contract building to add to their road and sewer work. It was an obvious progression now that Barney Robinson had come to join them – at Rosie's behest.

They'd cut prices to the bone to get the Boswell Court job, if only for the prestige it would bring. How Brindle, who wasn't interested in prestige, could have come in exactly one per cent under their price was a mystery to George. But not to Ernie.

Brindle had already signed the contract forms before he had his prices checked by a quantity surveyor. He was banking on the fact that George Metcalf knew what he was doing and that the prices smuggled out by Ernie would show a fair profit. He didn't mind slicing one per cent off, he could soon get that back by cutting corners. On a building site there were plenty of corners to cut and it made it so much easier when the building inspector was in your pocket.

When the costings came back from the quantity surveyor, Brindle hammered a furious fist through the plasterboard wall of his office and sent out a summons for Ernie to come round to see him. He grabbed the hapless man by the scruff of his neck as he came through the door.

'What're yer bloody playin' at, Ernie?' He waved the contract under Ernie's nose. 'I've just had these prices checked. I'll be lucky ter bloody break even.'

'Hey! Don't go blamin' me. You asked me ter show yer our prices and I did. I'd no idea what our profit margins were.'

'Profit margin? What profit margin?' snarled Brindle. 'Your firm went in at cost.'

Ernie flinched and took a step back. 'I know, I heard George mention it this morning.'

Brindle had him by the throat again. 'This mornin'? What did he say?'

'Gerroff, yer mad bugger, yer chokin' me, Joe!'

Joe let him go and stood back. 'Just tell me what were said.'

Ernie rubbed his neck and drew his brows together as he collected his confused thoughts. There was a note of petulance in his voice, 'Metcalf were disappointed not to have got it, but he couldn't understand how anyone, especially you, could have gone in under him. He wanted it to be a bit of a show piece with it being on the main road.'

'Show piece? How'd yer mean, show piece?'

'Well,' explained Ernie, 'he was going ter put a massive advertising board out so everyone driving past could see it. Put BJK on the map, like. He went in at cost ter make sure he got it.'

'And he only told you that today?'

'He never tells me nowt. I heard him telling Barney Robinson.'

Brindle nodded. Ernie's explanation made sense to him, even if he didn't share George's attitude toward business.

'Well, I've signed the contract. I can't back out of it now or it'll cost me an arm an' a bloody leg in penalties. We'll just have ter keep our costs down.'

'What about me, er, me fee?'

'Yer what? Yer set me up ter do six months work for bugger all an' you expect ter be paid? Do I look silly?'

'It's what was agreed,' grumbled Ernie. 'I'll do nowt more fer yer.'

Brindle had hold of him again. Oozing menace. 'You'll do as yer told or Hopalong bloody Cassidy'll find out more about you than yer'd like him ter know.'

'What're yer talkin' about?'

'I'm talkin' about you ordering materials on BJK's accounts an' having 'em dropped off on sites what's got nowt ter do wi' BJK. An' you pocketing a load o' cash – that's what I'm talkin' about.'

Ernie paled. He didn't think anyone knew about this.

'How much have yer fiddled out of him?' enquired Brindle, scornfully. 'Hundreds, thousands?'

'Nowt I'm not entitled to. He treats me like shit.'

'Oh dear, I wonder why?' Brindle pushed him away. 'On the other hand, if this is the sort of information yer gonna bring me, I can't see yer being any use ter me, neither.'

Rosie had called on site to drop off some plans and save George a journey. It was a remark by Barney Robinson that set her mind whirring.

'I reckon Brindle's kickin' himself for coming under our price on the Boswell Court job.'

'Surely he had the same idea as George,' she said. 'Go in at cost and do it as a prestige job.'

The very idea made Barney laugh outloud. 'Prestige? Brindle? Rosie, love, Joe Brindle wouldn't know prestige if it kicked him up the jacksie. I reckon he just made a cock-up with his pricing. Knowin' Brindle, he'll be cuttin' corners. No way will he lose money on a job if he can help it.'

'Cutting corners? That's interesting. You will tell me if you hear anything definite?'

Barney gave her a grin. 'You'll be the first to know.'

*

He picked up his first tit-bit in The Wellie where one of Brindle's Irish ground-workers called in for a pint after work.

'Finished the foundations?' asked Barney, innocently.

'Finished a week ago. We'll have the footings up ter damp-course level by this weekend.'

'By heck! He's a right slave driver, your gaffer,' said Barney. 'Are you making it pay?'

'Ah we're on good money right enough. But he's the feller what's making it pay.'

'How d'yer mean?'

The Irishman grinned. 'Well, I nivver knowed a feller want a bag o' cement ter go as far as Brindle. He's a mean man wid the cement.'

'Oh, he's allus been a bit careful. Can I get you a drink?'

The man needed no second asking.

'So,' said Barney. 'I suppose the concrete's up to strength. He wouldn't get away with it otherwise.'

The Irishman grinned again and looked sideways at Barney. 'I seen Yorkshire Puddings made out of a stronger mix than we're usin'.'

'Bloody hell! How's he gettin' away with that?'

The man laughed. 'How d'yer tink? I reckon the buildin' inspector's on better money than we are.'

Barney laughed along with him. 'Hey! Tell me summat I don't know. He was giving 'em back-handers when I was with him. Still, good luck to him, that's what I say.' Taking a pint of bitter from the barman, he handed it to his new friend. 'Is the building inspector taking concrete samples for testing, then?' He gave the Irishman a knowing wink which brought a grin to the man's grizzled face.

'I don't know what he's sendin' away fer testing, but it never came out of our trenches.'

'Is that right?' said Barney. 'The crafty beggar.'

'I'll tell yer something else as well.' The Irishman held the back of a confidential hand to his mouth. 'He's putting class B engineering bricks in the footings. The brickie reckons they should be class A. I tell yer, yer man'll be in some kind o' trouble if anyone ever found out.'

'Still,' said Barney. 'Couple o' weeks an' you'll be flyin'. No one ever goes back to check what's under the ground. Not if it's been passed by the building inspector.'

Rosie didn't ring the council straight away. The higher the building the deeper the hole; and Brindle was digging himself in deep. The job was almost complete before she made the call.

'I wish to speak to whoever's in charge of your building inspectors.'

'That'll be Mr Evans, the senior inspector. Can I say who's calling?'

'My name is Metcalf.'

'From ...?'

'BJK Ltd.'

'Hold the line, please.'

A gruff voice said, 'Building Inspectors – Evans speaking.'

'Hello, Mr Evans. I was just checking that you've heard the nasty rumour about the building inspector on the Boswell Court site who's been taking money from Mr Brindle,' she said, cheerfully.

There was a long silence as this revelation was digested. 'Who did you say you were?'

'My name is Metcalf, from BJK Ltd.'

He knew who she was. 'Er, this is a serious accusation, Mrs Metcalf.'

'Oh, it's not an accusation. I'm just relaying a very strong rumour. I felt it was my public duty.'

'Do you have any, er ... any proof of this?'

'None at all, Mr Evans. Why don't you send someone out to inspect the type of bricks used in the footings and re-check the strength of the concrete foundations and check the cement content in the mortar – that sort of stuff. Would you object if I rang the papers?'

He sounded horror struck. 'Papers? You mean *newspapers*?'

'*Daily Mirror*, that sort of thing. I thought it'd make a good read. People like a good read nowadays.'

'I'd prefer it if you didn't. At least until we've checked.'

'Fair enough. We all have to work together, don't we? Tell you one thing, Mr Evans.'

'What's that?'

She was really enjoying this. 'Sometimes it's a mistake to take the lowest tender.'

'I'll, er . . . I'll send someone out straight away.'

Rosie put the phone down as George came into the office. 'Who was that?' he asked.

'It was me shopping Joe Brindle to the council.'

It was the first George knew about it, but she never told him lies. She now told him all she knew. 'Sorry, love,' she concluded. 'It's something I needed to get out of my system. I'll never forgive Brindle for what he did.'

He looked at her, reproachfully. 'You still look upon Sean as Eddie's father, don't you? That's what you can't get out of your system.'

'It's not like that . . . George, please don't be annoyed with me.'

'Look, Rosie, this thing you have against Brindle. It's all to do with Eddie's real father. Have you any idea how that makes me feel? It's impossible for me to feel I'm Eddie's real dad while all this is going on.'

'I'm sorry, George . . . I didn't know. Perhaps you should have said . . .'

He interrupted her and snapped, 'I shouldn't have needed to.' Then he turned to go, adding, 'If you've got your facts wrong, you'll have seriously damaged this company's credibility with the council!'

His chastened wife looked at the angrily slammed door and she knew he was right. She should have checked with him, checked her facts, and done nothing without his agreement. Rosie had to work at her marriage to George, but

152

sometimes she fell down on the job. Sometimes she just didn't think. After a brief period of self-recrimination she picked up the phone and rang Barney on site.

'I've shopped Brindle to the council.'

'Does George know?'

'He does now, and he's not too pleased.'

'I can imagine.'

'Can you? Maybe you should have warned me.'

'Rosie, you've got a mind of your own. You shouldn't need telling.'

'That's more or less what George said. Anyway, what's done's done.' There was a silence as a disturbing thought crossed her mind. 'Barney,' she asked. 'How sure are you that Brindle was doing all those things?'

'It's like I said, Rosie. I was only telling you what one of his lads was telling me.'

'Supposing this bloke was wrong?'

'Rosie, after what you've just done, it doesn't bear thinking about.'

She sighed. 'Oh heck! We might have done a lot of damage. Maybe we should have made absolutely certain of our facts.'

'Rosie, what's all this "we" business?'

'Don't worry,' she assured him. 'If things go wrong, I'll keep your name out of it.'

'That's good of you.'

'There's one way to find out,' she decided. 'I'll ring Brindle.'

'Rosie . . .!' shouted Barney.

But she'd put the phone down.

Joe Brindle was on his way out of his office when the phone rang. He cursed. In two minds whether to answer it. His secretary-cum-dogsbody was out of the office for some reason or other, and he was late for a site meeting to agree a final account for the Boswell Court contract. Sod's law. It would only be important if he didn't answer it. He stepped

153

back into the room, snatched up the phone and growled: 'Whatever it is, be quick. I'm in a rush.'

'Mr Brindle?'

'Who are you?'

'Rosie Metcalf. I'm ringing on behalf of the late Sean Quinnan. You do remember Sean Quinnan, don't you, Mr Brindle? Just to refresh your memory, he's the young man you murdered three years ago.'

'It's Rosie Jones, innit?' he sneered. 'Once a slag allus a slag.'

She ignored this. 'I just thought you might be interested to know that the council have found out all about the corners you've been cutting on the Boswell Court site and they're on their way out to check the foundations as we speak.'

Rosie could hear him choking on the other end of the line. She pressed on, 'If the concrete's the wrong strength or the bricks and mortar of an inferior quality I'm afraid the whole building will have to come down. Oh, and do you want to warn the building inspector of his imminent arrest or shall I? . . . Mr Brindle, are you there?'

The phone had dropped from his lifeless grip, no blood was left in his face. This phone call spelt his total ruination. Had she not mentioned Sean Quinnan he might have thought it was some sort of cheap hoax. But he knew that this woman, this poisonous bitch carried a grudge against him for Sean's death. He couldn't get his breath. Brindle collapsed, choking in a chair. Rosie could hear him gasping. She called down the phone, 'Mr Brindle?'

Someone come into his office room. There was a rustling sound as his secretary put a paper bag to his mouth to stop him hyperventilating. The woman's voice came on the phone. 'Hello?' she said. 'Who is this?'

'I was speaking to Mr Brindle.'

'Well, I don't know what you've said to him, but I think you've said enough. He's not able to come to the phone right now.'

'Oh, I am sorry,' said Rosie. All doubt had now been dispelled by Brindle's reaction. She sat back and breathed a long sigh of relief, then rang Barney again. 'We're in the clear – I've just rung Brindle and he seemed quite upset.'

'I suppose that's a relief for us both.'

'I feel bad about upsetting George, though. Sometimes I think he deserves better than me.'

Barney didn't trust himself to comment on this. 'I expect you feel a bit better though,' he said. 'Dropping Brindle in it like that. You realise he'll do time for it, don't you?'

'I did it for Sean. Brindle needs punishing for what he did to Sean.'

Barney asked, 'Is it enough?'

'Not really. Still, it's over now.'

'What are you going to do about George?'

'He never stays mad at me for long.'

'Now why doesn't that surprise me?'

Chapter Fifteen

'I'm sorry, George.'

'I should think you are.'

'Are you still mad at me?'

'Rosie, you're impetuous. Impetuosity tends to leave you when you get to my age. You learn to tread more carefully when you get older.'

'Sounds boring.'

'It is boring – but it's also a lot safer. There comes a time when getting into trouble is, well ... too much trouble.'

'George, I've been impetuous again.'

'Rosie, what have you done now? And how much is it going to cost me?'

'Depends. I've paid for the flight – but you'll have to stump up for the rest of it. You're taking me to Paris so you can forgive me properly.'

'Paris? How long for?'

'Just a few days.'

'How many's a few?'

'Seven.'

'I can't afford to take the time off.'

'Yes, you can, I've organised things for you. If there's one thing I've learned from you, George, it's the art of delegation.'

'Delegation?'

'Delegation. My mam's looking after Eddie.'

'You know, Paris is expensive.'

'It is where we're going.'

'When do we go?'

'Your suitcase is packed. The taxi'll be here shortly.'

'Have I got time for a shave?'

'You've got twenty minutes.'

'Rosie . . . promise me I'll never have to forgive you for anything really bad. I don't think I could afford it.'

'George, you're supposed to keep your face still.'

'I'm having a job sitting on this chair with the amount of brandy you've poured into me.'

The artist held a vertical pencil out at arm's length, then turned it horizontal as he compared the width of George's head against the length of his nose. An accordionist played *Plaisir D'Amour* and a fat waitress at the pavement café began singing in a plaintive voice, totally at odds with her appearance. The setting sun reflected off the white dome of the Sacre Coeur, just visible through the cobbled streets. They were in Montmartre and were having a magical time.

Rosie looked at George and smiled; wondering if their relationship would have been as easy had she truly loved him. True love, as they say, never runs smooth. Unlike their marriage.

'She's been plying me with drink,' George said to the ancient artist, who wore a beret and black-and-white hooped shirt. All he needed to complete the picture was a string of onions around his neck. 'I think she has designs on my body. She's a very naughty lady.'

The artist, who didn't speak a word of English, smiled benevolently.

Rosie called out, 'George, will you be forgiving me again tonight?'

'Young lady, I forgave you twice last night. I'm not a machine, you know.'

157

The artist held up the finished drawing to show them both. Rosie exploded into fits of giggles. George angled his head appreciatively.

'Take no notice of my wife, she's a Philistine. I think it's very good.'

'It's Errol Flynn!' said Rosie. 'I bet he makes all the men look like Errol Flynn, so they won't grumble.'

The artist recognised the name Errol Flynn and looked guilty. He was banking on the drink clouding George's judgement.

'That's not Errol Flynn – Errol Flynn's got a tash,' said George. 'I happen to think it's a very good likeness.'

Rosie took a stick of charcoal from the artist's box and drew a moustache on to George's portrait. Twinkling eyes and dashing smile, it was Errol Flynn at his most handsome. George examined it carefully.

'Apart from the tash,' he decided, 'it's the dead spit of me. Now I'll have to grow one, so I look like my picture.'

Rosie took his hand and squeezed it. 'Don't you dare change anything, George Metcalf.'

'You're right, of course,' he said. 'You can't improve on perfection.'

'I might improve the shape of your nose, if you keep talking like that.'

'Stop it, woman! You're getting me over-excited.'

'You know I love you, don't you, George?'

'I know you do your best, and that's all I can ever hope for.'

Chapter Sixteen

27 July 1952

Rosie shrugged her dressing gown to the bedroom carpet and glanced, critically at herself in the cheval mirror. Little Eddie was four years old now and she still hadn't got back to her original weight. George walked in from the bathroom and stood behind her.

'You're determined to make me late for work, you shameless hussy. Put some clothes on and get me my breakfast before I fling you onto the bed and have my way with you.'

She drew her stomach in. 'Do you think I'm fat?'

'I think you're my ideal woman and I wouldn't want there to be any less of you.' The sight of his naked wife, posing seductively in front of him ignited a desire that surprised and pleased him. Considering what they'd been up to only half an hour ago. 'Please put some clothes on, woman. You're disturbing Jimmy and the twins.'

Rosie grinned and reached out a hand to caress the restless trio. 'I think you should bring them out to play before you go to work.'

'They've already had their morning recreation. They must learn to live in the real world like the rest of us.'

Rosie pulled him on to the bed. 'You know what they say about all work and no play.'

'All right, you insatiable woman. I can give you three minutes, no longer.'

'That long, eh? This could be a personal best for you.'

Twenty minutes later, George released a satisfied sigh and closed his eyes, blotting out the sight of his naked wife sitting astride him, still moving slowly up and down as she brought their energetic love making to a gentle conclusion. She was heavier than she'd been on their wedding day, but George could see nothing but beauty in her. The more of her the better as far as he was concerned.

Rosie eased herself slowly off him and switched on the bedside radio in time to catch a news bulletin about Eva Peron dying of cancer at the age of thirty-three.

'Thirty-three,' she said. 'My God, that's no age.'

George nodded. 'Her old man'll be gutted. He thought the world of her.'

'Would you be gutted if anything happened to me?' she teased, leaning over him.

'Gutted wouldn't cover it. I think I'd jump under a bus if anything happened to you.'

'You mustn't talk like that. You'd have to look after Eddie.'

'Just make sure you take good care of yourself, Mrs Metcalf.' He swung his tin leg off the bed. 'Can I go now, please?'

'I'll come with you,' she said. 'I can drop Eddie off at the nursery school on the way.'

George looked at the clock which was showing ten-past-eight. 'The nursery doesn't open till nine, I should be on site now. Sam's off sick, so I'm doing the setting out down at Oakenshawe Fields.'

'I'll drop Eddie off and follow you down. In fact I'll do the setting-out if you like.'

George laughed, 'I might just hold you to that, then I can get on with something more useful. There's a tender to drop off at Harrogate.'

'Couldn't Ernie do that?'

Her husband gave her a look that said it all.

'Sorry, daft question,' she said.

*

160

George was whistling as he drove on to the site. In the distance, a tractor and scraper were cutting away the topsoil from the field and depositing it in heaps to be used later for landscaping. Below the topsoil, the clay would then be cut down to the formation level of the new road they were building to connect Oakenshawe Fields Reservoir with the main road. He parked beside a gang of men who were off-loading concrete kerbs from a wagon.

'Where are the setting-out pins?' he enquired of Barney, who approached him. 'Sam's off sick today, I'll set the kerb-line out for you.'

'Rather you than Ernie,' said Barney. 'At least yer'll get it right.'

'So, you don't fancy having Ernie set out for you?'

'I do not. He keeps callin' on site an' pokin' his nose in. I wish he'd stick ter what he knows.'

'And what's that?' grinned George, adding, 'Don't answer that, Barney. I might have to sack you for in-subordination.'

'I think he's a bit put out that Rosie can set out an' he can't. The lads reckon she's a better engineer than Sam.'

'I wouldn't say that,' grinned George, happy at the compliment being paid to Rosie. 'There's a bit more to being an engineer than setting out a line of kerbs.'

Ernie had had a heavy night, which wasn't unusual for him. He was in the office, slurping a mug of tea whilst trying to focus on a letter attached to a Yorkshire Electricity Board plan showing a live cable running under the site which George was working on. The final paragraph caught his drink-sodden eyes:

Note: Live 11kv cable marked red on plan no. OR/JT/7. This will be disconnected and taken out of service 29/7/52.

He looked at the calendar and saw today was the twenty-seventh. The cable was still live. First thing that morning Barney had rung and asked him to check that no live cables were running across the site and Ernie had promised to ring him back if there were any. There was no rush. Life wasn't too bad – apart from Joe Brindle's imminent release. He'd got two years and had lost any remission he was due because of his behaviour whilst inside. Ernie put his feet up and opened the *Daily Mirror*. Within ten minutes he was fast asleep. He was still asleep two hours later when the phone call came through from the site.

George and Barney had been busy for over an hour when Rosie arrived in her Ford Popular. She parked it on a concrete apron beside the cement store and got out to look down on the site. George hadn't heard her car arrive, but he looked up, somehow aware of her presence, as he always was. Rosie waved to him as she went to the boot to get her Wellingtons. She then went back inside the car and took a penknife from the glove box. George had left it at home. There was a gadget on it that he needed for his beloved pipe, and George was lost without his penknife. Rosie smiled to herself as she slipped it into her pocket. It would be the first thing he asked for when she got down to him. The site was suffering from overnight rain and despite the warming sunshine, it was still quite muddy. George waved back. He always felt better when his wife was nearby. The last four years had been the happiest of his life.

He had also forgotten his rubber boots and was periodically scraping the caked mud off his shoes with a setting-out pin. Rubber boots had an insulating quality which would have created a safe barrier between his body and the wet ground. But George wasn't to know he'd need insulating. Afterwards, some people said his tin leg couldn't have helped much. Tin being a better conductor than flesh and bone.

Tucking his false leg beneath him with a skill he'd

162

acquired over the years, he bent down and squinted down the string line that ran along the curved row of pins to give the kerb-layers a line and level to work to.

'Throw me another pin,' he called out to Barney. 'I just need to sweeten the far end out a bit.'

He took the three-foot long, half-inch diameter bar and placed it against the string line, looking back for Barney's approval.

'About there.'

George held the pin vertical and hit it three times with a lump hammer, sending it deep into the soft clay.

Rosie had taken off her shoes and was about to put her Wellington boots on when a dull thud made her look up. She frowned when she saw George lying on his back several feet away from the smoking hole where he'd just driven the pin into the ground. Then she gasped as she saw Barney dashing towards her husband, kneeling beside him, slapping his face and pummelling his body.

With bootless feet and racing heart she ran across the muddy ground shouting, 'Oh God! What's happened?' She flung herself beside her husband. His eyes were still open which gave her false hope. 'George!' she screamed. 'What's happened?'

'He must 'ave 'it an electric cable, missis,' explained one of the men. Barney was already on his way to the telephone.

She looked up at the man, pleading, 'He's going to be all right, isn't he?'

But the man was out of his depth in this situation. He stood up and backed away, removing his cap and joining his companions who all stared down at Rosie as she held George's lifeless head in her arms; dripping tears all down his face.

There was a silent procession across the site to the ambulance, which didn't want to risk getting bogged down in the soft ground. George was being carried on a stretcher with a sheet completely covering him as the ambulancemen struggled carefully through the muddy patches with a policeman on either side and the workmen straggling along behind, with caps off and heads bowed. The sun came out from behind a cloud and lit their way, respectfully. Rosie walked immediately behind the stretcher, helped by Barney, who wanted to be of comfort to her but he didn't have the words.

As they'd waited for the ambulance to arrive she'd knelt beside George and held his lifeless hand until long after the warmth had drained away. A police examiner had satisfied himself as to the cause of death and gently persuaded her to step away. After George had been placed in the ambulance, a policeman turned to her and asked, 'Do you want to go with him?'

She stared at the man, thinking what a stupid question. 'Of course I want to go with him, he's my husband!'

'Only they'll be taking him straight to the, er . . .'

Mortuary! The word entered her head before it left his mouth. The strength she had been summoning from somewhere, left her body and Barney flung an arm around her to stop her falling.

'I think I'd best take you home, Rosie.'

'In a minute.'

There was comfort in Barney's arms that she was grateful for at a time like this. She climbed into the ambulance and drew back the sheet covering George's head. His face was pale and expressionless, his eyes were closed and the colour gone from his lips. She kissed them deeply; transferring her own warmth into them and allowing her tears to fall on to his face. It was the last time she'd see it. Not for her the waxen, sanitised image, lying in a silken shroud. Her husband had gone when he was still handsome and full of life. And that was the only way for heroes.

'Goodbye, my darling,' she whispered. 'And thank you for everything.'

As soon as Ernie heard the news he took out his lighter and

set fire to the letter from the Yorkshire Electricity Board. As far as he was concerned it had never arrived.

Ethel had volunteered to bring Eddie home. Rosie was sitting in the large living room when they came in. Her mother looked at her as Eddie struggled to take off his coat.

'Do you want me to stay?'

'Yes please, Mam.'

She held out her hand for Eddie, who came charging across the room to her and flung himself into her arms as he usually did when she picked him up from the nursery.

'I'll make us a cuppa,' said Ethel. 'Take yer time, love.'

Rosie held on to her son until he became restless and made it obvious he had better things to do. She let him go and ruffled his hair.

'Eddie,' she said. 'I've got something very important to tell you. Do you know what important means?'

Eddie nodded his head, unsurely, hoping she wasn't going to ask for a definition of the word.

'It means I want you to listen very carefully to what I have to say.'

Another nod.

Rosie took in a deep breath and Ethel stood by the door as she waited for the kettle to boil. 'Your daddy had an accident at work.'

Eddie stared at her with innocent brown eyes that had known no sorrow or heartbreak. Yet.

'Has he bumped himself? Poor Daddy.'

'Yes, he bumped himself. And sometimes you can bump yourself so badly that you can't come home.'

'Poor Daddy. Shall I kiss him better?'

'Well, Daddy would love you to kiss him better but . . .' Words had deserted her.

Ethel came in and took over: 'Your daddy can't come home, Eddie. They've had to send him to Heaven to get better.'

'Where's Heaven? Can I go and see him?'

165

'Well, that's just it, Eddie,' she continued, 'you won't be able to see him, neither will your mum. Sometimes it happens that daddies have to go away and they can't come back.'

Rosie couldn't stand all this. She grasped her son by his shoulders. 'Eddie,' she said, her voice still husky from hours of crying. 'Your daddy died today.'

Eddie stood there for a while trying to understand what he'd been told. He didn't cry, he just went quiet and allowed Rosie to take him back in her arms.

'Will you stay with me?' he asked.

'Yes, my darling, I'll stay with you.'

'And you'll never leave me?'

'Never.'

The notable absentee at George's funeral was Barbara. Hers was the biggest spray of flowers which, in Rosie's eyes, did not excuse her absence. She could have flown home in time for the funeral. Rosie felt like sending the flowers back. Instead she sent a terse note of thanks ending:

> *Your father told me he loved you. It would have been nice had you brought the flowers in person.*

In his will, George had left the house and his share of the business to Rosie. The remainder of his assets he left in equal proportions to Eddie and Barbara. Barbara sent a caustic letter complaining that Rosie had deprived her of her rightful heritage, Oak House. There was also a thinly veiled remark which cast doubt on Eddie's parentage. It had an irate Rosie almost buying a ticket on the next flight to Australia. She settled for another letter:

> *. . . next time I visit George's grave I'll tell him you said thanks for remembering you in his will. Your father was so happy with his son, Eddie. What a pity you couldn't have respected this.*

Barbara wrote back but Rosie returned the letter unopened. A slanging match such as this wasn't what George would have wanted.

The morning after the reading of the will, Ernie Scrimshaw rang her up. 'We, er. We need ter meet. I er . . .'

'It's okay, Ernie,' she said. 'Can you come round? I'm still not thinking straight.'

Ernie's tone brightened. 'Give me half an hour.'

Twenty minutes later he knocked and let himself in. Rosie knew she'd somehow have to step into George's shoes, but she wasn't ready just yet. Her husband's death was beginning to hit her hard. He had been the rock on which her life had stabilised. Eddie missed him terribly. She was holding her son's hand when she stepped out of the living room to greet Ernie. 'Come through, Ernie. Eddie and I were just about to have tea and teacakes, weren't we, Eddie?'

'Yes,' said Eddie, then by way of explanation added, 'Daddy can't come.'

If Ernie felt any sense of guilt he didn't show it. 'Look, Mrs Metcalf . . .'

'Please, call me Rosie.'

'Rosie. I, er, yer need ter sign a few cheques. We're a bit hamstrung at the moment.'

'Yes, I didn't think. Do you have them with you?'

Ernie laid a briefcase on the coffee table and took out four cheques which Rosie perused casually. George had often questioned his competence, never his honesty. She smiled at him and asked, 'Do you have a pen?'

He produced a fountain pen with which she signed all four cheques without really having a clue what they were for. She handed them back to him. 'There,' she said. 'Anything else?'

He stood there, awkwardly. 'There is, actually. Yer see, there are cheques ter sign nearly every day, plus all sorts of other stuff. Contracts and things. George ran the company pretty much his own way.'

Rosie nodded. 'I know, but I've also learned a lot about the business myself over the last four years. I'm sure you and I can keep it going.' She really had Barney in mind as her right hand man, but there was no need to go into that right now.

'I don't want ter seem unsympathetic,' said Scrimshaw, 'but the question is, when?'

'I'm sorry, Ernie. I'm still in shock.' She looked down at Eddie. 'I need time to get my act together. You just have to bear with m . . .'

Ernie interrupted her. 'If it helps I can take over every-thing in the short term. I just need your consent fer me to sign various things.' He saw the doubt creep into her eyes. 'I, er . . . Robert Hilton thought it was a good idea. In the short term . . .'

Rosie nodded. What Ernie was saying would have made a lot more sense had he been halfway competent. 'I'll ring Robert and sort something out,' she said.

'Well, actually, I've, er, I've got him in me car. Picked him up on the way, ter save yer any bother, at a time like this.'

'You'd better bring him in.'

Rosie should have been suspicious at Ernie's uncharacteristic alacrity, but she saw no reason to be. George had never had a bad word to say about the company solicitor. Robert Hilton entered in the suit he'd worn at the funeral the day before. The only difference being a grey silk tie instead of black. He handed Rosie a document.

'This is for the bank,' he said. 'It authorises Mr Scrimshaw to issue cheques on his signature alone. It can be countermanded by you at any time.'

Rosie signed it and smiled up at Ernie. 'At times like this we have to trust each other. Mind you,' she warned. 'In a week I intend taking over.'

'I think yer can trust me not to bankrupt the company in a week,' laughed Ernie. His smile faded when he saw the lack of humour in her eyes.

'Anything else?' she asked.

'Just this,' said the solicitor, handing her another document. 'It gives Mr Scrimshaw or me the authority to sign contracts. There's one due to be signed later this week or I wouldn't bother you.'

Rosie signed it without reading it. 'As I said. It's only for a week.'

'This way you can take as long as you want,' said Hilton, then added, meaningfully: 'I'll keep an eye on things, keep the company on the right track.'

Chapter Seventeen

It was nearly a month since the funeral and Rosie still hadn't come to terms with George's death. A light had shone from within him that had always seemed so unquenchable. He'd survived the horrors in the first world war and had gone on to share his indomitable spirit with her. And somehow he was dead. How could that be?

She'd entombed herself in the house all that August, unwisely leaving the business in the hands of Ernie who had already stepped up his illicit dealings. She didn't care about the business. All she wanted was her husband back; and the odd thing was that she had never been passionately in love with him. Despite him being one of life's winners he was also decent and honest and kind. A seductive combination. Rosie missed his humour and his love for her. Perhaps most of all his love for her.

She'd been tempted to sell up and move away but that would have been an insult to George's memory. A complete waste of all the nights he'd spent teaching her about the business. He wouldn't have wanted that. She stood at the bedroom window and looked at the oak tree in the garden where they'd spent so many happy hours. Tomorrow she'd go into work and repair any cock-ups that Ernie had made. Barney Robinson would be her number two. She smiled to herself and enjoyed a sense of optimism for the first time in weeks.

It was a warm evening and Ethel had called round and volunteered to babysit as she always did, fully expecting her daughter to refuse. As she always did. They would never be close, but each had a need for the other. And Ethel was very much taken with her grandson.

'Thanks, Mam, I might go out for a walk. Clear the cobwebs.'

'Good girl. Take as long as yer want. Call for a drink somewhere. Yer need ter get out of yerself.'

'I don't go in pubs on my own.'

'Right.'

Ethel knew that Rosie had few friends her own age. The girlfriends she'd had as a teenager were all married with lives of their own, including Susan Clarkson who was now married with two children.

How long she'd been walking she'd no idea. Had she not been lost in thought she'd have noticed the man tracking her; about fifty yards away. A tram slowed to a halt beside her. One of the big ex-London trams – she'd never actually been on one of them. Since she'd married George she'd gone everywhere by car. Rosie smiled inanely at it. There was something friendly about a tram. Something non-threatening and straightforward. You knew where you were with a tram. Trams reminded her of Sean. Trams stayed where they were put, on the tracks. There was a lot to be said for staying on the tracks. But that night her own life would become totally derailed. For no reason she could think of, she jumped on. She was halfway up the stairs to the top deck and the tram was moving when a latecomer jumped on. The conductor followed her up and called out, 'Fares please.' Rosie held out a shilling.

'Where to, love?'

'I don't know.'

The conductor sighed, he'd had a long day. 'I'll come back when yer've made yer mind up, shall I? Only yer choices are a bit limited, with this being a tram.'

'Where are you going?' enquired Rosie.

'Pudsey.'

'Well, that's where I want to go.'

'Whereabouts in Pudsey?'

'Pudsey terminus,' said Rosie. 'I assume there is a terminus in Pudsey.'

'There's many strange things in Pudsey, love – including my mother-in-law – ninepence, please.'

The tram trundled towards the city centre prior to heading out to the western suburbs. A fat man on the seat in front of Rosie was engrossed in the *Yorkshire Evening Post*. Apparently an aeroplane called DH 110 had crashed during an airshow and killed the pilot and twenty-five people. Twenty-six families, each mourning a loved one. Just like Rosie. No doubt they'd get on with their lives, re-adjust. Forget in some cases. The man folded up his paper, got up to go and pushed his way down the aisle, apologising as he bumped into shoulders on either side. Rosie felt sorry for him; having to constantly apologise for something that wasn't his fault. He wore just a shirt, pullover and trousers with two large back pockets, which were stretched tight across his gigantic backside. A newly-arrived passenger had to squeeze to one side to let him pass. The passenger grinned and winked at the people around him and said in a voice loud enough for the departing man to hear, 'Last time I saw a pair o' pockets that wide apart were on a snooker table.'

There was a lot of laughter and banter and Rosie didn't want to be part of it. She suddenly became aware of her own burgeoning girth.

'I'd rather be fat than be ignorant!' she blurted.

There was an embarrassed silence and Rosie decided it would be a good time to get off. She hadn't meant for this to happen. Get a grip of yourself, Rosie Jones . . . Jones? Why did she call herself Jones? She was insulting George's memory now. She went down the stairs to the lower deck where she had to stand on the bottom step because the fat man was taking up all the platform. He turned and grinned at her.

'There was no need for yer ter stick up fer me, love. I'm a club comic – I like a good gag. Might use that one in me act.'

'Sorry,' said Rosie, although she didn't know what she was apologising for.

The tram had stopped outside the Odeon Cinema. *Singin' In The Rain* was on. She and George had intended seeing that together. No doubt he'd have tapped out the tunes on his tin leg on the way home. After George's death, she'd had to rely on her mother. Ethel wasn't much, but she was the only mother she had. Ethel had been to the wedding, if only to express her disappointment that it was such a low-key affair, before leaving early with a stomach upset, which she put down to the prawns. Since then she'd visited them only on Eddie's birthday, accepting him as her grandson, but uncomfortable with George as a son-in-law, due to him being five years older than her.

'I'm amazed he could have fathered a child at his age,' she'd commented, sourly. 'And I'm certainly surprised you let him. Still, you made your bed, now you can lie on it.' Ethel had thought fleetingly of Tommy as these words came out. He used to say that. Didn't follow his own advice though.

'It's a very comfortable bed, Mam,' Rosie had assured her. 'And George is a wonderful father.' The secret of Eddie's parentage would go with her to the grave, not even Eddie would ever know the truth. It was better that way.

Something Ethel had said to her at the funeral had helped. As the coffin clumped against the bottom of the grave with an eerie finality, she had squeezed Rosie's arm.

'Well, love, you gave him the happiest four years of his life. That's what he told me, anyway.'

Rosie threw a single rose on to the coffin. She had no tears left, just a frightening emptiness.

'Did he say that, Mam? Really?'

She knew her mother was telling the truth. Ethel wouldn't tell a lie that favoured George, not even at his funeral.

'He did, love. He told me a couple of months ago, on

173

Eddie's birthday. He said, marrying you was the only really clever thing he'd ever done. I must admit I didn't feel like agreeing with him at the time. But that's what he said all right.'

Rosie set off down Briggate. The man who had followed her on to the tram alighted a few seconds behind her. A queue had gathered outside the Empire. The advertising boarding said *Issy Bonn, The Wisecracking Songster*. George would have liked him. She stopped outside the jewellers where George had taken her to choose their wedding rings. God! Was that really four years ago? How her life had changed in four years. She stood there for a while, happy just to be on her own with her memories; memories mainly of George, but Sean kept creeping into her thoughts. Dear, lovely young Sean. At least George had had a full life and gone out while still in his prime, but poor Sean hadn't seen or done much at all. Well, thanks to her he'd made a start. In fact she'd given them both a good send off. Then she felt guilty about Billy and for the hundredth time wished she'd said 'yes' to him that night.

In an alleyway, just off Briggate, stood Whitelocks, or the Turks Head, to give the pub its proper name, where she'd spent many an evening drinking with Janice Haddock, prior to them going dancing in the Mecca or maybe paying a visit to the Empire Theatre. They'd sit in a booth and discuss the rich and handsome men they intended marrying, but before then they'd both see something of the world, beginning with a month in the South of France and then they'd try their luck in Hollywood; and at the very least marry a film star. Neither of them managed more than a week in Blackpool. Janice married a gas fitter and now had three children. Rosie hadn't seen her for years. Her mother was right, she'd lost touch with all her old friends.

Only a certain type of girl went into pubs unaccompanied and Rosie didn't want to be thought one of them. On the other hand, Whitelocks held a special place in her heart, maybe Harry, the old barman, was still there. Maybe even some of her old friends. She'd just have the one. Eddie would be fast asleep and Ethel had encouraged her to go for a drink, so why not?

The long bar was about half full. Three old, pipe-smoking men sat around a heavy table, drinking dark beer and reminiscing about amusing events of long ago. A young couple in a smoky booth were having an intimate conversation, foreheads touching, kissing every other word and Rosie felt oddly jealous. She'd never had that sort of a relationship with a man. Twenty-six years old and she'd never been really passionately in love. Maybe she wasn't capable of it. Like mother like daughter. A cheerful Salvation Army woman came in the top door rattling her tin and embarrassing the sinful drinkers into buying the War Cry.

Before the woman left through the bottom door a few guilty people had parted with loose change then stuffed the newspaper under their seat to be left unread.

'What can I get my favourite customer?'

Harry came walking up the bar with a broad beam on his face. Rosie returned his smile. 'Surprised you remember me,' she said. 'It's been so long.'

'Never forget a pretty face ... usual?'

'Don't tell me you remember.'

He held a brandy glass up to an optic. 'Courvoisier – nothing with it.' He pressed it up twice for a double and set it in front of her. 'On me,' he said. 'Now then, I've heard all about your troubles, so do you want me to commiserate with you or shall I tell you a mucky joke instead?'

'Mucky joke please. I've had enough commiserating to last me a lifetime.'

'Right. Now I heard this at the Licenced Victuallers last week so it's a good un, is this ... Did you hear that the Amalgamated Union of, er ...' he snapped his fingers in exasperation. 'What do they call them fellers without any, er ... things down there?' he pointed to his groin. 'You know, they work in harems.'

'Eunuchs?' suggested Rosie.

'Them's the fellers. Well, did you hear that they've called the lads out on strike?'

Harry waited for her reply but Rosie just looked at him with a half-smile of expectance.

'You're supposed to ask why,' he prompted.

'Oh, sorry . . . why?'

'There's a dispute over severance pay . . . do you get it? Severance pay . . . eunuchs.'

Rosie did her best to laugh.

'Never mind,' said Harry. 'It went down ever so well at the Licenced Victuallers.'

'No, it was very funny,' said Rosie. 'Don't mind me – I'm a difficult audience at the moment.' She held out her glass and said: 'Same again, please.'

'Maybe you should call it a night,' suggested Harry, an hour later when it was obvious that Rosie wasn't enjoying herself. She was becoming maudlin drunk. 'Do you want me to get you a taxi?'

She shook her head. 'No thanks, Harry. I'm depressing you, aren't I?'

'You could never depress me. I just think you should go home.'

She tipped the rest of her drink down her throat. 'Okay. I'll stagger to the taxi rank. G'night, Harry . . . and I think your joke was very funny.'

She came out on to Briggate and turned right to where the taxis were parked. A bus had stopped just in front of her. The destination board said Killingbeck. George was at Killingbeck; six feet under the ground, but nevertheless that's where he was. Rosie climbed on board and went upstairs so that she could smoke and think. The man following her went downstairs.

She was wearing the coat she'd had on the day he died; short, smart and sensible. It was the first time she'd worn it since that day; she hadn't even emptied the pockets. George had always liked it.

The long, summer twilight had faded to darkness by the

176

time the bus dropped her off at the cemetery gates. The moonlight was scattered by thin clouds, but enough to see by. Rosie picked her way along stony paths, trying to remember where they'd buried her husband. The day of his funeral had been a blur but she remembered the grave was near a wall and it should have a new headstone by now. She hadn't actually seen the headstone yet but it should be nice for what it cost. Rosie searched round for half an hour and was crying in frustration by the time she found it. Black marble with gold lettering.

George Metcalf
Died 1952 aged 51 years
Beloved husband of Rosie and father of Barbara and Edward

How she had fought the temptation to exclude the name 'Barbara'. Barney had finally persuaded her with: 'It's what George would have wanted.'

Good old Barney. He was right of course. She clasped her hands and looked down at the mound beneath her feet.

'I don't seem to be handling things very well, George.' Her voice was amplified by the several brandies she'd drunk.

The night wind sighed through the trees as if in answer. Rosie smiled. 'You picked me up when I'd nowhere to turn and no one to turn to. It was such a lovely thing to do ...'

There was a raucous laugh from behind her; loud enough and sharp enough to send a spasm of fright through her body. She turned and saw the shadowy figure of a man leaning against a nearby gravestone. He struck a match to light a cigarette and illuminated his unmistakeable face.

'Is that you, Joe Brindle?' she called out.

'Who else did yer think it was? Or had yer forgotten about our little date?'

'I don't know what you're talking about.'

'I'm talkin' about you arranging ter meet me here. I

naturally assumed yer wanted ter make up fer kickin' me in me goolies all them years ago.'

'Go away and leave me alone!'

'Don't tell me yer've forgotten.'

'I haven't forgotten what you did to Sean.' The drink had given her courage she might not otherwise have shown.

'Still goin' on about that, eh?'

'Just leave me alone – murderer!'

'Watch yer mouth, Rosie Jones!'

'Why? What will you do? Murder me like you murdered Sean? You're a bully and a coward, Joe Brindle!'

A roar of rage began somewhere deep down in his gut and rumbled up his throat before exploding through his broken teeth. He moved forward into the light of a nearby gas-lamp. His heavy brow was furled over his eyes, casting them into shadow, from which shone a gleaming speck of violence. His thick neck puffed out, with crimson veins almost bursting through his skin.

Rosie's dutch courage froze into fear. She took a step back and fell on George's grave; banging her head against the headstone. Brindle let out a hoot of harsh amusement and looked down on her with lust and hatred. Here was the woman he'd always wanted. The bitch who'd had him sent to prison. The one who had spurned his advances and pushed him to the ground all those years ago. He knelt in front of her and pulled at her skirt, ripping it away from her terrified body. Within seconds he had stripped her naked from the waist down, exposing her pale flesh to the moonlight and his lust-crazed eyes. Rosie wanted to scream, but terror had stolen her voice and forced her into abject surrender.

Brindle pulled her legs apart and roughly forced himself inside her; grunting and thrusting and glorying at his power over her. He yanked at her hair and tried to kiss her but she managed to spit in his face and earned herself a vicious slap, which she didn't feel because the shock of his attack had anaesthetised her. She stretched her neck away from him and fixed her eyes on the upside-down inscription on

George's headstone as Brindle thrust away, maniacally, biting at her neck. The pain and foulness of the situation was almost unbearable. Her hands were clawing frantically at the ground and her fingers touched George's penknife that had been in her pocket since the day he died, and had fallen out in the turmoil. Brindle let out a moan of brutal ecstasy, then collapsed on her; still inside her, but spent. Rosie's heart was thundering as she lay trapped beneath his crushing weight. As she waited, her mind became detached from her body, floating in a world of its own. It was the only way she could deal with this. She joined her hands around his back, unclasped the blade.

And waited.

She waited until he withdrew and pushed himself upwards. He leaned over her, supported himself on his arms and leered: 'See what yer've been missin' all these years?'

It was a dis-embodied Rosie who jabbed the knife upwards. The sharp blade cut a deep groove up his cheek and became embedded in his left eye. Brindle's howl of agony rent the night air. It sent a nearby treeful of slumbering starlings flapping noisily into the black sky and jerked Rosie back into the real world. The world of rape and pain and suffering. What the hell had she done?

She rolled out from under him. Her mind was now in a blank shock as she gathered her torn skirt and put it on as best she could, before staggering away from this screeching, blood-soaked rapist. All she wanted to do was to get home, away from this evil. Home to a world of safety. Home to her boy.

Going straight to the police after the assault would have helped her cause, but all she wanted to do was shut herself away from the horror of that night. Rosie crouched, weeping in the bottom of the shower, wanting the steaming water to wash away all trace of him. Bewildered with mixed emotions. She had stabbed him in the eye. Maybe she had killed him. Why had she done that? He'd had his way with her, all she had to do was run away. Why had she inflicted so much pain on him? Did this make her as bad as him? Worse even?

She locked herself in her bedroom without a word to Ethel, who had heard her come in and run straight up the stairs. Her mother had chosen not to interfere. If Rosie wanted to talk she knew where she was.

Brindle's cries had been heard by passers-by and within half an hour of the attack he was on his way to Leeds Infirmary. The police were waiting to interview him when he came out of anaesthetic.

'Who did this to you, Mr Brindle?'

He was mumbling, almost incoherently. 'A bitch called Rosie Jones . . . got me locked up once an' now she does this . . . calls herself Metcalf now . . . bitch!' He nodded off again.

Rosie was in custody before he came round again. A sergeant had made the connection. In the car on the way to the police station she'd remained silent in response to their caution; shrinking away from them. Wary of their proximity.

'He raped me,' she sobbed, when asked why she'd stabbed him.

'Raped you? I see – and why didn't you report it?' asked one of the interviewing officers.

'I intended to . . . I . . .'

'What?'

'I don't know what . . . I just felt so awful.'

'Mr Brindle says you enticed him to have sex, then you stabbed him.'

Her voice was halting between sobs. 'Have sex with him? . . . That's just . . . just ridiculous . . . I stabbed him because he raped me.'

'Really – and do you always carry a knife?'

'What? . . . No, of course I don't.'

'I understand you held him responsible for the death of one of your former lovers.' The policeman looked at his notes. 'Sean Quinnan?'

'He raped me.'

180

'So you keep telling us. Mr Brindle seems to come off very much the worst. He's lost an eye, did you know that?'

Rosie felt a perverse satisfaction in this knowledge; so when she said, 'I'm sorry, I didn't mean to,' she lowered her eyes lest her insincerity be seen.

'It's a bit late for sorry. You hate him, don't you, Mrs Metcalf?'

She examined her feelings for the first time since it happened. Joe Brindle had subjected her to the vilest of crimes. Stripping her of her dignity and her self-esteem. He'd violated, degraded and humiliated her. And then in one brief, brutal second she'd redressed the balance. Expunged the shame. The policeman was right. Brindle had come off worst. But more importantly it had been at *her* hands. It had to be so, in order for her to live with herself. No court could punish him on her behalf. If there was a price to pay for this, then so be it.

'Mrs Metcalf, are you listening to me?'

'What?'

'I said you hate him for what he did to Sean Quinnan.'

'Yes,' she admitted, unwisely. 'I do hate him. He raped me . . . on my husband's grave.'

The questioner's tone remained calm and infuriatingly measured. 'Why were you at your husband's grave at such a late hour, Mrs Metcalf?'

'I don't know . . . why does anyone visit a grave?'

'It's unusual to take a knife with you. Why *did* you take a knife?' enquired the second policeman.

'I don't know. It was in my pocket. It was George's knife . . . why don't you people just leave me alone!' She got up from the chair and banged her fists in frustration against the wall. 'For God's sake, I've just been raped! Why don't you believe me?'

The senior policeman shrugged and looked up at Rosie. 'I think you'd be well advised to call your solicitor, Mrs Metcalf. In the meantime we'll have to keep you here until we carry out further investigations.'

Chapter Eighteen

It was a grey, drizzling day when Rosie walked down The Headrow towards Leeds Town Hall. She wore a black gaberdine raincoat over her new two-piece in dark blue barathea with gold buttons and a butterfly brooch. The rain pattered on to the umbrella protecting her recently permed hair. She didn't wear a hat because she felt that milliners didn't design hats with the round-faced woman in mind. A horse-drawn cart clopped towards her. Four white shire horses were pulling a Tetley's beer wagon. The driver and his mate, bowler-hatted and leather-aproned, braved the weather as they headed for the one of the city's many Tetley Houses; normally they'd earn a smile from Rosie. Not today though.

The last three months had been bad; going through the motions of running the company. How could the law have read the situation so wrong? Barney Robinson and the four site agents had done most of the work with Rosie trying to concentrate as much as she could. Barney had been a rock. Reliable, always there, with a hundred per cent belief in her story. Sustaining her in her periods of self doubt.

'But I maimed him for life, Barney. And the horrible thing is, I don't feel guilty – I took another human being's eye out and I don't feel a morsel of regret.'

'How can you regret it? It's your way of coping with what he did to you.'

She smiled. He understood. He was the only one who did.

'Brindle should think himself lucky to be alive after what he did to you.'

'What will happen to me, Barney?'

'Rosie, I wish I knew. If I could take your place, I would.'

And she knew he meant it. But to take advantage of his feelings for her at such a time would have been wrong. It was bad enough that she had damaged her own life without adding his marriage to her catalogue of destruction. Every man she came into contact with seemed to become cursed. Her dad, Billy, Sean, George. It would be unfair to add Barney to the list.

Ernie Scrimshaw had kept a low profile but had continued to run his illicit scam. Not enough to cause concern, but enough to add fifty per cent to his weekly wage. Other than that he was polite and helpful and had given Rosie no reason to countermand the arrangement for him to sign cheques. In fact, from time to time she had found the arrangement to be very convenient.

Had she kept as close an eye on him as Brindle had, her future might have been different.

Rosie was glad it was raining. If she had to leave the world behind for a while, and there seemed a fair chance of that, she didn't want to leave it on a sunny day. Robert Hilton was with her, carrying a heavy briefcase containing her file. She'd been charged with causing Grievous Bodily Harm. A charge of Attempted Murder had apparently been considered, but dropped as being too hard to prove. Her counter-accusation of rape had been left on file, pending the outcome of this trial.

She looked at her solicitor and asked, 'Do you think it'll last the full two weeks?'

'Probably, maybe a bit less.'

'So, I'll be kept in a cell for all that time?' It was a point she hadn't clarified with anyone. Too many other things on her mind.

'It's up to the judge. He'll probably let you go home on a night during the trial.'

'Only probably?'

'And after the trial you'll be kept in, er, custody, until the jury reaches its verdict.'

'What do you think my chances are?'

Hilton chose that moment for them to cross the Headrow, thus avoiding the question that Rosie had asked him a dozen times. Her case was touch and go. The clock beneath the Town Hall dome began to strike nine o'clock and the four stone lions guarding architect Cuthbert Broderick's grimy edifice gazed impassively at a point way above Rosie's head. The light rain suddenly turned heavy and noisy and unexpected as though some practical joker had reached behind the shower curtain and turned up the pressure, causing her to hurry the last few steps into the Bridewell to surrender herself to bail. She nodded grimly at the re-assuring words from Robert Hilton, like a boxer listening to the advice of his trainer between rounds; then she was taken by a policewoman along a dusty corridor that echoed both their footsteps, and through a barred doorway that led to the cells. Her escort selected a key from a bundle hanging from her belt and opened a cell door with the politeness of an hotel porter. Rosie paused in the doorway as she felt the blood drain from her face. The cell was small, square and windowless; with walls of cream painted brick, lit by a dismal light.

'I don't suppose you could leave the door open, could you?'

The policewoman gave a sympathetic smile. 'Sorry, love. I wish I could.' She closed the door gently, leaving Rosie alone with just a bed, a toilet and her thoughts.

Although the prosecution had opposed bail, it had been set at five thousand pounds. A sizeable sum, equivalent to the price of two decent houses. Rosie had put George's house up as surety. Her house now. It had bought her three months of freedom as she awaited trial in the Leeds

184

Assizes. She was weeping when the cell door was opened by the same policewoman.

'Time to go, love,' she said. 'It's not far, straight up these steps.'

Rosie walked beside her up the granite stairs that led to Court Number One. The steps had been worn down by the reluctant feet of countless thieves and thugs and murderers. Some having to be carried back down after having received the ultimate sentence; the gallows in Armley jail was only a short ride away. Rosie was just another potential criminal. No better, no worse, in the eyes of the law.

The murmur of the court drifted down the steps to meet her and curious eyes turned to look as she emerged in the dock. Only one eye in Joe Brindle's case. Then the eyes returned to the business in hand. She was just another part of their working day. The judge had yet to make an appearance.

A black-gowned clerk called out, 'All stand,' and there was a shuffling of feet as everyone stood to pay their respect to the judge as he made his entrance through a side door. He nodded his appreciation to the court then lowered himself into an ornate, high-backed chair. Everybody bowed their obeisance and sat down.

It was a dark place. Illuminated by three high windows down one wall allowing in dismal light from the dismal street outside. A street Rosie might not be allowed to walk down for some time to come. Everything inside was made of dark wood. The clerk and lawyers and ushers all wore various shades of dark grey or black. The only colour came from the plaque on the wall behind the judge, bearing the motto, *Dieu et Mon Droit*; and from the judge himself, who wore a red robe. It was all designed to suppress any sense of mis-placed optimism from the accused. Rosie noticed a chair in the dock. She turned to the policewoman and enquired:

'Can I sit down?'

'Only if the judge says you can.'

'You may sit down,' said the judge, who wouldn't have

185

allowed the same privilege to a man. He had a preconceived opinion of the case which he mustn't reveal. Joe Brindle was not unknown to him, and the phrase, 'An eye for an eye' kept springing to his Lordship's mind. The trial would last ten days.

On day three, Brindle, wearing a dark, sober suit, a military tie and a black, heroic-looking eye patch, was called to the witness box. He wouldn't have looked out of place marching at a Remembrance Day Parade. All that was missing was the row of medal ribbons (his brother's), which the prosecutor's solicitor had advised him to remove as it might be construed as overdoing things a bit. Brindle's attitude was that of a bewildered victim as he told the court how Rosie had telephoned him and arranged to meet him at the cemetery gates. The prosecuting barrister looked very young to be doing such a job. He wore a horsehair wig which looked older than him. In fact he had bought it second-hand when he'd been called to the bar, in order to give him the gravitas denied him by his youth.

'For what purpose?' he had enquired of Brindle.

'She said summat about lettin' bygones be bygones. Yer see, we used to go out with each other when we were a lot younger. I thought she might want ter take up where we'd left off – now that her husband was gone.'

'But wasn't Mrs Metcalf instrumental in your once being jailed for corruption?'

Brindle managed a sheepish grin. 'Look, that were business. I held me hands up to it; served me time and I bear no grudge.'

'Please tell the court what happened when you met Mrs Metcalf.'

'Well,' said Brindle. 'She dragged me into t' cemetery ter see George's new headstone. Ter be honest I think she'd had a fair bit ter drink. When we got there we started snoggin' . . . and next thing I knew . . . we were at it.'

The judge looked at him, balefully. 'What do you mean by "at it"?'

'Yer know ... havin' sex an' all that. On her husband's grave. Ter be honest, I thought it were a bit kinky.'

'He raped me!' screamed Rosie. 'He followed me there and raped me.'

'Mrs Metcalf!' cautioned the judge, sharply. Then to Brindle he said, 'Please continue.'

'Well, after we'd finished she give me this funny look and started laughin' like a maniac. Next thing I knew were this pain in me eye. Jesus! I've never known nowt like it.' He puffed his cheeks and blew out a mouthful of air as if the memory of the moment was too painful for him to recall.

Rosie's defence counsel couldn't budge him from his well-rehearsed story and Brindle gave the judge a respectful bow of his head as he left the witness box. Next up was Ernie Scrimshaw, who had been nervously pacing up and down inside the witness room; his recent instructions from Brindle still scarred into his brain: 'Yer do as I told yer, or I'll blow the whistle on all the fiddlin' yer've been doin'. It'll cost yer money and a fair stretch inside.'

Ernie heard his name called and cleared his throat noisily, in the optimistic hope that it might cure his nerves. Rosie watched him all the way to the witness box, at a loss to know why the prosecution had called him. He stumbled through the oath and faced the prosecuting counsel.

'Did Mrs Metcalf ever talk about Mr Brindle?'

'She never shut up about him.'

'Would you tell the court about a conversation you had with Mrs Metcalf on the day before the attack took place?'

Ernie looked away from Rosie's quizzical gaze. 'I'd popped round to the house ter tell her about a new contract. All she could talk about were Joe Brindle.'

'That's not true!' protested Rosie. 'I never mentioned Brindle. Ernie, I hardly spoke two words to you ...!'

'Mrs Metcalf,' scolded the judge. 'Would you please keep quiet, you'll have your say later.'

'But he's lying ... Ernie? What are you doing this for?'

'Mrs Metcalf ... I won't tell you again.' The judge

glared at her then nodded to the prosecuting counsel to continue.

'Would you tell the court what Mrs Metcalf said about Mr Brindle?'

'She were in a right state,' said Ernie. 'Evidently she'd been blowin' hot an' cold ever since George's death. Anyway, she started goin' on about Brindle, an' how she'd make him pay for killin' this boyfriend of hers.'

'Boyfriend?' enquired the prosecutor. 'Would this be a young man called . . .' he picked up a piece of paper from his notes and read out the name. 'Sean Quinnan?'

'Aye, that were his name. She reckoned Joe Brindle were responsible fer him bein' killed. She's had this bee in her bonnet about him fer years. Did yer know she got Brindle locked up once . . .?'

'Yes, the court has already heard about that. Tell me, Mr Scrimshaw, how did Mrs Metcalf feel about Mr Brindle going to prison and losing his business?'

'She thought he'd got off far too lightly.'

'Really? Did she say what punishment would have satisfied her?'

Ernie averted his eyes from Rosie's gaze and said, 'She reckoned she wanted him dead!'

'Dead? . . . Tell me, Mr Scrimshaw, do you mean "figure of speech" dead – or really dead?'

'Oh *really* dead,' Ernie assured the prosecutor. 'I told her ter forget Joe Brindle. I told her get on with her life . . . but she give me this funny smile and then she tapped her nose like this.' He gave a demonstration. 'Then she said, "I'll fix him once and for all, tomorrow night".'

'This is just a pack of lies!' shouted Rosie. 'I never said anything of the sort.'

'I'm warning you for the last time, Mrs Metcalf!' stormed the judge. 'One more outburst and I'll hold you in contempt of court, which could make you liable to a prison sentence whether you are convicted or not.'

*

As usual, after the day's proceedings, Rosie went home in Robert Hilton's car.

'I want to countermand Scrimshaw's right to sign cheques and contracts,' she snapped as she was closing the door. 'And I want him out of the company as from now.'

Her solicitor listened to her raging about the way Ernie had lied and betrayed her.

'Rosie,' he said, at length. 'I'm as disgusted as you are with Scrimshaw. I anticipated what you'd want to do and I went straight out and rang up the bank, as soon as he'd finished giving evidence.'

'So, he can't sign any more cheques?'

His face was grave. Rosie looked at him, concerned. 'I am right, aren't I? He can't sign any more cheques?'

Hilton said nothing; he just looked straight forward. They were stuck in heavy, rush hour traffic, still in the centre of Leeds. An impatient horn hooted behind him as he slid his Austin into gear and moved off. 'He doesn't have to sign any more cheques,' he sighed. 'The final payment from the Burmantofts Street job came in a couple of days ago. Yesterday, Ernie wrote himself cheques for every last penny in the BJK accounts.'

Rosie sat there, shocked. 'Surely he can't do that. The bank will just have to replace the money . . .'

The traffic came to a halt again. 'I'm sorry, Rosie. But you gave him written permission – on my advice, I'm ashamed to say.'

'Can't you stop it? If he only did it yesterday it . . .'

'He cleared the cheques express,' said Robert. 'The money's gone, and so has he.'

'Gone? Gone where?'

'No idea. If we could find him, at least we could get him back into court and question him about it. And no doubt discredit his testimony and have his assets frozen while the police decide what to do with him.'

The lights ahead turned green and Robert turned left up Vicar Lane. They drove in silence for a while as Rosie digested what she'd been told.

'Do you know where he's gone?' she asked.

'He apparently got a taxi from the Town Hall to the station.'

'Taxi? He could have walked it in five minutes.'

'By the state of him he didn't *have* five minutes. The policeman on the door said he'd never seen a man in such a hurry. So I rang a chief inspector friend of mine – the police have been trying to track him down all afternoon.'

'And?'

'And he's disappeared off the face of the Earth.'

The traffic thinned out as they headed north up Harrogate Road. Rosie tried to think straight. 'Where does that leave us, Robert?'

He took a deep breath. 'I don't think this was a spur-of-the-moment thing. It looks to me as if Ernie has been planning this for a while – and he could well have gone abroad. Which means we'll be hard-pressed to get your money back.'

'Where does that leave me?'

'I, er . . . I spoke to your accountant. I'm afraid BJK may well be insolvent.'

'You mean broke?'

'I mean you can't pay your bills.'

'What about wages?'

'I'll speak to Barney Robinson. He'll have to lay everyone off tomorrow. The men will be after Scrimshaw's blood when they find out what happened.'

'Make sure they're told the truth . . . and, Robert.'

'What?'

'How do I pay you for all this?'

He reddened slightly. 'In cases like this it's standard practice for a law firm to place itself in funds before the case starts. I, er . . . I did mention it to you at the start.'

'Did you? Maybe I had other things on my mind. So Scrimshaw gave you a cheque, did he?'

'Yes. I must say he did seem a little reluctant.'

'I'll bet he did,' said Rosie, grimly. 'It'll have been like handing over his own money. Is there any way I can get the firm's money back?'

'Not in the short term. And if he spends it I'm not sure what we can do in the long term.'

She gave a long, despairing sigh. In the space of a few months her whole world had been destroyed. 'Jesus, Robert. What a mess.'

'I'll do all I can to help.'

Rosie squeezed his hand. 'I thought Ernie Scrimshaw was okay,' she said. 'Dim as the proverbial Toc H lamp, but I didn't think he was a thief.'

'Neither did I. Otherwise . . .'

'I don't blame you, Robert. He fooled us both. At least I don't have to worry about paying you.'

Rosie's barrister opened the defence with a statement about Ernie.

'My Lord, a serious matter has arisen which could cast doubt on the evidence of one of the prosecution witnesses.'

'Really?' said the judge.

'Yes, My Lord. I suggest it's a matter which should be dealt with in the absence of the jury.'

'Do you indeed?' The judge stared at him for a moment, then turned to the jury. 'Would you vacate the court until we sort this matter out?'

The two barristers waited for the jury to file out before approaching the bench. The prosecutor looked puzzled and annoyed as Rosie's barrister said: 'My Lord, one of the prosecution's key witnesses, Mr Ernest Scrimshaw, has in the last few days, betrayed a trust placed in him by my client. He has withdrawn cheques from my client's company account to the extent of twenty-five-thousand pounds and has disappeared with the money. The police are searching for him, but so far without success. In light of this I request that this witness's evidence be struck from the record.'

The judge frowned, stroked his chin and gave an unconvinced 'Hmmm.' Then looked at the prosecuting counsel, 'Does the prosecution have any comments?'

'I do, My Lord. This case cannot be influenced by what are mere allegations at this point. Mr Scrimshaw, as far as I know, has not been found guilty of any crime. In fact, I understand he was given written permission by the accused to withdraw money from the company accounts.'

'My Lord,' argued Rosie's counsel, 'Mr Scrimshaw grossly exceeded his authority and has left my client's company insolvent.'

The judge weighed up the pros and cons of the situation with more rubbing of his chin, then said, 'I agree. It is an unfortunate situation ... but a matter for another court to decide upon.'

The defence barrister stood his ground as the prosecutor walked back to his seat.

'But, My Lord – this witness's evidence could sway the balance of the whole case.'

'Perhaps so. But I cannot dismiss evidence on mere allegations. It would throw the whole trial system into a complete turmoil.'

The final nail in Rosie's coffin came during her time giving evidence in her own defence. She'd told her own counsel the truth of what had happened then faced the prosecuting barrister. Unfortunately for Rosie, his youth belied his ability.

'Oddly enough, I find parts of your story quite plausible, Mrs Metcalf,' he said. 'Apart from one small thing. You took a knife with you to visit your husband's grave. An unusual item for a mourner to have about their person, don't you think? Of course you have explained what the knife was doing in your pocket and the more gullible members of the jury may choose to believe you.' He looked at the jury and studied them through half-closed eyes. Then he shook his head and turned to Rosie. 'I suspect you may be out of luck, they don't look all that gullible to me.'

192

The prosecutor stared at her, hoping to force her to look down, but she held his gaze, defiantly. He continued, 'You took the knife specifically to attack Mr Brindle. You took advantage of him at his weakest moment – after he'd had sex with you. Then you stabbed him. Isn't that the truth of the matter, Mrs Metcalf?'

'He raped me!' screamed Rosie, her eyes blurry with tears.

'Your plan was to seduce him, murder him, then to say you did it in self-defence because he raped you. A masterly plan if I may say so. But you slipped up, didn't you, Mrs Metcalf? You failed to kill him.'

Rosie's barrister sprang to his feet. 'Objection, M' Lord. My learned friend appears to be prosecuting a case of Attempted Murder. Perhaps he is in the wrong court?'

'Quite so,' agreed the judge. 'I would be obliged if the prosecution could keep the questioning within the limits of the offence as charged.'

'I apologise, M' Lud,' said the prosecuting barrister. 'I'm just stating the facts as I see them.'

'He *did* rape me,' sobbed Rosie. '. . . He raped me.'

The young barrister smiled and shook his head. 'Mrs Metcalf, had you succeeded in your plan we would have been forced to believe you – as Mr Brindle wouldn't have been around to defend himself. Had you killed him, you might have got away with it. It must have been an awful shock to find out he was still alive.'

'He raped me,' wept Rosie.

'I have no further questions, M' Lud.'

Rosie had been in the cells for twenty-two hours. The jury had been unable to reach a verdict and had been put up in an hotel for the night. She looked at her watch for the hundredth time, five-past-two. Her heart lurched as she heard footsteps outside her cell. The door rattled open.

'The jury's coming back, Rosie,' said the policewoman. 'Are you okay?'

Rosie nodded, not trusting herself to speak, lest she started blubbing. Her heart was pounding like a steam hammer. Her counsel, in his summing-up, had pointed out to the jury the implausibility of her having sex with Brindle on her husband's grave, as a ploy to murder him – and afterwards to accuse him of rape. He'd made Brindle's story sound laughable. So why had the jury taken so long?

'Good luck, Rosie,' said the policewoman.

Rosie smiled thinly and allowed herself to be guided up the steps for what would be the last time, no matter what the outcome. Would she be coming back down them? Or would she walk out of the Town Hall doors a free woman? She'd know in a couple of minutes. The judge arrived a few seconds after her. The court officials stood up, bowed their heads and sat down just as the jury began to file in. Rosie studied their faces for encouraging signs; a friendly wink or a smile. But each juror stared blankly ahead, studiously avoiding eye contact with the accused.

Rosie inadvertently caught Joe Brindle's lone eye. His face contorted into a cruel smirk and he drew a finger across his throat as though he knew something. Ethel and Barney were sitting behind him, both giving her encouraging smiles which Rosie didn't see.

'Will the foreman of the jury please stand,' called out the clerk of the court.

The foreman stood up. Rosie's eyes were glued to his face. Fiftyish, balding, dark brown sports jacket, fat fingers resting almost casually on the rail in front of him. Casual was good, she told herself.

'Have you reached a verdict upon which you are all agreed?' enquired the clerk.

'Yes, we have.'

'With respect to the charge of causing grievous bodily harm, do you find the defendant guilty or not guilty?'

Rosie looked away, she sensed the word forming in the man's mouth. Her mind went numb.

'Guilty.'

Brindle whooped and raised a triumphant fist. The policewoman standing behind Rosie saw her body slump so she guided her down into the chair.

'Okay, Rosie?' she whispered.

Rosie looked back at her through eyes half-blinded by tears and shook her head. 'What's going to happen to me?'

There was a sympathetic silence in the court, broken only by Brindle's coarse laughter.

'Could we have that person removed?' demanded the judge.

A policeman took Brindle's arm and led him sniggering and jeering from the courtroom, causing some of the jurors to exchange glances, and wonder. Had they got it right? The judge allowed Rosie time to collect herself. After an appropriate moment he nodded at the clerk, who said:

'Would the defendant please rise.'

Rosie pushed herself to her feet and gripped the edge of the dock with white knuckles. She didn't hear the judge's opening remarks, her brain didn't clear until he arrived at the sentencing bit.

'... Rosemary Anne Metcalf. The jury have found you guilty of a serious criminal offence. Despite your previously unblemished record I would be failing in my duty if I exercised undue leniency. Justice in my court must be seen to be done. I hereby sentence you to three years imprisonment.' His eyes dropped, as though not wanting to gaze upon Rosie's deeply shocked face.

'Take her down,' he said, brusquely.

Chapter Nineteen

The word 'guilty' rang in her ears as its dreadful implications slowly unfolded over the ensuing twenty-four hours: her first night locked up in the Bridewell under Leeds Town Hall, knowing there was worse ahead of her; the crippling ache inside her at being parted from Eddie; being handcuffed and led in a line of felons of both sexes to climb into the back of the Black Maria which would drop the male convicts off at Armley and take the women on to Ashinghurst; and then Ashinghurst itself and the finality of the prison gates as they banged shut, leaving the world she knew outside.

Then she'd had to submit to an ignominious strip search, then a lukewarm shower before standing in line in her underwear to be issued with her prison uniform. She'd felt a strange, comical relief that the grey outdoor jacket wasn't covered in arrows. All her belongings of any value had been confiscated, her diamond engagement ring, even her gold watch.

'It's for your own good,' she'd been told. 'You wouldn't keep this stuff two minutes in this place.'

She didn't sleep the first night. Partly through the shock to her system and partly because of the incessant noise. The spasmodic shouting and crying and clanging of doors and gates. And the snoring of her cellmate, Mags Outhwaite.

At first, Rosie spoke only when spoken to and sometimes

not even then. Some of the inmates seemed to have come from a different strata of society, some sort of sub-culture. She wasn't prepared for the expletives constantly assaulting her ears and she vowed not to become one of them. Mags seemed okay though. She was an accomplished thief, serving time for a string of burglaries. It was a trade she'd taken over when her husband suffered what she euphemistically called an 'industrial injury'. He'd fallen from a collapsing drainpipe and damaged his spine. Fortunately his injury occurred on the way to, rather than from work, otherwise he might well have ended up in a prison hospital instead of St James's.

Rosie had been advised not to appeal unless she could provide any new evidence. Her punishment had been lenient in view of Brindle's injury, and losing an appeal could mean an increased sentence. As things stood, with remission she could be out in two years. She tried to be philosophical about the injustice of it all. A punishment for something she'd actually done was easier to endure. At least she'd struck another blow for Sean. She was losing two years of her life but she'd now cost Brindle the same two years plus an eye. Against which he'd added a rape to his crimes. Barney's question sprang to her mind. 'Is it enough?'

And she knew it wasn't.

As the weeks went by, she became inured to the obscenity of the prison and took each day as it came. But it wasn't easy.

Breakfast at Ashinghurst consisted of porridge and toast, better known as stodge and scrape, which pretty much described it. At the beginning, Rosie generally missed this meal, telling herself that such abstinence would have two useful side effects. One, she would lose unwanted weight and two, she wouldn't choke to death on her own vomit. Hunger sometimes got the better of her, although she would have been better off staying in her cell on that particular morning in March, just three months into her sentence.

Gobby Grogan was one of two officers on meal duty and her constant ranting and sneering finally got to Rosie; despite Mags's advice:

'Some screws'll boss yer because of *who* they are, not what they are. Then there's them what hides behind their uniform – Gobby's one o' them. When she starts on yer, throw a deaf un. Everybody knows what a little shit she is – even the other screws.'

Rosie saw the sense in this and usually switched off whenever she was within earshot of Grogan.

'An' she's as bent as a nine-bob-note,' Mags had warned her.

'What? You mean she's some sort of crook?' Rosie was naïve in some things.

'No she's, yer know ... a dyke.'

'Oh, I see.'

'Just ignore her.'

But Rosie found it difficult when the insults were shouted from within range of Grogan's spittle.

'Thought yer'd grace us with yer presence, did yer, Metcalf?' she snarled in her ear. 'Well, get it down yer, and as yer eating it, think on. Yer on bog cleaning duty straight after this.'

Cleaning out the water closets in the main toilet block was the least popular job of all, as many inmates had un-hygienic sanitary habits.

'I did my stint in the toilet block last week,' protested Rosie. 'I'm supposed to be in the laundry this week.'

'Yer s'posed ter share bog duty out,' called out Mags, in support of her cellmate.

Grogan sniggered, 'Well, I've changed the work sheets.' She stuck her finger in Rosie's porridge and licked it. 'Hmmm ... you should be seeing a lot more of this later on.'

'Hey, Miss Grogan. You're one of nature's gentlemen,' called out Mags and everyone laughed except Rosie, who got to her feet and said, defiantly, 'You're an ignorant pig!'

Mags gave her a warning glance but Rosie took no notice. The buzz in the dining room subsided as people craned to hear Rosie's outburst. Her contempt for the officer was written in large letters, all over her face.

Grogan met her gaze, then turned away. 'I think Miss Inchbold might be interested to hear about your little tantrum. Being disrespectful to a prison officer is a punishable offence.'

'Respect's something you have to earn,' said Rosie. 'No one in this place has any respect for you. Without that uniform you'd be a nobody.'

Grogan suddenly turned and slapped her across the side of her head and Rosie found herself instinctively squaring up to the officer, with clenched fists.

A gleeful voice shouted, 'Watch out, Gobby! She'll have yer bleedin' eye out.'

'Leave it, Rosie!' cautioned Mags. 'She's tryin' ter get yer in trouble.'

Rosie nodded and took a step back. 'It's okay,' she said. 'I wouldn't soil my hands on her.'

'Inchbold's office, now,' said the officer, with little authority left in her voice.

Mags was sitting on her bed, smoking, when Rosie arrived back in the cell. 'Well?' she asked.

'Seven days loss of privileges. I wasn't aware we had any privileges. What are they?'

'Recreation, visits, letters, stuff like that.'

'Could be worse. I thought for one awful minute that I was going to get expelled.'

Mags grinned and offered Rosie a cigarette, as Rosie added, 'Tell you what, bog duty was never mentioned. I reckon Grogan was overstepping her authority by altering the sheets. All in all, it could have been worse.'

'It could have been a lot worse if yer'd belted her. Which yer nearly did.'

'Oh, I wouldn't have done anything,' Rosie said. She

took a deep drag on her cigarette. 'I'm not really a violent person. I just don't like being picked on, that's all.'

'Really? ... And what was it yer doin' time for?'

'I'd just been raped,' said Rosie, sharply. 'I wasn't quite myself.'

Mags laughed. 'Yer did yerself no harm today, Rosie lass. The girls are beginning ter think yer one o' them.'

'Oh my God, Mags! I'm not, am I?'

Chapter Twenty

It was fifteen months since the day of her conviction. Rosie glanced at the cheap watch which Ethel had bought her because it wasn't worth stealing, then took a last deep drag on a slender, hand-rolled cigarette, almost burning her fingers. She swung her legs off the bottom bunk and flicked the stub in the general direction of the chemical toilet. At the back of which, scrawled in red crayon on the wall, *For Emergency Use Only*.

'I make it lunchtime, Mags,' she announced to the prostrate body in the bed opposite. The top bunk was unoccupied, as it had been since the day of her arrival.

'Eat mine for me, than bring it back up here and throw it up,' said the body. 'It shouldn't taste much different.'

Rosie grinned. Mags Outhwaite kept her sane. The regime inside the prison was erratic, some of the warders were okay, some were worse than the inmates and the food was a criminal offence in itself. 'It's been good for my waistline, coming here,' she said, pulling at the loose waistband of her prison blues. 'I've lost a good four inches around the old belly. My mam reckons prison's doing me good.'

Living on your own is a poor life for a hypochondriac and Ethel had had a frustrating few years since Rosie had left home. But she now enjoyed the self-sacrifice of her monthly trips to see her daughter, who wasn't aware of the sweet suffering which Ethel endured during these visits. She was used to her mother's pained expression, but felt it polite to ask, 'Are you feeling all right, Mam?'

Ethel didn't want to have to say she was suffering for her daughter. She smiled bravely and said, 'I'll be all right, love. Don't you worry about me.' So Rosie didn't.

Her mother never brought Eddie on Rosie's instructions. He was old enough to remember things and she didn't want a picture of his mum in prison being imprinted on the boy's memory. But she missed him so much it physically hurt. Only the thought of seeing him again kept her going. The visits Rosie enjoyed were Barney's. There was something about Barney she'd always liked. He was a man who would never let her down. The trouble was, he probably wasn't the type to let his wife down either.

She looked at the calendar on the wall. With remission, another nine months and she'd be home. Apart from Gobby Grogan, the main blot on her horizon was Miss Inchbold, the assistant governor. A prisoner officer arrived at the door just as Rosie was about to leave.

'Miss Inchbold would like a word with you.'

'She'll have to wait, I've got a very important lunch date.'

'Now!'

'Keep your hair on, I'm going.'

Miss Inchbold had a soft spot for the governor, Martin McDowell, who, in turn, had a soft spot for Rosie. McDowell had once worked at the prison where Brindle had served his time and he had some sympathy for Rosie's predicament. This irritated the hell out of Miss Inchbold. Any chance she got of putting Rosie down, she grabbed at with both hands. McDowell was on three weeks leave, leaving Miss Inchbold in charge.

Rosie walked across the yard to the administration block and enjoyed a rare moment of solitude. Normally her walks outside were in the company of other prisoners; there was little time to be alone in jail, unless you were being punished. Enforced solitude is no solitude at all. She sat on a coal bunker out of sight of prying eyes and took a cigarette from her pocket. High brown walls surrounded her, and fences and gates and bars. All designed to keep her away from a world which she was entitled to inhabit. Most of all they kept her away from Eddie.

What would he look like now? Would he remember her? What was the point of her being here? What good was her imprisonment doing anyone? She wasn't a danger to society. The law had failed society in not punishing Brindle for what he did to Sean. All she'd done was to punish him for raping her; and look what the law had done to her.

A scruffy pigeon patrolled the ridge of a low roof, keeping a wary eye on her. It reached the end and considered its options. Should it turn around and continue its stroll or should it fly away, over the high, spiked wall? The latter option wasn't available to Rosie. The bird looked down, as if contemplating the reversal of fortunes between Rosie and some of its more colourful, caged cousins.

'Fly away, birdie,' she called out. 'Get out of this dump while you can.'

The pigeon seemed to heed her advice and with a noisy flutter it rose into the air, circled the prison yard then flew over the wall. She watched it disappear and smiled, ruefully. In a few months time she'd be just as free.

A bin wagon went past and stopped at the outer gates for the duty gate officer to swing them open. It would have been dead easy to slide open a door in the wagon and climb in with the rubbish. The guard was supposed to check but he never did. She'd noticed that. Spindly rain began to fall. Rosie squinted up at the darkening sky, nipped the cigarette out and stuck the stub in her pocket, then made her way up the steps to the governor's office. She knocked lightly on the door.

'Come.'

She smiled to herself at Inchbold's pretentiousness and pushed the door open. The assistant governor had her head in the *Daily Herald*. Inchbold was a big-boned, mean-eyed woman with close-cropped, greying hair, and halitosis.

'You sent for me, Miss Inchbold.'

The officer didn't bother to look up as she said, starchily, 'I've had a phone call to say your mother's ill, I thought you should know.'

'Ill?' said Rosie, concerned. 'What's the matter with her?'

Inchbold turned a page of the newspaper and became instantly engrossed. Rosie took a step forward and snatched the paper away from her. 'What's the matter with my mother?' she shouted.

Inchbold slammed an angry fist down on the desk. 'Don't throw one of your tantrums in here, Metcalf!'

Rosie held up an apologetic hand, aware she'd overstepped the mark. 'I'm sorry, Miss. I just want to know what's wrong with my mother.'

'If you were anything of a daughter you'd be out there looking after her,' snapped Inchbold. 'Not rotting away in here. You should have thought about your mother before you got yourself locked up!'

Rosie had long since given up protesting her innocence. Especially to those in charge.

'Please,' she said, as civilly as she could. 'I just want to know what's wrong with her.'

'How the hell should I know? I'm a prison officer not a nurse. I've told you all I know, now get back to what you were doing.'

'I just want to know what's wrong with my mother!' Rosie stood her ground; but her voice was shaking with frustration. 'I'm – I'm entitled to know.'

The governor got slowly to her feet, walked round her desk and stood face to face with her distressed prisoner. 'And I said get out of my office before I have you locked up in solitary. I can do that, you know.'

Inchbold's heavy face was inches from Rosie's. The stench in her stomach came out on her breath, making

204

Rosie grimace with disgust. It was a mixture of disgust and anger that made her push the woman away from her. Just like she'd pushed Joe Brindle all those years ago. Inchbold fell back against her desk and knocked over an inkwell with her hand. Papers on the desk became stained with dark blue Stephen's ink and Inchbold's face contorted with rage.

'Mr Green!' she screamed. 'In here, now!'

A male prison officer rushed in. Rosie was standing with her back to a filing cabinet, her face pale with a mixture of emotions. Inchbold was trying to blot away a pool of ink spreading across her desk.

'Mr Green, take this animal to the secure unit!' she snarled. 'Before she does any more damage.'

Rosie turned her pleas on the man. 'I'm sorry, it was an accident ... I just want to know what's wrong with my mother. She's ill and Miss Inchbold won't tell me what's wrong with her.'

The prison officer looked at his boss as if to confirm Rosie's story. If it was true, Rosie had a point.

'She's just attacked me, you idiot!' seethed Inchbold. 'Don't just stand there looking at me. Take her away from me.'

The officer took Rosie back to the main block, up to the middle landing and through a long corridor to the secure unit.

'I'll try and find out what's wrong with your mother,' he said, as he took her into a bare cell.

On her first visit, Ethel had approved of her stabbing Brindle. 'Men like that deserve all they get. Yer've nowt ter chastise yerself for, our Rosie.'

'Mam, I can't help chastising myself for getting into this mess because of someone like him. I shouldn't have done it. I should have just gone to the police. If I had, maybe he'd have been locked up instead of me.'

'Well, there is that, I suppose,' Ethel had conceded. 'But you are what you are and yer've never been no different.' She'd grinned at her daughter. 'Do you remember letting

one o' the coalman's tyres down because he swore at yer
for getting in his way?'

'I thought no one knew about that.'

'Knew about it?' chuckled Ethel. 'I watched yer doin' it.
I nearly had a word with the foul-mouthed bugger meself
but I hung back ter see what you'd do about it. My God!
Yer can't have been more than eight. When I told yer dad
he laughed like a drain.'

'I sometimes do things without thinking, Mam.'

'I know, love. But yer'll come out the other end none the
worse if I know you.'

Her support had been welcome. Especially the way she
had automatically taken charge of Eddie's welfare. He had
gone to live with her in Duck Street, a world away from the
house he'd lived in with Rosie and George, but Rosie knew
he'd be happy there. Now her mother was ill. How ill?

'It's probably neither nowt nor summat,' comforted the
officer. 'You've most likely got yourself into a load o'
bother over a dose o' flu.'

Rosie sank her head into her hands as the door clunked
shut. He was right; if it was anything serious, Inchbold
would have told her straight away. She'd probably done
this on purpose to get Rosie going and she'd fallen for it,
hook line and sinker. What an idiot? Christ! What would
happen now? If Inchbold made a meal of it she could be
charged with assaulting the assistant governor. Loss of
remission and another sentence added on top. An hour later
she was still assessing the damage she'd done to herself
when the door opened again. It was Mr Green; he looked
grave.

'What is it?'

He hesitated. 'Apparently your mother's got, er ...
She's got pneumonia, love,' he said, gruffly.

Rosie stared at him for a second then grabbed him by his
lapels. 'Please, I need to see her. You've got to let me see
her.'

He eased her hands away. 'Metcalf, er, Rosie, it's not up to me. You can't go without Miss Inchbold's permission.'

'She won't give me permission, you know she won't. Not after what I just did.'

'I know. That's why there's nothing I can do.' His heart went out to her. 'Look, I'll, er, I'll try to keep you informed of how she's doing. I'm sure she'll be all right.'

'What about Eddie?'

'Eddie? Who's Eddie?'

'He's my son. My mother looks after him.'

'Oh, right. Well, I'm sure he's being well looked after.'

'I just want to see my baby.' She had her face to the wall. Her tears were private, not to be shared with him.

He stood there for a while, feeling quite useless and hating his job. A flash of overhead thunder and lightning disturbed his thoughts. It seemed to trigger a rushing downpour just in time for him to be riding home on his bike. He said, 'Damn and blast it,' to himself then left the cell and closed the door quietly out of respect for Rosie's feelings.

Ethel would have been wiser to take herself to the doctor's instead of to bed. She'd self-diagnosed the headache and temperature as a dose of flu. To her, it was just another illness to be endured and enjoyed. Marlene Gedge had been looking after Eddie; old enmities put to one side in the face of adversity. Ethel's neighbour had taken her a bowl of hot soup.

'How're yer feelin' Ethel?' she enquired, her eyes concentrating more on not spilling the soup than on the patient. Ethel gave a scouring cough, causing Marlene to look up and exclaim, 'Jesus Christ! Yer should be in hospital.'

Sweat was pouring down Ethel's face, her breathing sounded heavy and painful. The neighbour set the soup down on the bedside table and ran downstairs to the telephone. By the time Ethel got to hospital, nothing could save her. She died a few hours later of bacterial pneumonia.

*

Mr Green stood six feet behind Rosie, who was standing in front of Inchbold's desk. His eyes were fixed on his boss. If the callous woman didn't do this properly he'd give her a roasting himself and sod the consequences. Inchbold looked up at Rosie.

'First of all, I wish to tell you that under the circumstances I've decided to take no further action against you for what you did yesterday. You will be returned to your cell.'

Rosie was confused. This was totally out of character for Miss Inchbold, but she wasn't going to argue. 'Thank you, Miss. Have you heard any more about my mother?' she enquired. 'I was wondering if it would be possible for me to go and see her. Pneumonia can be serious. I know Mr McDowell would let me go.'

Inchbold shook her head. 'I, er ... I'm afraid I have some bad news for you, Metcalf.'

'Bad news? What sort of bad news?' Rosie was worried. 'She's okay, isn't she?'

'I'm sorry. Apparently the doctors did all they could. She passed away peacefully, so I'm told.'

'You mean she's dead?'

'I'm sorry.'

Rosie squeezed her eyes together trying to make sense of what she'd been told. Her mother, who had visited her in the best of health only two weeks ago, was dead. And this pig of a woman had taken it upon herself to tell her.

'How dare you!' she trembled.

Inchbold frowned, 'What do you mean?'

'How dare you presume to tell me mother's dead. What right have you got?'

'Be careful, Metcalf,' warned Inchbold. 'I appreciate you've had bad news, but don't push me too far. I've already been lenient on you.'

'Lenient? My mother's dead and you're talking about leniency.' Senseless words poured out in a torrent, releasing Rosie's anger and sorrow and frustration. 'My mam had her faults, but she deserved better than you ... you lousy pig! People like you shouldn't be allowed to tell anyone their mother's dead.'

Inchbold got to her feet, her face blazing. 'Mr Green, take her back to her cell, before she says something she really regrets!'

'Yes, Ma'am,' said the officer, with ill-concealed scorn, as he led a dejected Rosie out of the office.

Mags Outhwaite sat on the toilet lid, smoking and staring at Rosie who had hardly spoken for three days. Mr Green had been round to tell her that the funeral had been arranged for the following day, Friday; and that Eddie had been taken into foster care. Rosie hadn't reacted. Her eyes stared blankly at the ceiling.

'Yer should eat summat,' advised Mags. 'Yer'll need ter get yer strength up for t' funeral.'

'The bastard won't let me go.'

Mags raised an eyebrow at this uncharacteristic expletive, then tried a joke.

'Ah! So yer *can* talk. I thought yer'd been struck dumb.'

Rosie spoke to the ceiling. 'If I'd been with her, she wouldn't have died. I'd have seen to that.'

Mags was in no position to advise, only to listen.

'Inchbold said if I'd been a proper daughter I'd have been with her, not locked up in here,' Rosie went on. 'My little boy's living in some home with people he doesn't know, all because of me. Maybe Inchbold's right. I'm not a fit person.'

'Inchbold's a pig,' said Mags. 'Yer worth ten of Inchbold. Anyway, who says yer can't go? Course yer can go. Yer entitled.'

'She won't let me go. She probably thinks I'm stupid enough to try and escape ... and she's probably right.'

'Well, I'll go and ask her,' said Mags. 'We've all got entitlements an' it's only fair yer should be allowed ter go.'

Raised voices approached along the landing. Mags was berating a female officer. The officer was protesting.

'Don't go blaming me. I'm only doing my job. If it's anyone's fault it's your mate's, she's her own worst enemy. She can't go pushing governors about and still expect favours.'

'She's just lost her mam, she's bound to be a bit upset.'

Rosie's gaze was still on the ceiling as they arrived at the cell door.

'Go on,' insisted Mags, pushing the warder into the cell. 'Tell her what bloody Inchbold said!'

The officer cleared her throat. 'Er ... Metcalf. I've been asked to tell ...'

'Save your breath,' cut in Rosie. 'Inchbold won't let me go to my mother's funeral.'

'It creates problems. You see we're understaffed at the moment and we'd have to send someone to escort you ...'

'Could you go away, please?'

Rosie hadn't taken her eyes off the ceiling, so the officer addressed herself to Mags.

'She brought it on herself. If she'd behaved properly she might have been allowed to go.'

'I pushed her away because I couldn't stand her bad breath,' Rosie said.

'I've noticed that,' sympathised Mags, looking at the officer for her support.

'It's okay,' said Rosie. 'Forget it.' She eased herself off her bunk and stood up. 'I think I'm hungry.'

The officer left. Mags grabbed Rosie's wrist and examined her watch. 'Couple of hours till teatime. I've got half a bar o' Fruit and Nut.' She slid open the top drawer of a two drawer chest and felt around under a disarray of underwear. 'Here,' she said, handing the chocolate to Rosie. 'Get yer choppers round that.'

Rosie bit into it, hungrily. Mags watched for a while then she suddenly grinned. 'Hey! What's long and black and hangs from an arsehole?'

Rosie continued chewing, she wasn't ready for riddles. 'What?' she asked, at length.

'Inchbold's tie.'

Rosie didn't react. She looked quizzically in Mags' general direction, but her eyes were somewhere else. '*You're* a burglar,' she said.

Mags was taken aback. 'I were actually a school dinner lady. Burglary were a more of a side-line. I had to make ends meet after Charlie had his injury.'

'Funny line of work for a woman,' commented Rosie.

'Well, I did think about becomin' a prozzie but yer need ter look the part. I used ter have trouble givin' it away, so I had no chance sellin' it. Anyway, there's a lot of walkin' up an' down and I've got fallen arches.'

'So you took over your husband's burglary business.'

'I suppose I did. Yer see, we figured they'd never suspect a woman and they never did for long enough until this night watchman locked me in these offices. I wouldn't care but I were bustin' for a pee an' this daft old bugger wouldn't let me out. That was the worst bit about it. I couldn't last out any longer so I dropped me drawers behind this desk an' I was halfway through when the police burst in. Well, yer just can't stop peein' halfway through, can yer? I mean they had their truncheons out as though they were expectin' some big bloke, an' all they got were me squattin' down over a waste paper bin. It didn't half make a row ...'

'But you know about breaking into places. Picking locks and stuff.'

'I don't know about picking lo ... hey! If yer thinkin' o' breakin' out, yer on yer own. When I walk out of here it'll be as a free woman. Anyroad, t' locks in this place'd baffle Houdini.'

'I need to go to Mam's funeral,' said Rosie. 'And to see that Eddie's okay.'

'Fair enough,' conceded Mags. 'What d' yer want me ter do?'

'Aren't you on cleaning roster this week?'

'What if I am?'

'Could you pick a lock on a cupboard door?'

'Mebbe,' said Mags. 'What cupboard are yer talkin' about?'

'The one in the screw's room,' said Rosie. 'There's a spare uniform in there. I noticed it when I was in there cleaning last week. Gobby Grogan went on leave and left it there. Trouble is, they normally keep it locked.'

Mags grinned, 'Yer thinkin' o' walkin' out dressed as Gobby?'

'I'm not *walking* anywhere,' smiled Rosie. 'There'll be a van coming tomorrow morning with a new intake of guests. I'll cadge a lift. Mebbe cadge a decent fag as well.'

Mags laughed loudly at the audacity of Rosie's plan. 'I'd best get yer that uniform before I go ter breakfast.'

Chapter Twenty-One

The weight that Rosie had shed since coming into prison came to her aid as she squeezed into Gobby Grogan's uniform. Mags stood back and simpered,

'Oh, madam, it really is you.'

'Thank you,' said Rosie. 'I'll take it. Do you have it in pale lilac?'

'No, madam, only in the dyke blue. Which is this season's colour. As chosen by her Majesty the Queen for her summer holidays in Skeggy.'

'May I try the hat?'

'Certainly, madam.'

Rosie suddenly stopped laughing. 'This isn't right,' she said.

'What's up?' asked Mags.

'They're burying my mother in a couple of hours and here I am, laughing like I don't care.'

'Rosie love, yer've just spent three days moping around with a face like a smacked arse. It's about time yer cheered up. Anyroad, yer'll be seeing yer son today with a bit o' luck. That's why yer so cheerful.'

'I know,' admitted Rosie. 'I just feel a bit guilty that's all.'

'I'm sure your mam wouldn't have minded.'

'You don't know my mam. She enjoyed a good funeral nearly as much as a good ailment. My mam could have made a living as a professional mourner.'

'Oh heck,' said Mags.

They heard Jack Green's unmistakeable footsteps and Mags pushed the cell door shut. The officer rapped as he usually did before entering. He was one of only three male officers in the whole prison; dealing with the opposite sex had its disadvantages.

'I'm undressed,' shouted Rosie. 'You can't come in.'

'That's okay. I've, er ... I've had another word with Inchbold about the funeral. She won't budge. Just thought I'd give it a last try.'

'Thanks, Mr Green,' said Rosie. 'I didn't think she would. What time does it start?'

'Half-past-eleven. Do you want to go to the chapel or something?'

'Not really. Thanks anyway.'

'If you want to complain to Mr McDowell when he gets back I'll back you up. What she's doing is wrong.'

'It won't be necessary. By the way, Mr Green?'

'What?'

'Is there a delivery of new clients due today?'

'About ten o'clock. Don't worry, there's none down for your cell.'

'Just checking.'

His footsteps faded into the distance as Rosie donned her prison garb over the officer's uniform. She looked at her watch, nine-thirty.

'Right,' said Mags. 'I'd best get back to me cleaning. I've had a word with all them as I can trust. We can probably cover for yer till teatime, then it's all hell let loose. Did yer ring that bloke?'

'Barney? Yes, he tried to talk me out of it but he'll be there.'

'He sounds like a good pal.'

'He's the best is Barney.'

'I suppose he's married?'

'You suppose right.'

'Pity.'

214

Mags kissed Rosie on her cheek and pressed a fistful of loose change into her hand. 'We had a bit of a whip round. Figured yer might need some dosh.'

'Thanks, Mags. And thank the girls.'

'Be lucky, love. An' make sure yer give yerself up before they catch yer. It'll make a big difference.'

'I know. See you when I see you.'

'Give my love ter little Eddie,' said Mags, uncertain as to whether she'd ever see her friend again.

Rosie hid her prison clothes behind the dustbins then adjusted Gobby Grogan's cap which she'd lined with paper to make it fit. As she waited, her adrenalin began to surge, preparing her body for what was to come. Her pulse raced as she tuned her ears to the sounds coming from round the corner, and tried to picture what was happening.

The van had already arrived and was disgorging its unhappy cargo. The escorting officers would remain in the prison and the driver would probably leave straight away, although sometimes he stopped for a cup of tea. Rosie hoped he wouldn't today, the longer she was there, the more chance there was of her being discovered. She was supposed to be on gardening duty. Spring was only a fortnight away and there were things to do, but hopefully someone was covering for her. The day was dull and cold and Rosie was glad of the serge, prison officer's jacket which was a tight fit when fully buttoned, but to leave it unbuttoned might invite a question and she didn't want that.

The van doors slammed shut and a minute later the engine fired into life. Good, the timing was crucial now. She took a deep, calming breath and strolled round the corner of the admin block just as the empty van approached from behind her. The driver slowed as she stuck out a thumb. He wound down his window.

'You're not going anywhere near Leeds, are you?' she asked casually, knowing full well that was exactly where he was headed.

'Yeah. Wanna lift?'

'Please. Save my bus fare.'

Rosie's eyes glanced up momentarily to a first-floor window where Mags and two other faces were grinning down at her. She began to wave back then smiled at the driver and quickly disguised the wave as tucking her hair under officer Grogan's cap. 'I'm off to visit my mam,' she explained. 'Haven't seen her for ages.'

'Whereabouts does she live?'

'Moortown.'

He looked at his watch. 'I'm okay fer time, I can drop yer somewhere near.'

'Don't get yourself into trouble on my account.'

The driver drove beyond the inner gate which had been left open for the van's return, and pulled up outside the gatehouse. Rosie slumped low in her seat and looked away as Albert, the gate-officer stared at her. He couldn't fail to recognise her as a prisoner.

'What's this,' he shouted. 'Thought yer'd run off wi' one of our lasses without us noticing, did yer?'

Rosie's heart sank. It was all over before it had started. She pushed down the door handle, wondering what to say when she got out. Maybe she could pass it off as a practical joke. The driver was shouting back to the gate-officer.

'Be fair, Albert. I'm only takin' one.'

'Don't let yer missis find out.'

'What my missis dunt know won't hurt her. She's a lot like your missis in that respect.'

Albert laughed and swung the gate open. Rosie slowly released her pent up breath as the van moved through. The driver turned to her and grinned. 'No offence, love. Albert thinks everyone's as sex-mad as him. Mind you, I suppose yer know that yerself.'

'That's right,' she agreed, wishing her heart would calm down. Beads of sweat appeared on her forehead in the aftermath of the adrenalin rush, then her face creased into a broad smile as the van turned into an open road. She'd done it.

Chapter Twenty-Two

The door to Oak House opened as she hurried up the path. Barney Robinson had been standing at the window for an hour, getting more depressed by the minute. However the day turned out, she'd end up serving more time. Prisons didn't like their inmates to come and go as they pleased without permission.

With a quick, 'Hiya, Barney,' she darted past him as he glanced around to make sure no one had seen her. He closed the door and followed her through to the kitchen. She was putting the kettle on.

'Any problems?' he enquired.

'No, you?'

'Me? Why should I have problems?'

'I don't know, getting time off work.'

'I work for myself now.'

Rosie smiled at him. 'Oh really? I didn't know.' She was casually spooning tea leaves in to the teapot as though nothing was amiss in her life. There were many things about her which exasperated him.

'Leave that, Rosie, I'll do it. You just get yerself changed.' He looked at his watch, 'It starts in thirty-five minutes, we'll have ter set off in about quarter of an hour.'

'Right, thanks for this, Barney. I just needed you to let me in. I won't involve you any more, I promise.'

'Rosie, I'm already involved. Just get yerself changed and let's get off.'

She looked at him for a second to check if he was angry with her for asking him to do something illegal.

'Are you mad at me?'

He stared back at her then grinned. 'Go on wi' yer. When were I ever mad at you?'

She dashed upstairs and smiled at the way Barney had already laid out everything suitable for a funeral on the bed. Normally she'd take an hour to get ready to go anywhere special, but prison had knocked a lot of the fussiness out of her. Ten minutes later she was ready and back in the kitchen sipping tea with Barney.

'Where's Eddie?' she asked. 'Will he be coming?'

'No,' said Barney. 'I rang the foster home last night just after you rang me. They said it'd only upset him.'

Rosie couldn't hide her disappointment. 'Did they now? Have you seen him?' Her eyes darted across his face.

'Aye,' he muttered. 'The little beggar's taken it hard. He thought a lot about her.' He smiled to himself. 'He used ter call me Uncle Barney.'

'I'm going to call in and see him.'

'Thought you might. I'll take you there after the funeral.'

'You're not coming to the funeral. I don't want you getting into trouble on my account. Just give me Eddie's address. If I'm caught I want to be on my own, without an accomplice.'

'But ...'

'No buts, Barney. I've got enough to worry about, without worrying about you.'

'I didn't know you cared,' he grinned.

She looked at him and smiled. 'I've always cared about you, Barney. You're the one solid thing in my life.'

Their eyes met for a brief second then Barney looked away, leaving Rosie staring at him. Wondering.

George's car had been sold to pay off creditors so she drove to the cemetery in her Ford Popular, which had been gathering dust in the garage. The day turned bleak and chilly with rain threatening; Rosie had chosen a dark-blue, double-breasted rain-coat to cater for such an eventuality, plus the black, pill-box hat she'd worn at George's funeral. Ethel had been paying one and nine a month into the Leeds Co-op funeral insurance scheme for twelve years. Going before her time meant she'd shown a nice profit on her arrangement, this would have pleased her. The hearse was already there, a black Daimler. Behind it was a Morris Eight belonging to Ethel's cousin, Stewart, who had reluctantly made all the arrangements; and an Austin Seven containing a curate and two of Ethel's neighbours. Rosie drove up the narrow, cemetery road and parked her Ford at the back of them, then watched as the coffin was carried to the grave on the shoulders of four Co-op coffin carriers.

The flowers on the coffin looked a bit pathetic, her mother deserved better. She cast an eye around the cemetery. One fairly recent grave was heaped with rotting blooms, others had potted plants, yet to flower. Most had nothing. Beneath a stone angel about thirty yards away she caught a flash of colour. Rosie got out of the car for a better look and saw what looked to be a pristine wreath. Shielded by the line of cars, she sneaked between the graves and stood by the flowers, hands together, ostensibly in prayer, as she looked furtively around to make sure no one was looking.

It was the grave of Charles (Charlie) Poskitt. Born 1828 died 1903, and his beloved wife, Agnes (Aggie), who was twenty-five years his junior and had died as recently as 1944. Forty years a widow and all because she'd married an older man. The significance wasn't lost on Rosie. Still, today was the tenth anniversary of Aggie's death, so the flowers were fresh. She bowed her head, solemnly.

'Sorry, Aggie, but I'm sure you understand.'

She picked up the wreath and backed away, respectfully, until she was far enough not to be a suspected grave robber but just another mourner. Then she turned and headed towards the funeral party.

219

As she approached her mother's grave, a gust of cold wind shook the trees and showered her with last night's rain which had been clinging to the bare branches. She looked upwards, apologetically, and it crossed her mind that this might be some sort of retribution for her most recent crime.

Turning up the collar of her coat, Rosie stepped between the bowed heads of the mourners to reverently place the flowers on top of the coffin as a damp-looking curate prayed mournfully for the repose of Ethel's soul. She looked around and felt sad that her mother had so few friends to see her off; apart from the curate and the Co-op undertakers, just four people. Marlene Gedge looked up, her eyes widening; first in surprise, then in acknowledgement as Rosie nodded her recognition and mouthed, 'Thank you for coming'.

The curate droned on, then he stopped and raised his eyebrows to the two men who were holding on to the ropes supporting the coffin. The men looked back, then at each other, then realising that this was the signal, began to lower Ethel into the ground and Rosie felt a sense of loss for the second time in eighteen months. The excitement of the morning had, up until then, superseded any sense of sadness, but it released itself now in a sudden flood of quiet tears. The other mourners backed away leaving her to her private grief. Rosie stood there and blinked her eyes dry.

'Bye, Mam.'

She stared down at the coffin as fine spots of rain fell on the polished wood and clung to it in tiny beads until joined by others which formed into narrow rivulets that ran off down the side. The sun pushed a narrow ray of its light through a gap in the clouds, reflecting off the brass plaque, which was economically inscribed:

Ethel Jones
Age 47

Not much of an epitaph but Rosie would remedy this when she organised the headstone. She said a last quick prayer then picked up a handful of damp earth and threw it on the coffin where it mingled with the stolen flowers. Without thinking, she wiped her hand on her expensive raincoat then said, 'Damn' when she realised what she'd done. Prison had instilled too many bad habits into her. She sensed someone at her elbow.

'Let yer out for the day, did they, love?' enquired Marlene.

'Something like that.'

'I were with her at the end.'

'So I understand. Thanks for that, Mrs Gedge.'

'Marlene, call me Marlene.'

They stared down at the coffin; both with hands clasped as if in prayer.

'She were better fer knowin' were yer mam.'

Rosie nodded.

'I thought yer might have brought the lad wi' yer.'

'It would have been too upsetting. I'm calling in to see him on my way back.'

'Oh ... I must say, love, I think it's a bugger the way yer've been treated. Nobody'll think any the less of yer when yer come out.'

'That's good to know, Mrs Gedge.'

'Marlene.'

'Sorry – Marlene.'

'So ... yer've nowt arranged then?'

'In what way?' enquired Rosie.

'Funeral tea – I don't suppose you could arrange owt like that.'

'Well, I haven't. I don't know about anybody else.' She glanced towards her cousin.

'No, he hasn't either. Never mind.' Mrs Gedge inclined her head down to the coffin. 'It's not as though she'll be any the wiser. I'll, er ... I'll be off then.'

'Thanks for coming Mrs ... er, Marlene.'

As Rosie watched the woman walk away, her thoughts turned to her son. Somehow she must get to see him before

221

she was caught and taken back inside.

Number Ninety-Four Branwell Avenue had seven bedrooms and three reception rooms and it housed anywhere between six and ten fostered children in reasonable comfort. Most kids considered it a vast improvement on the squalor they'd left, but they found the house-mother, the eccentric Mrs Gittings, quite hard to fathom. Eddie had taken an instant dislike to her.

'The little bugger thinks I'm an evil old witch,' she told Rosie.

'It's hard to imagine what's going through his mind right now,' said Rosie. She glanced up the stairs. Somewhere up there was her baby boy. Mrs Gittings had suggested they have a chat downstairs before she brought Eddie to meet her. She shooed a small, runny-nosed boy from a large, comfortably furnished living room. As the boy left he wiped his nose on his sleeve with an exaggerated movement of his arm, designed to annoy Mrs Gittings. She ignored him and turned to Rosie.

'I gave the little bugger a handkerchief but he made a toy parachute out of it, so he can go round wi' snot on his sleeve as far as I'm concerned. The other kids'll laugh at him ... that'll soon teach him a lesson.'

'Right,' said Rosie, wondering how this unusual treatment would project itself on to Eddie. She accepted the house-mother's invitation to sit down.

'By the way,' began Mrs Gittings. 'In case yer wondering. I never lay a finger on any of 'em. Most of 'em have had enough ter put up with without me adding to it. I have me own ways, but I never hit 'em.'

'I'm sure he's in good hands.'

The house-mother accepted the compliment with a nod, then asked: 'Does he know yer in ...?' She tactfully chose not to finish the question.

Rosie jumped in quickly. 'No. He's been told I've had to go away for a while.'

222

'Good of 'em ter let yer out, I suppose.'

'It's only what I'm entitled to.'

'You weren't entitled ter go ter jail in the first place if what I've heard's right. I were talking ter Mr Robinson yesterday. He told me all about it.'

'Barney?' smiled Rosie.

'He thinks a lot about yer, does Barney.'

'He's married, Mrs Gittings.'

'Married or not, he thinks a lot about yer.'

Rosie changed the subject. 'How is Eddie? Is he happy?'

'He's a bit quiet, but it's only to be expected. Now his grandma's dead, he really misses his mam.'

'I miss *him*. I miss him terribly.'

'I think he's takin' a bit of stick from the kids at school. They've obviously found out about you.'

'Oh no.' Rosie felt dreadful.

'Sooner yer get out the better.' Mrs Gittings got to her feet. 'I'll get him, shall I?'

'Please.'

Rosie smoothed her skirt and patted her hair in readiness to greet the son she hadn't seen in over a year and she felt almost as nervous as she had earlier that morning when she was waiting for the prison van to whisk her to a temporary freedom.

She heard them coming down the stairs. Mrs Gittings was chatting in a low voice, but no response was coming from Eddie. Rosie felt suddenly frightened. Suppose he'd forgotten her? A year was a huge chunk of his life and this was a very formative time for him. A time when his thoughts began to mould into memories. What memories would he have of her? He appeared at the door looking apprehensive and wary. Mrs Gittings stood behind him, gently prodding him into the room. Rosie was frozen to her chair, not wanting to overwhelm him with the gushing love she felt for him. She gave him a smile that only a mother can give to her child. He'd grown and had lost some of his chubbiness; his features were becoming more defined and

Rosie had been deprived of being with him when all this happened, which saddened her.

The boy frowned when he saw her, then he took a step forward and asked indignantly, 'Where did you go?'

She ran to him and swept him up in her arms. At first he allowed himself to be held limply, as children do, then his arms came around his mother's neck. She hugged him as she walked around the room, smothering him with kisses. Then she set him down and held his hands as she examined every inch of his face. She wanted to remember this. To keep it locked in her memory until she was free to come back to him. Eddie's eyes were reproachful.

'You said you'd never leave me.' It was one of the few things in his memory.

His words stabbed into her. 'I know I did, darling. I meant it. I'll be home soon and I'll never leave you again.'

'I didn't think you were coming back,' he said. 'I thought you'd gone to stay with daddy. Grandma's not coming back.'

She ached with guilt. 'I know, love, Grandma had to go.'

'I'm glad you came, Mum. Can we go home? I don't like it here.'

Rosie looked up at Mrs Gittings for help, then back at Eddie. 'Look, Eddie. I've got to go away again for a little while, but when I come back, I'll be staying with you for good.'

His face dropped. 'Have you got to go back to jail?'

'What do you know about that?' she asked, gently.

'Some boys at school were laughing at me.'

Her mind raced for an answer. 'Well, you can tell those boys it's where, I, er ... where I work. And if I hear they've been laughing at you, tell them I'll have them locked up as well.'

'Will you lock Peter Buttershawe up?'

'Tell him from me he'll be the first one if he doesn't watch his step.'

Eddie grinned at the prospect of this and Mrs Gittings shook her head, disapprovingly.

Rosie looked up at her and shrugged, then smiled at her

son. 'I want you to be a good boy for Mrs Gittings because she's a good friend of mine.'

Eddie looked at the house-mother in a new light. 'Are you a friend of Uncle Barney's?'

Mrs Gittings smiled through gritted teeth, 'Oh yes, your Uncle Barney's one of my best pals.'

This seemed to satisfy Eddie. He held his mum's hand. 'Can we go to Butlin's on holiday when you come home?'

'Definitely,' promised Rosie. Although Butlin's wouldn't have been her first choice.

A police car siren wailed in the distance; probably nothing to do with her, but it was getting nearer. She got to her feet. If she was going to be caught she didn't want her son to witness it.

'I've got to go.' She hugged Eddie and fought back the tears.

'Best way,' agreed Mrs Gittings. 'Longer you stay, the harder it gets to leave.'

'I'll be back before you know it, my darling.'

Eddie stood there, dumbly as she left him. He was used to people leaving him. But he didn't like it.

The wailing police car came down the street. For a second she thought it was going to screech to a halt outside Mrs Gittings' house and disgorge a gang of policemen. But it howled by and brought a sigh of relief from her. She looked back and saw Eddie at the window. His hand was waving slowly, and he looked so sad. Rosie had to force herself to get in the car. Every instinct told her to rush in and grab him; to take him away with her. Away from these people who were making their lives such a misery. But commonsense won the battle. She drove away, drowned in tears and headed back to Oak House from where she planned to ring for a taxi to take her back to jail. To face the consequences.

Barney was waiting for her. Sitting in an armchair facing the door as she came in. 'I was worried about you,' he said. 'How did it go?'

Suddenly the events of the day overtook her: the escape from jail; her mother's funeral; seeing Eddie. Her face began to crumple.

'Hold me, Barney.'

Barney didn't need asking twice. He got up and folded his arms around her as she sobbed against his chest. There was an unspoken need inside them both. A need for each other, which they'd denied themselves for years. They kissed; gently at first, then with passion. Then they led each other up the stairs. Not saying a word. Not needing to. Each heart pounding in anticipation of what lay ahead.

They made wordless love. Hiding their guilt behind the silence. Especially Barney, the married one. But the guilt, the danger, the need and passion they felt for each other all added to the excitement of the moment. A moment they would never quite repeat.

Afterwards Rosie stretched her naked body and realised it had never been like this since that night with Sean. The night he'd made her pregnant. With George she'd never worried about pregnancy; if it happened it would be a nice surprise. But she couldn't afford any such surprises right now.

'Oh heck!' she said.

'What?'

'We didn't use anything, that's what.'

Barney said nothing for a while, then he turned to her. 'I, er, I shouldn't worry love. Me and Eileen have been trying for years – in fact we've given up trying. At least she has. She reckons it's my fault.'

'That's what she reckons, is it? Barney, I think it's a bit more scientific than that.'

'She said she had a test and there's nothing wrong with her.'

'Have you had a test?'

Barney grimaced, 'Ter be honest, I didn't fancy the idea. Anyway, Eileen reckoned there was no need. Process of elimination and all that.'

'Right.' Rosie thought it all sounded very odd.

'So, yer've no need to worry,' he said.

'If you say so ... Barney, don't you and Eileen ... you know, do it anymore?'

'Not for a while. I think she might have a boyfriend.'

'And do you mind?'

Barney had to think. 'Not right this second ... but yes, I do mind.'

'Do you love her?'

A car door slammed, cutting off Barney's answer. Rosie got out of bed and walked over to the drawn curtains as he leaned up on one elbow and enjoyed the naked view of her. She pulled one curtain back just far enough to see through.

'There's someone inside!' shouted a voice from the driveway. 'I can see the curtain twitching.'

'Oh Jesus!' gasped Rosie. 'I don't believe this.'

Barney was already out of bed, pulling on his underpants. 'What is it?'

'It's the police!'

A loud banging on the door had him hopping around on one leg as he tried to get his trousers on. 'They must have found out you've escaped.'

'The important thing is that they don't find *you* here,' said Rosie.

'I suppose you could give yourself up?'

'I want to hand myself in, rather than have them catch me. And I don't want you to get into trouble.'

The banging became more persistent.

'They'll have a job breaking the door down,' said Rosie, glad she'd remembered to lock the door to the garage. 'This house is built like a fortress.'

'Pity you don't have an escape tunnel,' said Barney, fastening his shirt.

Rosie's face brightened. 'There is sort of an escape *route*,' she said, pulling on her dress. 'George worked out how we should escape in case of fire.'

The shouting outside was now loud and urgent. 'This is the police, open up or we'll break down the door.'

'Landing window,' decided Rosie, urgently. 'They shouldn't be able to see us from the ground.' She put on her raincoat, grabbed Barney's hand and dragged him from the bedroom, down a short flight of stairs on to a half-landing where she cautiously opened a stained-glass window. He was struggling to put on his jacket as she looked out.

'It's okay,' she whispered. 'We can get on to the garage roof.'

He helped her out and lowered her the short distance on to the flat roof, then leaped out after her, landing noisily. There were shouts from below:

'What was that?'

'I think there's somebody on the garage roof!'

Rosie pressed a finger to her lips and moved on all fours to the other side of the roof, which bounded next door's garden. Almost without breaking stride she jumped to the soft earth of a flower bed and rolled clear of Barney as he landed beside her.

'Okay?' she enquired.

'I will be when we get away from here. Where to now?'

With Barney hard on her heels she ran around the back of her neighbour's house, down a gravel path and scrambled over a fence into another garden. A woman's face came to the house window but by the time she'd opened it Barney and Rosie were halfway across the next garden where they hid in a bush.

'Where's the nearest phone box?' he whispered.

'There's a footpath runs along the side of here,' Rosie said. 'The phone box is at the end.'

'Right, I'll ring for a taxi.'

She kissed him hard on the lips. He responded and pulled her to the ground. Through the leaves he saw a policeman's helmet on the far side of the fence, then a face peered into the bushes. Barney pressed his hand over her mouth.

'Nothing here, Sarge,' called out the face beneath the helmet. Heavy footsteps faded away down the path as the fugitives released their pent-up breath.

'Wait here,' instructed Barney. 'I'll be back in a minute. No one's looking for me.' He stood up to leave.

'Hold it. Your shirt's hanging out of your trousers,' giggled Rosie. 'You look as suspicious as hell.'

'What about you? Your coat's covered in mud.'

They tried to make themselves look presentable and Barney suddenly grinned. 'Did you put your knickers back on?'

She took them out of her coat pocket. 'They'll be on by the time you get back.'

'Pity.'

She watched him climb over the fence and felt as good as she could under the circumstances. Even at a time like this she felt easy in his company. Whatever it was she felt for him, it was special. Barney nodded at a uniformed policeman as he arrived at the phone box.

'I don't suppose you've got change for the phone,' he asked, holding out a half-crown.

The policeman said: 'Sorry, sir, I haven't got time ... I don't suppose you've seen anyone acting suspiciously, have you?'

Barney shrugged. 'Suspicious, in what way?'

'There's been a break in.' He didn't elaborate. 'If you see anything, call the station, sir.'

'I would if I had any change.'

'Oh, right.'

The policeman took a handful of coins from his pocket and changed Barney's half-crown for him. A few minutes later, as he came out of the box, a black Wolseley drove past with two policemen inside. They'd obviously given up their search. Barney whistled as he walked back up the path, alerting Rosie to his approach. He leaned over the fence and called out in a stage whisper: 'Have you got them on yet?'

Her smiling face appeared through the leaves. 'Less of your smutty talk, Mr Robinson. Can I come out now?'

'Yes, the police aren't actually looking for you. They think there's been a break-in.'

'At my house?'

'I assume so.'

'Nice to know the law's looking after me so well.'

She climbed over the fence and linked his arm as they walked back down the path. Being with this man felt so right, but they couldn't be together. She had always known that.

'That'll be just five bob,' said the taxi driver as they pulled up at a telephone box, two hundred yards from the prison.

She'd come on her own. There'd been no more kisses; that would have been too painful. Rosie realised the impossibility of their situation and knew she had to be the strong one. She'd put both Barney's freedom and his marriage in jeopardy.

'Thanks for everything,' she'd said, climbing in to the cab with her emotions held in check.

'My pleasure. I'll pop in on Eddie as often as I can and keep you posted.'

'That'd be lovely. See you, Barney.'

The sky was as sombre as her mood as she walked along the street. Rosie stared up at the high walls which would keep her from the outside world for God knows how long, and she felt suddenly out of place. There were other people in the street who had every right to be there, unlike her. A man on a bicycle rode past, with a cigarette in his mouth and a shopping bag hanging from the handlebars. A free man, just like the two cackling women across the street and the short-trousered boy licking a lollipop. Even the scruffy dog peeing against the lamp post was freer than her.

She arrived at the prison gate. It was huge and imposing, with a small, personal door cut into it; beside which was an ordinary doorbell and a sign saying, Ring Once For Attention. It was just like Lazarus's doorbell. A sudden thought brought a smile to Rosie's lips as she compared the hospitality extended by the two places and concluded there was not much to choose. The absurdity of her whole situation hit her as she pressed the bell.

After a few seconds a hatch in the small door slid open. The officer on the other side didn't immediately recognise her.

'What do you want?'

'I seem to have forgotten my key, could you let me in, please.'

'And who are you?'

'Rosie Metcalf. I live here.'

He recognised her. 'Oh hell!'

The door opened and she stepped inside to confront Albert, the gate officer. He took her arm and hurried her into his office.

'What the hell's happening? What the hell d'yer think yer doing?'

'I popped out to my mother's funeral. You should know, it was you who let me out this morning.'

'I did no such thing.'

'You did, actually. I came out in the prison van. Admittedly I was dressed as a warder, but I didn't think you'd let me out otherwise. Mrs Inchbold said I couldn't go, so I had to take matters into my own hands.'

He scratched his head, worried. 'Aw, bloody hell! This could cost me my job.'

Rosie brightened. 'Are you saying no one knows I'm missing?'

'Not as far as I know,' he said. 'Why?'

'Maybe we can do each other a favour. My prison uniform's hidden behind admin block bins. If you could get it for me, I could sneak back to the main block.'

'I don't believe this. Yer want me to help yer?'

'You'd be helping us both,' she pointed out.

He thought about it for a few seconds. 'I'm not supposed ter leave the gate.'

'It'll only take a few seconds. I'll look after the gate for you.'

'Back of the bins?'

She nodded. 'Admin block – middle bin.'

'Just sit there and keep quiet. Don't answer the phone, don't open the hatch. Do nothing till I get back. Do you understand?'

She nodded her head, meekly, and Albert shook his at the folly of what he was about to do; then he walked quickly out of the office, leaving her to reflect on the events of this unusual day. Mainly reflecting on Barney.

Two minutes later, Albert came back with her prison clothes and Jack Green. Both men looked grave. Rosie's face dropped.

'Another five minutes and the balloon would have gone up,' Jack said. 'At the moment you're just missing, and I've been sent to track you down and take you to Inchbold's office for a bollocking – so get a move on!'

'Turn your backs,' said Rosie as she slipped out of her clothes. The men obeyed, with not a little irritation.

'You can turn round now.' Rosie handed Jack the clothes she'd just changed out of. 'You'd better get rid of these.'

Jack took them and said, 'Inchbold thinks you're deliberately causing trouble because of not being allowed to go to your mother's funeral.'

'So, that's my story, is it?'

'It is – so stick to it, or we're all in trouble ... and don't give any cheek. Be humble and tell her you're very sorry.'

'I'll do that.'

'I wish I could believe you.'

'You can. Thanks, fellers.'

'Rosie, you can tell me. How the hell did you get back in?' enquired Mags as the cell doors slammed them in for the night.

'Mags, I can't tell you. I've promised I won't tell anyone.'

'Not even yer best mate?'

'Don't make me feel rotten.' Rosie stretched out on her bed and stared at the white-washed ceiling. 'I tell you what, Mags,' she said, 'what with one thing and another, it's been a very unusual sort of day.'

Chapter Twenty-Three

Rosie and Miss Inchbold faced each other across the desk. She'd been summoned to the governor's office after breakfast and on her way there she passed a worried Jack Green.

'What's it about?' she whispered.

'I don't know.'

'I won't drop you in it.'

He went on his way knowing she might not have any option. Grogan was back off leave. She sidled up to him. 'In trouble again, is she?'

'I've no idea what the problem is.' Jack moved away from her, but she followed.

'I hope she gets her arse kicked this time.'

'You'll be getting your arse kicked if you don't find that uniform,' he warned. 'They'll make you pay for it, you know.'

'Somebody nicked it, why should I pay for it?'

'Who's going to nick a uniform?' said Jack.

'Somebody who's damaged their own,' grumbled Grogan. 'Don't worry, I'll find out who it is. For a start it's somebody my size, which narrows it down. I've got a couple of ideas.'

'Do you think it's another guard?'

Grogan shook her head and flashed him a despairing look. 'Well, it's hardly likely to be an inmate.'

*

'The police have been in contact with us,' said Inchbold. 'Apparently there's been an intruder in your house.'

Rosie's relief must have been visible to the assistant governor, who frowned.

'When did this happen, Miss?' enquired Rosie, respectfully. Her eyes suddenly focused on Inchbold's black, prison officer's tie and she remembered Mags's joke. She hid her smile behind her hand and manufactured a cough. Inchbold cleared her throat, Rosie should have been told much earlier.

'Er ... a few days ago. The sixteenth to be precise.'

'The sixteenth? That's the day they buried my mother. I'd have liked to have gone.'

'Yes, well. I think that day's best forgotten. You're lucky to have escaped punishment for going missing the way you did.'

'I was having a hard time ... and I did apologise.'

'Quite,' said Inchbold, fiddling with a fountain pen. 'The police would need your permission to enter the house and check if anything's missing.'

'How will they know, Miss?'

'Well, you won't be allowed out, if that's what you're angling for.'

'I somehow didn't think I would be, Miss.'

'Is there anyone we can contact who might be able to help?'

Ideally, Rosie didn't want to pursue the matter. But she also didn't want to arouse any suspicion. Then an idea struck her. Rebelling against the system was helping her cope with the injustice being done to her. All opportunities must be seized.

'There's a man called Barney Robinson, he has a key. I can give you his telephone number if you like.'

'That would be satisfactory. Write down his number then you may go.'

Rosie picked up a pen from the desk and wrote down Barney's number on a notepad. As she handed it to

234

Inchbold, she said, 'There's something I wish to say. It's ... it's a complaint.'

Inchbold drew in a deep breath. 'If it's to do with your mother's funeral you must take it up with the governor when he returns from leave.'

'No, it's not that.'

'Well, spit it out, I haven't got all day.' Inchbold seemed relieved that it wasn't to do with the funeral. A complaint about that might take some defending.

'It's Miss Grogan, she's had a down on me since the day I came in here. It's as though she's trying to goad me into hitting her and losing my remission. I don't know what she's got against me.'

'So you'd thought you'd tell me, so that when you do hit her I'll be more lenient with you, is that it?'

'No, Miss. I was hoping you'd have a word with her. The women on my wing will all back me up. Grogan hates me for some reason.'

'Your complaint is noted.'

'Will you be having a word with her, Miss?' pressed Rosie.

'I said your complaint is noted,' repeated Inchbold, testily.

'Thank you, Miss.'

That evening, Rosie and her cell-mate stood in line for the telephone. 'Are you sure about this?' asked Mags.

'How can I possibly get into trouble?' said Rosie. 'I've been locked up in here for over a year.'

She fed two pennies in the slot and dialled Barney's number. 'Barney? It's Rosie. Have the police been in touch? Honestly, there's nothing to worry about. Just let them in so they can have a look round the place. Tell them nothing's missing and make sure they have a good look in my wardrobe. I left something interesting in there. You'll know when you see it. Make sure they find it ... yes, I'm definitely sure. And, Barney ... thanks for everything – and I mean *everything*.'

*

She put the phone down and grinned at Mags. 'Get out of that, Grogan,' she said.

Mags stared at her with a suspicious smile on her lips. 'What was all this, "I mean *everything*"? Did you an' him ...?' she nodded, meaningfully.

Rosie blushed. 'I don't know what you mean, I'm sure.'

'Oh, I think you do ... and what's more I think you did.'

Rosie and Mags were in the exercise yard when two uniformed policemen made their way from the main gate to the prison building; one of them carried a bag. Rosie called out through the wire fence, 'Excuse me. Can I have a word?'

The men looked at each other, unsure of the wisdom in talking to a prisoner. One of them gazed keenly at Rosie and was persuaded to peel off and walk over to her. 'What?' he enquired, brusquely.

'I'm Rosie Metcalf. I gather my house was broken into, but no one's told me if anything was missing.'

The policeman hesitated. His colleague had stopped and was waiting impatiently for him. 'Er ... nothing was actually, er, missing,' he assured her.

Rosie repeated his words: 'Nothing *actually* missing. It sounds as though something was amiss.'

'We found evidence of an intruder,' admitted the policeman.

'Was any damage done?'

'None at all,' he said, turning to go.

'I hope you catch this intruder,' she called out after him. 'There's too many criminals walking around free.'

Grogan frowned at the sight of two policemen standing by the window of Inchbold's office. The assistant governor's face was twitching with anxiety. She looked up at her subordinate.

'Miss Grogan, this is Sergeant Smithson and PC Bloice.'

'Hello,' smiled Grogan. It didn't occur to her that she was in trouble personally.

On Inchbold's desk was a brown-paper carrier bag. She opened it and took out Grogan's uniform. 'Miss Grogan, is this your uniform?'

Grogan took a step forward and picked it up. The label inside the collar had her number written on it in ink. 'Yes, ma'am. Where did you find it?'

'How long has it been missing?' enquired Inchbold.

'How long?' puzzled Grogan. 'I first missed it when I came back off leave.'

'That was what? Four days ago. Why didn't you report it missing?'

'I, er, I thought it'd turn up.'

'You thought it would turn up?' Inchbold sat back in her chair and tapped her teeth with her fountain pen. 'Miss Grogan, mislaying a prison uniform isn't something we take lightly. Any more than the police would if one of their uniforms went missing.' Nods of agreement came from the policemen. 'It should have been reported. Or was there another reason you didn't report it missing?'

'I don't know what you're talking about.'

Inchbold got to her feet and joined the two men at the window. 'I had a complaint about you the other day, Miss Grogan. From one of the prisoners.'

Grogan was unsettled, there was more to this than a missing uniform. 'Oh, who?' she asked.

'Metcalf.'

'Oh, her. She's always moaning about something.'

Inchbold looked at the sergeant. 'I'll let you take it from here, Sergeant.'

The man nodded and looked keenly at Grogan. 'Miss Grogan, could you explain why your uniform was found in Mrs Metcalf's house just after an intruder had been seen there?'

'Which was during the time you were on leave,' added the constable.

Grogan was flabbergasted by this accusation. 'I ... I don't know anything about it!'

'Miss Grogan, where were you between the hours of one

237

and two pm on the sixteenth of this month?' enquired the sergeant.

'One and two? I've no idea. I'd have to check. At home probably.'

'Would anyone be able to verify this?'

'I, er ... not really. I live on my own.'

The sergeant looked at Inchbold, who shrugged. 'Miss Grogan,' he said, 'I think this would be best sorted out down at the station.'

Jack Green tugged on Rosie's sleeve as she walked past him the next morning. He caught her up and spoke from the side of his mouth. 'You set her up, you bugger. They've had her down at the nick all night.'

'Have they charged her with anything?'

'Not that I know of. None of it'll make sense to the coppers – and they don't like things that don't make sense.'

'She's getting what she deserves,' said Rosie. 'Which is more than some of us get.'

Grogan was released without charge due to lack of evidence; but it left a big, unexplained mystery. When the governor came back off leave he invited her to apply for a transfer and she grudgingly accepted the invitation. Martin McDowell, did not suffer fools gladly, or bullies. It made Rosie's life more bearable. Until the next problem came along. It was three months later when she said to Mags: 'I've got a little problem.'

Mags hugged her. 'Rosie, I doubt if yer've ever had a little problem in yer life. Yer don't have problems, you have disasters. How big a disaster is this?'

'Well, at the moment it's only a small disaster. But it's growing bigger every day.'

Mags frowned, she didn't understand until Rosie pointed to her stomach. 'Give over!' Mags gasped. 'How the? I mean, when?'

'When I went to Mam's funeral,' said Rosie. 'And as if you didn't know, the father's Barney and I don't want this to go any further.'

238

'Bloody hell, Rosie!' Mags paced up and down the limited confines of the cell. 'I reckoned you had more sense.'

'It's hard to be sensible at a time like that, especially after being locked up in here for over a year. It just happened – we've never done it before.'

'Does this Barney know he's going to be a dad?'

'No, he doesn't. In fact he thinks he's sterile.'

'Sterile? One out of one's hardly bloody sterile.'

'I know. His wife must be a real bitch telling him something like that. If it's not him it must be her.'

'Why would she say it's him?' asked Mags.

'I don't know – pride, I suppose.'

'She's no right telling him it's his fault.'

Rosie nodded. 'I think it's because she wants to get one over on him – make him feel inadequate. Men do feel inadequate if they can't have children.'

'Funny buggers are blokes,' said Mags.

'I don't want you to mention this to anyone.' Rosie was adamant.'

'If you say so.' Mags plucked Rosie's cigarette from between her fingers. 'Give us a drag while I think.' She drew deeply, before handing back the remaining half inch. 'I take it yer about three months gone?'

Rosie nodded. 'It's due the week I get out.'

'This is gonna take some explaining.'

'I'll cross that bridge when I come to it. Maybe they'll let me out early under the circumstances.'

'They're gonna want ter know who the father is.'

'I won't tell them. What can they do if I keep my mouth shut?'

Mags grinned. 'I've no idea. What *can* they do?'

'They'll blame it on one of the male warders.'

'Not necessarily,' said Mags. 'There's all sorts of blokes comin' in and out of here. Could even be the doctor.'

'You what?' exclaimed Rosie. 'Doctor Crippen? I'd sooner do it with Inchbold's dog.'

'Inchbold's dog? I didn't know Inchbold had a dog.'

'You know what I mean.'

They sat in silence for a while. Beyond the open cell door were the sounds of the prison. Coarse laughter, shouting, the echoing clang of steel doors shutting, and the footsteps running up and down the steel staircase. Always running. As though the staircase was not a place to loiter. Sounds they'd become so inured to that they didn't hear them any more.

It was the only way to survive.

Chapter Twenty-Four

Summer came and went, Eddie had his sixth birthday in the care of Mrs Gittings. One day she answered a knock on the door and found a smiling, sun-tanned woman on her front step.

'You don't know me,' said the woman. 'My name's Barbara Hawkins. I was given your address by Robert Hilton, my late father's solicitor.' The puzzled expression on the foster mother's face prompted further explanation: 'My father was George Metcalf ... I believe his son is living with you.'

'Oh, you mean Eddie.'

On first impressions Myrtle Gittings didn't much like her. The woman's smile hadn't budged. It could have been painted on.

'That's right, Eddie,' said Barbara, as if she'd forgotten her half-brother's name. 'I wonder if I could see him.'

'Well, he's at school right this minute, love. Yer welcome ter come in an' wait, but it'll be a while before he's home.'

'School? Ah, how time flies. I'd forgotten how old he was ... No, I'll call back over the weekend if it's all right by you.'

Mrs Gittings shrugged. 'I don't see why not.'

'I'm staying at the Park House Hotel if you need to phone me.'

'Park House Hotel, right.'

Barbara walked away, not quite sure why she'd bothered, other than that Eddie was her closest blood relative. That's if he *was* a blood relative. There had always been a doubt at the back of her mind. She missed her husband more than she thought she would; but before long he'd come after her, with his tail between his legs. After all, they'd agreed at the outset that if one of them didn't like Australia they'd both come home. As far as she was concerned, his argument that she'd left it a bit late to decide she didn't like the place was neither here nor there. *He* was breaking their agreement not her. What did she care that he'd established a promising career for himself. He could establish another career over here.

A suspicious Mrs Gittings had made a couple of phone calls to check on Barbara Hawkins, and she was almost disappointed to find the woman was genuine.

'Someone came to see you today,' she said to Eddie when he came home. 'A lady called Barbara Hawkins. She's your half-sister apparently. I said she could call in and see you over the weekend.'

'I think my mum told me about her,' he said. 'What's for tea?'

The only woman in his thoughts was his mother, who would be home for Christmas when they'd move back to Oak House. He viewed that with mixed feelings. His memory of his old home was very misty and, by and large, he was beginning to find life in the foster home almost enjoyable. This was in no small way down to two brothers, Alan and Brian Craven; who would spend most of their boyhoods labelled Craven A and Craven B – a joke inflicted on them by parents who had since gone their separate ways.

He'd had many good times with the brothers, but the following Sunday would stand out in his memory. It began with the brothers nagging Mrs Gittings, whom they called Auntie Myrtle – or Owd Git when she wasn't around.

'Auntie Myrtle, can we go ter Paradine Woods ter get some conkers?' asked Alan, who was nine.

'And can Eddie come with us?' added Brian. He was a year younger.

'So long as yer back before tea,' said Myrtle Gittings, who was a great believer in boys having their freedom, especially if it got them out from under her feet on a Saturday afternoon. 'And look after Eddie; try and bring him back in one piece.'

The brothers laughed at the thought of bringing Eddie back in several pieces and the happy trio went on its way. Each clad in short trousers, socks at half-mast and boots with the toes all but kicked through. It was their favourite time of year.

The trees in Paradine Park were at that point where the tips of the leaves were turning to rust in readiness for the autumn display of brilliant yellows and shimmering golds that would have visitors saying, 'Isn't this a grand time of year?' Then a week later, the display would be over and those same people who had looked up in wonder would be looking down in wariness as they sloshed through the sea of fallen leaves; their ephemeral beauty spent. And the older visitors might draw gloomy analogies with their own lives.

The way to the woods took the boys past Battye's Bakery on Wilmslow Street. The smell of fresh pastry wafted up their noses, prompting Brian to enquire, 'Anybody got any dosh?'

Six hands went into six pockets. Three with holes, all six empty. 'We don't need dosh,' said Alan. 'Keep yer gobs shut an' get ready ter run.'

The bakery was in the cellar of a converted end-of-terrace house and several pies had been left to cool just inside an open, ground level window that looked out onto a small yard. Alan quietly opened the gate and whispered, 'Keep a look-out.'

Eddie and Brian, with hearts in their mouths and eyes all over the place, stood by the gate as Alan walked swiftly up to the window and took two large pies. A shout from inside had the three of them running.

'Oy! Yer thievin' little bugger!'

Eddie and Brian had difficulty keeping up with Alan, despite the fact that he was balancing a pie in each hand as he ran, whooping and laughing. A shout from behind told them they hadn't got clean away.

'Split up!' shouted Alan. 'I'll meet yer at the tree.'

He darted up a ginnel between two rows of houses and the two smaller boys carried straight on, not daring to look back at their pursuer, who had momentarily stopped, before setting off after Alan, the pie carrier.

Eddie and Brian didn't stop running. They ran till they got to Paradine Woods, then collapsed, exhausted, behind a broad elm. It was several minutes before Eddie could pluck up the courage to look back.

'I can't see anyone,' he reported.

'He's mad is our kid,' grumbled Brian. 'I wasn't all that bothered about a pie.'

'They smelled all right,' said Eddie. 'What shall we do now?'

'He says ter meet him at the tree.'

'D'you know where it is?'

Brian nodded. 'Through here, follow me.'

The two boys trudged, single file, along a barely defined pathway with the autumn sun flickering down through the leaves on to their Fair-Isle jumpers.

'D'you think he got caught?' asked Eddie.

Brian shrugged. 'He's never got caught before. Still, there's allus a first time. Owd Git says that.'

'Yeah. My mum used to say that as well.'

The pathway ran beside a shallow stream which disappeared into a round, concrete culvert, big enough for a small boy to walk through without having to crouch down. With their legs splayed out into the shallower water at either side, they made their way through the tunnel, shouting and laughing as their echoing voices came back to meet them. Brian ran forward and started to pee in the water which then ran under Eddie's feet and made him shout out in disgust. 'You dirty dog! I'll have yellow shoes now!'

Brian screamed with laughter. His voice mingled with the echoes as he shouted, 'Yer'll have brown shoes in a minute.' He pulled down his trousers and pretended that he was going to pollute the stream in a much more serious way. Eddie ran forward and pushed past, knocking his pal into the water; this time it was Eddie's turn to laugh. Brian got to his feet, dripping, but with his grin still intact. He pulled up his trousers and suddenly went for Eddie, who ran away up the middle of the culvert as fast as he could, with water splashing all over his clothes until he was as wet as Brian.

They emerged into the daylight; breathless, wet through and laughing. It had taken them under a road into more woods at the far side. They climbed out of the stream and took off their shoes and socks, wringing them as dry as they could.

'Owd Git'll go potty when she sees us,' said Brian, putting wet socks back on to his wet feet. 'We'll get a crack round us ear'oles if we're not careful.'

Eddie had never had a crack round his earhole and he viewed the prospect with some trepidation. 'We might be dry by the time we get back,' he said, hopefully.

'Mebbe, come on.'

They pushed their way through the heavy bracken growing between the trees. A movement ahead made them stop. A young man stood up out of the undergrowth and stared at the boys, whose eyes became transfixed on the man's exposed penis which he was holding in his hand. His trousers were round his ankles.

'Come here, lads.' It was more of a command than an invitation.

The boys didn't move. Their hearts fluttered with fear.

'Come here. I won't hurt yer. D' yer want ter earn a bit o' pocket money?'

Neither of them could talk, nor could their legs obey his command.

'How come yer wet through? Have yer fell in t' stream? Yer should take yer clothes off and dry 'em out, else yer'll catch yer death.'

The boys shivered but still said nothing. The man's tone grew harsher.

'Yer not gonna make me come down there, are yer? If I have ter come over there, yer'll be for it.'

'Me mum says I haven't ter.' Eddie's's voice was little more than a croak. Brian nodded his agreement.

'What's yer mam got ter do with it? Come on, I'll give yer a tanner each.'

The boys' eyes widened. He hadn't said what they had to do to earn their sixpences, but neither wanted to have anything to do with him. The thing in his hand was growing bigger and the man began to walk towards them. Something flew past them and struck the man, splattering all over his chest. Eddie recognised it as one of the stolen pies.

'Gerraway, yer mucky bugger!'

The second pie followed and landed on the man's exposed groin. Eddie and Brian looked round and saw Alan standing halfway up a slope to their right. He now had a large stone in his hand which he hurled down at the man, hitting him on the shoulder and producing a cry of pain. The two younger boys had stones now. The path was littered with them. They hurled them with all their might at the half-naked man who cowered, crying, beneath the onslaught. A rock from Alan caught him flush in the face and blood gushed from the man's nose.

'Come on!' yelled Alan, and the other two needed no second bidding. They ran through the woods, with a mixture of triumph and terror. Alan took up the rear and encouraged them along with loud whoops and warning shouts of 'He's catchin' up!' Eventually they came to an exhausted halt at the foot of the horse chestnut tree, where they all sat on the ground to catch their breath.

246

'Have we lost him?' enquired Brian.

Alan grinned 'He never even chased us.'

'But I thought . . . ' said Eddie.

Alan's grin widened. 'Yer know what thought did.'

Eddie didn't, but he didn't ask. He was just relieved to be free of the man.

'Listen,' warned Alan, at length, 'if yer tell anybody about that feller, we'll not be allowed ter come here any more.'

'I don't want to come here any more,' said Eddie.

'Nor me.'

'Don't be so daft,' said Alan. 'That feller won't ever come here again. He'll go somewhere else. They never go to t' same place twice. That's why they never get caught.'

This seemed a plausible argument. 'Do you think he's gone, now?' asked Eddie.

'Course he has,' said Alan, confidently. 'He'll be a million miles away now. 'Specially if he thinks we might recognise him.'

'My mum told me there were funny fellers in these woods,' said Eddie.

'There's funny fellers in all woods,' argued Alan. 'That's where funny fellers go. Yer can't just stop goin' ter woods cos there's funny fellers there.'

Brian said, 'He had a big dick.'

The other two nodded and Alan explained, sagely: 'When yer body stops growin', yer dick carries on.'

'Blimey!' said Brian. 'I wonder how big me granddad's is?'

The three of them laughed as they made exaggerated guesses, then they laughed even louder when Alan pointed out that Grandad Craven's had been growing for nearly seventy years so he must have it wrapped around his waist and it's a wonder he didn't pee in his pocket. He looked at their wet clothes and said: 'Have yer been muckin' about in t' tunnel?'

'Yeah,' admitted Brian.

'Owd Git'll go spare when she's sees yer.'

'We might be dry by then,' said Eddie.

'What sort o' pies were they?' enquired Brian.

'Apple. I'd just had a bite when I saw that mucky bugger.'

His brother licked his lips. 'I right fancy an apple pie.'

'I don't want to go nicking pies again,' said Eddie. 'I bags we get some conkers.'

'Fair enough,' agreed Alan. 'We can nick another pie on t' way home.'

'Are you sure he won't have followed us?'

'Course I'm sure.'

The tree grew right on the edge of the park. Some of its branches were bent with horsechestnuts over the park railings, one of the few stretches of railings which hadn't been commandeered during the war for re-cycling as weapons. Hurling sticks high up into the branches brought a number of horsechestnuts tumbling to the ground with a satisfying volley of thuds. The three boys scrambled for the biggest ones and oohed with excitement as they peeled back the spiky case to reveal the shiny sienna nut inside. One of the great joys of childhood. But the conker harvest, although bountiful, was not enough.

It was Alan's idea for one of them to climb the tree and shake the conkers down. The two brothers looked at each other. The two strongest would have to give the other one a leg up.

'D'yer want me to have a go?' volunteered Eddie.

It seemed much less dangerous than stealing pies or throwing rocks at funny fellers. The other boys had in mind Mrs Gittings' warning about bringing Eddie back in one piece, but their guilt was far outweighed by the likely rewards.

'We'll give yer a leg up on ter t' railings,' said Alan. 'Then yer can grab that branch an' pull yerself up. I'd do it meself only I'm a bit heavier than you an' it might not take my weight. It'll hold you all right.'

The branch in question was flimsy but Eddie took his pal's word for it. He put a foot in Brian's cupped hand and climbed on Alan's shoulders, and thence on to the top of the railings, one foot either side of the protruding spikes. The branch was just beyond his reach.

'Jump up an' grab it,' suggested Alan.

'Right,' said Eddie. 'I will.'

'Go on then!'

'I'm going to.'

'When I count three,' said Alan. 'You jump up.'

Together his two pals counted. 'One ... two ... THREE!'

Eddie jumped up and made a desperate lunge for the branch. He managed to grab it and made to hoist himself up, noisily encouraged by the others. As he struggled up into the tree he disturbed a shower of conkers which came thumping down, to the delight of the brothers.

Neither was looking at him when they heard the sharp crack of a snapping branch. Eddie almost fell on top of them, gashing his leg on a railing spike just before he hit the ground. Blood spurted from the vicious wound and dripped on to the bed of soft earth beneath him. He howled with pain as his two pals stood over him, white-faced and panicking.

'You stay with him,' said a shocked Alan. 'I'll go knock on someone's door.'

Any self-respecting nine-year-old boy would be able to spot a police car when he saw one and Alan Craven was no different. He recognised the black Wolseley the second it came over the brow of a hill, a quarter of a mile away. He was standing in the middle of the road as it screeched to an angry halt just in front of him. The passenger door opened and a stony-faced policeman got out. From where Alan stood, he looked to be at least seven feet tall and he wondered if they might be out looking for a gang of pie thieves. He summoned up whatever courage he had left.

'Me pal's cut his leg right bad.'

'Has he now? Where is he?'

Alan pointed. 'Over there. I think he'll have ter go to hospital.'

The policeman called out to the driver. 'Park up, Des, I'll take a look.'

Alan led the constable to where Eddie lay, with blood pumping from his wound. Within a second the policeman took off his belt and lashed it around Eddie's leg, just above the knee. He turned to Alan. 'I want you to run to the car and tell the driver to call an ambulance and bring the first aid kit. Tell him I need a tourniquet. Did you get that? A tour- ni- quet.' He spoke the word slowly as he pulled the belt tight, slowing the flow of blood.

Eddie had already passed out as the second policeman arrived. He came round in St James's hospital. The two brothers sat with the first policeman as they waited for their friend to be sewn together. Mrs Gittings arrived and was greeted by a nurse.

'Are you his mother?'

'I'm looking after him while his mother's away. Is he all right?'

'Looking after him, eh?' The nurse's tone was reproving. Mrs Gittings went on the attack.

'I'm a foster mother. And I haven't got eyes in the back of me head, young lady!'

The nurse stood her ground: 'Had it not been for a bit of quick thinking by his pals and this policeman he'd have lost a dangerous amount of blood. As it is, he's had to have a transfusion.'

'But he's going to be all right?'

'We'll have to keep an eye on him for a while, but he should be able to go home in a few days.'

It was Brian who noticed the man with the bandaged head approaching down the corridor. He nudged Alan.

'Hey up, our kid!' he whispered, nervously. 'It's that mucky bloke.'

The policeman's ears pricked up. He looked from boy to

man and back. 'What mucky bloke?'

The man stopped momentarily. His eyes darted round, recognised the boys and widened in alarm before he quickened his pace.

'Him,' said Brian, pointing at the departing figure. 'He were in the woods ... bein' mucky.'

Without further explanation the policeman got to his feet and hurried after the man. Alan looked daggers at his brother, knowing that Paradine Woods would now be out of bounds. Mrs Gittings asked them, softly but firmly. 'Tell me what happened?'

'He were wavin' his willy at me and Eddie, then our Alan started throwin' pies at him.'

Alan was nudging his younger brother into silence about the pies when the policeman came back.

'I've told the man not to leave the hospital until I've had a further word with him. 'He's with a security man at the moment.' To Mrs Gittings he explained: 'He's known to us for, er ... that sort of thing.'

'He's apparently known ter the lads as well,' said the foster mother. 'According ter them he was er, exposing himself.'

'He were goin' ter give me an' Eddie a tanner each – then our kid turned up an' started chuckin' pies at him,' said Brian.

Mrs Gittings patted Alan on his head as a reward for his brave intervention.

'What sort of pies?' enquired the policeman.

'Apple,' said Brian, unaware of his brother's glare.

The policeman said, 'Apple pies, how very interesting.'

'I had ter do summat 'cos he were frightening 'em,' said Alan, trying to divert the conversation away from apple pies.

'We chucked some stones at him as well,' said Brian. 'Our Alan caught him a right clout wi' one.'

'What did the man do then?' asked the policeman.

'He started cryin' so we ran away,' said Alan. 'We went ter get some conks.'

'That's when Eddie fell outa t' tree,' added Brian.

The policeman glanced at Mrs Gittings. 'They lead very full lives, your boys.'

'I don't like to wrap them up in cotton wool. Life comes as a shock when you wrap kids up in cotton wool.'

'I assume they brought these apple pies from home?'

'Yes, we did,' Alan assured him, hoping his foster mother wouldn't contradict. She nodded and the boy knew this nod would cost him dearly when she got him home.

'I thought you must,' said the policeman. 'I mean, where else would three small boys get apple pies from?'

'Will they have to go to be witnesses in court?' asked Mrs Gittings.

'I don't think it'll go that far. I think our friend might plead guilty when confronted with such damning evidence. He's a pathetic sort of an individual.'

A nurse approached and said to Mrs Gittings, 'You can see him now, he's sitting up, giving us cheek.'

'Wait there, you two,' commanded the foster mother. 'And don't get into any more mischief.' She held out her hand to the policeman. 'Thanks for everything yer did for the lad.'

'That's okay, just doing my job.' The policeman looked down at the two boys. 'Right, I'll be off ... and the next time any pies go missing, I'll know just where to look.'

Alan glared at his younger brother again. All in all it had been a most unsatisfactory day.

Myrtle Gittings rang Barbara out of courtesy and told her about Eddie's accident. 'He's in St James's, he'll probably be home in a few days. But I can't guarantee when.'

'Thank you, Mrs Gittings,' said Barbara, sweetly. 'I'll pop in and see him tomorrow, if it's convenient.'

'Well, I don't suppose he'll be goin' far, the state he's in, love.'

Up until that moment, Barbara's interest in Eddie had been more out of curiosity than sisterly love. Calling round to see him had been simply something to do as she waited for Paul's letter to say he was coming back to England. But now another idea formed in her mind. A way of solving a nagging doubt. The following afternoon she sat by Eddie's bed and switched on her smile as he popped a toffee into his mouth.

'Don't eat them all at once,' she cautioned. 'You'll get me into trouble with the nurses.'

A nurse came past and smiled at Barbara. 'Are you his mum?'

Barbara and Eddie both laughed. 'No,' said Barbara. 'Believe it or not, I'm his sister ... well, his half-sister. His mum won't be able to visit him. She's, er, she's been unavoidably detained.'

'Pity,' said the nurse. 'At times like this, a boy needs his mum. He lost quite a lot of blood did this young man.'

'Oh dear,' said Barbara. 'Did you have to give him a transfusion or anything?'

'As a matter of fact we did. Just a pint but – it's enough for a small chap like him.' She checked Eddie's pulse and blood pressure, then gave him a wink. 'You'll be as good as new in a few days.' Then she jotted a few additions to Eddie's notes. 'Good job you haven't got an obscure blood group.'

'What is his blood group?' enquired Barbara, casually.

'I ... don't think I'm allowed to tell you. Patient confidentiality and all that stuff. If you like I could ...'

Barbara cut her off mid-sentence. 'It's not important – I was only making conversation.'

The nurse smiled, placed Eddie's notes in the folder at the bottom of his bed and walked away. Within seconds, Barbara was reading them.

'You're blood group O,' she said to Eddie. 'Common as muck, fortunately for you.'

Eddie grinned. He didn't quite know what to make of this woman. On the face of it she seemed pleasant enough; but he didn't see her remove one of the notes and place it in her handbag.

On her way out, Barbara tapped on the half-open door of the matron's office.

'Excuse me, matron, sorry to trouble you – I've just been to visit my brother, Eddie Metcalf and, er ... well, I wonder if you could solve a little mystery.'

'I'll do my best.'

'Could someone with Blood type AB have a child with Blood Type O?'

'Let me think ... er, no; that's one of the impossible groups for an AB parent.'

'Even if the other parent's type O?'

'Doesn't make any difference.' The matron became suddenly curious. 'Why do you ask?'

'It's just something I needed to know. Thank you, matron. You've been unbelievably helpful.'

Chapter Twenty-Five

If anyone noticed Rosie's weight gain they probably thought she was putting back on what she'd lost when she first came in. But at seven months the bulge was becoming recognisable for what it was. Of course to suspect such a thing was ridiculous. How could anyone get pregnant in a place like this? Barney Robinson, the one person who had good reason to suspect, didn't.

Seeing his face once a month was one of the things that kept her going. He was already sitting there as she came into the visitor's room. She'd heard about Eddie's accident and had been overcome with guilt at not being there for him.

'How's Eddie?'

'Right as rain. Came out of hospital yesterday.'

'How did it happen?'

'Oh, just a lad's thing. He was up a tree collecting conkers and he fell down on some railings and cut his leg. Needed a few stitches, that's all.'

'Stitches? Oh my God! How many?'

'Rosie, I don't rightly know how many. But honestly, the lad's as right as a bobbin. You can't stop lads getting' up to tricks like that.'

'But he's only six.'

'Aye, and he can apparently shin up trees like a monkey,' he grinned.

'Apart from that, how is he?' she asked.

'Thriving. Missing his mam but I've told him she's coming home soon.'

'Sooner the better by the sound of things.'

'He's okay, Rosie, stop worrying.' He took out a packet of State Express and offered her one.

'No, thanks, I'm trying to give up.'

Barney shrugged and took one for himself, then he looked around the room; taking in the buzz of conversation. Hurried words passing across bare tables. Everyone smoking, the only pleasure. Beneath a suspension of tobacco smoke was a hum of different, muted emotions. Anger, despair, love, hope – and some laughter. Barney suddenly grinned.

'Hey – I still can't believe you got back inside without the gaffers findin' out.'

Rosie produced a grin of her own. 'I know. Apparently I'd have lost all my remission, with another six months stuck on as well.'

'Would it have been worth it?'

He placed a hand on top of hers. She knew what he was getting at. To tell him the truth and say, 'Yes, every second', would have jeopardised his marriage. Instead she asked: 'How's your wife?'

His smile disappeared. 'Eileen? Okay, I suppose. You didn't answer my question.'

'What question was that?'

'Rosie, yer know what I'm talking about. You've only to say the word.'

Rosie had anticipated this. On each of his visits since the day of her mother's funeral he'd dropped strong hints. It would have been so easy to give him some encouragement. But would it have been fair? She didn't even know how she felt about him. Being locked up had confused her emotions, damaged her self-esteem. Was Barney simply a lifeline she was grabbing at? She had to be sure before she made up her mind about him. Besides, there was something else holding her back. Every man she'd ever loved had come to grief. What right did she have to add Barney to the list?

'Barney, I'm no good for you. Please, just take my word for it.'

'You *are* good for me,' he insisted.

There was a way of putting paid to all this nonsense. She'd thought long and hard about it. Barney believing he was sterile made her task simpler.

'I promise you, I'm not.' She withdrew her hand from under his and said, quietly, 'I'm pregnant!'

His eyes lit up and a smile creased his face. 'I knew it! I knew there was nothing wrong with me.'

Before he got too carried away, Rosie added the killer lie: 'Barney ... I don't think it's yours!'

He stared at her as the implications whirled around in his brain. 'I don't understand ... how ... I mean, who?'

'Someone in here,' she said. 'How do you think I got back in without being caught?'

The hurt in his eyes tore at her heart. 'Jesus, Rosie! Did you have to?'

'It was either that or another year or two inside – separated from Eddie.'

'Bloody hell! Rosie, I didn't think you were ...' He stopped himself, realising he had no right to criticise her.

'Didn't think I was like that? ... Barney, I'm not like that, not normally anyway. With you it was different, a lot different. With him,' she shrugged, 'it was just a price I had to pay.'

'The lousy sod!'

He had now forgiven her, magnifying her guilt at telling him such an awful lie.

'Has it got you into much trouble?'

'What? Oh, not yet. I haven't told anyone yet. Well, only Mags.'

He was desperately hurt, but felt he had no right to show it. After all, he was a married man and she was a prisoner trying to make the best of things. What she'd done had

257

really cut into him, but it had saved her eighteen months inside. No, he'd no right to criticise.

'Don't think too badly of me, Barney.'

'You did what yer thought you had to do, Rosie. And I'll help all I can.'

He looked at her bulge for the first time: 'I reckon they'll find out for themselves before much longer. I should get yourself checked out as soon as you can.'

'I intend to. Then the shit'll really hit the fan!'

He frowned at her language. Prison had taken its toll of her and he knew she needed him more now than ever. He changed the subject and discussed what she'd be doing when she got out. Would she live in Oak House? Would she sell the house in Duck Street which was now hers? Or vice versa? The bell for the end of visiting hour was ringing when he remembered his bit of news: 'Oh, I knew there was something,' he said. 'A woman came round to the foster home the other day and said she was George's daughter, Eddie's half-sister. She reckoned your solicitor had given her the address.'

'You mean Barbara?'

'I assume so. Mrs Gittings didn't like her ... thought she were a bit hard-faced.'

'Sounds like Barbara. What the devil's she doing here? She lives in Australia. What did she say?'

'Well, she just asked if she could see Eddie because she was his half-sister. She was supposed ter call in to see him at the weekend.'

'And what did you think of her?

'Me? I never actually saw her. Apparently Mrs Gittings rang her and told her about Eddie being taken to hospital. She called in to see him the next day ... so she can't be all that bad.'

'George thought she was a pain in the arse.'

'Well, like I said, Mrs Gittings wasn't all that struck on her.'

'She's a strange woman but she's not a bad judge. What

did Barbara have to say for herself? Did she say what she was doing here?'

'Not that I know of ... she rang me up this morning and asked if she could borrow the keys to Oak House, but I said she'd need the solicitor's permission.'

'Good. If she got into the house I'd never get rid of her, especially if she's over here for good.'

'I must admit, I got that impression meself,' said Barney. 'Anyway, I called round to check and she's not in residence.'

'Keep checking, Barney. I don't trust that woman.'

Barney nodded and said, 'Look after yourself. You know what I mean ... and I don't think any less of you for what you did. In your shoes I might have done the same.'

'What? ... With a man?' she teased.

He grinned, sheepishly. 'Well, no ... I think I'd have had to do the time.'

She went round the table and kissed him, contrary to the rules, which were there to be broken, especially in the visitor's room.

First thing the following morning, Rosie asked to see the prison doctor on the pretext that she wasn't feeling well. The usual procession of malingerers trudged in and out of his surgery and Rosie waited until they'd all gone. She wanted to be last. As she went in, he didn't even look up from writing up his notes. 'What is it?' He sounded bored, with no hint of compassion.

'I've missed six periods and I think I might be pregnant.'

She had his attention now, his eyes fixed on her bump. 'Bloody hell! How on Earth did you manage that?'

'To be honest, I thought you might know, you being a doctor.'

'I'll, er ... I'll need a urine sample.'

'You're welcome to all I've got.'

He gave her a sample bottle and sent her off to the toilet. By the time she got back, Inchbold was waiting for her. She looked at the full bottle Rosie handed over to the doctor. 'I do hope you're not taking the piss out of us as well!'

259

'Why should I do that, Miss?' enquired Rosie, innocently.

'Because to get pregnant in this jail is virtually impossible.'

'You'd think so, wouldn't you?' agreed Rosie, earnestly. 'Came as a bit of a shock to me as well. I always thought virgin births were a myth. How do you suppose it happened, Doctor? I need to know because no one will believe me.'

'There is no such thing as a virgin birth,' said the doctor, lamely.

'Ah! There is if you're a Catholic,' Rosie pointed out. She assumed an air of sexual naivety and made up her story as she went along, realising that if she stuck to it, no matter how impossible it sounded, there was nothing they could do about it.

'Metcalf!' thundered Inchbold. 'Who is the father of this child?'

'You tell me,' said Rosie. 'There's not much to choose from in this place.' She looked at the doctor. 'Maybe it's him! Maybe I should make a complaint to someone. What do you think, Miss?'

'I think you're playing a very dangerous game.'

Rosie smiled sweetly. 'Not to worry, I should be out by the time my baby's born, so it won't be your problem.'

'I wouldn't be so confident if I were you,' said Inchbold. 'There'll be an inquiry about this. Let's see where your cheek gets you with them.'

Rosie dropped her gaze so that Inchbold couldn't see she was worried. But the assistant governor had already spotted the concern on her face. She smirked, 'Metcalf, I imagine you'll need a damn good explanation.'

Martin McDowell sat back in his chair and fixed Inchbold with a questioning stare. 'The only thing that Metcalf's admitting to is that the time of conception coincides with the time I was away on leave. The doctor confirms this.'

Inchbold began to feel uncomfortable as he continued: 'So the ultimate responsibility lies with you. What the hell was happening while I was away? We had an officer apparently breaking into an inmate's house and that same inmate becoming pregnant.'

'She's a troublemaker,' protested Inchbold. 'She once struck me.'

'Yes, I heard about that. And don't look so surprised, not much gets past me in this place. Why didn't you do anything about it? Striking a prison officer is a serious offence.'

'Well, she ...'

McDowell got to his feet and went to the window. With his back to her he said: 'She was upset because you wouldn't let her visit her dying mother. Then to cap it all you refused her permission to go to her mother's funeral. I don't wonder she's a troublemaker. It's a wonder we didn't have a prison riot on our hands if you treated everyone like that.'

'We still need to find out who the father is,' Inchbold said, uncertainly.

'Metcalf refuses to tell us and we can't force her.'

'Pity,' muttered Inchbold. 'He's the real culprit in this.'

'So, you accept that Metcalf isn't the culprit?'

'Well, she must take her share of the blame, of course.'

'Miss Inchbold ...' He always used her surname to maintain a distance between them. 'There are only four men who could possibly be the father. Three of them are prison officers and the other is the doctor.'

'I know who the hot favourite is.' Inchbold was thinking of Albert.

McDowell read her thoughts: 'I've already had a quiet word with the hot favourite and he denies it emphatically.' He turned to face her. 'I've also had a quiet word with individual members of the prison board. They'll be recommending Metcalf's early release on medical grounds.'

'You can't do that ...!'

'I can and I am!' His tone forced her to back off.

261

'But ...' she was clutching at straws now. 'Can we trust her to keep her mouth shut once she's out?'

'She'll be out on licence,' pointed out McDowell, 'so she knows she has to watch her step or she'll be back inside.' He turned his back on her again, and watched a noisy game of netball in the yard below. 'Metcalf isn't a recidivist, she didn't belong here in the first place. She'll say she became pregnant by an old boyfriend during the time she was let out on trust to attend her mother's funeral – her story, not ours. We will say nothing about it if questioned.'

'How do you know she'll say that?'

'Because it was her own suggestion. And, on balance, it clears up a messy business which doesn't exactly cover you with glory.'

Rosie was sitting up in bed reading *Woman's Own* when Mags came to visit.

'How did you get in here?' asked Rosie. 'I'm not allowed visitors until I go.'

'They know I know about you,' grinned Mags.

'Did they ask if you knew who the father was?'

'I told Inchbold I thought it were Gobby Grogan, but she didn't think that were very funny.'

'I'm forced to agree with Inchbold.'

Mags laughed. 'I reckon I'll be due for early release as well, if I keep me mouth shut. Blimey, Rosie. Yer've come up smelling o' roses. When do yer get out?'

Rosie couldn't keep the smile off her face. 'The prison board's meeting tomorrow. I could be sleeping in my own bed tomorrow night with a bit of luck. They can't get shut of me fast enough. I'm an embarrassment to them.'

Mags leaned over the bed and gave her friend a hug. 'I'll miss yer, Rosie. Yer a bit of a one-off, yer know that, don't yer.'

Rosie laughed. 'At the moment I'd rather be an embarrassment, the payoff's better.' Mags looked suddenly sad. 'Hey!' soothed Rosie. 'Don't be so soft. Come and see me when you get out. I'll introduce you to Eddie. He'll like you.'

'Most kids do,' said Mags. 'I make 'em feel superior.'

'Best of luck, Rosie,' said Albert as he opened the prison gates for her. 'And thanks for ... you know, keepin' quiet.'

'Thank you.' Rosie planted a kiss on his cheek. 'Maybe we'll meet under more pleasant circumstances.'

'I'd like that.'

A watery autumn sun peered through the clouds as Rosie stepped outside to freedom. It was an odd feeling. Returning to the world to which she rightfully belonged. But it was time to put any resentment behind her, that's what Martin McDowell had advised.

'You're not the first customer I've had who didn't belong inside,' he said. 'And you won't be the last. Don't continue punishing yourself once you're out.'

'Thank you, Sir. You do know that the baddies in here aren't all locked up in cells.'

'Let's not go into that, Metcalf.'

'I think I'm back to being Mrs Metcalf now, Sir.'

'Not until you walk through that gate, you're not.'

'So long as you know about the baddies, Sir.'

'I'm not stupid, Metcalf.'

A maroon Rover, parked nearby, parped its horn. Rosie hadn't been sure who to expect, but she was pleased it was Robert Hilton. She waved and strode to the car. 'Thanks for coming. I thought I might have to catch a bus.' She climbed into the car and gave her solicitor a peck on his cheek. Today was a day for kissing old and trusted friends.

'Barney was going to come but he's busy at work,' he said.

'Barney's done more than enough for me.'

'Yes, he's a good man.'

'God! I can't believe I'm going to see my Eddie again. I've been dreaming of this moment ever since ...'

'... Since the last time you saw him?' put in Robert, knowingly. 'Just after your mother's funeral?'

'You knew about that?' said Rosie. 'How?'

'Barney told me in the strictest confidence. He thought I'd need to be prepared just in case you got into trouble.'

'What else has Barney told you about me?' she asked. Her hand went, unconsciously, to the bump beneath her coat.

'What else is there to know?'

'Oh, nothing. Just how I got out and back in without anyone seeing me.'

He smiled. 'Actually I don't think I want to know all the details. As an officer of the court I have certain legal obligations which I don't want to compromise.'

He hadn't noticed her bump and Rosie would tell him in her own time about her pregnancy, today she just wanted to enjoy her freedom. As he steered the car out on to the main road she felt the constrictions of prison life dropping. This time she was just as free as the people they passed. As free as the passengers on the bus which had stopped beside them, some glancing sideways with envy; at her being in an expensive car whilst they had to settle for an LCT bus. She turned her head away and allowed them their envy because she knew she looked good. Her last hour inside had been spent in front of a mirror. One of the nurses on the prison ward had lent her some make-up and another had done her hair. All in all, Rosie was one of the most unlikely looking prisoners who ever stepped out of a jail.

'Rosie,' said Robert. 'Before I take you, er ... home, I'd like you to call in my office for a few minutes.'

'Oh, why?'

He paused. 'There have been a few developments over the past couple of days and I need to protect your back.'

'Against who? Not Brindle?'

He shook his head.

'What? ... Is it to do with the business? Do I owe money to anyone?'

264

'On the contrary. As a matter of fact your accountant has good news on that score. What Scrimshaw stole from the company was basically its trading capital. Although this, and the fact that no one was around to run the company, forced it to stop trading, the company wasn't actually insolvent. Not quite anyway. After selling off all the assets and paying the bills, you're left with just over five hundred pounds. And if it's any consolation, the company still exists – albeit in name only.'

'Five hundred quid? Robert, that's marvellous. I've been worried how I was going to manage until I got back on my feet. I was thinking of selling one of the houses. Duck Street probably. Selling Oak House would be betraying George's memory in a way.'

'Rosie,' said Robert, seriously, 'at the moment you can't touch Oak House. George's daughter has taken out an injunction preventing you from entering it.'

'Barbara?' said Rosie angrily. 'What the hell's Barbara got to do with it?'

'She's contesting George's will.'

'On what grounds?'

Robert took a breath. 'She's claiming that Eddie isn't his son which disqualifies him from his inheritance. She's contesting the will on the grounds that George was the victim of a deception.'

Rosie's heart sank. 'Oh Jesus.'

Robert looked at her. 'Rosie,' he asked, quietly, 'is it true?'

'Is what true?'

'Is Eddie George's son?'

Rosie was miles away. Were all her hopes being snatched away at the last minute? All the time she'd been in prison she'd been able to count her blessings. Many of them financial. Oak House was worth a small fortune and would guarantee her and Eddie some sort of security. Duck Street, although much more modest would fetch a decent price. What did all this mean?

'Rosie, I need to know.'

'George knew all about Eddie,' she said, quietly. 'He married me to give me and my son some sort of life. Of course he knew he wasn't Eddie's father, George wasn't an idiot. Eddie's father's dead. How the hell did Barbara find out? Maybe she's guessing. Maybe we should call her bluff.'

'Somehow she's got hold of Eddie's blood type. It apparently proves that George couldn't be the father. Look, if we can prove that George *knew* that Eddie wasn't his natural son it would prove he hadn't been deceived and blow her case right out of the water.'

Rosie nodded, then shook her head. 'The trouble is, I don't know how to do that. You see, George and I went to great lengths to cover the fact that Eddie wasn't his son. The real father's dead and the only people who knew were me and George. Not even Eddie knew. And we'd no intention of ever telling him. I'd no idea you could prove something like this from a blood test.'

'Did George confide in anyone ... anyone at all?'

She shook her head again. 'I'm pretty sure he didn't.'

'Then we've got a fight on our hands,' said Robert. 'The court will have to take your word for it.'

'The word of a convicted criminal?'

Robert sighed. 'It won't be easy. We can line up a couple of dozen people who'll tell the court how happy George was after he married you. And what a marvellous father he was to Eddie. And as you say, George wasn't an idiot. He wasn't a man who was easily fooled.'

Rosie thought for a while. 'But I was George's wife. Surely she can't be seriously trying to cut me out of the will altogether?'

'That's just it – she isn't cutting you out altogether. She's going for the house because it was her childhood home and for Eddie's share because he's not George's son. The rest is yours.'

'So she's not going for the business, that's big of her considering it's worthless at the moment.'

'Oh, she's being very clever. When George left it to you, the business comprised more than half his total estate. What you did with it afterwards is not her problem. At the time it still left you as the main beneficiary.'

She rested her hands on her unborn child, deriving some comfort from its presence. Allowing the feel of it to put things into perspective. 'What do you think my chances are?' she asked, at length.

'Fifty-fifty. My guess is she'll want an out of court deal.'

'Which will be a sort of admission that I did trick George into marrying me!' snorted Rosie. 'Well, she can stuff that!'

'I thought you might say that. Look, forget the office, I'll take you back to Duck Street.'

'Good, let's get on with the important things, like me seeing my son again.'

'That's something else we need to talk about.'

'What?'

'Regaining custody of your son isn't automatic. You need to prove you're a fit and proper person, with the means to provide for him.'

Rosie panicked. Losing Oak House was bad news. Being locked up hadn't been a picnic, but losing Eddie would be like the end of her world. And what about her unborn child? What would happen to that?

Robert saw the abject look on her face and smiled. 'Try not to worry,' he said. 'I've already set wheels in motion. You have money and a home and a flawless record as a mother. We're seeing the magistrates in the morning. It should be a formality.'

She hid her pregnancy behind a double-breasted raincoat. Neither the magistrates nor Robert Hilton suspected she was seven months pregnant, otherwise it might not have been the formality Robert had promised. The senior magistrate, a bilious looking woman glared in Rosie's general direction without actually looking at her.

'And how can we be sure Mrs Metcalf is a fit person to be a mother?' she boomed.

267

Rosie bit her lip in anger as Robert Hilton replied. 'It's worth pointing out that the only harm that has ever befallen her son, occurred while he was *not* in her care. Not to return him into his mother's care would be doing the child irreparable harm.'

There was a muttered consultation followed by nods and a look at the clock by the senior magistrate. 'The court will allow this application,' she said, curtly, writing the court's decision down in a ledger.

Mrs Gittings opened the door and gave Rosie a suspicious look when Barney took her to collect her son.

'Prison food must be a lot better than I thought,' she commented, drily.

'How's my son's leg?'

'I'm sorry about that, but it wasn't my fault.'

'I'm not blaming you, Mrs Gittings,' smiled Rosie, magnanimously. 'You have a difficult job to do.'

'Mum?' called out Eddie from inside. 'Is that you?'

Rosie ran past the house-mother and into the room where Eddie sat with his bandaged leg resting on a stool. The bad times were surely behind her now. Nothing life could throw at her could ever be as bad as losing her boy. She knelt beside him and hugged him to her.

'I'm back for good, Eddie.'

'Promise?'

'I promise.'

Barney and Mrs Gittings allowed them a moment together before they entered the room. Eddie looked up at his foster mother, worried.

'Are we going back home, Mum?'

'Not straight away.'

'But you just said ...'

'We're going to live in Grandma's old house in Duck Street.'

'Now?'

'Yes.'

He squeezed her as hard as he could. It was the best she'd felt for a long time.

'Just me and you?' he asked.

'For the time being. Someone else will be coming to join us shortly.'

Eddie looked hopefully at Barney, who held up his hands. 'Hey, not me, lad,' he grinned. Eddie's face dropped. 'Who's coming?' he asked his mother.

'I'd perhaps better explain it to you later.'

'Rather you than me,' said Mrs Gittings. 'Still, it's none of my business what folk get up to.'

'That's right,' said Rosie, still hugging her son. 'And I'll thank you to keep it that way.'

The house-mother looked accusingly at Barney. 'So long as them responsible do the right thing by you.'

Barney said nothing. He wished the baby inside Rosie was his, and if Mrs Gittings wanted to think that way, then so be it.

Chapter Twenty-Six

They were back in Duck Street, Barney had made a fire and the three of them gazed into the flames. Each with their own dreams. Barney's and Rosie's coinciding more than they cared to admit to each other. Eddie had his leg resting on a stool. He adjusted it and winced.

'His leg's a lot worse than I thought,' said Rosie.

Barney shrugged. 'He was enjoying himself and he fell. Lads are supposed to fall now and again.'

'I suppose so.'

'Evidently his mate was a bit of a hero. Had he not jumped into the road and stopped a cop car it might have been a lot worse for Eddie.'

'I didn't know that,' said Rosie. 'It seems to me there's a lot more to this story than I've been told.'

'Well, there is a bit more,' admitted Barney, in whom Eddie had confided everything, including the pie theft.

Rosie smiled at her son once again. 'Well, we've got all the time in the world to catch up.' She got up and went over to him. 'Just one more hug to keep me going for a while. I've got a lot of hugs to catch up on.' She held him to her, knowing the time was now ripe to tell him her own little secret before anyone else did.

'Eddie,' she began, 'you know this big bump in my stomach?'

He nodded.

'Do you know what it is?'

'You've been eating too much.'

Rosie and Barney laughed. 'Well, as a matter of fact I haven't, young man. As a matter of fact I'm having a baby.'

She held on to him, trying to gauge his reaction, but there was none. 'Did you hear what I said?' she asked.

'You said you're going to have a baby. Derek Smith's mum's having a baby.'

'Oh, is she now? Well, I'm having one as well.'

The boy seemed unimpressed. 'Will it be a boy or a girl?'

'I don't know yet. We have to have what we're given.'

Eddie shrugged, then asked, 'Can I listen to the wireless please?'

'Course yer can,' said his mother. 'Though I don't know what's on at this time o' day for a young lad like you.'

'There might be Worker's Playtime,' said Eddie. 'I'd like it to be a boy.'

'I'll do what I can,' promised Rosie. She got up and stood beside Barney. 'So far so good, eh?'

'Yeah,' agreed Barney, twiddling with the radio knobs. 'Kids don't complicate your lives. They just trust you if you treat 'em right.' Static whistled from the bakelite box as he tried to tune into the Light Programme. A blast of music, a garble of foreign voices, then more static. He retraced the tuning needle past the static and the voices, then with a delicate touch, he balanced it to where the music was clearest. Much to Eddie's satisfaction.

Rosie smiled at Barney and wondered if she was doing the right thing keeping their baby a secret from him. 'Eileen okay?' she asked, innocently.

'Fine,' he replied, flatly. He never spoke of his wife unless asked; why was that? Did Rosie have any right to question him? Did she have any rights at all over him?

'Is she, er ...,' she lowered her voice, 'still seeing the boyfriend?'

271

Barney grinned. 'Not since I had a word with his wife. Eileen went mad. She swore blind he was only a friend.'

'Maybe he was.'

'Pigs might fly.'

'So ... you and Eileen are trying to make a go of it?'

'Yeah,' he said, without enthusiasm. 'We're even tryin' for a kiddie again – you never know.'

Rosie felt a twinge of disquiet at the thought of him making love to Eileen. It was an avenue of thought she didn't want to explore.

'Barney, you've been a big help.'

'Any time, Rosie. You've only to ask.'

She felt like asking him to leave his unfaithful wife, who had obviously lied to him about his sterility, and come to live with her and Eddie – and the baby. His baby. To look after them. Instead she gazed into the fire again. 'Do you know what I've missed most during the time I was inside? Apart from Eddie.'

'What's that?'

'Buttered toast. Done on a toasting fork in front of the fire. It never tastes the same in one of them electric toasters.'

Barney gave a broad smile. 'I think I can manage that. Have you got a toasting fork?'

Rosie hadn't finished. 'And fresh pikelets from Freeman's, and fish and chips from Wormald's. Even when I lived with George, I used to go back there for my fish and chips.'

Rosie still had mixed memories of Wormald's chip shop. That was where she first heard about Billy.

'It's changed hands,' Barney said. 'It's Faraday's chip shop now. The batter's like rubber and I don't know what they do to the chips. I reckon they fry 'em in sump oil. I go to that one on Ashley Road, now.'

'I don't know,' grumbled Rosie. 'I'm gone less than two years and civilisation's crumbling around me.'

Chapter Twenty-Seven

Barbara cursed as she opened up the letter from her solicitor. She'd made an offer for the contested part of George's will but Rosie wasn't going to play ball. She hated Australia, whereas Paul was settled there. If she won possession of Oak House she was sure she'd tempt him back.

Relieving Eddie of his inheritance would have been a bonus, but she'd settle for the house. That was her offer. She got the house and Eddie got to keep his share of the will. Rosie had turned her down flat. It was to be a straight fight, winner takes all. Loser pays the costs. Barbara picked up the phone and looked out of the window as the first snow of winter fluttered on to the garden of her hotel.

'I got your letter, Mr Greaves,' she said, on being put through. 'What do you think my chances are?'

'Ah,' said her solicitor. 'Since I dictated that letter, events seem to have overtaken us.'

'In what why?'

'Did you know that Mrs Metcalf managed to get herself pregnant whilst she was in jail?'

'Pregnant? No, I didn't. I've actually had no contact with her.'

'We have contacts and apparently she is. And no one appears to know who the father is.'

'She's probably not too sure herself. I'm not sure how this affects things?'

'Well, this whole case hangs on whether or not George Metcalf thought he was the biological father of Mrs Metcalf's child. As there is no solid evidence on either side of this case, Mrs Metcalf's general character – honesty, decency and reliability – will come under close scrutiny. She will no doubt be bringing many character witnesses to speak on her behalf. It would be our job to bring all these traits into question. Up until now we've had little to go on. I intended making as much as I could of her attack on Brindle, but many people think she was harshly treated in this. Perhaps even the judge.'

'So, what are you saying? That the bitch getting herself up the spout while she's doing time goes against her?'

'You appear to have picked up a smattering of antipodean slang, but you've more or less hit the nail on the head,' said Greaves. 'I can assure you that this will go heavily in our favour when we bring her promiscuity to the attention of the court.'

Barbara smiled for the first time in weeks. 'If I'd known this, I wouldn't have made her an offer.'

'I'd have advised you to withdraw it,' said Greaves. 'I'm quite surprised she turned you down.'

'I'm glad she has,' said Barbara. 'I'm going for the lot. Plus costs. When that whore walks out of that court I want her to be penniless! How soon can we start?'

'I've already issued the necessary papers to Robert Hilton. We should get it into court early in the new year. I must say, I think she's being very badly advised; perhaps Hilton doesn't know about her pregnancy? Would you like me to speak to him and offer her a small ex-gratia sum to keep it out of court?'

'Offer her nothing,' said Barbara, sharply. 'I want her to regret turning down my offer. Even though I would have withdrawn it.'

'Perhaps I should appraise him of her pregnancy. He might advise her to drop her claim altogether.'

'Do that,' said Barbara.

*

Rosie felt her unborn baby kick, as though reminding her that it would probably be arriving in the world in less than a fortnight. She thought of Barney and how she should be sharing things like this with him. The banging of Robert Hilton's car door awoke her from her daydreams. She was sitting in the front room, trying to concentrate on reading her book despite the building noise all around her. Barney was converting the store back into a shop. This was to be her livelihood once the baby was born. A grocery shop. The five hundred pounds left in BJK Ltd would be enough to pay for the conversion and stock.

As she went to answer his knock it occurred to her that she hadn't told Robert about the baby. He wouldn't need telling once he saw the size of her. His face was grave when she opened the door to him.

'Hmmm,' he said, glancing at her stomach and walking past her. 'I wish you'd told me a little earlier. This is a bit of a shock.'

Rosie grinned, sheepishly, as she closed the door. 'Sorry, Robert, I, er, I didn't know what to say to you on the day you brought me home. I suppose I was a bit pre-occupied with what you told me about Barbara. And I thought it best not to let the court know when I went for custody of Eddie.'

'A wise decision. Perhaps it's as well I was kept in the dark.'

'Do you think badly of me?' she enquired, tentatively.

'In my profession it's best not to judge people.'

'Judge not, and ye shall not be judged, eh?' said Rosie.

'Luke six, verse thirty-seven,' he said.

'I'm impressed.'

'Don't be,' smiled Robert. 'There are quite a few biblical quotations that get thrown at us lawyers; over the years I've heard them all.'

'How're things going, by the way? Have we got a hearing date yet?'

Robert sat down without being invited and Rosie sat

opposite. He rested his elbows on his knees and placed his palms together. His well manicured fingers spread apart. 'This ...' he cleared his throat, noisily. 'This pregnancy has thrown a different light on things.'

'Oh, how?' enquired Rosie.

'Barbara's solicitor rang me this afternoon to ask if you wanted to avoid the embarrassment of a court hearing and all the ensuing publicity. He said he would be bringing your mysterious pregnancy to the notice of the court.'

'I see.'

'What he meant was that he now had the ammunition to do a character assassination of you which would persuade the judge to rule in Barbara's favour.'

'You mean he's using my pregnancy against me? The lousy pig!'

'It's a rough business, Rosie. I'd do the same in his shoes. It's his job to use every means at his disposal to secure a win for his client. Anything less and he'd be doing her a disservice.'

Rosie leaned forward and rubbed her back as she looked at him. 'Do you think I should take her offer?'

Robert shook his head. 'I doubt if that offer's still on the table. They didn't know about this when they made it. I could try them if you like.'

'No,' said Rosie firmly. 'Don't give her the satisfaction. What are my chances?'

He shrugged. 'Unless you can find absolute proof that George knew Eddie wasn't his natural son I'd say we have a real fight on our hands.'

'But it's not hopeless?'

'Not entirely. It would depend a lot on the judge. If you revealed how you became pregnant it might help. Explain that you simply stole a moment of passion with a man you loved.' He looked at her. 'It, er ... it doesn't have to be the absolute truth. I just need to be able to assure the court that you're not simply a promiscuous woman.'

'Maybe it *is* the absolute truth, Robert. Maybe I *did* steal

276

a moment of passion with a man I love. The trouble is I also stole out of jail and stole back in.'

'That's a lot of stealing,' admitted Robert, 'And I don't know a biblical quotation that caters for it.'

'Pity.'

Rosie thought of all the implications attached to her telling the court the story of that particular day. Perjury wasn't an option, so what about the truth? ... Well, what happened your honour, is that I escaped from jail to go to my mother's funeral. While I was out, I had it off with Barney Robinson. How did I get back in? Well, your honour, I persuaded a couple of prison officers to help me – and do you want a real laugh, your honour? The prison governor got me an early release because he thought one of his own officers was the father of my child. So he and I concocted a story about how I really had been allowed out on that day and got pregnant with a friend of mine on the outside. What do you think of that, your honour?

No question of it. If perjury wasn't an option, neither was the truth.

'I don't think I can do that, Robert.'

'I agree. But I think it's my duty to tell you that you're probably throwing good money after bad; however, I'll do my best for you.'

'Hey,' said Rosie. 'Did I tell you I'm opening up a new business? All that banging is Barney Robinson converting the store back to a shop.'

Ever the professional, Robert said, 'You need planning permission for change of use. Do you want me to organise it?'

'Didn't realise it was necessary – and, yes, please. In the meantime, I'd like to keep Barbara simmering. I'd like her to think we've got something up our sleeve.'

'Mr Greaves, please.' Robert tapped his fingers on his desk as he formulated what he was about to tell Barbara's solicitor.

'Mr Greaves? Robert Hilton ... good morning. I've had a word with my client and she's still refusing your offer ... has she really?'

Greaves was telling him that Barbara had now withdrawn her offer. He went on to suggest that Rosie save her money and withdraw from the dispute.

'It occurred to me to suggest that to her myself.' Robert's tone indicated exasperation with his client. 'I've warned her to expect a real hatchet job when she gets on the witness stand, but she didn't seem to care. I suspect this thing isn't as straightforward as it seems, but getting information out of her is like getting blood out of a stone. I don't mind telling you that I was more than a little annoyed that I had to find out about her pregnancy from you.'

'Are you saying there's something else she isn't telling you?' enquired Greaves. His voice was flat, disguising any worry he might have.

Robert noticed this and smiled to himself. 'Well, I wouldn't put it past her,' he said.

Greaves reminded him of his obligation to let them have a copy of all relevant documents or he would have it ruled inadmissible. Both of them knew that this was a flexible rule and a judge would probably allow such evidence rather than have it brought up at Appeal.

'I'll do my best,' Robert assured him. 'But I'm afraid she's a law unto herself. She doesn't seem to trust our legal system; and after her experiences, who can blame her?' He grinned at the blustering coming from the other end. Lawyers hate the unexpected, especially after telling their client they've got an open and shut case. Telling Greaves that Rosie was still refusing Barbara's offer was a nice piece of gamesmanship. But that was all they had.

Christopher was so called because he was born on Christmas Day. It was Barney's suggestion and Rosie felt she owed him this at least. A month later she opened Duck Street Stores with Marlene Gedge behind the counter and

Rosie mainly behind the scenes, looking after the business and the baby. Life was okay but there were problems to be settled. It was late February when the disputed will got to court.

Barbara took a taxi to the Town Hall. She could afford it, George had left her £5,000 in his will and the same amount on trust for Eddie. It was the equivalent of ten years wages for the average working man. But she wanted what was rightfully hers, every last penny of it; and this included the house and Eddie's share. No way in the world would her dad have married Rosie Jones had he known he wasn't the father of her child. Barbara had convinced herself of that.

Bitter memories returned as Rosie and Barney walked up the stone steps towards the pillared entrance. At least she wasn't about to lose her liberty this time; you couldn't put a price on that. She said hello to Robert Hilton who was waiting with her barrister, then she turned to go inside and almost bumped into Barbara, who said, 'Oh! ... hello,' obviously embarrassed to come face to face with her adversary. She hurried off and Rosie watched her go, suddenly feeling sorry for her. Barbara was alone. Her husband was ten thousand miles away and she had no friends worthy of the name. When you're a pain in the arse you don't have friends, only acquaintances. Whatever she won today wouldn't amount to much against what Rosie had. Which was friends and a small family and a future. The thought crossed her mind again. A future which would be much brighter with a certain person on the horizon.

Inside the busy entrance hall there was a low-voiced buzz amongst the host of urgent figures, hurrying backwards and forwards and across and through doors and up and down the marble steps to and from the upper courts. Discussions were taking place between gowned and be-wigged barristers and their worried-looking clients who looked as though they'd prefer to be anywhere but here. Rosie included.

Various young men, obviously here to see their fates

decided by the criminal courts, stood around dressed in suits which didn't quite fit. They had slicked-back hair and shiny faces as if they'd been trying to scrub away their villainy in a vain attempt to reveal a layer of respectability beneath. Some, who looked like butter wouldn't melt in their mouths, might be treated leniently; others appeared to come from a mutant underclass which would never know right from wrong. Their fate had been decided at birth.

A familiar face puzzled her, then she smiled as she identified him as an Ashinghurst prison guard. He was looking lost for a while until he spotted the court lists pinned to a line of notice boards; he strode across to them. Rosie walked over and tapped him on the shoulder.

'Albert?' she said.

He turned round. 'Metcalf ... er, Rosie,' he said. There was a look of relief on his face. He glanced at Robert standing beside her, than back at Rosie. 'Er ... could I have a quiet word before yer go into court?'

Rosie looked at her solicitor. 'Have I got time?'

Robert donned his glasses and scrutinised the lists. 'We're in third, but don't go far. The other two might be formalities.'

Albert and Rosie went outside and stood on the top of the steps beside one of the white lions. Rosie looked down on Victoria Square beneath her and caught a flash of memory which brought a smile. A memory of cheering crowds and marching men. And Billy Tomelty.

'The last time I stood here it was Salute the Soldier Week,' she recalled. 'I was in the WVS. It was something to do with National Savings. My boyfriend came with me; we were engaged. I remember him telling me about how he couldn't wait to go abroad. That was his one big ambition – to go abroad.' She paused for a long time, staring at the traffic moving up and down the Headrow. 'He was killed in Normandy a month later. He hadn't even reached dry land.' She stared at the grey sky. 'I've often wondered if it counted as going abroad.'

'I was in the RAF meself,' said Albert, after a respectful silence. 'Never went overseas. Mind you, it were warm enough where I were stationed. Lost a lot o' mates.'

Rosie turned to him. It was the first time she had seen him in his civvies. He looked ordinary in his sports jacket and flannels. And that tie? His wife must have missed that or she wouldn't have let him out of the house.

'Well?' she asked.

'I've just come to ask yer one question.'

'Let me guess. You want to know if I'm going to drop you in it?'

Albert looked down at his shoes and nodded. Then he looked up at her. 'What are yer going to tell the court about the day yer got pregnant?'

'The truth.'

He looked worried.

'Well, up to a point,' she added.

'What point's that?'

'I'm going to tell them I became pregnant by an old boyfriend on the day of my mother's funeral.'

'And are yer going to tell them how yer got out?'

'Why would they ask? They're hardly going to think I broke out and got back in without anyone knowing. They'll naturally assume I was out on compassionate grounds.'

Albert nodded. 'That's right.'

'So you can go back and tell everyone they've nothing to worry about – I'm not stupid.'

'I never thought yer were,' he said. 'But yer get carried away sometimes.'

He had a point, 'Thanks for your concern.' She wasn't being completely sarcastic. Her getting carried away could cost a lot of people dearly; herself included. She heard Robert Hilton calling her from the doorway. 'Right,' she said. 'Looks like I'm on.'

'I'll come in and cheer you on if yer don't mind.'

'Keep an eye on me more like.'

*

The significance of the judge's words didn't hit her at first. The case had taken the best part of four hours. Rosie had assembled a formidable array of character witnesses who had testified as to the happiness of her marriage to George. Against this, Barbara had several big guns in her armoury: Eddie wasn't George's son; Rosie's criminal record; the fact that George had left her the business which constituted more than half his estate – or had when he died; and that she'd managed to lose the business within a few months of his death. But most of all, Barbara's barrister dwelt upon her recent pregnancy. She'd conceived a child to a mystery man whilst serving a prison sentence for violence. Could the court rely on the word of a promiscuous woman such as this? He had painted a picture of an inept, scheming Jezebel that at one point had Rosie screaming at him with anger and the judge threatening to have her removed. Albert's heart was in his mouth and a court reporter scribbled furiously.

The judgement came as no surprise. It ended with the words:

'. . . *I find for the plaintiff in this case. A full written copy of this judgement can be obtained from the court office. Costs to be paid by the defendant.*'

'All rise,' ordered the clerk, as the judge got up to leave. The door to his room had barely shut when Barbara said to her lawyers, a lot louder than was necessary: 'What he means is that whores get what they deserve in the end!'

Rosie went cold with fury and sadness. It wasn't so much the money or the house, it was the desecration of the memory of her time with George. How she hated courts and their distorted version of justice. Even the magistrates court, which had grudgingly returned her son to her. This judgement had told the world that the happiest four years of her life had really been something seedy and dishonest. How would she explain this to Eddie, who still thought George was his dad? She turned to Robert Hilton.

'Can I appeal?'

'We can apply.'

'I want to appeal.'

'Okay.' Robert was humouring her. 'We'll discuss it when we've had time to think.' He knew that if it went to appeal the result would be the same. When she'd had time to think, he'd advise her to drop the matter. It was a pity she'd had to suffer such humiliation. But he *had* warned her.

Her case finished too late to catch the *Yorkshire Evening Post* and a train crash just outside Wakefield took up the first three pages of the next day's local papers. Three people were killed and Rosie's misfortune went unreported.

Chapter Twenty-Eight

Rosie was sitting in the front room in Duck Street, bouncing Christopher on her knee to the beat of 'Blue Suede Shoes' coming from the Dansette record player. Life wasn't bad but it could have been better. It was coming up to Eddie's seventh birthday and she still hadn't said anything to him about George not being his real father. It wasn't an easy thing to explain. Barbara was ensconced in Oak House with her husband, and Eddie's trust fund had been handed over. The shop had got off to a fair start but money was tight. It was Barney Robinson who re-kindled her interest in Ernie Scrimshaw. He had called in on his way home from work, as he often did.

'Guess who I bumped into today? ... Joe Brindle.'

'Tell me something I'm interested in.'

'You'll be interested to know who his partner is.'

'Will I?'

'Yes, you will.'

'Go on then,' she challenged. 'Interest me.'

'Ernie Scrimshaw.'

'Is he now? Well, you're right, I am interested.'

'Sleeping partner away,' went on Barney. 'I don't think Joe trusts him with any proper work. Brindle's in a big way over in Huddersfield and the word is that Ernie put the money up.'

She handed Christopher over to him. He smiled with

284

pleasure at the boy; his own son if he did but know it. Rosie felt more guilt.

'He's getting a bit sturdy.'

'Takes after his mother,' smiled Rosie. The weight she'd lost in prison had all returned.

'Now then,' said Barney. 'I wouldn't say that. Better than being a stick insect. At least that's what I keep tellin' Eileen.'

It was the first time she'd heard him make an unsolicited remark about his wife. 'How is Eileen?' she enquired.

'Puttin' weight on, an' moanin' about it.'

'Still ... trying for a baby?' Rosie had to force the question through her lips, so reluctant was it to come out.

He shook his head. 'Things are a bit dead in that department.'

Rosie liked the idea of things being dead in that department, whatever it meant. She knew she could destroy his marriage in a moment by simply telling him the truth about Christopher. But did she have the right? She changed the subject rather than press him for further explanation.

'Are you saying Ernie's a director of Brindle's company?'

Barney was humming and rocking Christopher in his arms. The boy beamed up at him. Rosie smiled.

'Barney, I asked you a question.'

'What? Oh, sorry ... when I said a sleeping partner, that's really what he is. It's supposed to be a secret. The bloke who does my accounts told me. Apparently he once crossed swords with Brindle and he's got no great love for him. I think he told me because he knew I'd pass it on to you.'

'Thanks for the information, Barney.'

He handed Christopher back to her. 'What are you going to do about Ernie?'

'He ran off with twenty-five thousand pounds of the firm's money – what do you suggest?' There was a trace of sarcasm in her voice.

Barney said, 'You know if you go for Ernie, you'll be takin' Brindle on as well, don't you? I reckon if one goes down they'll both go. D'you want my advice?'

'No.'

'I think you've got a good thing goin' with your shop and you don't want to do anything to spoil it.'

'What did you tell me for, then?'

'I just thought you had a right to know. Personally I think you should leave well alone.' He paused for a second then added: 'I'm wasting me breath, aren't I?'

She gazed down at her son, then without looking up said, 'Yes.'

'We can sue for misappropriation of funds,' said Hilton. Rosie could smell cigars on his breath even from across his desk. It seemed an expensive form of halitosis. She sat back in her chair as he continued: 'It could be long and drawn out. And very costly. Civil actions always are.'

'He owes me a lot of money,' Rosie reminded him. 'Do you think I'd win?'

'Common justice is on your side, but we're not dealing with justice. We're dealing with the law.'

She pulled a face. 'I haven't had much luck with the law recently. Maybe I should hire someone to break a few of his bones.'

Robert glanced at her to check that she was joking. Her expression gave nothing away, so he gave her the benefit of the doubt. 'I'm not sure what his defence will be,' he said. 'If we could put him in criminal court first, we'd stand a better chance.' He looked steadily into Rosie's eyes. 'You know that George didn't trust him, don't you?'

'Well,' said Rosie, 'I know he thought Ernie was incompetent. He never said anything about not actually trusting him.'

'Nor did he to me,' agreed Robert. 'Otherwise I would never have agreed to giving Ernie permission to sign cheques. After he'd run off with your money, Mrs

286

Drysdale rang me. Obviously she was in a bit of a state, knowing her job was in jeopardy. She told me about a conversation she'd had with George just before he died.'

'Conversation? What about?'

Robert stretched his arms and pulled out his cuffs, showing off a pair of gold links. They caught Rosie's eye, but she ignored them. 'Apparently Ernie had made some sort of cock-up,' he explained. 'He tried to blame it on her and she went steaming in to George about it, telling him either Ernie goes or she goes ... and George had tried to calm her down.'

'Blimey! It must have been serious, she was besotted with George.'

'Oh, you noticed as well, did you?' he grinned.

'I'm not stupid; anyway, what happened?'

'Apparently George told her to bide her time. He said he was adding up the money Ernie was creaming off the company and when the time was right he'd get him to hand over his shares or face the consequences ... or words to that effect.'

'So George thought Ernie was fiddling money?'

'I think so, but Mrs Drysdale wasn't sure how.'

'Pity she didn't mention it before my trial.'

'She didn't think it was relevant. Not until Ernie ran off with the money.'

'Perhaps not,' conceded Rosie. 'The books are still around, aren't they?'

Robert nodded and took a cigar from a wooden box on the desk.

'Do you mind ...?' he asked.

'Go ahead, I love the smell of cigar smoke.' She could have added, 'but not cigar breath'. But she didn't.

He cut off the end with some sort of tool designed for the job, then struck a match and spent a self-indulgent few seconds bringing the Cuban weed to life. Rosie was too polite to waft away the cloud of smoke that came her way.

'The liquidator will have sent them back to your

accountant, but I doubt if they'll turn anything up.'

'It's somewhere to start,' she said. 'In the meantime if you could send him a writ for the money he took, plus interest.'

'We'll probably need a private detective to get his address. This isn't going to be cheap, Rosie.'

'You mean you want to be put in funds before you do anything?'

Robert smiled. 'Sorry, business is business.'

'Any money I've got's tied up in my business. I'll sell the car,' she said.

Robert nodded. 'There is one other thing,' he said, getting to his feet to escort Rosie to the door. 'When George was killed I wrote to the Yorkshire Electricity Board telling them to expect action to be taken against them for leaving a live cable running across a building site.'

Rosie stopped halfway across the room. 'You didn't tell me.'

'You had other things to worry about,' he explained. 'Besides, nothing came of it. They sent me a copy of a letter they'd sent to BJK, warning them about the cable. It was apparently sent two days before George was killed. We wouldn't have a leg to stand on if we sued, so I dropped it. Just thought I'd tell you in case you ever wondered.'

Rosie pondered his words for a few seconds. 'I'll tell you what I am wondering,' she said. 'I'm wondering why George wasn't told about the cable?'

Robert shrugged. 'I don't know,' he said. 'You tell me.'

'Someone at the office should have contacted the site and told them,' said Rosie. 'It was standard practice.'

'It'd do no harm to check things out,' said Robert. 'If someone's to blame, we ought to know who.' He looked at Rosie and read her thoughts. 'Was there anyone at the office who ignored standard practices?'

'Ernie was in the office!' Rosie's face flushed with anger. 'Something like that would have been his responsibility.'

There was déjà vu here. Was Ernie as responsible for

288

George's death as Brindle was for Sean's? If so, she had much unfinished business to take care of.

Rosie lay awake that night. In the dark, quiet of her bed the anger she'd felt that day had magnified and filled her full of unrequited vengeance. Brindle and Scrimshaw had stolen the lives of two men she loved. Okay, loved but not *in love*; otherwise she couldn't have coped. As she tossed and turned she devised many versions of gruesome revenge. She felt herself going round in circles unable to rid her restless mind of these two awful men who had caused her so much pain. Maybe it was as well that she hadn't become involved with Barney. Maybe he'd have fallen victim to them as well. Christopher, who was in the same room, woke up bang on time for his two o'clock feed. Rosie switched on the electric heater, picked him up out of his cot and walked to the window. His eyes were still closed but his tiny mouth was reaching out – goldfish-like – for food, bringing a smile to his mother's face.

'Hold your horses, greedy guts.'

Her night nadgers, as she called them, were soothed as soon as she put him to her breast. She pulled back the curtains just far enough for her to see out. The street was deserted. Just above Mrs Craddock's chimney pot was a full moon. 'Shining like a tanner on a sweep's arse,' her dad would have said.

Someone had left a bike leaning against a yard wall. They were taking a big risk. A few years ago it would have been safe but things were changing. Honesty wasn't what it used to be.

A man appeared from round the corner, struggling under the weight of a heavily-laden rucksack. Mostin Craddock. For a jobless young man he did remarkably well for himself, having evolved from a nit-ridden child into a bespectacled Teddy Boy with money to burn. Rumours abounded about his nocturnal activities but nothing had ever been proved. He leaned against the street lamp, as if to

289

catch his breath, then hurried on his way. His glasses winked in the lamplight, which also reflected off his heavily Brylcreemed hair, styled in a DA; duck's anatomy if you're polite, duck's arse if you're not. He wore black, drainpipe trousers that accentuated his knock-knees and the light picked out his pink, fluorescent socks – the latest craze; and on his feet were a pair of beetle crushers with thick crepe soles. A deeply suspicious Rosie watched him disappear towards the Craddock back yard. Should she alert the police? Not likely. The law had never done her any favours and there'd been no burglaries round here. Not much to steal. Mostin obviously plied his trade in the more affluent areas! Chapeltown, Moortown, Alwoodley. Maybe he'd paid Barbara a visit that evening. The thought amused Rosie.

A lonely light shone in Mrs Gedge's downstairs room. What would she be doing at this time of night with her husband gone? Despite old enmities she'd turned up trumps when Rosie's mother needed someone. Perhaps that's what neighbours were; friendly enemies. She'd jumped at Rosie's offer of a job and had turned out to be surprisingly good at it. Just as well; Rosie wouldn't have dared sack her.

The following morning a brief phone conversation with Barney brought her vague plan into focus.

'Barney, I've just heard a story about how Ernie was creaming off BJK's profits before George died. Did George ever say anything to you about it?'

'Well, he didn't have much time for Ernie, but he never mentioned anything to me about him fiddling.'

'Nor me,' said Rosie. 'The only person he mentioned it to was Mrs Drysdale and he didn't tell her much. What do you think Ernie was up to?'

'Well, I did hear the odd rumour that stuff was being bought on BJK's account at some builder's merchant's or other and flogged off round the sites for cash. That could have been down to Ernie.'

'Why didn't you say something at the time?' Her tone was reproachful. His response was defensive:

'I didn't hear about it until after the firm had gone bust.'

'Wouldn't he have needed an accomplice with a wagon?'

'There'd have been no shortages of accomplices in this business,' Barney assured her.

Rosie considered the value of what she'd been told. 'So, a lot of people out there will know all about his fiddles?'

'I imagine so,' said Barney. 'Getting them to own up to it might be a bit tricky though.'

'Yes, I imagine it would, but that might not matter. I don't suppose you know where Ernie lives, do you?'

'I can ask around.'

Two days later, Barney rang her. 'I don't know where he lives but I know where he drinks. It's a pub called the Crown at Mirfield. He's there every Friday night apparently – gets himself absolutely pi ... er, plastered. Rosie, we still don't have actual proof that he was fiddling.'

'Ah, but he doesn't know that. All I have to do is tell him I know all about his fiddles and if I know Ernie, he'll be so shocked he'll do the rest for me. It's human nature.'

'I hope you're right.'

'I am right. Ernie's a big daft baby. Will he be there on Friday night?'

'As far as I know ...' He paused and added. 'I'd better come with you.'

'I can look after myself.'

'No arguments. Pick me up at seven o'clock.'

'Thanks, Barney.'

She paced up and down the room as an idea formulated in her head. Then she nodded to herself, as though giving her idea the seal of approval. Picking up the phone, she dialled Robert Hilton.

The pub was crowded as Barney pushed his way to the bar with Rosie in his wake. She spotted Ernie almost instantly, leaning against a piano, drinking alone.

291

'He's over there.'

Barney looked and nodded, 'I see him.'

'Get me a brandy,' said Rosie. 'I'm going to collar him before he sees us and slopes off.'

'I'll make myself scarce then, shall I?'

'Not too scarce. I want you to be there, as and when I need you.'

'*If only*,' thought Barney.

She stood with her back to Ernie, half-shielding Barney, who was keeping an eye on their prey as he ordered the drinks. 'He's looking old,' he said. 'Old and bald. And he's got no mates by the look of things.'

'He never did have,' Rosie said.

Ernie was now fifty-five and looked seventy. His face was crumpled like an old, brown-paper bag, but without the usual symmetry to the wrinkles which would betray evidence of humour, gravitas, compassion or intelligence. His face had no story to tell. It was an empty face. His lumpen frame was clad in a tweed sports jacket that had been made to measure for someone a different shape from him, and a cravat that he didn't know how to tie properly; and in an attempt to give himself character he'd grown a nicotine-stained moustache that hung over his top lip like a neglected grass verge. He jumped and spilled his beer when Rosie planted herself in front of him.

'Long time no see, Ernie.' She held out a hand. 'Where's my money?'

'What?'

'I've come for my money,' said Rosie. 'You must have known you couldn't get away with something like that. Come on, where's my money? Do you want me to shout out what you did, so that all and sundry can hear me? Because I will.'

'I haven't got yer money.' His manner was sullen.

'Well, in that case you're going to prison,' Rosie said, matter-of-factly.

Ernie plucked up enough courage to grin. 'They don't

lock yer up fer that. It's what's known as a civil dispute.'

'Oh, I wasn't talking about that,' said Rosie. 'I was talking about all the fiddling you did when yer worked for BJK.'

Ernie became guarded. 'What fiddling?'

'Sending a wagon to pick up gear on BJK's account and selling it off for cash.'

Guilt was written all over his face.

'Sorry, Ernie,' lied Rosie, 'but I know all about it. Practically down to the last penny. And I've got more proof than I need.'

Ernie became flustered. 'I were a partner in BJK. Why should I want ter fiddle meself?'

'Because you only had a minority of the shares.'

A man pushed between them, placed a pint of beer on top of the piano, lifted up the lid and said, cheerfully: 'C'mon, you two. Let the dog see the rabbit.'

He then pulled out a stool, sat down and cracked his knuckles which was something that always made Rosie cringe. He launched into a passable version of 'Black and White Rag' that had people tapping feet and drumming fingers against tables.

Rosie took Ernie's elbow and led him across the room. Barney followed and stood with his back to them both.

'George gave you a lousy job with a lousy wage.' She was shouting above the noise. 'And you thought you'd make up the difference. Only you got too greedy. It all showed up when the liquidator moved in.'

A young couple who obviously didn't appreciate having their tête-à-tête drowned out by the piano player, vacated a table, which Rosie grabbed and the two of them were seated before Ernie could protest. Rosie took a sip of her drink without taking her eyes off him. He squirmed under her gaze. Much to her enjoyment.

'I've got all the evidence I need to get you sent down for this,' said Rosie. 'Too many people knew what you were doing, Ernie. And they're all dropping you in it, to save their own skins. At least they will when it gets to court. According to my solicitor,' she went on, 'if you're lucky, you'll get the same as I got – three years.'

The noise from the piano forced her to shout in Ernie's ear. 'Could be as much as five ... especially if they take into account all the money stolen from BJK.'

Ernie looked suspicious. 'What yer doin' here then? Why haven't yer been ter t' police already?'

'Because I'm sick to death of courts and lawyers. I just want what's owed to me. Pay me what you owe and I'll take it no further.'

'Why should I trust you?'

She fixed him with an offended glare. 'Ernie!' she snapped. 'Who's the most trustworthy here, me or you? If I got you locked up, I could still sue you. And what chance do you think you'd have then? You'd lose the lot *and* you'd be locked up.'

'How do I know yer not bluffin'?' he challenged, half-heartedly.

She ignored him and countered with. 'How much of the money's tied up with Joe Brindle?'

'Yer what?'

People were singing now, which made conversation even more difficult. It wasn't the ideal venue for such a confrontation, but they hadn't chosen it. A passing woman spilled her drink on Ernie's jacket.

'Oops!' she sniggered. 'Can't stop. Nature calls.'

She disappeared into the Ladies clutching what was left of her drink. There was a lull in the singing.

'How much of my money's tied up with Brindle?' repeated Rosie.

Ernie seemed surprised at the extent of her knowledge. 'Just about all of it, if yer must know,' he admitted, glumly.

'That's what I figured.'

A well-dressed man took up a position directly behind Ernie. She gave him an imperceptible nod.

'Ernie,' Rosie asked. 'Just between you and me. Why did you lie about me in court? I never said any of those things about Brindle. I never even spoke to you about Brindle.'

Ernie lowered his eyes and shrugged. 'Because I had no option, that's why. Somebody said he'd shop me if I didn't do as he said.'

'Who was that? Brindle?'

'I'm sayin' nowt.'

'But you do admit to lying in court about me?' she pressed.

'I just said so, didn't I?' he admitted, petulantly. 'But I'll not admit to it in any court. That'd be admittin' perjury. And as fer the rest of it, I think yer bluffin'. Yer know nowt.'

Rosie looked up and spoke to the man standing behind Ernie. 'What do you think?'

Ernie looked round and blanched as he recognised Robert Hilton standing behind him. 'I think we have enough to have your conviction quashed,' said Robert. 'And to have this man and his crony put behind bars for a long time.'

Rosie looked at Ernie. 'Robert's an officer of the court. His evidence probably carries more weight than yours and mine put together.'

'There's also my evidence,' said Barney, sitting down beside Ernie. 'You're a slimy creep, Scrimshaw.' He grabbed Ernie by the scruff of the neck and almost hoisted him from his chair. 'If I had my way I'd ...'

'Leave him!' said Robert, sharply. 'We don't want him claiming he confessed under duress.'

Ernie was utterly deflated. Dejection clouded his rheumy eyes. 'What do you want me ter do?' he asked.

'Like I said. I just want my money.'

Robert and Barney were by now sitting at either side of Ernie. 'Well, he's admitted to everything,' Rosie summed up. 'Including perjury. So I think he's ready to do a deal – aren't you, Ernie?'

He nodded, dismally.

'I want you to sign everything over to me. And I mean everything. The papers are already drawn up.' She sensed Barney's questioning glance, but she ignored it. She wanted Ernie to think she was two steps in front of him.

'Some o' that money were mine.'

'Okay. I don't want to be unfair. I want my share of the money, plus interest, plus compensation for spending two years in jail.'

'That's a lot of compensation,' said Barney.

Rosie looked at Ernie with distaste. 'It's more money than you'll ever have. So, it's every penny you've got, or I'll report you to the police ... and I'll still sue you.'

Ernie looked undecided, so she threw in her trump card. 'We also know about how you failed to notify anyone about the live electric cable that killed George.'

'Hey! Now that were nowt ter do wi' me!'

'George knew about your fiddling,' said Rosie. 'So it won't take the police long to put two and two together to work a motive for you not notifying him about the cable.'

'I didn't kill him! That were an accident. Definitely!'

'Well, the police'll be looking into it now we've got evidence to prove that BJK had *definitely* been notified,' said Rosie. 'What did you do with the letter from the YEB – burn it? Whoever's responsible will cop for it. *If* I choose to take it any further.'

'It was criminal negligence at the very least,' said Robert.

'Could even be manslaughter,' added Rosie.

'Or even murder,' suggested Barney. 'If the police link it with all your fiddles. You're in a lot of trouble, Ernie. And Rosie's offering you a way out that you don't deserve.'

Ernie thought for a while, with sweat glistening on his pallid cheeks. The woman came out of the toilet, leaned over his shoulder and said, 'Sorry about that, love, but I were nearly wettin' me knickers.'

Ernie looked completely bemused. He finished his beer

and said, petulantly, 'Well, I can't do owt over t' weekend. It'll have ter wait till Monday.'

'You've got an appointment at Robert's office at ten o'clock on Monday morning,' Rosie informed him, coldly. 'Bring all your stuff. If you're not there on the dot, I'll be ringing the police up at five-past. We know where you live. In fact, we know everything there is to know about you.'

Barney whispered in his ear. 'Ernie, lad, do yourself a favour. She knows more about you than you know about yourself.'

The three of them got up and left Ernie sitting there with an open mouth and an empty glass. A Salvation Army woman rattled a tin under his nose.

'War Cry?'

'Piss off!' said Ernie.

'You worry me, you know that, don't you?' Barney said, as she drove them both back to Leeds. 'God knows what Brindle's gonna do when he finds out about this.'

'If Ernie's got any sense,' said Rosie, 'he won't tell him till he's signed the money across to me. Then we'll have Brindle over a barrel.'

'Are you really gonna let Scrimshaw off the hook?'

'I didn't actually *promise* him anything. If he's got hold of the wrong end of the stick, that's his problem.' She pressed her hand on Barney's. 'I couldn't do any of this without you – you know that, don't you?'

'That doesn't make me feel any better, Rosie.'

Chapter Twenty-Nine

Ernie's financial affairs were in the hands of two people. Joe Brindle, and an accountant who didn't trust Brindle as far as he could throw him. Placing his finances in the hands of his father's old accountant was one of the few intelligent things Ernie had ever done. Brindle, who had blackmailed Ernie into investing in his company, had fumed when he realised financial control wasn't entirely in his own hands. Ernie's wisest course of action would have been to deal with Rosie through his accountant; instead he chose to go to Brindle's office the following morning. Ernie told him everything apart from the bit where Robert Hilton had witnessed him admitting to perjury. He didn't know how Joe would take that.

'They're bluffin',' sneered Brindle. 'How could she know about all yer fiddles?'

'I'm tellin' yer, she does. She know all sorts o' stuff about me. Honest, Joe, I'm bloody scared! If I don't do as she says, I'm goin' down.'

'And I'm tellin' you I don't want that bitch getting' her hands on my company!' roared Brindle. 'She'll ruin me, soon as look at me.' He had Ernie by the scruff of his neck. 'I'm warning yer, yer useless pillock. You give in to her and yer'll have me ter worry about. So what d'yer think's worse, eh? Me or her?'

It wasn't as obvious a choice as Brindle thought it was.

Being beaten up by Joe seemed preferable to prison, but Ernie didn't say so. Brindle saw his uncertainty and realised that threats weren't always the answer.

'Look, Ernie, just leave the bitch ter me,' he said, calming down and thinking straight. 'She's got some sort o' shop in Leeds by all accounts. Tell yer what. You come wi' me ternight and I'll put the wind up her a bit. Let her know who she's *really* dealing with.'

'I don't know about that, Joe.'

'Yer want ter keep yer money, don't yer?'

'Well, course I do, but ...'

'What'll yer do if yer've got no brass, eh?' Joe sneered. 'Yer'll not get a job, not at your age. Yer'll be livin' off t' pancrack with yer arse hangin' out o' yer trousers like all t' other dossers. Is that what yer want?'

'Well, no ...'

'Drinkin' meths an' scrabbling in bins fer food. Is that what yer want?'

'Course I don't, Joe.'

'Well, frame yersen then! Stop whinin' about what that bitch might do and let's get our two penn'orth in first. Fight fire wi' bloody fire.' Up until then, Joe hadn't thought of an exact plan. But he had now.

Ernie had a Standard Vanguard. It was a heavy, pugnacious vehicle, which he hoped would make up for certain deficiencies in his character. Duck Street Stores had been closed an hour, after its busiest day yet. Brindle and Ernie were driving down the Huddersfield Road past a sign indicating that they were now in Leeds. It was still light, which didn't suit Brindle, so he instructed Ernie to stop at a pub to kill some time. Ernie was troubled.

'She'll know who did it, yer know.'

Joe grinned as he let Ernie buy the drinks. 'Did what?'

'Yer know what – whatever yer've got in mind.'

'Course she'll know who did it. That's the whole bloody point. It'll be like a warning shot across her bows. She'll get a phone call tomorrow tellin' her that her kids'll be next.'

299

'Aw, Jesus, Joe! I'll have no part in harmin' kids.'

'Yer won't have ter. D'yer know what's gonna get yer out of all this mess yer in?'

'What?'

'My reputation, that's what. The bitch'll not risk me harmin' her kids.' Brindle gave an evil grin and threw a whisky back. 'And yer'll owe me fer this. After tonight I don't want that accountant o' yours meddlin' in my affairs.' He thrust his face into Ernie's, causing him to flinch. 'Do yer hear me?'

Ernie swallowed, 'No problem, Joe.'

'Good lad.' Brindle looked at the watch on his thick wrist, then glanced out of the window. 'Right, drink up, we're off. Should be dark when we get there. All yer've got ter do is drive, I'll do the rest. An' drive nice an' steady. We don't want ter go breakin' no speed limits.'

Joe sat in the back and put on a pair of gloves. Ernie watched through the mirror. 'What're they for, Joe? Yer not gonna get up to no rough stuff, are yer?'

'Precautions, Ernie lad.'

He reached into a haversack he'd brought with him and took out two lemonade bottles. He unscrewed the tops and a smell of petrol pervaded the car.

'Christ! Joe, what're yer doin'?'

'Preparin' a couple o' drinks.'

Brindle took two lengths of rag from his bag and stuffed one into each bottle. 'Molotov Cocktails. Just ter liven their shop up a bit.'

'Oh, bloody hell, Joe!'

'Don't be so soft,' sneered Brindle. 'What did yer think I were gonna do, shout rude names through her letter box? That bitch needs a proper scare – and this'll do the trick.'

Rosie was just coming in from the pictures and her babysitter, Marlene Gedge, was slumbering in the armchair. There was a play on the wireless that she'd started listening to, but her tiredness had got the better of her. It had been a long, hard day and it had been her idea that Rosie went to the cinema.

Upstairs, Eddie and Christopher were fast asleep. Rosie's shop had given Mrs Gedge a whole new lease of life. Something to get up for on a morning. Her husband had left her before the war; gone off to live in Heckmondwike with a woman from his work and Marlene had become embittered. He'd been called up into the RAF, and that had given her hope. Maybe being parted from both his wife and his fancy-piece might make him see the error of his ways – see which side his bread was buttered. Apparently his bread was being buttered by a WAAF from Macclesfield, so at least Marlene had the satisfaction of knowing his fancy-piece was in the same boat as her. A war widow's pension would have given her greater satisfaction.

The smashing of glass woke her up. At first she thought it might have come from the wireless. She listened for a while and realised it couldn't have been. Rosie came through the back door and shouted. 'I'm back.'

'Did you hear a noise?' asked Marlene.

'What sort of noise?'

'Like glass breakin'. I were asleep an' I thought I heard a noise.'

'I didn't hear it,' said Rosie. 'Maybe something's fallen over in the shop. I'll just have a look.'

She left her coat on and walked through the short passage that led to the connecting door to the shop. There was a crackling beyond it that should have told her all was not well. Without thinking, she pulled the door open and was met by a wall of flames that had her staggering backwards with her coat on fire. Rosie ran into the kitchen, with Marlene close behind. She ripped off Rosie's coat and threw it on the floor, then she opened the back door and pushed her outside.

They both stood in the middle of the street shouting for help as the flames lit up the downstairs of the house. Windows scraped open and people came to doors. Rosie screamed, 'My babies!' and ran back to the house. Marlene grabbed her from behind and pushed her into the arms of Mrs Craddock, who had appeared on the scene with her son.

'They're upstairs,' screamed Rosie. 'Please, someone help my babies!'

Within seconds, Mostin was halfway up the cast-iron drainpipe.

'Don't, Mostin! We've sent for t' Fire Brigade,' yelled his mother.

But he'd smashed his fist through the bedroom window and, with a bleeding hand, was unfastening the catch. He climbed inside, with all the expertise of his nocturnal trade. Within seconds Eddie's white face appeared beside him at the window.

'Yer'll have ter catch him,' shouted Mostin.

Rosie broke away from Mrs Craddock and ran into the yard, with Marlene two steps behind her. They both held out their arms as Mostin threw the struggling boy out. Rosie broke Eddie's fall and lurched into Mrs Gedge, sending her to the ground. Christopher followed, landing on top of them. They managed to drag the two boys from the yard just before the downstairs window shattered and flames roared out.

Mrs Craddock was too paralysed with horror to help. She was watching her son struggling to get back out of the window. His shirt and hair were on fire and she couldn't see his face. He was just a black, melting shadow against a background of flames. Then there was a crash as the floor beneath him collapsed and he disappeared completely.

'Mostin!' shouted his mother.

He'd caused her much grief in his life, but none more than this.

Ernie was shaking as he drove off. He'd stopped the car just long enough for Brindle to open the back door and hurl one of the home-made petrol bombs through the shop window, before accelerating away. They'd seen it explode

302

but had no idea of how much damage they'd done.

Brindle laughed loudly. 'That'll make 'em think twice about messin' wi us. There'll not be much left o' their shop after tonight's piece o' work.'

'Christ, Joe! I hope nobody's been hurt.'

'Nah. There'll have been no bugger in t' shop. Serve 'em bloody right if they were.'

An ambulance arrived before the fire brigade and Beryl Craddock was persuaded to sit inside, rather than watch the horror of the house burning with her son inside. She sat on a bed with Rosie, Marlene and the two boys. Beryl's senses were dulled by the sudden, unexpected horror of the situation.

'D'yer think he's all right?' she asked.

'I don't know, Mrs Craddock,' lied Rosie. Tears of relief and shock made white rivulets down her smoke-blackened cheeks. 'He saved my boys, I know that much.'

'Bravest thing I've ever seen,' said Marlene.

'I hope he's all right. He's allus doin' summat daft is our Mostin.'

Her voice was flat. The shock had robbed her of any emotion. They sat for an hour before the fire was declared under control. Silently, Beryl Craddock climbed out.

A large crowd had gathered and the air was thick with damp, acrid smoke. People parted as she made her way forward. A fireman turned round and held out an arm. 'You can't go any nearer, love. The whole place might fall down.'

'My lad's inside,' she said. 'I just want ter see if he's all right.'

Men were inside, damping down. One shouted, loud enough for Rosie to hear, 'There's someone here.'

Mrs Craddock made to rush in but was held back, screaming and struggling. A fireman went inside and said, 'Don't bring him out just yet.' Then he came back out and spoke to a policeman, who went up to Beryl. 'I'm afraid the

303

person inside's dead, love.' There was no gentle way to tell her. 'I take it he was your son.'

Beryl collapsed in his arms as Rosie looked on, clutching her baby and her boy as tightly as she could.

Brindle looked at Ernie's sweating face. 'Get a grip of yersen, man.'

'I've never done nowt like this before, Joe. What if somebody got hurt?'

'I'm tellin' yer, there were no one in t' shop,' said Brindle. The lights of a pub came into view. 'We'll call in here.'

Inside the pub, Ernie's hand was shaking as he held his glass to his lips. 'I think we should go back and see what happened,' he said. 'I'd be a bit happier if we went back.'

'Aye, why not?' grinned Brindle. 'I wouldn't mind takin' a look meself.'

'What if someone recognises us?'

'Who the hell knows us round there?'

Ernie looked at Joe's distinctive black eye-patch. 'I wish yer'd wear yer glass eye.'

'Tell yer what, Ernie,' laughed Joe. 'I'll stick it in, just fer you.

He took out a small, cloth bag from which he brought a glass eye. With a deft movement he lifted up his patch and stuck it into his empty socket, then he turned to Ernie and grinned. 'How do I look?'

Ernie flinched. The artificial eye glared, unnervingly, at him as the good eye swivelled all round.

'I wish yer wouldn't do that,' he muttered.

An ambulance, now containing Mostin's charred body, was just driving away as they pulled up a few yards down the road from Duck Street. There were still crowds milling around. Joe wound down his window and called out to a passing youth. 'What's been goin' on, pal?'

The young man came up to the passenger window. Ernie

turned his face away and watched the ambulance pass by; its bell ominously quiet and its headlights glinting in Joe's glass eye. The youth pointed to Rosie's smoking house and shop.

'There's been a big fire over yon.'

'Oh dear. Anybody hurt?' enquired Joe.

'Yeah. Mostin Craddock – burnt to a cinder,' announced the youth, macabrely.

Ernie gave a shocked sob, attracting the youth's attention, so Joe wound up the window. 'Drive,' he ordered. 'I want ter get as far away from here as possible.'

They drove back to Huddersfield with Ernie sobbing all the way. 'Oh Christ, Joe! This is murder. We're gonna get hung fer this.'

'Just keep drivin' while I think.'

They didn't stop at Huddersfield, they carried straight on along the Rochdale Road, then Joe told Ernie to take a turn that took them up into the Pennines. Ernie didn't argue, his mind was in a turmoil. Visions of a noose dangled in front of his eyes. He knew the police would catch him eventually.

'She'll tell the police it were me,' he snivelled. 'She'll tell 'em about what were said last Saturday.'

'Shut up!' roared Joe. 'I'm sick of yer bloody whinin'. All we've got ter do is back each other up. Stick to our guns and they'll be able ter prove nowt.'

'They know I were fiddlin' BJK.'

'It's your word against hers.'

Ernie's common sense had long since deserted him. 'There's summat I didn't tell yer Joe. About when I saw Rosie in t' pub.'

'What?' snarled Joe. 'What're yer trying ter tell me?'

Ernie was totally dejected. Tears rolled down his face. 'She knows I lied in court about her.'

'Course she bloody knows, yer thick bugger!'

'I mean it's not just her. Robert Hilton were there an' all He heard me admit it.'

'Oh aye – an' who's this Robert Hilton?'

'Her solicitor. I think he heard everything.'

'Oh Jesus!'

'Hey – I never brought you into it, Joe. She asked me why I'd lied in court an' I kept me mouth shut about you.'

'An' I'm supposed ter believe that, am I?'

'As God is my judge, Joe, I never said nowt about you.'

Brindle lapsed into deep thought. They were driving high in the hills now, along narrow moorland roads. Every time Ernie opened his mouth to speak, Joe snapped him into silence. The road took them beside a deep, wooded ravine.

'Here, pull up,' commanded Brindle. 'I'll bloody drive.'

Ernie drew the car to a halt. Joe put his gloves back on, got out and walked around the car as Ernie shuffled into the passenger seat. The remaining petrol bomb was on the floor at the back. Joe opened the rear door and reached inside to pick it up.

'We don't want ter get caught wi' this, Ernie lad.'

Joe's tone was friendly and Ernie felt oddly reassured. Maybe they'd get away with it after all. He forced out a half smile.

'I don't want ter get caught at all, Joe.'

His world went black as Brindle smashed him over the head with the petrol filled bottle. As Ernie slumped, unconscious, Joe opened the driver's door and pulled him back behind the wheel.

'Sorry, Ernie lad. Yer just too much of a bloody liability.'

He took off the handbrake, turned the wheel to the left, then gave the heavy car a heave. It ran down a slight slope, gathering speed before it plunged down the steep ravine, bouncing off trees growing out of the side which would shield the car and Ernie's body for several days. There was a silence as it took off into mid-air, then a loud crash as it hit a rocky stream at the bottom. Brindle's face curled into a grin. It hadn't burst into flames, that was good. The smashed petrol bomb would no doubt tell its own incriminating tale. All in all, things had worked out quite well for him.

He set off walking back to Huddersfield, ducking out of sight of the occasional passing car. Police would be asking questions of anyone in the area, so he needed to put some miles between him and Ernie's car before he thumbed the lift that would take him home. His grin broadened as he weighed up the advantages of his partner no longer being around. Ernie had never been a director or share holder in Joe's company, his share of the profits was guaranteed by a legal contract; but when Ernie expired, so did the contract. There was even a mutual life insurance on which Joe would collect in the event of Ernie's death. And best of all, that bitch who had taken his eye out could whistle for the money Ernie had fleeced out of her. No way could she get her hands on it now. After an hour, he stuck out his thumb and stopped a passing wagon.

Chapter Thirty

It was two days before Rosie could bring herself to look at her old home. The Fire Brigade had managed to stop it from spreading into Number Four but there was little left of the house in which she'd spent most of her life. Just a shell. Scarred windows stared down at her like empty eye sockets, the paint blistered door hung on one hinge and the roof spars stood stark against the sky like charred ribs. Eddie and Christopher were both being looked after by Marlene Gedge as Rosie began the slow process of getting her life back together. She stood beside Mr Wicks, the insurance assessor, who had just told her that the company suspected arson.

'We think it was started by petrol in the shop,' he told her.

'So the police say,' Rosie replied. 'Who would do a thing like that?'

'I've got no idea, but it means we can't process your claim just yet.'

'Why not?' That's my home we're looking at. My premiums were up to date, weren't they?'

'It's company policy, Mrs Metcalf ...'

'Is it company policy or is it because I've got a criminal record and you think I might have started the fire on purpose to collect on the insurance?'

'As I say, it's company policy.'

'The shop had only been open a couple of months. We were just beginning to get established. Why should I set fire to it? Why should I put my children's lives in danger? If the police thought I did it they'd have arrested me for murder.'

'No one's saying you did it, Mrs Metcalf.'

'Well, can I have my money then?'

'It's not as simple as that.'

'Look, forget it. Deal with my solicitor, would you? It'll make a wonderful advert for your company when this gets into the papers.'

'I didn't say we wouldn't ...'

'You haven't said anything of any comfort to me, Mr Wicks. I've just lost my home and my livelihood and a very brave young man has lost his life. Right now I need words of comfort or I'll go mad. I'll get my solicitor to give you a ring.' Rosie began to walk away when a thought struck her. She turned and shouted back to him.

'There's a builder in Huddersfield called Joe Brindle, the odds are that he did it. Me and him have a long-running feud. Mostin Craddock wouldn't be the first person he's killed. And if he uses a man called Scrimshaw as his alibi, don't be taken in. Scrimshaw is up to his neck in all this as well.'

'Perhaps you should tell the police.'

'I have, Mr Wicks. I might as well tell the man in the moon.'

Rosie went back to Marlene Gedge's house, because she had nowhere else to go.

'It's a right old mess is all this, Marlene. All Friday and Saturday's takings went up with the house. Apart from the little matter of having nowhere to live, there's hardly any money in the bank and there's a funeral pay for.'

'What? Yer payin' fer Mostin's funeral?'

'Well, Mrs Craddock said not to, but it was the least I could do. The Craddock's haven't got two ha'pennies to scratch together. I offered them something out of the insurance money, but they said no. What do you think I should do?'

'It's Mostin who deserves paying,' said Marlene, 'not his mam and dad.'

'That's more or less what they said.'

'The lad died a hero,' Marlene commented. 'You paying money out might take the gloss off it a bit.'

'If the insurance money doesn't come through in time to pay for the funeral, I'll have to sell the car. I'll owe you a tidy sum by then.'

'It'll wait till yer get yersen sorted.'

'Thanks, Marlene.'

Rosie took out her cigarettes and offered the packet to Mrs Gedge, who took one and grinned. 'I never forget that time when Mostin wrote Traitor on your wall. By God it hurt when yer mam hit me with that brush. Mind you, I probably deserved it. Hero, yer dad was. Him an' young Mostin alike – funny that.'

'God, what Mostin did was so unbelievably brave,' Rosie said. 'Eddie and Christopher wouldn't be here if it wasn't for him.'

Marlene blew out an untidy puff of smoke. 'Did yer know he fancied yer?'

'Who?'

'Young Mostin – his mam once told me. We used to have a right laugh about it. We teased him summat rotten, me an' Beryl. I kept threatening I'd tell you.'

'Oh my God! Do you think that's why he …?'

'Why he helped you?' Marlene gave it some thought. 'Could be.'

Rosie buried her head in her hands. Every man who ever had any feelings for her had died. Every single one of them, including her dad – and now Mostin.

That afternoon Barney knocked on the door. 'Is Rosie about?'

'She's about all right,' said Mrs Gedge. 'I'd say she's about knackered.'

He walked in and stood beside Rosie's chair. 'I thought

I'd ring Robert Hilton, just on the off chance.'

'Robert Hilton?'

'About Ernie going to see him today at ten o'clock.'

'Oh, I'd forgotten about that ... and?'

'And he didn't turn up,' said Barney.

'No, well, he wouldn't, would he?'

Three boys found Ernie's car. The stream at the bottom of the ravine was popular haunt for local lads. One of them was violently sick when he saw Ernie's bloodied head poking through the shattered windscreen. The Leeds Police had already put feelers out to their Huddersfield counterparts about Ernie, so his discovery solved many things; especially as they'd found the remains of the petrol bomb in the car. On Friday morning, the day of Mostin's funeral, a policeman knocked on Mrs Gedge's door.

'Sorry to call at a time like this, but is Mrs Metcalf in?'

Rosie appeared at her neighbour's shoulder. The policeman removed his helmet and stepped inside.

'I thought you should know that we've found Mr Scrimshaw.'

'Well, at least that's something,' said Rosie 'Maybe I can get my money out of him now.'

The policeman hesitated, not sure how his second bit of news would be received.

'He was found dead in his car yesterday afternoon.'

Rosie stared at him. Unable to unravel the complications of all this. 'Dead?' she said. 'What happened to him?'

'His car went down a ravine.'

'When did this happen?'

'We're not absolutely sure. Could have been as long ago as last Saturday night.'

'Last Saturday?'

'And there was evidence in the car to tie him to the fire at your shop.'

'What sort of evidence?'

'Evidence of a petrol tomb. Scrimshaw's clothes were

soaked in petrol and there was a smashed bottle that had obviously contained petrol, in the car.'

'So, what do you think happened?'

The policeman shrugged. 'Hard to say at this stage. He could have lost control of the car.'

'Or someone could have killed him, and pushed the car down the ravine,' suggested Rosie. 'Someone like Joe Brindle.'

'Mr Brindle was apparently in Huddersfield at the time.'

'Was he really?' There was heavy cynicism in Rosie's voice.

'How does that leave you?' enquired Mrs Gedge. 'With him owing yer all that money.'

'I've no idea,' said Rosie. She looked at the policeman. 'Can you sue a dead man?'

'I shouldn't have thought so, love.'

With Barney's help, Rosie sold her car for a hundred and fifty pounds, sixty of which went to the undertaker. The insurance claim was stuck in the system, she'd even been asked about her movements on the night of the fire. The questioner had gone off with a flea in his ear.

Chapter Thirty-One

It was the day after the 1955 May General Election and Rosie had been living with Marlene for over two months when it arrived. The surplus money from the sale of her car was just about gone and she was on the verge of pawning her engagement ring. Marlene watched with interest as her lodger opened the envelope. Rosie looked at the printed name on the front. *Northern Star Insurance Co Ltd.*

'This looks like it.'

She took out the cheque and stretched it between thumbs and forefingers as she read out the figures, slowly. 'One-thousand-three-hundred-and-seventy-three pounds, fourteen and six.' She checked the numbers with the written amount, then examined the signature. All was in order and she was in business.

'Must be like coming up on the Pools,' said Marlene, trying to hide any jealousy she might feel. 'It'd pay the rent on this place for donkeys years.'

'It's supposed to cover the re-building cost of the house and shop.'

'Is that what yer gonna do, re-build it?'

Rosie nodded. 'Re-build the house and re-build my life, Marlene. In the meantime what would you say to putting us up until I get back on my feet?'

'Well, I must say, it's been a lot more lively round here since you lot arrived ...'

'I'll pay the rent and food bills – and I'll have a phone put in.'

'I've allus fancied a phone,' said Marlene.

Rosie saw Barney in the Wellington Arms on his way home from work.

'Thought I'd catch you,' she smiled. 'Doesn't your wife mind you not coming straight home?'

'I need this to give me Dutch courage before I face her,' he grinned.

'Surely she's not that bad?'

He shrugged, dismissively. 'Nothing we can't put right.'

Rosie wondered if she was wrong in taking such pleasure out of Barney's marital difficulties. She wanted to ask him if they still slept together, but tact prevailed.

'I've just got my insurance money through,' she said. 'And I've got a proposition for you.'

His eyes twinkled at the ambiguity of her statement. 'I'm not cheap,' he said. 'And I don't go in for kinky stuff.'

She slapped him, playfully. 'Smutty boy! Go to your room . . . it's a business proposition.'

'Shame . . . go on, I'm listening.'

Rosie unfolded her scheme to him. 'What's left of the Duck Street house and shop, plus the land it stands on are still mine. The insurance money's apparently sufficient to re-build, re-stock and re-furnish everything. Only I don't intend re-stocking and re-furnishing because I want to sell it when it's finished.'

'Oh yes, and where will you live?'

'We're staying on at Marlene's for the time being. There'll be some surplus money if all I'm doing is the building. I'll live off that until the work's done.'

'Then what?'

'Then you and I can move on to the next job.'

'So, you want me to do the building work?'

'I want you to do more than that. I want you as a partner. You put in the work, I put in the land and the money. You

314

draw a living wage and we'll split the profits down the middle.'

His hand was already outstretched. 'You've got yourself a deal.'

'Oh, and there's just one other thing.'

'What's that?'

'BJK Ltd still exists as a company. I want that to be us.'

'It'd be an honour. With the reputation George gave it, we should get off to a flyer.'

As soon as he heard about the resurrection of BJK Ltd, Joe Brindle was magnetically drawn to Duck Street; just to see with his own eyes what was going on, and to perhaps ensure there was no threat to him from that direction. It was mid-July and Barney was supervising the demolition of Rosie's old home. Rosie was at the doctor's with Christopher, who had a skin infection. Her local man had failed to find a cure so Rosie had travelled the extra miles to visit George's old G.P. A man she knew and trusted. Doctor Rowell was in his seventies but still going strong with no intention of retiring. He examined Christopher and wrote out a prescription for a jar of ointment.

'This should do the trick. If it doesn't, bring him back and we'll try him on something else.'

'If this works we might start to bring our custom here, doctor. It'll be worth the extra journey.'

He looked at her over his glasses. 'You know I've missed treating the Metcalf family. I've looked after them all, at one time or another.'

Rosie smiled. 'I'm glad you still look upon me as a Metcalf. There are those in George's family who don't.'

'I assume you mean his daughter?'

'Who else?'

He cleared this throat, nervously. 'She came round to see me, you know,' he said. 'She asked me about George's blood group.'

'Did she now? Pity you had to tell her. It cost me my

home, and made a mockery of our marriage.'

'Yes,' the doctor said. 'I heard about that. I often wondered if I should have intervened. But there was a question of patient confidentiality, so I decided to keep out of it.'

'I don't understand.'

The doctor sighed. He'd said too much now to back out. Sitting back in his chair, he wrestled with his conscience. His shaggy brow was knitted in deep thought. At length, he said, 'On balance perhaps I should have come forward, but your husband trusted me with a confidentiality that I should have taken to my grave. I never suspected he would go before me.'

Rosie searched his rumpled old face for clues. 'Doctor, I haven't the foggiest idea what you're talking about.'

'No, my dear, of course you don't. No one does.' He laced his fingers together and held them in front of his mouth as though fervently praying. 'Of course George knew Eddie wasn't his son. I'm quite sure he went into his marriage with you with his eyes wide open.'

'So, he told you?'

'He didn't have to. You see, George couldn't have children.'

Rosie looked at him, the significance didn't instantly sink in. 'Couldn't have children? Why ever not?' was all she could think to say.

'When he lost his leg, he also lost the ability to father children. George was rendered sterile.'

Rosie picked Christopher up and sat him on her knee. 'But ... he never told me. Why wouldn't he tell me a thing like that?'

The doctor shrugged. 'Who knows? At his age, maybe he didn't feel he had to. Perhaps he didn't want to kill off all your hopes of having a family with him.'

'It didn't surprise me when we didn't have children,' admitted Rosie. 'But I thought he might have mentioned it.'

'He loved you very much. Maybe it was a risk he didn't want to take.'

'It wouldn't have made any difference,' said Rosie. 'Hang on! What are we talking about? You say it was caused by his wound in the war, so . . . ' She shook her head, trying to make sense of things. 'How come Barbara . . . ?'

The doctor held up his hands. 'I know what you're going to say. And that's where patient confidentiality comes in.'

'Is Barbara one of your patients?'

'No.'

'And does patient confidentiality extend to patients who are now dead?'

'Possibly.'

Rosie ignored this. 'You're saying Barbara isn't his daughter. She was adopted?'

'All I'm saying is that George couldn't have children and that he was well aware of it.'

She looked at him, keenly. 'Would you be prepared to tell this to a court?'

His shoulders sagged and he shook his head, uncertainly. Then he looked up at her. 'If it rights a wrong, then I suppose it's my duty to do so.'

'It's what George would have wanted,' Rosie pointed out. 'It wasn't just the house and Eddie's money. The court ruling made a complete mockery of the happiest years of his life. Barbara made him out to be a gullible fool.'

Faced with such damning truth, the old doctor's eyes grew sad. 'I should have come forward at the time, I realise that now. I'm dreadfully sorry.'

'It's not too late, doctor. Could you write me a letter to give to my solicitor? I need to set some wheels in motion.'

Rosie stopped off at Duck Street to give Barney the good news. A sharp wind whistled through the telephone wires and, high above, scattered the summer clouds, leaving patches of blue for the first time in weeks; an optimistic omen. Rosie looked up and smiled. 'Oh look, blue sky.'

'Just enough to make a sailor a pair of trousers,' said Barney.

'What?'

'It was something my mother used to say,' he explained. 'To what do I owe the honour of this visit?'

'Ah, this is brilliant news. I've just been to the doctor's and ... morning, Mrs Craddock.'

Mostin's mother appeared, carrying a shopping bag; her face still drawn. 'Sooner yer get this shop opened, the better,' she said. 'It were right handy.'

Rosie felt guilty. She'd sworn Marlene Gedge to secrecy about her selling the house and shop as soon as it was finished. She changed her mind there and then. If Mrs Craddock wanted a grocer's at the end of her street, then Mrs Craddock must have a grocer's.

'We'll have it opened before you know it,' Rosie promised. 'In fact, we'll let you cut the string on the opening ceremony – and free groceries for a month.'

'Nay, I don't need yer charity, Rosie. Our Mostin didn't do what he did for a few lumps o' sugar. He did it because he were a daft bugger.'

'A very brave daft bugger,' said Rosie. 'And I'm sorry. I didn't mean to insult his memory. But I'll never forget what he did for as long as I live.'

Mrs Craddock set her face into a frown lest she display any unbecoming emotion. She patted Christopher on the head and went on her way.

Barney joined them after Mrs Craddock had gone. 'I thought we were supposed to be selling the lot.'

'I'll just have to work something out,' said Rosie. 'I owe that family so much.'

Barney smiled. 'Whatever you do's okay by me. Now, what was this news?'

Brindle's car pulled up alongside. Neither Rosie nor Barney recognised it until the man got out. Barney scowled and Rosie's face set in anger. She pointed at Mrs Craddock's departing back.

'It was her son you killed. He died saving my boys.'

Brindle held up protesting hands and walked around his

car towards them. 'Hey! Don't blame me for that. I wasn't even in Leeds that night.'

'Just stay away from me and my boys,' hissed Rosie.

Brindle stopped and shrugged. 'The bloke who did that got what were comin' to him. I reckon yer must have said summat to Ernie to upset him. The coppers think he set fire ter this place then topped hisself.'

'You've got all the money he stole from Rosie,' said Barney, stepping in front of Brindle.

Brindle smirked. 'What makes yer think that?'

'Because he told us, that's why.'

'Ah, so yer did speak to him just before he died. This tells me yer brought all this on yerself. If yer'd kept yer mouths shut mebbe none o' this would have happened.'

Barney stepped right into Brindle's face, his anger rising. 'What about Rosie's money?'

Brindle thrust his face forward until their noses were touching. 'If yer think yer've got a leg ter stand on – bloody sue me.'

All the while, a youth who was working on the demolition, had been staring at Brindle, as though trying to place him. He made his way to Barney's side as the situation between the two men became apparent to him. Then he looked, questioningly at Rosie, who shook her head as if to say, 'keep out of it'. The young man returned his gaze to Brindle, who saw him staring.

'What're you gawpin' at?'

'Nowt,' said the youth. 'I just thought I'd seen yer somewhere before, that's all – don't know where, though.'

'His name's Joe Brindle,' said Barney. 'He reckons he's a builder. Mebbe you've come across him on a site somewhere. It's not a face you'd forget in a hurry.'

'He's never worked for me, I can tell yer that,' sneered Brindle. 'I don't employ dozy-lookin' pillocks like him ... I leave that to you.'

The youth snapped his fingers. 'It were that night,' he said. 'I remember now.'

Brindle scowled. 'What bloody night?'

'The night this place got burned. Yer were here wi' that other bloke. Yer asked me what had happened.' He pointed at Brindle's car. 'Yer weren't in that car, though, yer were in a Standard Vanguard. I remember 'cos I've allus wanted a Standard Vanguard. It were black ...'

'You saw him ... here?' said Barney.

The youth nodded. 'Yeah, there were two of 'em, him and this other bloke.'

Joe Brindle suddenly realised the implications of what had just happened. Barney grabbed him by his collar and Brindle punched him, fiercely. Rosie backed away, her child in her arms. Brindle was already back in his car. Barney banged on the roof as the car screeched away and Rosie fiercely held on to Christopher. The nightmare wasn't over.

By the time the youth had given the police his statement and the police in Huddersfield had been alerted, Brindle had cleaned out his bank accounts and was long gone. That afternoon Rosie went to see Robert Hilton.

'Thanks for seeing me at such short notice but a couple of interesting things happened to me this morning.'

'Interesting things to you are usually Earth-shattering to us mere mortals,' commented Robert. 'Will I need a drink to steady my nerves?'

'No, it's all good news, really. Joe Brindle turned up at Duck Street ...'

'The cheek of the man!'

'No, I'm glad he did. You see one of the men said he'd seen him on the night of the fire, with Ernie in Ernie's car.'

'You mean they were at the scene?'

'Yes, this lad's made a statement to the police. They went off to arrest him in Huddersfield but evidently he's done a bunk. Barney tried to stop him, but he's a big, nasty bloke is Brindle.'

'Rosie, this is good news. Coupled with Scrimshaw's admission to perjury, I think we can get your conviction quashed. If Brindle's convicted of this, his evidence won't count for anything at a re-trial.'

'What about my money? The money Scrimshaw stole from me?'

Robert made to take a cigar out of a box but stopped when he caught the look in Rosie's eyes. 'I can't see any legal way of recovering that from Brindle – but I could add it to the claim for compensation, as and when you get your conviction quashed.'

'Really?'

'Plus damages for wrongful imprisonment, loss of earnings, psychological damage, et cetera et cetera. Should add up to a tidy sum. Should more than make up for you losing your case against Barbara.'

'Which brings me to my other bit of news.'

She gave Robert the letter from George's doctor. His eyes opened wide as he read it. He folded it up and crossed his arms.

'Hmm ... I don't think "interesting" is a word I'd have used to describe your morning. I think I'll stick to Earth-shattering. Would you like me to inform Barbara's solicitor and set the wheels in motion?'

'Do you think I can get Oak House back?'

'I think it's a formality. George obviously knew exactly what the situation was. His wishes must be honoured.'

'I want to tell Barbara myself.'

'I thought you might ... Rosie.'

'What?'

'Take care in everything you do. After today these people are going to hate you. I don't know how dangerous Barbara is, but we do know about Brindle. Maybe you should go away until he's caught.'

'I can take care of myself, Robert. I have friends.'

'You worry me, Rosie. You know that, don't you?'

'May I come in?' asked Rosie, politely.

The smile that had been on Barbara's face vanished when

she realised who was at the door. 'No, you may not. Just tell me what you want and clear off!'

Rosie smiled, sweetly. 'I think you might want to be nice to me in view of what I've brought to show you.'

'Oh yes?'

Rosie handed her the doctor's letter. As Barbara read it, her fingers began to shake. Her husband appeared behind her.

'What is it, love?' he asked. Then to Rosie, 'Who are you?'

'Rosie Metcalf, I assume you're Paul?'

He took her offered hand and shook it through force of habit. 'I think Barbara was just about to invite me in,' said Rosie. 'Weren't you, Barbara?'

Barbara nodded, dumbly, as Rosie followed Paul through to the living room where she had spent such happy times with George. All of the old furniture was still there – it was all part and parcel of George's will, and Rosie felt so strange; as though she was in her own home yet somehow didn't belong there.

'I spent many happy hours in this house,' she said, sitting down in the chair that had always been hers; but was now Barbara's.

'What's this all about?' enquired Paul, surprised at his wife not objecting to Rosie making herself at home. Barbara sat on a window seat and gazed out. Her world suddenly shattered. The letter was still in her hand.

'I think you should look at the letter,' advised Rosie.

He gently took the sheet of crumpled paper from his wife's frozen grip and read it.

'I see,' he said, at length.

Paul looked at his wife's ashen face, then back at Rosie. 'I'm sorry,' he said, 'but I must ask you to leave. This house legally belongs to my wife.'

'Legally but not morally – and it won't be legally hers for much longer.'

Barbara was sobbing now. Paul sat beside her and put an

arm around her. Rosie waited, quietly and patiently for her to speak.

'I spent my childhood in this house,' Barbara said, at length. 'Just me and my dad.'

'But he wasn't your dad, was he?' said Rosie. 'He wasn't physically capable of being anyone's dad.' The hurt Barbara had inflicted on her had hardened her for this moment.

'You know, he never told me I was adopted.' Barbara sounded distant. 'No one did.'

'I suppose it could explain why you didn't feel very close to him,' Rosie said. 'Why you hardly bothered with him, once you left home.'

Barbara shook her head. 'What you're saying doesn't actually make sense.'

'No? Then what *does* make sense?' asked Rosie, who tended to agree it didn't make sense; but she couldn't think of any other reason for Barbara shunning a lovely man like George.

Barbara went quiet again before saying, 'If I hardly bothered with him, it was because ...' she paused for a long time. 'It was because I *knew* he wasn't my real dad!'

Rosie and Paul looked at each other.

'You knew?' Paul said. 'Why didn't you tell me?'

His wife stared out of the window, with her back to them. 'Oh, I don't know – maybe I didn't want to admit it to myself. He never told me, so why should I tell you?'

'But ... how did you find out?' Paul asked, gently. Rosie could see he had deep feelings for his wife. There was obviously more to her than met Rosie's eye.

'Because I saw my own adoption papers when I was six years old, that's how. He kept all his private stuff in a locked drawer in his bedroom ... but one day it wasn't locked.'

'It must have been a hell of a shock,' ventured her husband, squeezing her to him.

'Not really,' said Barbara. 'Not at the time. It was just a big word that I didn't understand. It only caught my eye because I saw my own name written down there as well. I remember feeling really important seeing my name written down in proper typing. I found a piece of paper and wrote the word down. Adoption.' She gave a thin, humourless laugh. 'I couldn't even pronounce it properly. I asked one of my friends what adopteeyon meant – she didn't know ... give me a ciggy, Paul.'

Paul picked up a silver cigarette case from a glass-topped coffee table and took out a cigarette. He offered the open case to Rosie, who refused. They both waited for Barbara to light up and continue her story:

'I didn't say anything to Dad because I was frightened of getting told off for going in his private drawer. Then as I got older, I became aware of what it meant.' Rosie felt an unexpected twinge of sympathy for her. 'When I was about nine I managed to sneak another look. Just to make sure I hadn't imagined it. But I hadn't. I think that's when it hit me. And that's why I resented my dad so much.' She looked at Rosie. 'Always did, to his dying day. I just wanted him to tell me. I had a right to know.'

'Is that why you contested the will?' Rosie asked.

Barbara took time to consider her reply. 'I never knew why I was adopted. Maybe I always assumed he couldn't have children of his own. So when I found out he'd made you pregnant, I ...'

'You what?'

'I felt incredibly bitter. The whole thing was so confusing. Then he died and left most of his stuff to you and your son. So when I found out Eddie wasn't really my father's son ... and when I heard you'd been locked up for assault, I thought someone like you had no right to his money.'

'Someone like me, eh? Your father loved me.'

'He would never have married you if he'd known what you were capable of.'

Rosie should have felt angry, but somehow she under-stood and felt obliged to explain herself.

'Joe Brindle, the man I'm supposed to have attacked is being sought by the police for burning my house down and

324

killing two men, including Ernie Scrimshaw, your Dad's old partner.'

'We knew about the fire,' Paul said.

'The night before the fire,' Rosie went on, 'we got Scrimshaw to admit to perjury. It was his evidence that got me locked up. Brindle put him up to it, the same as Brindle burned my house down.'

Barbara shook her head and blew smoke against the windowpane. 'What's all this got to do with anything?'

'It means I *was* being raped by Brindle when I stabbed him. I was being raped on your father's grave.'

'If that's the case,' Paul said. 'You should get your conviction ... reversed.'

'Quashed,' said Rosie. 'That's the term my solicitor used a few hours ago.'

'Congratulations,' he sounded sincere. 'It must be a relief after all you've been through. Look, if this letter's genuine ...'

'It *is* genuine.'

'We won't fight you in court, will we, Barbara?'

Barbara was staring out of the window. Her thoughts were a million miles away.

'It's been a mixed sort of a day for us,' smiled Paul, wryly. 'Barbara's just found out she's pregnant.'

Rosie allowed the news to sink in. Pregnant. It had happened to her twice. Each time it had come as unwelcome news. For these people the news had been welcome. She remembered the smile on Barbara's face as she opened the door. She'd probably ruined a joyous moment.

Barbara suddenly turned and looked her. 'I'm sorry,' she said. 'After all you'd been through, the last thing you needed was me taking your home away from you.' Her sincerity was unexpected but unmistakeable.

Rosie accepted her apology with a nod and said, 'Barbara, it wasn't so much the house, it was my marriage to your father. You cheapened that. You persuaded the courts that it had been a sham. I happened to know that the

325

years your father spent with me were the happiest years of his life. Your father was a lovely man. Perhaps you should have told him you knew about being adopted. He meant no harm by not telling you. As a matter of fact neither of us had any intention of telling Eddie he wasn't George's son. But you blew that out of the water.'

'How did the boy take it when you told him?' enquired Paul.

'I haven't told him ... yet. The court case never got reported, so it's not exactly common knowledge and Eddie's still only seven years old.' Rosie stood up and walked over to Barbara. 'Have you any idea how much damage you did to me?'

'I said, I'm sorry.' Barbara was beginning to get annoyed. Losing her house was bad enough without being forced into so much humbling contrition. 'At the time I really believed you'd tricked him into marriage.'

Rosie said nothing. She'd come prepared for a confrontation; to get things off her chest and to tell Barbara exactly what she thought of her. But she could see Barbara's point of view and she felt irrationally cheated. She settled for: 'I didn't trick him into anything. You're insulting your father's intelligence just by thinking that.'

There was no condemnation in her voice, but Paul, who couldn't see her face, anticipated a flare up between the women. The last thing he wanted, with his wife in her present state.

'You'll have to give us time to find somewhere to live,' he said, firmly.

'Why's that?' enquired Rosie, almost pleasantly.

His tone hardened. 'Because if you don't, we'll drag this thing out for as long as we can; which could be months, maybe even years.'

Rosie shook her head. 'I meant, why would you want to find somewhere else to live when you've got a perfectly good house here?'

'What?'

326

Rosie sat back down again. Her need for revenge on Barbara was now extinguished. Barbara wasn't evil. Her story of how she'd found out she was adopted explained her behaviour to a certain extent. Explained but not excused. And George had loved her; which was something else in her favour.

'All I want is Eddie's trust fund restored to him,' she said. 'You have my word that I'll sign the house back over to you just as soon as you've reinstated George's will to what it was – that's very important to me.'

Paul looked gobsmacked, 'I don't know what to say.'

'Neither does she,' observed Rosie, looking at the shocked expression on Barbara's face. She suddenly grinned. 'Look, Barbara, maybe you had every right to be a pain in the arse. I just wish you'd told George you knew you'd been adopted. You know how stupid men can be at times.'

'Don't answer that,' said Paul.

Barbara smiled, 'Thank you, Rosie.'

'Don't mention it,' said Rosie. 'And by the way ... congratulations.'

'It healed a rift between me and his daughter,' she explained to Barney. 'Small price to pay because I'm sure it's what George would have wanted.' She was watching Barney and his men clear away the last of her old home; shovelling a lifetime of memories on to the back of a wagon.

'Small price?' he commented. 'That house is worth a fortune.'

'Yes. But it was George's fortune. I intend making my own, with a little help from you.'

'A little help, eh?' Barney said. 'Some people call it hard graft.' He tapped the side of his head. 'And know-how.'

'I've got every faith in you, now get back to work, my man, or do I have to take my whip to you?'

He grinned and touched a subservient forelock. 'Yes, boss. Anything you say, boss.'

Chapter Thirty-Two

Joe Brindle cursed violently. He stamped around his room and ripped the *Daily Mirror* into shreds. His picture took up most of page two, under the heading: BRITAIN'S MOST WANTED MAN.

The wagon driver who had given him a lift that night had now come forward, and the evidence against him was damning. What had given him away was his scarred face and glass eye. The one he'd got courtesy of that bloody woman.

He was still okay for cash, but he hadn't dared leave the country. Certainly not now that his picture was in the nationals; no disguise under the sun could hide his glass eye. He tried sunglasses, but that seemed to attract even more suspicious looks, especially in October in Newcastle. Very few Geordies wear sunglasses in the middle of summer – much less October – and never in a pub.

He'd rung his father and had been given short shrift. No help would be forthcoming from that direction; not that he'd expected any. He was on his own in this. That woman had been the cause of all his problems. Had she not been a friend of that idiot Irishman who hadn't the sense to grab the swinging slab, his life would have been plain sailing. Joe Brindle had been doing well. Okay he'd cut a few corners here and there, but who doesn't? She'd set him up on that Boswell Court job. He didn't know how, but somehow she had. His hatred for Rosie festered and finally bubbled over that morning in his room. If he was going down, he was taking her with him.

Barney was on the top lift of scaffold when he read the paper. One of the roofers had bought it that morning.

'Looks like your old gaffer's on borrowed time. Shouldn't be long afore he's caught. I mean he doesn't exactly blend in ter the background.'

'Sooner the better,' Barney said. 'The man's a waste o' good breath.'

'I don't know,' smirked the roofer's labourer. 'He gorrus this job. Weren't it him what burned this place down?'

'Do you want this job or don't you?' snapped Barney.

'Keep yer hair on,' said the roofer.

It was evening when Brindle pointed his Humber Hawk towards Leeds. His life was a thing of the past. He had never married, so there were no ties there. The only person he'd ever loved was his brother. Ralph's death had twisted him up inside. Made him hate the world and everything in it. He stopped at Scotch Corner and called in to a pub for a drink and to gather his thoughts, such as they were. The world had done him no favours so he owed nobody nothing. If they wanted to hang him, so be it, but the bastards would have to catch him first. And before they did, he'd make sure there was one less person in this lousy world.

The boys were fast asleep and Rosie and Marlene had spent the evening in front of the new television; another of Rosie's additions to the house. They had watched *The Makepeace Story*, *Café Continental* and the *News*. And when programmes closed down they'd felt guilty at not standing to the National Anthem as everyone did at the pictures; then they'd watched the screen shrivel up into a tiny white dot before Rosie turned the dial that switched the set off.

'What d'you think?' she asked Marlene.

'I think I shall have ter get one of me own when yer've gone.'

'No need,' Rosie said. 'I'll be leaving this one here. You've been good to us, Marlene. If I can give Barbara a house, I can give you a telly.'

'Yer a right one fer throwin' yer brass about, but I'll not say no.'

'Hopefully there should be a lot of money coming my way, what with one thing and another. I'll be due for a nice bit of compensation as and when my conviction gets quashed.'

'Is it definite then?'

'Nothing's definite as far as the law's concerned, Marlene. I need to convince the court I was being raped when I stabbed him. I might have to wait until he's caught and convicted of murder. That should be enough to convince a jury what he's capable of. What the . . . !'

The front door burst open and Brindle appeared in the room. A wild, unbalanced look on his face. He was smiling through broken teeth, his glass eye stared blankly ahead as his good eye swivelled all around, before settling on Rosie. Marlene got to her feet and advanced on him. Without bothering to look at her he punched her in the jaw and sent her sprawling and unconscious to the floor. Her dress had ridden up her fat legs, revealing her laddered stocking as far as her knickers. There was blood on her face and she looked ominously still. Rosie's mind went back to the time he raped her and she knew by the look in his eyes it was going to happen again – only this time it would be worse. Much worse. Picking up a brass poker from the fireside companion set, she held it, uncertainly, in front of her. Brindle sneered and lunged forwards. She swung the poker in a half-hearted arc that missed his face by a foot; then she backed away, gripping the poker tightly.

'What do you want?' she asked; her voice was muted by fear.

'I think yer know what I want – I want you, yer bitch!'

His voice was malevolent, his one eye drink-sodden and

330

dissolute and his manner menacing and intent on ravishing her and torturing her until death came as a merciful release. Rosie knew this and knew there was no escape.

Then, for no explicable reason, her mind suddenly jerked back to when she was fourteen and he was just a big, awkward bully; trying it on with her round the back of Vinery Place Primitive Methodist Chapel, and she wasn't scared of him any more. Just angry. Her pupils dilated and her pulse speeded up as nature prepared her body for emergency action. A rush of adrenalin pumped extra blood into her muscles and her grip tightened on the poker. She was ready for him.

'How come you never got a proper girlfriend, Joe Brindle? One who actually wanted you?' She could hear herself talking, but her voice seemed far away. Her obvious contempt stopped him, momentarily.

'Get out of this house, Brindle!' She jabbed the poker, viciously, into his face and moved round to his blind side.

He exploded with rage, but he didn't move quickly enough to avoid a ferocious blow to the side of his head. Brindle stumbled into her and brought her down. The poker flew from her grasp and his face touched hers. She tried to turn away in disgust, but he grabbed her hair and held her there.

'One last time fer you, bitch. So yer might as well enjoy it!' He ripped at her blouse, tearing it and her brassiere off in one vicious pull. Then he leered at her exposed breasts.

'Didn't get ter see these last time.'

Taking both of her wrists in one huge hand, he pinned her arms to the floor behind her head. With his free hand he slapped her as she writhed and kicked and screamed at him.

'Keep still, yer bloody bitch!'

His blow knocked her into semi-consciousness and he tore at her skirt. The elastic waistband cut into her skin as it came away from her body. Then he let go of her hands as he pulled her skirt and pants down. Rosie came to just as he had her naked. She rained savage punches at his face, but lust had now anaesthetised him against anything she could

331

throw at him. He slapped her into stillness again. Joe Brindle had her where he wanted her.

Barney was still cursing himself as he drove back to Duck Street. His tool kit would probably have vanished by now, such was the level of dishonesty in that area. He grinned to himself. Had Mostin got his hands on it, he would have already sold it and probably spent the money in some pub. Mostin would have been welcome to it. Heroes such as him were few and far between. Barney hadn't met many heroes during his five years in the army. Self-preservation was the order of the day. Volunteer for nothing and keep your feet dry were the two golden rules that brought Barney and thousands of others home safely. Rosie's dad had been a hero. Given his life to save an officer. Barney wasn't sure he was capable of that. The toolkit should be on the first floor in one of the bedrooms. He parked his car at the end of Duck Street and made to swing up the scaffold. The ladders had been padlocked for the night and he hadn't got the key. Brindle had left his car lights on or Barney might not have noticed it parked outside Marlene's house. He recognised it immediately.

Picking up a short length of scaffolding tube, he ran down the street, his heart thumping with apprehension bordering on panic. In Marlene's front room the curtains were drawn and the light was on. The front door was ajar, which was odd at that time of night. Barney stopped by the window and heard a woman crying, a man's rasping voice and sounds of blows being struck.

He kicked the door open and took in the scene with one horrified glance. Rosie, naked on the floor, with Joe Brindle kneeling over her.

Brindle gave a maniacal roar and leaped at Barney with a mixture of intense frustration and rage; superior in height and weight and natural aggression. Barney jabbed out with the scaffold tube, catching Brindle in his belly, knocking the wind out of him. Rosie scuttled backwards towards the

332

stairs, where she stayed to watch; torn between the safety of her boys and the safety of this man who had come to rescue her. Barney swung the tube down on Brindle's shoulder, who shrugged off the blow and hurled himself forward, sending Barney tumbling on to his back, grunting in pain as Brindle's heavy fists hammered into his face. Barney made a grab for Joe's legs, brought him to the floor and butted his head into the big man's nose. The two men rolled over and over, kicking, thumping, gouging, butting. Furniture smashed beneath them as the fight raged around the room. Then Brindle's crushing arms encircled Barney's neck. Rendering him helpless. Powerless. For the few seconds before his world went dark, Barney knew he couldn't survive this. He just hoped Rosie had managed to get away. He didn't feel the blows from the scaffold tube raining down on him. Smashing his ribs, his skull, his arms and his legs.

The sight of Barney being so savagely beaten concentrated Rosie's emotions into a Herculean surge of rage and strength. She picked up the poker and screamed, hysterically, at Brindle. He looked up at her just as she hit him with a single, ferocious blow, delivered with every ounce of power at her disposal. It cut deep into his skull and sent him sprawling, lifeless, over Barney's prostrate body.

Marlene came round and looked through a mist of semi-consciousness at a scene which would be imprinted on her mind forever. She rubbed her eyes and blinked away the haze. Her vision focused on Rosie, naked and splattered with blood, standing there; white-faced and wild-eyed, with a poker in her hand, over the bodies of two men. Neither of them moving. Marlene didn't recognise Barney's blood-caked face. She got to her knees and pushed herself up with the aid of a chair; then she shook her head and tried to switch her brain back on.

'Who's the other one?' she asked, at length.

But Rosie couldn't answer. Still clutching the poker, she sank to her knees beside Barney's head. She began to shake as Marlene recognised the face behind the mask of blood.

'Oh my God! It's Barney.' She knelt down and put her ear next to his mouth. 'I think he's still breathin' ... I'll ring for an ambulance.'

'Is he going to be all right?' There was desperation in Rosie's voice.

Marlene didn't think so, but said, 'He'll be okay. He's just knocked out, that's all. You get summat on.'

Rosie nodded, then looked at Brindle. 'What about him?' she asked, faintly. 'Is he dead?'

'I think he is, love.'

'I killed him.'

'You had ter, love. It were him or us.'

'He was hitting Barney.'

'I know, love.'

'He was going to rape me, Marlene.'

'I gathered that, love. Everything's all right now.'

'Barney's not all right, is he?'

Rosie heaved Brindle's body off Barney and cradled his bloodied, unconscious head in her arms. Marlene rang for an ambulance and the police, then went upstairs to bring Rosie down a change of clothes.

'Just one thing, Rosie love,' she said. 'Tell the police yer hit Brindle because he was comin' fer yer.'

'I hit him to stop him hurting Barney.'

'I know, love. But the police have a funny way o' lookin' at things. I just don't trust the buggers; they did yer no favours last time an' there's no point takin' any chances. Just say he were comin' fer yer, an' yer clocked him one. That's my story, so don't make me out ter be a liar.'

'All right, Marlene.'

'Promise?'

'I promise.'

'Yer kiddies seem to have slept through it ... thank God.'

'I'm glad they didn't have to see any of that,' Rosie murmured.

'Aye, lass. It's not a memory they'd treasure.'

Rosie stroked Barney's bloodied head. 'Don't die,

Barney. Please don't die.' She looked up at Marlene, with tears streaming down her face. 'I love him, you know.'

'Aye, love. I think I've known that fer a long time.'

Rosie was sitting in the back room in silent shock when Robert Hilton arrived. The front room, where the attack had taken place, was full of people, mainly police. Barney had been rushed to hospital. Marlene had made tea for her and Rosie and no one else.

'Good evening, Sergeant,' said Robert. 'My name is Hilton, I'm Mrs Metcalf's solicitor.'

'Are you really?' The policeman raised an eyebrow. 'And why on Earth would Mrs Metcalf need a solicitor, sir? I understand she's the victim – or one of them.'

'It's not the first time my client has been the victim of Mr Brindle's brutality,' retorted Hilton. 'The last time, she was jailed for her trouble.'

'It was the courts what jailed her, sir, not us.'

'She incriminated herself by answering police questions, which should never have been put to a woman who had just gone through such a severe trauma. Mrs Gedge rang to tell me what had happened and I'm here to ensure there's no repeat of such questioning.'

'We'll be the best judge of that, sir.'

'Yer weren't very good judges last time, were yer?' chipped in Marlene, scathingly. 'Anyway, this time there are witnesses. I saw him hittin' Barney and then he went for her ... so Rosie hit him ... in self defence. And if she hadn't, we'd all have been dead – an' no thanks ter the bloody police neither. If you lot'd framed yersens, he wouldn't have been able ter run round the flippin' country-side attackin' decent people.'

'We'll be taking a statement from you in due course, Mrs Gedge.'

'I should hope yer will.'

'I killed him, didn't I?' Rosie wept. Her promise to Marlene forgotten. 'I'm sorry. I didn't want him to hurt Barney.'

'Didn't want him ter hurt *you* more like,' said Marlene, quickly. 'If you hadn't have clocked him, yer wouldn't be here ter tell the tale.'

The sergeant looked at Rosie, keenly. 'I'd like you to come down to the station to make your statement, Mrs Metcalf.'

Marlene cursed under her breath and jabbed her elbow into Robert's ribs. He needed no urging.

'My client has just suffered a severe trauma. She's not going anywhere until she's been given the all clear by a doctor. And then she'll make a statement in the comfort of her own home.' Robert looked, balefully, at the sergeant. 'Unless of course, you intend to arrest her.'

'Now then, no one said anything about arresting her, sir. I just need to get a proper picture of what went on.'

'I'd have thought the picture was clear enough the minute you walked through the door,' Robert said, with ill-concealed sarcasm.

A police doctor came in from the front room and addressed the sergeant. 'I've just pronounced Mr Brindle dead. I assume your people will want to take a look at the scene before he's moved.'

'I wonder if you could take a look at this lady,' said Robert, pointing to Rosie.

'What's wrong with her?'

'She's one of the victims and she's suffering from trauma of the most severe nature.' Robert nodded towards the sergeant. 'This officer wants her to go to the police station to start answering questions. It's my opinion that she's suffered enough for one evening.'

The doctor shone a light in Rosie's eyes and did a few cursory checks. 'I want her admitted to hospital and kept under observation,' he said, brusquely.

Robert gave the sergeant a grim smile of triumph. 'You should be thanking her, Sergeant. She's just caught the most wanted man in Britain.'

Chapter Thirty-Three

If the police had any doubts about what exactly happened, they chose not to raise them, especially in view of Rosie's application to have her conviction quashed. The papers had got hold of her story and had made her into a heroine. The helpless young woman laying low the Most Wanted Man in Britain. But none of this was of any comfort to Rosie. It had been a week now and Barney hadn't regained consciousness. He was the only patient in a two-bed ward. To Eileen's irritation, Rosie had maintained an almost constant round the clock bedside vigil.

'I do have a job to go to,' Eileen pointed out. 'I can't just devote the time to him that you can.'

'I think someone he knows should be here when he comes round,' Rosie said. 'It's okay, Eileen. I owe it to him. He saved my life.'

'But ... he could be like that for weeks.'

'So be it,' said Rosie. 'I owe him the whole of my life. I can give him a few weeks.'

Eileen's irritation grew daily. Left to her own devices she would have seen no good reason to visit Barney until she heard that he'd regained consciousness. Staring at a sleeping man, encased in bandages wasn't her idea of a good time. But she could hardly *not* visit, with Rosie never leaving his bedside.

'You probably think I'm rotten, don't you, not waiting

by his bedside day and night.'

'I don't think you're rotten at all,' lied Rosie, who wondered what Barney had ever seen in her. He had been unconscious for five days. His wife had spent less than five hours at his bedside. Their conversation that night was, as usual, awkward. But it was the first time Rosie had heard her criticise her husband:

'He's lucky I've stood by him at all. I mean, he's not exactly what I expected when I married him.'

'Oh?' said Rosie.

'We can't have children, you know. And I know for a fact it's not my fault.'

'Really – you've had tests, have you?'

'Oh yes. I went to the top specialist. My father had to pay, of course. Barney never had two ha'pennies to scratch his backside with.'

'I thought he'd been doing all right recently.'

'Depends what you call all right.'

'Doesn't sound as if you love him very much.'

'Love?' scoffed Eileen. 'What's love when it's at home? My dad can't understand for the life of him why I haven't left Barney and married a proper man who could give me children.' She looked down at her husband. 'But it's like I said to him. Dad, we made our vows at the altar – 'til death us do part.'

Rosie's patience snapped. 'You don't really want children, do you?'

'I beg your pardon?'

'I reckon you're using Barney as an excuse.'

Eileen lost her temper and her guard dropped. 'Using him as an excuse? I don't need to *use* him as an excuse – let's face it, dear, he *is* a bloody excuse; an excuse for a man.'

'And you only stay with him because you can't get anyone else!'

'I'm leaving,' shouted Eileen. 'And when I come back, I don't want to see you here.'

'Then you'd better wear a blindfold.'

After seven days Rosie thought he moved a finger. She called a nurse, who called a doctor, who tapped on Barney's chest and shone a light in his eyes and listened to his heart – and shook his head.

'I'm sorry,' he said.

'So am I,' said Rosie.

'You should get some real sleep.'

'I'm okay, doctor.'

'Try talking to him,' advised the nurse. 'He might be able to hear you. No one quite knows what goes on in a coma such as this. I once talked to a coma patient and when he came round he remembered some of the things I'd said to him. Try and tell him something really exciting, even if you have to make it up. This chap was a mad Huddersfield Town supporter. I told him they'd just won the FA Cup. He came round three hours later. Then I had to tell him I'd been lying.' She laughed. 'Poor bloke nearly had a relapse.'

Rosie waited until the nurse's footsteps had clicked away down the ward, then she leaned over and kissed Barney on the lips. Not for the first time.

'They say I should talk to you,' she said. 'Tell you something exciting. Well ... Joe Brindle is dead. I killed him when he was hitting you ... Is that exciting enough? Actually, I'm not proud of it. I can't explain how I feel. Angry at him for driving me to it ... anyway, it's all over and done with. The police have accepted my version of events. They might want to confirm with you that he was about to rape me when you came on the scene.'

She sat back and thought for a while. If he could hear her, what she had to tell him next would change their lives. Was she sure she wanted to tell him? It was certainly more exciting than Huddersfield Town winning the FA Cup. To her anyway. But was she about to tell him just because she wanted him to wake up? Or did she, deep down, have an ulterior motive?

'There are two good reasons you must get better,' she began; her mouth was close to his ear. 'One is that I love you ... only I didn't want to admit it, with you being married to Eileen and trying to make a go of things.'

She watched for some sign of acknowledgement, but his chest rose and fell with the same depressing regularity. 'And there's something else I've been keeping from you – because of Eileen, who only comes to visit because I'm here all the time. Barney, I don't want to sound rotten, but I don't think she's putting her heart and soul into your marriage.'

She kissed him again then whispered in his ear. 'Barney, I made it up about having sex with a man in jail ... *you* are Christopher's dad.'

Then she sat back and waited for some indication that he'd heard her, but none came.

'Barney, Christopher is your son.'

His breathing remained steady and almost undetectable; his hands at rest and motionless; not a flicker of an eyelash, nothing. She felt dejected at his total lack of response to her life-shattering revelations. After a while, sleep overtook her.

She dreamed of Brindle attacking her on George's grave. Only it wasn't George's grave it was Sean's grave and Barney was there, lying beside her and he wouldn't wake up. And there was blood everywhere. She could smell blood; she could smell something. Stale, musty, like last night's drink on the breath. A hand was shaking her shoulder; roughly, impatiently. Rosie opened her eyes and wrinkled her nose at the smell of stale alcohol fumes. That, plus the look on Eileen's face told Rosie she'd been drinking more than her fair share. It was their first encounter since their exchange of harsh words.

'Still here?' Eileen slurred. 'I hope you're not doing anything you shouldn't to my husband while he's asleep.'

'Don't be so disgusting!'

Eileen laughed. '*Me* disgusting? Let's face it, dear, it's you who has all the bastard children. Would you mind

340

leaving me to a have a private moment with my dear husband?'

'Christopher's my son,' mumbled Barney.

'Barney!' shouted Rosie. Then to Eileen she said, excitedly, 'Did you hear that? He said something. He's coming round.'

She pressed the bell to summon a nurse, then leaned over Barney. Eileen was at the other side. Neither of them knew for sure what he had said.

'Christopher's my son.'

They both heard it this time. A nurse came in, quickly followed by a doctor.

'He said something, doctor,' said Rosie. 'It, er ... it didn't make sense, but he definitely spoke.'

'Christopher's my son,' said Barney.

'Has he said anything else?' enquired the doctor, who didn't know who Christopher was.

'I think he's said enough!' stormed Eileen who looked as though she was about to hit Rosie. 'It all makes sense now – you bloody whore!'

The doctor looked up and frowned. 'Could you ladies wait outside, please?'

As soon as they were out in the corridor, Eileen turned on Rosie. 'One question and one question only, madam, is it true?'

'How can it be true?' challenged Rosie. 'You told me Barney couldn't have children.'

The anger in Eileen's eyes magnified. 'You bloody bitch!' She slapped Rosie across the face and sent her staggering. She would have followed it with more blows had not a passing porter intervened.

'Ladies, ladies. This is neither the time nor the place.'

'Mind your own bloody business!' screamed Eileen, advancing on Rosie again. The porter bravely positioned himself between them, moving from side to side as Eileen tried to get at her. Rosie's feelings were mixed. Guilt, elation at Barney's recovery and relief that her secret was at last in

341

the open. She'd probably destroyed Barney's marriage, such as it was. Eileen's face was quivering with anger. But she didn't seem sad. If Rosie had just found out her husband had been unfaithful, she would have been sad as well as angry.

There was relief on the porter's face as reinforcements arrived in the shape of a formidable-looking matron. Eileen's mouth curled into a sneer.

'I'll divorce him for this. My dad'll make sure I take him for every penny he's got – you're bloody welcome to the dregs!' She laughed, maniacally. 'I hope he has a relapse and dies. Then I won't even have to divorce him. I'll get his money anyway.'

Rosie was shocked. 'Eileen, I'm sor . . .'

But Eileen was gone; which was fortunate, because Rosie wasn't really sorry. She went back into the room where the doctor was listening to Barney's chest.

'Is he going to be all right, doctor?'

'Well, he's regained consciousness, but he's not ready for any excitement. Has the other lady gone?'

'Yes, she has.'

'Perhaps that's just as well.'

Barney dropped off again and it was over an hour before he opened his eyes. Rosie summoned the doctor, who pronounced him fit enough to talk to her for while.

'So long as you don't overtax him.'

'I won't, doctor.'

'I thought I saw Eileen here,' said Barney, after the doctor had gone.

'She, er . . . she left.'

He squeezed his eyes together, trying to make sense of the confusion within his whirling mind. Then fragments of his memory began to return. At first, their conversation was punctuated by long silences as Barney worked out the questions he needed answering.

'How long have I been here?'

'A week.'

'Rosie, are you okay? Did Brindle . . .?'

342

'No, he didn't, thanks to you ... Brindle's dead, Barney.'

'Oh, Christ! I don't remember much about it. I just remember seeing you there ... and him ...'

'You saved my life, Barney.'

'And he's dead, you say?'

'Yes ... I killed him. He was trying to kill you.'

'So, you saved my life as well.'

'I suppose so.'

'Rosie, did you say ... Christopher was my son?'

'Yes, I did.'

'But you told me the father was a prison guard.'

'I was lying ... sorry.'

'Oh, that means I'm not ...'

'No, you're not,' confirmed Rosie. 'You're definitely not. Barney ... Eileen knows.'

'Does she?' He didn't seem too concerned.

'She's not best pleased,' said Rosie. 'She told me I was welcome to you.'

'She's right, you are welcome to me ... Why didn't you tell me about Christopher?'

'I didn't want to break your marriage up. There's been a lot going on in my life. I needed something to jolt some sense into me.'

'Like Brindle knocking seven bells outa me?'

Rosie leaned over and kissed an unbandaged part of his face. 'Like you nearly dying ... I love you, Barney Robinson. Maybe I always have.'

'Pity you didn't mention it earlier.'

'I suppose I couldn't see the wood for the trees.'

'I could,' said Barney. 'I've always loved you. Always have, always will. I love Christopher an' all. Couldn't be happier, knowing he's my ...' Tears suddenly streamed from his eyes, causing Rosie concern.

'Barney, what is it? Shall I get the doctor?'

'By heck, Rosie! This is the happiest bloody day of me life.'

Rosie stared at the heavily bandaged man and smiled at the incongruity of his words. Then she leaned over and kissed away his tears.

'And mine, Barney.'

She held his hand and they both fell silent, enjoying the moment. A wall clock quietly ticked away the seconds as, beyond the door, the bustle of the hospital went on unnoticed.

Barney never did explain how he managed it. Rosie suspected collusion between the nurses and some of his many pals. It happened the following afternoon when Rosie went to visit him again after she'd had a long and much needed sleep. The cold light of a new day brought several potential problems to her attention. Eileen had been drunk. And people sometimes regret what they say when they're drunk.

'Barney,' she said. 'I've been thinking about Eileen and I feel a bit guilty. I said some nasty things to her.'

'I reckon she must have deserved it, then,' said Barney. 'The only thing we've hurt is her pride. She always thought she was too good for me – so did her parents.'

'She said she wants a divorce, among other things.'

'Did she now?'

'I don't know if she meant it, she was a bit drunk.'

'Oh, she definitely meant it,' said Barney. 'Now that her darling husband, who can't have kids, has had a child by another woman.'

'I thought it was a bit rotten of her to tell you you can't have children.'

'I want me flipping head examining for believing her. Anyway,' he said. 'I've got a couple of bits of news. Eileen popped in last night to tell me she's divorcing me and intends taking me for every penny I've got.'

'Oh dear, she mentioned that to me as well.'

'So I took certain precautions,' he said.

'What sort of precautions?'

'I spent all me money this morning.'

Rosie couldn't begin to understand what he was talking about. 'Barney, are you feeling all right? You certainly don't sound all right.'

'Right as rain,' he said.

'What did you spend it on?'

He fixed her in his gaze. 'Rosie, I know I might be jumping the gun a bit here, but it seemed like a good idea at the time.'

From beneath the bedclothes he took out a black velvet box and handed it to Rosie. 'I bought you this,' he said.

It was a ring. A sapphire between two diamonds. A ring like this would have emptied Barney's bank account, and more.

'It's an engagement ring,' he said.

'I thought it might be. Barney, it's beautiful, but ... aren't you supposed to ask me something first?'

'What? Oh, right. It just seems a bit odd with me being already married.'

'It's always nice to be asked.'

He cleared his throat and asked, nervously, 'Rosie, will you marry me?'

Rosie was about to answer, but she hesitated and said, 'I might.'

'Might? How do you mean, might? What sort of answer's that?'

She took the wedding ring off her ring finger and placed it on the third finger of her right hand. Barney knew that George's memory would always be part of her. He could live with that.

'Barney, I need you to convince me that it's definitely all over between you and Eileen.'

'It is.'

'Barney, I need convincing.'

'Rosie, what can I tell you? Our marriage was a mistake. She'll not be back, I'll guarantee that.'

'You're sure – and you've got no regrets?'

345

'No.'

'None at all?'

'Rosie, you're going on at me. I'm not a well man. I'll report you to the doctor if you keep upsetting me.'

'I just want to know that you haven't got one single, solitary regret at your marriage breaking down.'

Barney's eyes suddenly became sad. 'Oh, all right then,' he admitted. 'I have to confess – there is one thing I regret.'

Rosie's heart sank. 'How big a thing?'

'A very big thing.'

She knew this had all been too good to be true. 'What is it?' she asked.

'Well,' said Barney, taking her left hand in his. 'When me and Eileen got married, her dad promised me an acre of land and a cow ...' He pushed the engagement ring firmly on to Rosie's finger.

'And I never did get me acre of land.'